I0674431

# WAYCALLER

D.J. McPhee

KANNON

Published by Kannon, an imprint of Timeless Awareness Publications
Bellingen, New South Wales, Australia

First published in 2017
New Edition 2026

Copyright © D.J. McPhee 2017

The right of D.J. McPhee to be identified as the author of this work has been asserted under the *Copyright Amendment (Moral Rights) Act 2000*.

This work is copyright. Apart from any use as permitted under the *Copyright Act 1968*, no part may be reproduced, copied, scanned, stored in a retrieval system, recorded, or transmitted, in any form or by any means, without the prior written permission of the publisher.

National Library of Australia Cataloguing-in-Publication entry:

McPhee, D.J. 1968–
Waycaller/D.J. McPhee.
9780994242570 (pbk.)
Fantasy--Fiction
Speculative fiction--Young adult fiction.
A823.4

Cover design by D.J. McPhee

Printed in the United States
ISBN: 9780994242570

*To Martin Galafassi*

# CONTENTS

Acknowledgments     i

Author's Note     ii

1   Out of the Dark     1

2   From the Lost Night     77

3   The Dark Prince     153

4   Night of Falling Leaves     253

About the Author     342

# ACKNOWLEDGMENTS

Huge thanks to all the people who have helped *The Druid Prince* duology get published, particularly Lorae Harbottle-Purs (copyeditor), Kerrie Le Lievre (proofreader), Shayla Olsen and Jessica Stewart. I would also like to acknowledge the following people who have read and made editorial comments on parts of earlier versions of *Waycaller*: Martin Galafassi, Sharon Dunne, Linda McConkey, Ondine Weate, Georgia Carter Mathers, Dionne Lister, Victoria Norton, Lauren Wynder and Selena Hanet-Hutchins.

# AUTHOR'S NOTE

Some books are like portals that drag us (willingly) into other worlds. We are more susceptible to this when we are young. The first book portal I crossed was J.R.R Tolkien's *The Hobbit*, which transported me at the age of eight to Middle Earth, right into the parlour of one Bilbo Baggins. Once there, I didn't want to come home. Mostly because the idea of second-breakfast appealed to me greatly, but also because I found that world so rich and engaging.

The world of my everyday existence was pale and uninteresting compared to Bilbo's world, though inarguably safer. My world had no Gandalf or Lady Galadriel, only soapie stars and dull politicians. On the upside, my everyday world had no orcs or mountain trolls to threaten me in the dark hours of the night. Still, I would have willingly forgone the safety of my run-of-the-mill existence for a little danger if it meant I could tramp in the Misty Mountains or visit the enchanted woods of Lothlórien.

My love for the world that Tolkien created was total and unquestioning. That changed one autumn morning when I was eighteen. I remember it vividly. It was a cool morning, the kind of morning perfect for reading in a patch of sunlight by a window. I'd settled myself by just such a window after breakfast to finish re-reading *The Lord of the Rings*. I hadn't picked up those books for many years and had thrown myself into the re-reading with some excitement. When I finished *The Return of the King* later that day I was left with an uneasy feeling.

By that point I had noticed the strong environmental messages of Tolkien's work. As a budding environmentalist myself I found that element of the books gratifying. But now, on this re-reading, I could not help but notice a few things that unsettled me. All the good characters, the heroes and heroines, were white people, some of them were even described that way – the White Lady Galadriel for example. Worse, all of the bad or evil characters were often described in language associated with non-white people. The only exception to this was, of course, Saruman, but his presence in the novels does not lessen the sense that the books present white people as good and black people as bad. Also, none of the main characters are female. Out of a cast of hundreds, the female characters are all secondary or incidental to the story. The single exception is Galadriel, but even she could not be described as a main character, appearing in only a handful of scenes.

This unease with a world I loved so much percolated over the years and deepened when I noticed the same things in a lot of other fantasy fiction. With the release of the first *Lord of the Rings* film in 2001, a film that made visual the concerns I'd had with the language of the books, my unease transformed into a desire to "write back" to Tolkien, to create a fantasy world in which women and girls were central and people of colour were represented fairly. It took me another handful of years to get started on the actual writing. The result of that "writing back" to Tolkien is *The Druid Prince*, a traditional fantasy duology that includes all the things we expect of the genre (elves, dragons, magic) but that features all different types of people.

*The Druid Prince* is not much of a departure from Tolkienesque fantasy. It isn't meant to be. It's not about creating something completely new. It's about celebrating Tolkien-inspired fantasy whilst making it more inclusive and appealing to young adult readers. It's "writing back" rather than simply writing. As one reviewer said: 'Reading *Waycaller* is like visiting a world you're familiar with and love but meeting a whole lot of interesting, fascinating and likeable new people.'

I do hope that each reader finds a character or two to love *The Druid Prince*, but mostly I hope they see themselves positively reflected in it.

# PART 1: OUT OF THE DARK

# MORRIGAN

*Cairnbawn Village, Scottish Highlands*

Eloise buried her head deeper under the blankets. The wind rattled the windows and moaned through the trees on the banks of Loch Cairnbawn. The sound made her imagine a whole troop of ghosts walking on the loch's grey waters, creeping along the cobblestone streets of the village towards her house. She huddled under the covers, picturing them tapping on the glass of her bedroom window with translucent fingers and gazing in at her with their milky, dead eyes.

She pulled her knees up towards her chest, making herself into a small ball and tugged the blankets in tightly around herself, mimicking the hedgehogs she sometimes found out in the wilds, who rolled themselves into bundles of warm quills at the first sign of danger. She considered calling out to her father, just for a moment, but she knew what he would say: *Eloise, you are sixteen years old and far, far too old to believe in ghosts and ghoulies!*

Her father was right. She *was* too old to believe in ghosts, too old to be afraid of the dark; but he didn't know about the nightmares. Every night for nearly a month now she'd woken sweating and trembling with fright. Her dreams teemed with monsters. Monsters that wanted to tear her limb from limb. Monsters that waited in the dark spaces of her mind for her to fall asleep. The second she drifted off, they were there, howling, baring their grisly teeth and chasing her through a landscape she didn't recognise.

The nightmares always ended the same way. The night before hadn't been any different. The monsters chased her for what seemed like hours, until she finally came to a broad valley. At the centre of the valley stood a circle of standing stones, tall and ancient. The stones reminded her of the ones in her own village, only much larger. She ran straight for them, believing, without knowing why, that they offered safety. As soon as she crossed the perimeter of the circle, the howling of the monsters behind her stopped. She spun on the spot, checking every direction for her pursuers. There was no sign of them. They were gone. The night was quiet and still.

She bent over double, hands on her hips, her chest aching with a stitch. She forced herself to breathe slowly and evenly. Relief spread over her like a pleasant wave. Before she had properly recovered, a soft breeze came up, cold on her sweaty skin. Perhaps because she was breathing so deeply, she caught a barely detectable scent on the wind. Her skin goose-pimpled as it hit her nose. A second later she realised what it was. The smell of death, of rot and decay. As soon as she knew what the smell was, it grew much stronger, making her gag. She staggered back from it, looking for its source in the direction of the breeze. It was coming from the far end of the valley where a copse of trees sat beneath a thin sliver of moon.

Eloise had only a moment to register the trees and the silvery moon above them before a figure emerged from the shadowy copse: a human figure that proceeded to walk slowly towards the circle of stones, towards her. Something about that pale figure, the way it moved, the way it reflected so much of the moonlight that it glowed in the dark, made Eloise feel as though a cold stone had dropped into her belly.

As the figure moved closer, Eloise saw that it was a woman; beautiful, yes, but terrible too, with long white hair in dreadlocks. The woman's eyes were so startlingly, luminously green that Eloise's breath caught in her throat and her knees went weak. The breathlessness was made worse when she noticed the woman's lips. They were blackened and scarred as if burned.

The woman walked silently to the edge of the stone circle, bringing with her the reek of death. Eloise covered her nose and mouth with one hand and clutched at her stomach with the other, trying desperately not to be sick. Then the woman's voice was in Eloise's mind: *Come to me, girl. I am*

*Morrigan, the Queen of Doom! Come out of the circle, come out of the circle to me!* With the voice came a powerful wave of nausea, so strong that Eloise's first impulse was to do anything this Morrigan asked just to make the nausea go away. But then she understood something. She was safe inside the circle.

Unable to speak, Eloise shook her head and took a few wobbly steps backwards, deeper into the circle. Morrigan's luminous green eyes flared and her face contorted with rage. She opened her blackened lips to scream. No sound came out, just a pulse of sickening energy that made Eloise lose her footing and fall to the ground.

When Eloise hit the damp earth she always woke, shaking and trembling, back in her own bed in the stone cottage in Cairnbawn where she lived with her father, where there were no monsters and no pale, terrifying women with breath-taking green eyes and blackened lips.

Eloise started drinking coffee to stay awake through the night. Sometimes she downed three or four cups a day. Anything to avoid the nightmares, to avoid another encounter with the emerald-eyed Morrigan, whom she had come to equate with death itself. But it wasn't working. No matter how much coffee she drank, she inevitably fell asleep, most often in that bitingly cold hour just before dawn. As soon as she nodded off, the race to the stone circle began all over again, with the monsters right on her heels, howling like hyenas mad with hunger.

That's why when she fell asleep under the covers this time she was surprised to find herself in a dream free of monsters. She was in the same unfamiliar landscape, only all alone, the night quiet except for the occasional hooting of an owl far off in the distance. She made her way to the stone circle at her leisure. When she reached it, she looked to the copse of trees off to the south, but no scent of death came on the breeze. The shining lady, Morrigan, didn't emerge from among the shadows.

Eloise sat on the soft grass at the centre of the stone circle and took in the surroundings – the wide grassy dell, the copse of trees in the distance, the broad starlit sky above. For the first time, she found the valley rather beautiful. She sat there until she lost all track of time, absorbed in the night sky and the way the grass on the hillside undulated with the breeze. Hours later, a strange sound intruded on the dream. She listened intently to it until she realised what it was: the sound of fingers tapping lightly on a window.

She woke, sat bolt upright and found herself caught in the tangle of her blankets, struggling to breathe. For a moment she didn't know where she was. She wrestled with the bedding and shook it off. She looked to the window, half expecting to see a ghost there, its translucent fingers rapping on the glass. What was at the window was not a ghost.

She went to scream but fear and surprise chocked off all sound. A woman was standing outside, so close to the glass of the window that her breath was misting it. Eloise scrambled backwards in the bed until she was pressed hard against the wall. The woman did not look human. Her eyes were a cat-like yellow. Her skin was as dark as the night, her hair a shiny mass of magenta dreadlocks.

The woman raised her hand to the glass and tapped again, her mouth forming a slight smile. The smile caused the woman's dreadlocks to shift, revealing her ears; ears that were long, thin and tapered to a fine point.

*No*, Eloise thought to herself. *No, she can't be real.*

"No, go away, you can't be real," she mumbled out loud.

The woman continued tapping on the window, still faintly smiling. She pressed her hands, palms open, to the glass. Eloise guessed this was meant to show that the woman meant her no harm, was unarmed, but Eloise didn't move, just shook her head some more, muttering, *No, no, no, no.*

"Child, Eloise." The woman's voice was deep but quiet. "I wish to speak to you."

"No," Eloise said again. "No, you're not real. You're just a dream."

"I *am* real, Eloise, and so are your nightmares."

"Who are you?"

"My name is Kashashem," the woman said, her voice misting the window pane.

"And ... and *what* are you?" Eloise looked from the woman's yellow eyes to her pointy ears before pulling the blankets back up to her chin.

"A friend." She tapped on the window again. "A friend who can teach you to rid yourself of nightmares, and to defend yourself against monsters; and against the Pale Mother, Morrigan."

# AUTUMN DARK

Jack Gordon ducked just in time to avoid getting smacked in the head by a rogue ball, kicked in his direction by a group of first-graders playing a wild game of football by the gate to the schoolyard. The girl he'd been kissing just moments before—Carlie or Kaelie or whatever her name was—saw the ball coming. She put her hands over her face, in terror for her near-perfect nose, and shrieked so loudly it almost burst Jack's eardrums. He spun her behind him to protect her from the ball, her blond hair flying like a silk banner, and then faced the first-graders, yelling.

"Hey, midgets, clear off!"

He glanced back over his shoulder at Carlie (or was it Kaelie?) to make sure she was alright. He wished he could remember her name, but as hard as he tried, he couldn't. He'd been so dazzled by her crystalline eyes when she'd come up to him, smiling and batting her eyelids, that he hadn't heard her properly when she introduced herself. She cowered behind him now, her hands still clamped tightly over her nose, her trance-inducing eyes wide with alarm.

"You clear off, *psycho!*" one of the first-graders shouted back, sounding like a rabid leprechaun. "We can play here if we want!" The kid grabbed the ball, stuck his tongue out at Jack and ran off to resume the game with his friends, half of whom were waggling their tongues at Jack as well and yelling: *Psycho, psycho, psycho!*

He didn't bother telling them off for calling him 'psycho'. What was the point? Everyone in the village called him that. They all thought he was like his mother, who everyone knew was mad. She'd believed in crazy things, really crazy things, like monsters and elves and trolls.

Jack turned back to Carlie or Kaelie and smiled, taking

her in his arms again, glad that she was new to the village and hadn't heard any of the whispers yet. She dropped her hands from her nose and looked up into his eyes. He leant in towards her, planning to kiss her some more.

"Is it true?" she asked, pulling away from him a little, her eyes fixed on his.

"Is what true?" His stomach tightened and his skin prickled. Did she know? Had she found out already?

"Is it true that you live at Cairnbawn House, the children's home, because your mother was, you know ..."

"Insane?" He looked into her eyes. They had a familiar look, a kind of dark fascination that made her eyes seem as hard as glass. He'd seen that look in the eyes of girls before. Girls who were a bit morbid, who liked the idea that he was kind of dangerous.

"I heard it from the neighbours. They said your mother lost her mind."

"Yeah, everyone likes to whisper about how my mum lost her mind. They love a good horror story around here."

"So, it's true? It's true that—"

"That when I was six years old my mother killed my father by breaking his neck with her bare hands and then drowned herself in the loch? That they never found her body, just her coat and shoes on the shore, at the edge of Cairnbawn circle? Yeah, it's true. All true."

He didn't want to look into her eyes again. He didn't want to see that hard glint there that proved that she saw him the way everyone else in the village did – a reminder of his mother, the lunatic who'd killed her husband and then herself, abandoning her two children.

"I'm not like her." His voice cracked. "I don't believe in elves or dragons. I don't keep a sharpened dagger under my bed to fight off monsters." He looked off into the distance. Anything to avoid seeing her looking at him like he was a zoo animal, interesting only because it was wild, dangerous.

He zipped up his leather jacket and put his hands in the pockets, realising as he did so that his black clothes, messy hair and taste for punk music didn't help his argument any. In the Highlands, anyone who looked different was automatically dubbed a lunatic.

He turned back to Carlie or Kaelie and smiled. She was new to Cairnbawn, maybe she would understand.

"Can I see it?" Her voice was a trembling whisper.

"What?"

"The mark, the mark everyone says you have."

"My birthmark? Why do you want to see that?"

"The old lady next door to us says you only get a mark like that when—"

"When what?"

"When you're touched by the fae."

"It's just a birthmark. You don't believe in that nonsense, do you?"

She slid the zipper on his jacket down a few inches and pulled at the neck of his t-shirt, revealing the mark in the hollow between his collar bones. Pale red, the birthmark had always looked to him like a tattoo, a tattoo of two almost identical circles, one tight inside the other. She touched the mark with a cool finger and he shivered. He moved in close to kiss her. Anything to stop her from talking about his mother and that mark.

She looked up into his face, the hard, fascinated look in her eyes now even stronger. He turned away again, gazing at the ground.

"What's wrong?" She tugged on his jacket sleeve, trying to turn him back towards her.

"Nothing's wrong. My little sister will be out of class soon." It wasn't a lie, but not entirely why he'd lost interest in kissing her. He couldn't tell her the truth, that she'd killed the mood by making him think of his lunatic, murderess mother.

"We could go down behind the ruined tower," she whispered, pouting her pink lips. "No-one ever goes down there."

He imagined the two of them alone in the ruins of the tower, on the shore of the loch, his fingers tangled in her hair, her body pressed against his. He was about to agree when the school bell rang. Moments later a door opened in the schoolhouse and a stream of kids came running out. "Sorry," he said, "I can't, Harrie will be here any minute."

"It's only four streets to the home, why can't she walk by herself?" She ran her finger up Jack's arm.

Jack pointed at the first-graders. "She's afraid of *them*, worried they'll attack her if she walks home alone."

"I'm afraid of them too. They're scary. But why would they attack her?"

"They don't like her."

"Why?"

"She's a Gordon. They dislike all Gordons on principle, but they dislike her especially. Mostly because she's smarter than the lot of them put together and she's a bit of a loudmouth."

"I'm sure they wouldn't really hurt her. Let her walk home by herself, just this once." She pouted her pretty, rose-coloured lips and looked up into his eyes. Jack's stomach fluttered with the urge to put his arms around her and do whatever she asked. He looked off towards the ruined tower on the shore of the loch, and then back at the stream of kids coming out of the schoolhouse.

"I can't, she's expecting me."

She moved a strand of blond hair away from where it had stuck to her lips, then stretched a trembling hand to the front of his shirt, pressing it flat against his chest.

"Your heart's pounding," she whispered, looking at him sideways, her cheeks flushed. The weight of her hand against Jack's skin made him sigh and reach out for her. She took her hand away and smiled coyly. "You can't tell me you don't like me, not with your heart beating so fast." She was trying to reassure herself.

"It's not that I don't like you, it's just that I can't hang out with you right now. I'm sorry, Carlie." He knew as soon as the name left his mouth that he'd gotten it wrong. Her face went suddenly tight, her eyes narrowing and her forehead creasing with a frown.

"Sorry, sorry, I know your name's not Carlie," he said quickly.

"What is it then?" she demanded. She wasn't running her finger up his arm now. She was looking at him as though he were something awful she'd stepped in.

"Kaelie?" He knew straight away that was wrong too. Her eyes narrowed even further. "Cassi?" he added weakly, hoping he'd finally got it right.

"My name is Tricia." Her voice was strained through clenched teeth. She spun on her heels and stalked away, her silky blond hair swinging like the tail of an angry cat. Jack pushed his jet-black hair out of his eyes and sighed, now annoyed more than ever that he had to walk his sister home.

Walking Harriett home was all the more tiresome because she was always late out of class. Five, then ten minutes passed and there was still no sign of her. Although Jack was used to her constant lateness, this time it was getting on his nerves. It had cost him a pleasant hour or two all alone with Tricia down behind the old tower. With each passing moment he grew more irritated.

He settled in to wait for Harriett to turn up, leaning against the low wall that separated the schoolyard from the street. A moment later, he sensed a reduction in light, as if a darker cloud had passed in front of an already veiled sun. He looked up to the sky, then out of nowhere he felt a strange stinging sensation in his left ear.

"What the hell?" He rubbed his ear, thinking maybe he'd been stung by a wasp. Though what a wasp was doing in his ear he had no idea. He stuck his finger in his ear and rubbed more vigorously, then stopped, startled, when he heard a barely audible hiss. He shook his head. Was he imagining things? He resumed rubbing his ear. This time he heard a faint voice whisper: *Jack.* He looked around. No-one was there. He rubbed at his ear again. Just as quickly as it had started, the stinging stopped.

"That was weird," he said to himself. Two ten year old

girls passing just at that moment overheard him and sped up, walking away from him as fast as they could. They glanced over their shoulders to make sure he wasn't about to lunge after them. One of them whispered to the other: "Talking to himself, what a total nutcase."

Just then Jack felt a small, warm hand slip into his own. He started with fright, shaking the hand away before looking down. It was Harriett, standing beside him, clutching a book in her free hand, her backpack slung loosely over one shoulder. Everyone said she and Jack shared a lot of the same genes. Harriett was thin, with lanky arms and legs, and had the same dark hair and sapphire blue eyes. Her skin was as milky-pale as his. But unlike Jack who, much to his embarrassment, got a lot of attention for his looks, Harriett was gangly, uncoordinated and scruffy-looking. Jack often teased her that she looked like a nine year old scarecrow.

"About time, Harrie, I've been waiting ages."

Harriett didn't respond, simply looked up at him with those big, cold blue eyes of hers.

"Why are you always late?" he asked, frowning.

"I don't mean to be late." She shrugged. "It just always works out that I am. But this time I have a good reason. I had to ask the teacher about this book." She showed him the book in her hand, a small, beaten-up hardback that looked a hundred years old at least.

"What did you need to ask about that old book that was more important than being on time?"

"Well, I asked if the teacher had heard of it because I wanted to know if it was a series, you know, to find out if there was a sequel—"

"Just look it up on the net."

"I did, but there wasn't anything. I've never done a search and had nothing come up, like nothing at all."

"It's probably just so old that nobody remembers it. What is it, some geeky fantasy novel?"

"No, it is not." She rolled her eyes. "Well, actually, it is a fantasy thing, but it's not geeky. It's kind of cool."

"Hate to break it to you, Harrie, but smelly old books aren't cool." He pushed off from the wall and headed down the street. "Where'd you get it anyway?"

"Out of that box of old stuff."

"What box of old stuff?"

"That box of stuff, you know—"

Jack stopped, facing her.

"Mum's old stuff?" he asked.

"Yes—"

"I've told you not to mess around with mum's stuff!"

Harriett fired up immediately. "That stuff's just as much mine as yours, Jack! I can read this book if I want to!"

Jack glared back at her a moment then just shook his head. He walked away. She was right, it was her stuff as much as his. He just didn't like anyone touching it because when someone touched it, he had to think about it, had to think about his mother. How she killed their father and herself and abandoned them.

He turned the corner and headed down the street towards Cairnbawn House. It was the last place he wanted to be right now. It reminded him day in and day out that he and Harriett were alone, but he had nowhere else to go. Harriett skipped forward and caught up with him, saying "Don't be mad at me, Jack." She tried to take his hand again. She was nothing if not determined.

Jack gritted his teeth, checking the street to make sure no-one was watching. "Don't do that, Harrie! I've told you, you're too old for holding hands!"

"I'm sick of you always pushing me away, Jack!" Now she was shrieking. "If you don't hold my hand, I'll scream!"

Jack held his temper. When it came to books and school work, Harriett was mature for her age, but in other ways she was deeply immature. Like with the walking home thing. She behaved like a toddler when it came to that. Jack knew it had something to do with her being abandoned by their mother, so he tried not to overreact to it.

"You're already screaming," he said. "And how old are

you? Five? Now come on, unless you want to walk home by yourself and risk being attacked by the first-graders?" He walked away, leaving Harriett fuming.

Jack reached the next corner and rounded it, pretending to look straight ahead, but quickly casting his eyes back to check on Harriett. She stood right where he'd left her, her face screwed up in indecision, looking nervously at the first-graders playing ball down the street. He'd only gone a few more paces when he heard her taking off toward him at a run, her school shoes slapping on the wet cobblestones. He smirked, knowing she'd given in.

When Harriett finally caught up with him, Jack gave her a stern look and she fell into step beside him and sulked. He suppressed a smile. As he slowed his pace a little, enough so that Harriett's knobbly legs could keep up, he cast his eye over the dank street leading to the children's home.

The cottages here were all made of stone and squeezed up against each other as if huddled against the biting wind, which blew day in and day out. The roofs were all tiled with slate. Everything in sight, every stone wall, every chimney stack, every front stoop, was covered in a layer of green moss.

The village sat at the head of a narrow valley containing glassy Loch Cairnbawn. There were about fifty cottages in total, as well as a tiny school and a grim-looking church. The sky and the loch mirrored each other, both a bitter, steel grey.

A gust of wind brought tears to Jack's eyes. He turned his head away from it, looking towards the shore of the loch, where the ruins of a narrow tower jutted into the grey sky, casting its shadow over the church and graveyard. It stood on the shore like a broken lighthouse. He could have been down there right now with Tricia. If only she hadn't already heard all the stories about him. Whispers travel fast in Cairnbawn, especially if they're about something dark. Like the stories about the tower itself. The local children said it was haunted. Jack thought that was rubbish. The kind of rubbish his mother had believed. The same children said that a lot of strange things happened in Cairnbawn, which they blamed on the ancient circle of standing stones that sat on the shore of the loch, in the churchyard. The Cairnbawn Circle, they said, was a gateway to another realm, the realm of magic and elves and dragons. Jack dismissed that as superstitious nonsense.

"Jack, it's really cold," Harriett whined. He looked down into her face. Her eyes were watering from the wind that was also buffeting her black hair.

"No, really?" he teased. "I hadn't noticed, but that does explain the icicle hanging off my nose."

"Ha, ha, ha," she said sharply. "I was just saying. I'm allowed to say things you know. I have rights." Harriett loved to regale Jack with her notion of human rights, which basically meant she should be allowed to do and say whatever she pleased. She'd been learning about that human rights stuff in school.

"You don't have to say everything that enters your head, you know," Jack said. "Especially if it's something that obvious."

"Don't be so mean, or I'll tell the welfare people that you're messing with my human rights."

"They couldn't care less," he said harshly.

"They might, they might come and lock you up."

He snorted. "If there's one thing I know for sure, it's that the welfare people don't give a damn about us."

"You think you're so smart, Jack," she said, trotting after him, "but I know lots of things you don't know!"

"Oh really? Do tell." Jack made sure he sounded as disinterested as possible.

"Well, for one thing, I know that Aggie McTavish has a crush on you."

Jack stopped still. "Who's Aggie McTavish? Is she cute?"

"Sure she's cute," Harriett said, "for an eight year old! She's a grade below me at school. She says you look like a pop star!"

Jack instantly started walking again. "Well you can tell Aggie for me that I don't care what she thinks. Like I care what some eight year old says."

"If only all the girls who think you're so handsome and dangerous knew how you felt about them." Harriett's voice had a waspish tone. "Maybe then they'd realise what a dweeb you are instead of thinking you're the biggest teen-hottie of the moment."

"Don't say hottie. You're too young."

"I'm not a baby, Jack. I'm nine, not six! I know all about hotties, and Aggie thinks that you're one, only she doesn't like your hair."

"What's wrong with my hair?" Jack's hand involuntarily went to where his hair stuck up at the crown. He worked hard to make his hair look like he'd just climbed out of bed.

"Well," Harriett began, clearly enjoying the fact that she had her brother's total attention, "she thinks it's a bit *too* punky."

"There's no such thing as *punky*, it's just punk," Jack growled.

"Don't snarl at me, I'm not the one who said it."

"Well, next time I see Aggie McTavish I'll snarl at her then."

Harriett giggled. Then the already grey street went totally black. Jack couldn't see a thing, barely able to make out Harriett who was right beside him. He looked up, searching for the sun.

"An eclipse," Harriett mumbled, pointing towards a patch of grey clouds where the sun should have made them lighter. Jack couldn't see the pavement beneath his feet. He felt like he was floating in space. The street lights hadn't come on. All the houses around them were lightless and eerily silent.

"It's so dark," Harriett said, infuriatingly stating the obvious again. Jack didn't respond. Something stopped him before he could say anything. He heard that voice in his ear again, this time as clear as a bell. *Be calm*, the voice said. He stopped short, thinking at first that whoever said it was standing behind him. He spun around but, once again, there was nobody there. Then he heard the voice again: *Be calm.*

This time he recognised the voice instantly. It was *his own* voice! This hadn't happened to him before. Sure, he often thought things to himself and talked to himself in his head, but this was different. The voice was coming out of nowhere, unrelated to what he was doing or thinking. Had his little sister finally driven him over the edge? Was something seriously wrong with him? Was he going nuts? Harriett looked up at him curiously, apparently noticing that something was not quite right. She reached out her hand and wrapped it in his. He was too distracted and worried to flick it away. He could tell by the sudden tightening of her grip that, because he hadn't pushed her hand away, she understood something was really wrong.

"What's the matter, Jack?" she whispered, as if hushed by the extreme dark.

Jack shook his head slightly, not sure what to say, looking down the street toward Cairnbawn House, scanning for anything that might explain what was happening. He knew that Harriett's eyes had followed his because he felt her hand clench with tension when she saw what he saw. She looked up to him for reassurance, but he couldn't pull his eyes away from the scene ahead of him to meet her gaze.

A police car was parked outside the stone building that was the children's home. Its emergency lights were on so that, as they flashed, they threw the end of the street into an eerie, pulsing light. The front door to the home was open. A tall, thin constable stood on the stoop. The constable's head was hung low, his face pale and his eyes downcast. The last time Jack saw a scene like this was the night of his father's murder.

"Jack," Harriett said, her voice quiet as a mouse and her hand shaking. Perhaps she was remembering the story Jack had told her so many times about the police coming to get them in the middle of the night. Without speaking they resumed walking toward Cairnbawn House, hand in hand.

As they got nearer the home, the constable saw them approaching. He came down the front stairs and headed towards them, using his hand to shield his eyes from the flashing emergency light. He stumbled at the gate, as if blinded by the flashing light. Harriett was positively shaking now. Her hand trembled in Jack's like a frightened bird. Jack felt worried but, for some reason, strangely calm, just as the voice had commanded.

The constable reached them and immediately took hold of Harriett's arm. He steered them toward the car. Normally something like this would make Jack panic. But he wasn't panicking at all. His mind was calm and clear.

"What's going on?" he asked. "Where are you taking us?"

The policeman glared at Jack before answering. "I'm not at liberty to tell you that, laddie. Just come with me and you'll soon find out."

"We want to go home," Harriett said.

The constable manoeuvred between the two of them and grabbed hold of Jack's arm as well. He increased his pace, practically dragging them toward the car. As they neared the vehicle its emergency lights flashed in quick succession. The constable released them as his hands shot to his face to protect his eyes. As he jerked away from the light, the constable hissed, like some kind of animal. Then the voice in Jack's ear, his own voice, came back again. This time it said: *Run!*

Jack felt a strong impulse to take Harriett by the arm and bolt. But he didn't. He resisted the urge. Why should he run? The children's home might not be much but he still wanted to know why they were being taken away from the only home they had. *Run!* the voice hissed again, this time more urgent. Again, Jack felt an overwhelming impulse to flee. He felt very confused. He didn't know what was going on.

He looked to the constable, to ask him again what was happening, just as the thin man shied away from another flash of light. For a split second, the constable's eyes glowed faintly green, a look of sheer malevolent hatred. The voice in Jack's head yelled once more: *Run! Run now!*

This time Jack couldn't resist. He grabbed Harriett by the

arm and ran. Harriett resisted at first, but Jack pulled her with such force that she was dragged along after him, her gangly legs working overtime.

"Jack, what are you doing?" she screeched. "Where are we going?"

Jack didn't have time to answer before the constable surged after them. He just missed catching hold of Harriet's schoolbag. Jack hurled his own bag at him, urging Harriett to run even faster. Jack's schoolbag didn't slow the constable down for long. He was soon pounding the pavement close behind them.

"Harrie, drop your bag!" Jack yelled.

"Are you crazy, Jack? My schoolbooks are in there!"

"Drop it, Harriett! Otherwise he's going to catch us!"

They rounded a corner into a small lane. As they did so, Jack glanced back at their pursuer. He was very close behind them. Now the hateful gleam in the constable's eyes was unmasked and full-blown. What was worse, his eyes had turned an awful murky green, like something rotten at the bottom of a swamp. Harriett looked back too, then she shed her schoolbag without a second thought. She put everything she had into spurring her legs to run faster, clutching their mother's old book to her chest with her free hand.

A few moments later they heard a skidding sound followed by a thump and then the clanging of rubbish tin lids. Jack looked back again and saw the constable sprawled on the ground. The shoulder-strap of Harriett's bag was tangled around both his ankles. He was maniacally trying to clear himself from the debris of a couple of toppled rubbish tins. The constable looked up and, staring straight into Jack's eyes, growled. It was a growl like a wild animal, but with something snake-like about it. Without a word, Jack and Harriett pelted down the lane as fast as they could.

The end of the lane opened onto another street running along the shore of the loch. The churchyard and the ancient ring of standing stones that encircled the cemetery were directly opposite them. The place where their father had died.

Darker shadows looming out of the gloom showed where the stones stood, tall and imposing. Jack bolted toward the gate to the churchyard, dragging Harriett behind him. He was headed toward a clump of trees backing onto the graveyard where he hoped they could hide.

"Jack! I'm not going in that graveyard!"

"It's either go in there or let that freak catch us!" He dragged her through the gate, heading to the back of the cemetery where a stand of trees and the shadow of the church offered some protection. Once there, the voice rang out in Jack's ear again: *To the oak! The oak!*

"Harrie, which of these trees is an oak?" Jack asked, panting, his voice sounding as desperate as he felt. "I can't tell one from the other."

"Are you flipping mad, Jack? This isn't the time for botany!"

"Which one, Harriett? I don't know why it's important, but it is!"

Harriett peered at the trees through the darkness, feeling the trunks to see which one was an oak.

"This one, its bark is all rough. I think this is an oak." She patted the trunk of an ancient looking tree just inside the outer circle of stones.

"Are you sure, Harrie?" Jack asked.

"Feel around on the ground! Oaks drop acorns!"

They both went down to their knees. Soon enough Jack's fingers closed on the familiar shape of an acorn, old and covered in muck but an acorn nevertheless.

"It's an oak!" Jack pulled Harriett close and they huddled up behind the tree, right beside an ancient tombstone marked with a skull and crossbones. Jack shuffled slightly away from the gravesite towards the very edge of the stone circle, thinking it bad luck to step on the dead. The voice hissed inside his head: *Stay well inside the circle, beneath the branches of the oak!* Jack shifted back, making sure that Harriett did too.

They crouched as low as they could behind the tombstone, looking back in the direction of the lane for their pursuer. Within seconds the constable emerged into the street fronting the churchyard. His face had transformed. His eyes were now a dark fleshy green, with no whites or pupil at all. His lips were pulled back, revealing a mouth of drooling fangs. His skin had changed to a rank grey. His constable's cap had fallen off, revealing a bald and mottled head covered with bruises. Jack thought he looked like a corpse, a corpse that was puffing and out of breath. But corpses couldn't run around and they didn't get short of breath. Jack wondered if he'd finally gone the way of his mother. Was he mad now?

The constable stopped for a moment, listening. He extended a long, forked tongue, like a snake's, and lapped at the air with it, sending streaks of spittle everywhere. Jack shivered. Images of a mad dog he'd seen on the nature channel once, with a mouth full of fangs and froth and filth, flashed through his mind. But this was worse because the constable was searching for them with his tongue, the way a snake senses its prey on the air. Harriett gasped at the sight of him, waving the old hardcover book in front of Jack. Her hand shook so much that Jack thought the cover might fall right off.

"Jack," she said, trembling all over, "that thing is exactly like the monsters in this book!"

The constable heard her. He looked right in their direction. The voice in Jack's ear hissed. *Skinwearer!* Then the monstrous policeman ran toward them at full pelt, eyes fixed right on the spot where they were hiding.

"Oh no," Jack moaned, "I think he's going to get us."

The policeman reached the churchyard gate, pausing just for a second as if afraid, before entering the graveyard at a loping run. The voice shrieked in Jack's ear: *It acts against the power of the stones!* Jack had no idea what that meant. He didn't know anything about these stones, or skinwearers for that matter. He didn't understand how he could be having these thoughts, how these words could be in his mind. But he didn't have time to ponder any deeper because the constable, the skinwearer, was bearing down on them.

"Should we run, Jack?" Harriett's voice was shaking. Jack listened. No voice.

"No, we stay."

"Jack, he's coming!"

"Stay put. I think we're safe here."

The skinwearer reached just a few feet away from them and stopped still, just outside the circle of stones, growling and spitting. *Stay inside the circle, beneath the oak! Wait for the light to return!* urged the voice in Jack's ear.

"Don't move, Harriett!" Jack held tightly onto his sister. The skinwearer prowled left and right, apparently trying to find a way around some invisible barrier. He circled around behind them and then came crashing toward them through the trees, his feet crushing fallen leaves and snapping twigs. But then, just as before, he stopped a few feet away, just outside the circle of stones and the shadow of the oak.

They could hardly see him now. He was hidden in the full shade of the trees. They could only make out his silhouette as he paced to and fro, like a caged animal. Suddenly, he hurled himself forward, yowling at the top of his voice. In terror, Harriett and Jack pressed back hard against the tombstone at the base of the oak, but the constable stopped just as suddenly as he started, growling, frothing and spitting furiously.

"Something is keeping him away from this oak," Jack said, almost to himself.

"What?" asked Harriett.

"I don't know, but while we're here I'm pretty sure he can't get us."

"I hope somebody will hear him and come and find us soon."

"Don't hope that!"

"Why?"

"Because whoever comes will be attacked!"

"Oh, no! But what are we going to do? We can't stay here forever."

"We don't have to. I think he hates light. As soon as the

eclipse is over, I think he'll go."

A terrible voice growled from amongst the shadows. "I will have you yet, little things. Don't you worry your little skins." His voice was a raspy lisp, hindered by the forked tongue. "The night comes before the eclipse is done, and I will wear down this enchantment." He spat on the ground. The spit sent up steam like water thrown on a skillet. "And then I will have your pretty skins to myself. No longer will they be yours!"

"You know what, Jack, that zombie thing is *really* scary." Harriett sounded so matter-of-fact that Jack shook his head in disbelief.

"You're unbelievable!"

"What? He *is* scary."

"Yes, Harrie, I had noticed that."

The skinwearer circled to the side of them, in-between them and the church, still searching for a way to get to them, a weak spot in the invisible barrier that was protecting them. After a moment of hissing and growling, he went down on his hands and knees and started digging. As he dug, he howled and giggled. The deeper he dug, the more he spat, growled and giggled.

"That doesn't sound good," Jack said. "He sounds happy about something."

"I will have your little skins very soon, little things." The skinwearer cackled and resumed digging.

The voice in Jack's head came back, more urgent than ever: *The bough above has withered. The roots below are weak. The skinwearer may break the shield! You must open a Way!*

The voice made Jack feel like a split personality, inside his own head and sounding like him yet speaking as if someone else. Open a way? He had no idea what that meant. Could it mean a way to escape? But how? What was he to do? As if in answer, the voice in his ear shouted: *Call! Call for a Way to open! Do it now!*

Once again, the internal voice took on a tone that forced him to act. He couldn't resist. Even though he didn't know what any of it meant, he knew he had to do what the voice said. So he opened his mouth and called out: "Please, please, open a way for us to escape!"

Harriett jumped with fright. She looked at him as if he'd lost his mind. Maybe he had. He didn't know who he was calling to, or what he was asking, but he put his whole being into it and called again. "Please, open a way for us to escape this place!"

The skinwearer growled, spitting a huge glob of drool in their direction. The spit hit the tombstone just inches away with a steaming sizzle.

"No! *My* little skins! Mine!" he growled.

Harriett screamed and got up to run. Jack grabbed her by her jacket and pulled her back to him. In that moment, every part of him just wanted his little sister to be safe. He couldn't bear it if anything happened to her, not after losing their parents. A sudden surge of determination filled him and he called out again: "Open a way! Open a way!"

The skinwearer resumed digging at a furious pace. Then, somehow, the sky grew slightly lighter. The skinwearer howled in a mad frenzy and, to Jack's horror, transformed before their eyes. His body grew larger as his arms thickened and elongated, much longer than his legs. His feet changed into paws and sprouted long claws. As he continued to change and grow, splotchy fur like a hyena's sprouted all over his body, his mouth turned into a maw full of razor-sharp teeth and his ears grew longer and pointier, like a jackal's. His spine—no *its* spine, for it was no longer human at all—stretched and widened until it could no longer stand upright but had to rest on all fours. Then its nose became a snotty muzzle and its hands turned to paws as well, with long, savage-looking claws.

Once transformed, it was a beast about the size of a bull, greatly resembling a monstrous hyena, only with a snake-like nose and tongue. It laughed a hideous, reverberating hyena cackle and bared its teeth at them. Then it growled, its hackles raised on end. It could no longer speak but Jack got the message. It wanted to tear them apart. Harriett screamed. Jack's heart stopped for a moment, then reluctantly started up again. Then he heard a small crack. It came from the headstone at the base of the oak. He looked at it in the shadows, thinking it must have cracked from their weight. But what he saw could not have been caused by their pressure on the stone, or by anything natural at all.

At the top of the headstone, right in the mouth of the skull and crossbones, a shaft of light was emanating from a tiny opening. With another crack, accompanied by a frenzied howl by the now much more horrifying skinwearer, the light grew brighter.

The monstrous thing was now shrieking non-stop, its head thrashing and arms flailing. It howled and growled and spat as it abandoned its digging and hurled itself toward them over and over, only to be stopped again and again by the invisible barrier.

As Jack and Harriett watched, the light emanating from the tombstone formed a small ball. Then, with another crack, a small silver branch appeared amidst the light. It was almost like a miniature tree. It flashed and tripled in dimension so that it was about the size of an umbrella. It hovered before them, glowing brilliantly silver for just a moment before the voice at Jack's ear commanded: *Take hold of the Silver Bough and the Way will be opened.* Without question or pause, Jack took Harriett's hand and stretched it out, with his, toward the bough of light.

"Jack, what's happening?" Harriett whispered.

"I don't know, but I just feel this is right."

Jack took hold of the Silver Bough. A wave of overwhelming pleasure rolled up his arm and spread through his entire body. Glittering silver light surrounded them, blocking all view of the cemetery and enfolding them in utter silence. The pleasure mounted as the glittering light increased. Jack closed his eyes to enjoy it and felt himself being forcefully pulled away, hurtling through the silver light to another place.

# HOB

When Jack opened his eyes, still tingling all over with the feeling that came with touching the Silver Bough, it was no longer pitch dark. It was twilight and it was warm. He and Harriett were now in an open field, in the middle of an ancient circle of standing stones, much like the one in the graveyard in Cairnbawn. But here there was no church, no graveyard and no stand of oak trees. This stone circle sat in a broad, grassy dell and was much, much bigger. It was easily twice the size of Stonehenge. The Silver Bough had vanished. And so had the thing that had chased them into the graveyard.

Harriett was beside him, her eyes closed. By the peaceful look on her face their abrupt arrival here, wherever they were, had not shaken her at all. Her rosy lips were stretched in a broad smile. He wondered if this was because, unlike him, Harriett had always believed such things were possible. She hadn't mocked the strange beliefs of the Cairnbawn children as he had. She was perfectly ready to believe in magic and hoped to see it for herself one day. He was fairly sure, however, that the hideous thing that chased them into the Cairnbawn cemetery wasn't the kind of magic she'd been hoping for.

He scanned the valley for any sign of movement, not quite trusting that they had really escaped from the skinwearer. He peered from one end of the valley to the other. Nothing moved; the valley was empty and quiet. Jack looked down at a tug on his sleeve. Harriett had opened her eyes and was looking up at him, smiling. He returned her smile with a weak one of his own, not quite able to muster a proper one.

"Don't try and tell me that touching that shiny twig didn't feel nice, Jack." She nudged him in the ribs, grinning.

He laughed despite himself.

"Always annoyingly stating the obvious, Harrie." He grinned back at her. "Even after being attacked by a ... by a ..." He couldn't quite bring himself to say 'monster'.

"By a freakazoid that turned into a monstrous hyena?" Harriett suggested helpfully. "And I'm not trying to annoy you. It's just that sometimes I feel like you're not really paying attention to me—"

"Are you serious?" he blurted. "We've just been chased by a, a—"

"Zombie hyena," she offered.

"Yeah, a zombie hyena, and we've, we've been—"

"Transported somewhere by a tingly, silver twig thing."

"Yeah, and yet you're still after more attention? When is enough going to be enough?"

"Well, excuse me, Jack." Her voice had a sarcastic tone he recognised all too well. "Sorry that I'm being too needy for you after a *monster* just tried to *eat* me! If being chased by a monster isn't reason enough for you to show me a little attention, then I don't know what is!"

Jack normally found her sarcasm infuriating, but not this time. Her sarcasm was reassuringly familiar in the face of the strange things they'd just experienced. After being chased by a zombie hyena and transported by a bough of light, familiar was what Jack wanted most. He smiled at her.

"Eat *us*, Harrie," he said matter-of-factly, still smiling. "It was trying to eat both of us."

"Eat *us*, then," she admitted begrudgingly, clearly thinking that it would be churlish of her not to grant him at least that.

Jack laughed again despite himself. He was still smiling when he resumed looking around. Harriett looked around as well.

"I don't see that thing that was chasing us anywhere," she whispered. She was right. It wasn't anywhere in sight. In fact, they were nowhere near where they were before they touched the Silver Bough. "I don't think we're in Cairnbawn anymore," she added.

"I don't think we are either," Jack said, continuing to look around.

Wherever they were, it was a long way from the old churchyard. The countryside was totally different. As far as Jack could see there were rolling green hills. Thickets of trees stood here and there, their leaves just taking on their autumn colours. In the distance, hedgerows formed boundaries between neatly-shaped meadows. It looked nothing like Cairnbawn, but Jack didn't mind this at all given that the monster was in Cairnbawn. The further away from it they were, the happier he felt.

"What should we do?" Harriett asked then.

"Find a phone and call the home. We need to know what the hell is going on and get back."

"I don't think it's going to be that simple to get back." Harriett's voice shook, the pleasant after-effects of the Silver Bough wearing off.

"We have to try anyway." He took her hand in his and squeezed it comfortingly.

That small consoling action was enough to make Harriett shudder and tear up. "Oh no," she said, wiping at her eyes, "if you're being nice to me, then things must be really bad."

"It's okay, Harrie." He squeezed her hand again. "We just have to find a phone and call someone to come get us."

Without speaking, he led Harriett out of the centre of the circle towards what looked like a trail heading away in the direction of a small copse of trees and beyond that a small hill. As they neared the huge standing stone directly in front of them, Harriett stopped still.

"Jack, look …" She pointed to the top of the stone.

"What?" Jack couldn't see anything but a tall stone lit by the sinking sun.

"That mark, at the top there."

Jack looked where she was pointing, at a strange sign carved into the stone. It was obviously very old, worn down by time and weather, and barely visible. Jack had to squint to make it out. It was like an eye, an eye with sunrays coming out of it.

"What about it?" he said.

"That mark is in mum's old book, Jack! It's right here on the first page!" She turned over the book and opened it to the first page. There was the sign, an eye emitting rays of light.

"Does the book say what it is?" Jack asked, looking over his shoulder and feeling uneasy. It couldn't be a coincidence that the same mark was in their mother's old book and on this ancient standing stone.

"Yes," Harriett said, trembling all over again. "In the book it's called the Mark of Thullu."

"The mark of what?"

"Not what, *who*. Thullu is ... Well, Thullu is ..." Harriett paled before Jack's eyes, shaking so much now that she looked as though she might throw a fit.

"What's the matter?"

Her knees went out from under her and she dropped to the ground.

"Harrie! Are you alright?" Jack bent down closer to her, looking into her eyes.

"Thullu," Harriett whispered, "is ... is ... one of the *fae*. Not just one of the fae, the first of the fae, like the first angel—"

"What?"

She didn't answer. She opened the book to the first pages and pushed it towards him, her eyes wide, urging him to read. He sat down beside her, took the book from her shaking fingers and started to read.

> *And in the beginning there was only emptiness, the infinite yet knowing void.*
> *And the first child of the void was Thullu: timeless, ageless, shapeless, faceless, neither dead nor living, neither bright nor dark, neither good nor evil.*

Jack stopped reading and looked up at Harriett. "You can't seriously believe this is real?" he asked her.

"I think it is, Jack. That mark on the stone is from the book and that hyena thing is in the book too, it's called a skinwearer."

Jack shuddered. That was what the voice in his ear had called the monster. That couldn't be a coincidence. His throat constricted and his heart started racing. He said nothing, just resumed reading.

*And Thullu sought to increase, to propagate, to create.*

*And so the knowing void allowed Thullu his will, sparking a great cataclysm that seared the void, bringing light (and shadow), creating space and time, forming blood, flesh and bone, enervating breath and mind.*

*In this way the universe was born and all the worlds made. All the worlds thereby owe a debt to Thullu and are under his ultimate and intimate dominion and ever will be.*

*And in the midst of this great creation, Thullu thought into existence many ageless children of his own, deathless and potent, male and female, Bright and Dark. These children, the Faeden, Thullu sent forth to bring awe and wonder to all the new races in all the new worlds, so that all beings might know and understand Thullu's true nature, both its Brightness and its Darkness, its limitlessness.*

*And thus the Faeden came to the realm of Anwynn, over which they reigned as if gods, as Thullu ruled over them as their god.*

Jack stopped reading, his skin prickling and his heart pounding. He didn't know why, but he knew that what he had just read was not just some story. It was more than that, it was—

A shadow stepped out from behind one of the nearest standing stones. Harriett reacted instinctively, scrabbling on her hands and knees behind her brother for protection and screaming so loudly that it echoed off the stones.

"Get away!" shouted Jack, jumping to his feet, putting himself between the shadow and Harriett. "If you hurt my sister I swear I'll tear you to shreds!"

"Such manners you display," the shadow said in a bored voice. "So positively base. I have no intention of hurting either you or your *sonorous* little sister. Though I fear she has burst my eardrum with that cow yodel of hers."

"Cow yodel!" Harriett peeked out from behind Jack to see who'd insulted her. The voice was that of a young man. He stepped out of the shadow of the stone. He looked no more than eighteen or nineteen years old and was, Jack had to admit, seriously good looking. His outfit looked like a fancy dress costume. He wore tight, shin-length pants of blue velvet, a white shirt with a lacy bit at the neck, a matching blue velvet waistcoat and a long, thigh-length blue velvet coat. His hair was long and black and tied back in a pony-tail with a blue satin ribbon. His shoes were also of blue satin, with a matching bow.

"Ooh, he's pretty," Harriett whispered, apparently distracted from the worry about what had just happened to them and where they were. "I like him."

"Thank you for the compliment, little one," the man said, "though I dare say I am already well aware of the perfection of my visage and the affect it has on others. I need not the judgment of little humans to assure me of that."

"Little humans? What do you mean *little humans?*" Jack asked, shoving Harriett back behind him as she crawled out from behind his legs, staring at the handsome man's clothes.

"Is that not what you are, members of the human breed?"

"Well, yes, but you make it sound like we're human and you're not," Jack said.

"It doesn't merely sound so, boy, it *is* so."

"What do you mean?" Jack asked.

"He said he wasn't human, Jack," Harriett explained.

"I heard him, Harriett, I just don't believe him."

"Believe what you will, little boy. It matters to me not at all what you believe. As for me, I hold no beliefs whatsoever. I find they drain one's energy and serve no useful purpose."

Jack didn't know what to say to that, and judging by the look of astonished disbelief on Harriett's face, neither did she. Ignoring that last statement, Jack turned to the most pressing question on his mind.

"Do you know how we got here?"

"I do indeed, little boy." He offered no more, just stood there looking at them blankly. A long moment passed.

"Well?" sputtered Harriett. "Are you going to tell us?"

"No, not at all. I will leave that ... pleasure ... to someone else." He yawned. "To provide explanations is not why I am here. I am here," he continued, motioning to the hills around them, "to guide you from this place."

"But where are we exactly?" Jack asked, unable to keep the rising dislike for the velvet-clad stranger out of his voice.

The man simply grinned and remained silent. Jack looked down at Harriett to share his disbelief. Harriett was still staring at the man, perhaps planning to do so for as long as it took for him to answer. Jack turned back and glared at him as well, demanding an answer with his eyes. Being stared at mulishly by two kids soon had the desired effect.

"Oh, fine," the young man said, "I will enlighten you as to your location. I have the distinct displeasure of informing you that you are on the edge of the halfling village of Bright. It is a positively pastoral and nauseatingly domestic place filled with beings that are themselves brimming with all kinds of beliefs, especially ones about etiquette and manners, which are, for the most part, used to quell all fun."

"So, do you live there then?" asked Harriett.

"How absurd you are, little girl," he snorted. "Do I look like a halfling?" Harriett shrugged, so he continued. "Am I only as tall as a barrel, as round as one too and dressed like a peasant? No, little human, I am certainly not a halfling."

"Sorry, but what are you then?" she insisted, ignoring the fact that he'd called her absurd.

"In your realm my kind has many names. Mostly, you call us faerie."

"You can say that again," Jack sniggered.

"My kind causes you amusement?"

"It's not that," Harriett explained, shooting a reproachful look at Jack. "It's just where we come from fairies are only in stories; they're tiny little ladies with wings."

"How strange. Are there no male faeries in your realm?"

"Sure." Jack chuckled. "But they're mostly hairdressers."

Harriett thumped Jack in the arm, throwing an apologetic smile at the finely dressed stranger. The young man pondered Jack's words for a minute and then took on a serious demeanour.

"Such things are of no importance," he said. "I have been coerced to come here to this," he paused and looked around with disdain, "*place* to collect you and escort you to a nearby safe haven. I am led to believe you are in need of such a haven—"

"Oh yes," Harriett said in a rush before Jack could say what was on his mind: that the velvet-clad man could take his refuge and shove it somewhere unmentionable. "We were being chased by this hideous zombie-type guy with a snake-tongue and a mouth full of spit!"

"Spit, you say?" the man repeated. "That sounds like a skinwearer. In their true form, they are monsters, misshapen things from the shadowy pits. It's strange for a creature of that type to be in your realm." He pondered this a moment before turning his attention back to Harriett. "It must be said that skinwearers are indeed vile. They may even reach degrees of rudeness beyond your brother's." He cast a sideways smirk at Jack.

"Ha, ha, very funny," Jack said. "What do you mean 'our realm'?"

"You have crossed the Way Between. You are no longer in your realm, but in ours."

"And what realm is that?" Jack asked, incredulous. He looked to Harriett to see that she was practically bursting to hear the answer.

"Why, this is Anwynn of course."

"Anwynn? I've read about that," Harriett said quickly, brandishing her book in the man's direction. "It's an island where elves live!"

"It is more than an ordinary island, it is a continent apart from the sea of time, a hidden place, but otherwise you aren't far from the mark," the man answered.

"But isn't this Anwynn just a fairy tale?" scoffed Jack. "Something grade-schoolers believe?"

"Sometimes fairy tales are real," the costumed man remarked without a hint of jest.

Jack, taken aback, stood there silent a moment.

"Are, are you," Harriett stuttered, "one of the ... the Faeden?"

The young man looked at Harriett with surprise, his eyebrows arched. "That is the name given to my kind in this realm, in Anwynn."

Jack and Harriett exchanged worried glances.

"How do you know that word?" the Faeden asked.

"It's in this book, *The Word of Thullu*," Harriett answered, showing him the book.

"Where did you get that?" The Faeden's eyes widened further.

"It was our mother's," Jack said. "Why?"

"No reason," the man replied, rearranging his face back into a look of disinterest. "I was just surprised that little creatures such as yourselves can read."

At that moment an owl hooted nearby, causing Jack and Harriett to jump. Harriett nervously looked over her shoulder. "Umm, I'd kind of like to know if there are any of those skinwearer things here?"

"Fear not, child," the Faeden said, "no such fiends can harm you while you are with me. But let me continue with my message, with no further interruption, for I am bound to deliver it." He sighed and took a deep breath, as if resigning himself to explain something very boring to very dull company.

"You have a friend nearby in the person of one Aelf Ethelwulf, a thoroughly irritating, and some might say manipulative, druid who wishes to see you brought to safety."

"Druid?" Jack interrupted, his voice full of disbelief.

"Yes, druid," the Faeden said. "A member of the Order of Druids, and this druid, or rather his Master, has very rudely diverted me from my normal ... pleasures ... and compelled me to bring you to him. He has found lodgings with an acquaintance in the nearby village of Bright where he awaits you. But let me make this clear: I cannot lead you out of this circle without your express permission. The druids have placed enchantments on the circle to guard those within, namely you. These enchantments prevent any being from taking you out without your wishing to be so taken."

"Can we go by ourselves?" Jack asked, not trusting the velvet-clad man. He didn't want to go anywhere with him.

"No. That would not be wise." He watched them a moment, waiting for Jack to say something more. When he didn't, he rolled his eyes. "I could easily remove any spell placed by the druids, their magic is nothing compared to my own power, but it would be swifter for you to do as I bid. So, what say you? Shall you come with me?"

Jack and Harriett looked at each other. Up until a few minutes ago, Jack would have thought this guy was an absolute lunatic and wouldn't have believed a word he said. But having seen the skinwearer, and having touched a silver bough that appeared out of a tombstone and then brought them here, clearly miles away, a whole continent away in fact, he was much more willing to accept the Faeden's version of things.

"What do you think, Harriett?" he asked quietly.

Harriett shrugged and said, "I kind of like this faerie guy and wouldn't mind seeing some halflings and this druid too. Besides, we need help getting home again. I don't think we have a choice. We have to go with him."

Jack thought about that. Despite mistrusting the velvet-clad Faeden, he agreed with Harriett that if they were ever going to find out what was happening to them, and keep out of the way of that skinwearer, then they definitely needed help.

"Okay, so maybe this Aelf will be able to help us," he said to Harriett. "He seems to know what's going on, and wants us to be safe, but," and he lowered his voice to a quiet whisper so that the Faeden couldn't hear, "his choice of friends leaves a lot to be desired. I mean, that faerie looks like he's out of an old movie, and he's positively full of himself."

"I think we should go," Harriett whispered back quickly, worried that the Faeden could hear them.

After just a few seconds more thought, Jack nodded. It was true that they didn't have any other options. He and Harriett turned back to the Faeden, who was leaning against a standing stone and polishing his nails on his velvet jacket. He seemed not to give two hoots if they went with him or not.

"Ok, we'll go with you." Jack tried to sound sure of his decision, for Harriett's sake.

"Wonderful," the Faeden replied, still focussed on his fingernails. "You need to stand on the edge of the circle and formally agree for me to escort you out."

Jack and Harriett moved to the edge of the circle and stopped, immediately feeling a strong pressure preventing them from going any further. "Repeat after me," said the Faeden. "We grant thee the power to lead us beyond this circle." They looked at each other nervously. The Faeden waited a brief moment and then snarled, "Little humans, even though I am immortal I would rather not spend my *entire* life waiting to ferry you to the house of a simple-minded halfling. Now, repeat the words I told you."

"We grant thee the power to lead us beyond this circle," Jack and Harriett said in unison. After they spoke the words, the voice was back in Jack's head again, whispering deep in his left ear. Jack jerked his head to the left, listening to the voice as it recited the same words that he and Harriett had just said. He looked at Harriett to see if she'd heard it that time. He wasn't able to ask her about it, though, because the Faeden interrupted him.

"Lovely," he drawled, smoothing his velvet jacket with a pale hand, "and delivered with such pizzazz." Without further ado he walked away, following a trail as thin as a cow path that led from the standing stones through some trees to a distant hill. Jack noticed that the invisible pressure had vanished, they could move forward. They stepped out from the circle and followed.

The minute they stepped out of the circle, the Faeden man stopped suddenly, turned and stared at them. He looked around, his pupils dilating as he scanned the air around them, as if searching for something hidden from view. Jack and Harriett both looked over their shoulders, wondering what he was looking for. Soon the Faeden seemed to decide that it was of no consequence, because he spun on his heels again and paced toward the trail. Once the Faeden was a few steps ahead, Jack caught hold of Harriett's arm and whispered in her ear.

"Have you been hearing a voice, Harrie? A voice in your head?"

"No, what kind of voice?"

"It sounds like me, like my own voice," he whispered, glad that she hadn't responded in the teasing way she normally would, perhaps because of the worry on his face, his fear of going crazy.

"What is the voice saying?"

"Different things. It told me to call for a Way to open, to escape that—"

"Zombie hyena."

"Yeah, and then, just now, it said exactly what I said, about granting the faerie the power to lead us beyond the circle."

Harriett's brow furrowed and she looked up at him out of the corner of her eyes. Maybe she thought he *was* going nuts.

"Look, Jack," she said in a calm voice, "I think you're

just stressed. I mean, that thing did try to eat us."

"Yeah, maybe. I guess." He was trying his best to believe it himself. The drawn look on Harriett's face told him that she was not much more convinced than he was.

"Will you be accompanying me or not?" the Faeden snapped from a dozen yards away.

Jack and Harriett jumped and immediately set off to join him.

"My name's Harriett," she said, breathless, having just caught up to the Faeden. "What's your name?"

"I am the autumn and the twilight," The Faeden answered off-handedly. "I am the wind on the water. I am the ember and the ash. I am the shadow by the hearth. I am dusk and I am dawn. I am life and I am—" He looked down at Harriett and Jack, who were both staring back at him aghast. He sighed, rolling his eyes. "You may call me Hob," he muttered.

"Hob?" Harriett said, recovering from the strangeness of the Faeden's last utterances. "That's a funny name."

"On the contrary, Harriett, it is a name that inspires little mirth." He smiled mysteriously.

"Is it a faerie name?" she pressed.

"Some of us, the Faeden, what you call faerie, have multitudes of names, for we are vast and no two the same."

"You said we could *call* you Hob," Jack noted, "but is that your real name?" There'd been something in Hob's tone when he said that they could *call* him Hob, as though the Faeden wasn't quite telling the whole truth.

"My real name," Hob said firmly, "is my own to know and not to be tainted by the lips of the likes of you, little boy. Hob has always sufficed for your kind. Now come." He stalked away.

Harriett had to practically run to keep stride with Hob, her legs not even a third the length of the Faeden's. He looked down at her as though he was being followed by a rather hideous puppy. He gave her a forced smile that looked more like a sneer. It crossed Jack's mind that Harriett was accustomed to that kind of look. It was the same look he often gave her himself. Sure enough, Harriett paid the look no mind. She kept pace with the Faeden no matter how much he sneered until finally he stopped and faced her.

"Tell me, child, are you brain-sick or merely mentally deficient?"

"I'm not sick," Harriett said, smiling up at him.

"And she's not mental," Jack said. "The staff at Cairnbawn House had her tested when she was six."

"And this test you speak of showed no gross abnormality of mind?" Hob was looking at Harriett closely, as though examining an interesting yet gruesome specimen.

"Nope." Harriett smiled. "The test showed that I'm of above average intelligence."

The Faeden looked unconvinced. "It may be so, but I hardly think that is boast-worthy. The bar is very low for your species. Most of you are little brighter than squirrels." He turned back towards the trail.

When they reached the path, Hob led them into the thicket of trees and then out the other side toward a distant hill. After a while following the path, they entered a more densely wooded area and Hob stopped suddenly again. He turned to Jack and said, "That stench, is that normal for your breed?"

Jack's face flushed. "What are you talking about?" He was deeply offended, and checked if he'd stepped in something just in case.

Hob made a great show of sniffing the air near Jack, his nostrils visibly contracting.

"It's not me!" Jack protested.

"Perhaps you are right," Hob said, angling his head this way and that, trying to figure out from which direction the smell was coming. "It is behind us," he said finally, just as Jack picked up the smell as well. It smelt like the muck at the bottom of a pond, a mixture of rotting vegetation and dead fish.

They all looked back in the direction they'd come. The

breeze was now blowing straight into their faces, bringing with it the awful stench. "That reek bodes ill," Hob said with a note of curiosity.

"No kidding." Jack pinched his nostrils firmly closed. Harriett, apparently finding the smell unbearable, used her jacket to cover her whole nose and mouth.

Hob stood stock still, staring at a thick stand of trees beyond the stone circle, his eyes and nostrils dilating. "How interesting," he said to himself. Before Jack could ask what was interesting the sound of hooves reached his ears. A herd of six horses burst out of the trees into the open valley.

"Bog nags!" Hob barked with surprise.

It took only a moment for Jack to realise that bog nags were not ordinary horses. They were solidly built, shaggy beasts of a dung colour with long, matted manes and tails. Their hides and hair were greenish, as if stained by swamp muck. Their wide eyes were a milky, viscous white. As they galloped across the field their hooves threw up clods of dirt. When he looked closely, Jack saw that the hooves were razor-sharp and smeared with something resembling congealed blood. As the herd pelted towards the stone circle, the horses neighed; a terrifying, otherworldly sound that made the hair on Jack's neck stand up.

"Look at their mouths," Harriett said shakily as the horses continued to neigh, their mouths open wide to reveal long, filthy fangs.

The monstrous horses reached the stone circle and paced around its edge, stamping and sniffing at the air and ground, which they pawed with their razor-sharp hooves.

"Bog nags are blind," Hob whispered, "they hunt their prey by scent, which is ironic given how they smell."

As soon as Hob finished speaking, the horses must have picked up the trio's scent because they launched themselves in a mad gallop towards the thicket of trees where Jack and the others were standing.

"Shouldn't we run?" Jack asked, his voice a little shaky.

"No," Hob replied. "Bog nags are fast, you could not

outrun them." The Faeden was quiet just a second before speaking again. "Wait here," he said before stalking off in the direction of the oncoming herd.

Harriett yelled after him. "Hob, no! Come back!"

Hob ignored her. He moved away from them unnaturally fast. He was soon obscured by a grove of yellow-leaved birch trees that stood between them and the horses. The bog nags galloped into the stand of trees and were lost to sight as well. Moments later, a bone-chilling chorus of vicious whinnying filled the air.

"They've found him," Jack said as the whinnying increased to frenzied screams and stomping of hooves. Jack and Harriett stared into the birch grove, trying to see what was happening, shivering at the terrifying sounds of the nags. A sudden flash of blue light caused them to turn away and shield their eyes. For a long moment they couldn't see, but they could hear that the whinnying and neighing had stopped. The whole valley went unusually quiet. Once his eyesight returned, Jack looked back towards the grove, searching for Hob. The quiet was oppressive now. Jack and Harriett took a few steps towards where Hob had disappeared, straining to hear any sound that might tell them the Faeden was alive. They glanced at each other, worry etched on their faces.

A blood-curdling whinny shattered the silence. Another bog nag burst out of the trees just to the right of them. It was huge and black, its mane and tail trailing weed and dripping wet. Its lifeless white eyes ablaze with an evil light. In an instant Jack knew that the other nags had been a diversion, to cover the approach of this much more ferocious one. The nag thundered towards them, its fangs bared and dripping with froth. Jack grabbed Harriett and staggered back, turning to run.

The bog nag changed direction and cut them off, lunging at them, rearing high over their heads, its razor-sharp hooves flashing out. Jack dropped to the ground, dragging Harriett with him and rolling away as the nag's hooves hit the ground where they had just been, cutting into the earth as though it were butter. Jack and Harriett scrambled towards a large tree, the sound of stamping hooves right behind them. Jack dove behind the tree and pushed Harriett down against the trunk, covering her with his back. He looked up to face the nag as it stamped around the tree and whinnied with sheer menace, drool quivering on the end of its huge fangs. It reared again, its mud-smeared hooves pawing at the air, and then it lunged.

Jack closed his eyes, bracing himself for the moment the hooves sheared into him and his life ended. There was a sizzling crack like lightning and a flash of blue light. Jack tensed and waited for the pain, for the blood and for death. He waited but it didn't come. He opened his eyes. The huge black nag was gone. The air in front of him where it had been was buzzing with energy. A few thin tendrils of smoke hung close to the ground, where the scars of the nag's hooves dug deep into the earth.

He looked around to see Hob calmly walking back towards them. From beneath him, Harriett let out an unmistakeable sigh of relief. He helped her onto her feet. She was shaking, her eyes wide with terror.

When Hob reached them he said, in a voice of unbelievable calm, "The bog nags will not harry us further. I have vanquished them."

"How did you do that?" Harriett gasped.

"A simple reorganisation of matter, my child, nothing terribly profound."

"What! Are you kidding?"

"Kidding? No, I am not kidding." The Faeden motioned for them to continue on their way.

"Seriously?" Harriett's mouth hung open. "You got rid of the whole herd just like that?" She clicked her fingers together.

"Indeed," Hob answered.

"That's so cool! Did you see that, Jack? Hob reorganised batter!"

"*Matter*," Hob interrupted, "matter, not batter."

"Oh, right, matter. But, what do you mean by matter

exactly?" Her head leant to the left, like a curious puppy dog.

"Anything that isn't empty space. In other words nearly everything, which I suppose does include batter."

"That's so cool." She beamed at the Faeden. "Did you see, Jack? Hob reorganised matter!"

"Yes, I saw it," Jack said, shocked by what had happened.

"Is it like witchcraft, what you did?" Harriett asked, awestruck.

"Witchcraft!" Hob snarled, his spine stiffening, his eyes sparking with danger.

"Yeah," Harriett said doubtfully, "like making potions or putting hexes on people."

"What you describe are the weak practices of lesser beings. My powers go far beyond that. Witchcraft is the pastime of fatals, those who can die. I am immortal, I am ageless and cannot die. I am above such trivial games."

"If you're so high and mighty," Jack said, "how come you can't tell us how we got here and what's going on?"

"It's not a question of can or can't," Hob said, "but a question of will or won't."

"So you're enjoying keeping us in the dark! You're tormenting us!" Jack fumed.

Hob faced him. "Your constant whining, though irritating, will not persuade me to tell you any more than I have. My task is to take you to the druid, Aelf Ethelwulf, and that is all. In fact, Ethelwulf specifically stated that I should not tell you anything important. But, seeing as how you refuse to be silent, and in the interests of peace and quiet, I will give you something to ponder. The real question is not where you are or what is happening. The real question is: who, or *what*, are you?"

Jack went to ask Hob to explain this but the Faeden cut him off. "Press me any further on this and you will go the way of those nags!" The steely look in Hob's dark blue eyes showed that he was serious. Jack shut his mouth.

The Faeden sighed in a satisfied way and moved off

again, toward the small hill. When Jack and Harriett caught up with him, the Faeden's mood had lightened again. He sniffed in Jack's direction, making a dramatic show of wrinkling his nose. Harriett failed to suppress a laugh.

"I do believe that reek was not only coming from the bog nags," Hob teased, sniffing Jack. "Yes, you do have a rather interesting stench, little boy, a smell only slightly better than that of those rank nags."

Harriett covered her mouth with her hand to stifle another laugh. Jack said nothing, just clenched his fists and held onto his temper. Hob chuckled heartily and then increased his stride, leaving Jack fuming and Harriett trying desperately not to look at her brother and thus burst into a peal of giggles.

"I hate that faerie," Jack muttered. "If he calls me 'boy' or 'little' one more time, I'll reorganise the matter of his stupid face."

"I think he's funny," Harriett said simply, before trotting after the Faeden.

After a short walk, they reached the grassy, thinly wooded hill and followed the trail upwards. As they moved in among the trees, Hob slowed his pace.

"We are close now," he said. "If we encounter anyone along the way, you must tell them that you are Pixish. The Pix have much the same appearance as you, except in clothing."

"What are Pix?" Harriett asked.

"They are fatals, or mortals, like yourselves." Hob whispered the word 'mortals' as though it were something to be ashamed of. "They are one of the nations of the human-kind here in Anwynn," he added in response to Harriett's blank expression. "They are an ancient people. Oldest among the four kingdoms of humans here in Anwynn. The Pixish all have dark hair and blue eyes like yours. You will easily pass for one of their younglings."

"So, they're just like ordinary people then? People from where we're from, I mean?" Jack asked.

"Basically, yes, but they have no knowledge of your

realm and so their ways are different to yours in many respects."

"Like what?" Jack's anger was overtaken by curiosity.

"They are more courteous, for one thing," Hob said pointedly, "and unlike the humans in your realm they do not know of machines. There are no machines anywhere in Anwynn. They would be considered the dark work of sorcerers. Oh, one other thing, by all means do not call me by my name in the village."

"Why can't we use your name?" Jack followed Hob as he stalked ahead.

"I prefer to remain anonymous," was all that Hob said in response.

Harriett grabbed her brother's arm. "Wait a minute, no machines?" She stopped in her tracks. "Does that mean no television?"

"Suppose so." Jack shrugged.

"No television! I think I'm going to be sick."

# BRIGHT

They came to the top of the hill and looked down onto a small village. A group of thatched cottages hugged the banks of a shallow river, their chimneys all working overtime sending white smoke up to mingle with a few clouds scudding westward. The sun was now setting and Jack thought the little village looked homey and comfortable.

"Feast your eyes on the halfling village of Bright," Hob yawned. "The most placid place in the universe."

In the centre of the village a little white cart, drawn by a very fat pig, headed toward what looked like an inn, a two-story thatched dwelling with dormer windows and four chimneys. The cart carried a tiny, plump woman wearing a large straw bonnet adorned with a long red feather.

"Is that ... a pig drawing that cart?" Jack asked, astounded.

"That it is," Hob answered. "Halflings are ridiculous in practically everything they do, even their means of transport. They saddle pigs instead of ponies for riding. This is because they consider the pig the most noble of animals, and, if you can believe it, the most handsome. If you ask me, when it comes to halflings and pigs, both steed and riders share a remarkable resemblance."

Jack couldn't tell if Hob was being sarcastic or serious, but he found the very idea of halflings alarming. Halflings, like monsters and elves and dragons, were not meant to be real. His mother had been called insane for believing in them. If they were real, had his mother been telling the truth all along?

Harriett sighed. "That pig looks really sweet. I can't wait to get down there!"

Hob looked at her as though she were a total imbecile. She smiled sweetly back at him until he shook his head in dismay and turned to gaze over the valley below. The halfling village sat in the middle of a wide dale with low, undulating hills at its edges. Surrounding the little town were ploughed fields and clover-filled meadows, dotted here and there with farmhouses and barns. Some of the fields had haystacks in their middles, formed into large conical shapes. At the base of the hill where they were standing was a row of beehives with bell-shaped tops made of straw. The hives were arranged on the banks of a pond under the shade of a glade of weeping willows. They looked like a miniature version of the village; a little bee town. In the eastern distance rose huge, snow-capped mountains whose peaks were ringed with clouds. Jack couldn't help but be impressed by how beautiful it all was.

Most of the cottages already had light in their windows. The distinct smell of home cooking wafted up from the town, carried on a lazy breeze. As the breeze reached them, bringing with it a bouquet of mouth-watering fragrances, Harriett gasped with joy. The sight and smell of the quaint little village was like something from one of the books she loved so much.

"Do you think Frodo's home?" she said, in all seriousness.

"He's not real, Harriett. This is real." Jack's eyebrows wrinkled as he took in the village below them. "At least I think it is." He was having trouble believing it himself.

"What is real and what is not real is a question of some importance in both our realms," Hob remarked. "For often it seems to us that your world is just a mirage, so temporary and strange, and ours must seem just as strange to you. Somewhere in the middle I expect can be found the truth, if there is such a thing. Now, let us go to the dwelling where Aelf Ethelwulf awaits and where a ridiculous halfling by the name of Dorothea Butters has, by the smell of it, prepared an array of confectionaries for your delectation."

They walked down the hill and skirted the edge of the village, heading towards a group of cottages on the other side of town, close to the shallow river. Jack trailed behind as Hob led him and his sister towards a small and unusual cottage in the distance, set apart from all the others on a road leading off into the hills. Unlike the other cottages in Bright, this one was not whitewashed but painted a vivid lilac.

As they approached this vibrantly painted house, Jack got the distinct feeling that Hob didn't want to be seen by any of the local inhabitants. When a small and very merry halfling man meandered down the lane toward them, Hob hid them behind a dry stone wall. The man, three-and-a-half feet tall, was wearing a tweed suit and shiny brown shoes. Perched atop his head was a grey hat with a bright red band and a long, white feather curling up from one side. The halfling swayed a little as he walked. Jack felt sure he was drunk. This was confirmed as the fellow passed by their hiding place, for he pulled a flask out of his pocket and took a long swig.

"Ooh, lovely dovely, warm whiskey lovelies," he said as he re-corked the flask and continued on his way. "I do hope there are lots of chubby-wubbly lovelies at the inn tonight."

Once sure that the tipsy halfling had passed by, Jack asked, "What is a chubby-wubbly?"

"I think he meant a lady," answered Harriett. "A really fat one."

"Indeed," Hob sneered. "Such horrors are common in these parts."

Hob led them out from behind the wall and they walked along the road to the garden gate of the cottage toward which they'd been heading in a circuitous fashion. The thatched dwelling with lilac walls had small porthole windows and was surrounded by a low hedge that contained an attractively overgrown garden filled with a multitude of flowering plants and bushes. Hob opened the gate and walked up the path towards the oak front door. Jack noticed that a sign on the gate read 'Butters Nob'. Harriett noticed this too and was still giggling to herself when she stopped half-way down the path to smell the flowers growing there. Soon she'd plucked a handful of them and wandered off the path towards a camellia pruned into the shape of a teapot, its white blossoms illuminated by the yellow light thrown by the cottage's porthole windows.

"Oh, they're all so pretty." She bent down to pick a tiny

bellflower.

A sound beyond the teapot camellia made them all look up. Something was coming out of the evening gloom. It looked big, lumbering towards them on four legs. As it got nearer, Jack could discern horns.

"Do not fret," Hob said, "it is nothing to fear."

Harriett took a few steps back anyway. A moment later, a rather shaggy-looking long-haired cow came out into the light, tan in colour with long horns that curved upwards. A large bunch of daisies were in its mouth and it chewed on them absent-mindedly, not unlike a farmer chewing on a stalk of straw. Its large brown eyes looked at them with mild curiosity as it sat down on its haunches just like a dog or cat might. It swished its tail and watched them, all the while chewing on the daisies.

"OMG, Jack, look at it! It's gorgeous!"

"Don't go near it, Harrie, it might be dangerous." Jack took Harriett by the shoulders and dragged her closer to him.

"Oh, Jack, he's not dangerous. Look at him, he's eating daisies!" She broke free of Jack and started towards the cow.

"Come along, child," Hob demanded from near the stoop. "You may chew the cud with your shaggy-haired kin after I have delivered you to those inside."

He rapped on the door and waited. Jack and Harriett crowded beside him, anxious to see the druid who had, somehow, predicted their arrival and organised for Hob to bring them here. They didn't need to wait long before they heard the muffled padding of small feet approaching the door. Hob manoeuvred the children in front of him and took a step back out of the light.

When the door opened, Jack was surprised to see not a druid, but a very plump, middle-aged lady of about three feet tall. Her physique was just about as round as she was tall. She was conservatively dressed in a tweed skirt and jacket, which were a size too small. She looked a bit like a wine barrel bulging against its metal hoops. Her hair, neatly tucked beneath a jaunty, tartan cap adorned with a long, greenish-black feather, was short and nut brown. Her eyes were soft and an appealing amber. Altogether, she had the appearance of a well-fed, middle-aged woman in miniature. If it weren't for the frosty-white icing adorning her top lip, she would've looked altogether prim and proper. A small peak of icing was also perched on the tip of her nose. Jack surmised this must be the halfling that Hob had mentioned, Miss Butters.

"Why, what have we here?" Her amber eyes blinked in the twilight as a deft finger scooped the icing from her lip and nose into her mouth. "Two half-grown Pix-kind, are you?" She looked them up and down, apparently trying to work out by their clothing and appearance what kind of beings they were. "Though I dare say I've never seen Pix-kind attired in your fashion. Well, I suppose I must say good evening to you, though I wasn't expecting *more* visitors. My friend Aelf has just arrived moments ago, he's a druid, don't you know." She nodded importantly before noticing Hob lurking in the background. "Oh, there's another fellow here I see? Who are you, might I ask?" She blinked as her eyes adjusted to the differing light outside.

"I am merely an escort, madam," Hob said, "I have brought this pair of younglings to the druid Ethelwulf who, I believe, waits within your walls." The sound of his voice and his way of speaking apparently triggered some memory in the little woman. These memories clearly disturbed her, for she started to quiver. She took hold of the door jamb as if for support.

"Step into the light, friend," she said, a tremble in her voice, "so I might lay my eyes on you."

Hob hesitated just a moment, then sighed ever so faintly and stepped forward into the door light. He made a small bow toward the little woman. Upon seeing Hob, the halfling's face paled. She screamed an earth-shaking scream, then spun around and tore back down the hall, bellowing to someone inside. "Aelf! Aelf! The demon Hob's at my door! Aelf, help! Demon! Help! We shall all be *throttled!*"

Jack glared at Hob, a very bad feeling rising in his

stomach. When Hob noticed Jack watching him he smiled somewhat wickedly.

"She doesn't like faeries very much, does she, Jack?" Harriett peered into the cottage, trying to see where the little woman had gone.

"Not this one anyway." Jack stood in front of Hob, glaring into the Faeden's cold blue eyes. "Who and what are you?"

"I told you, little boy. I am Faeden. We sometimes have this effect on the lesser breeds."

Jack's forehead tightened and his heart thumped. "Lesser breeds? We're not animals, you know, we're people, and so was that little lady. What makes you so superior?"

"Nothing *makes* me superior." Hob smiled. "I simply *am* superior. To my kind, you are only just a little better than animals. Certainly you have the scent of the barnyard." Though Hob's words were filled with venom, his eyes were cold and detached.

Jack was caught between two impulses – giving Hob a good smack on the mouth or grabbing Harriett and running into the house to look for help. He had a bad feeling about Hob and wanted to see the back of him. Before he made up his mind, the halfling woman, Miss Butters, hurtled back down the hallway, screeching like a hawk. Now she was armed with a flour-dusted rolling pin. When the halfling reached the stoop, she shoved Jack aside with a strength he wouldn't have expected of so small a person and he found himself flying through the air. He landed, sprawling, in a clump of blue flowers. He shook his head and jumped to his feet, just in time to see an arm reach out from inside the doorway and grab Miss Butters by the collar of her tweed jacket.

The arm belonged to a tall, angular-faced man with shoulder-length grey hair who looked about fifty years old. He towered over Miss Butters and had a pale but kind face. He wore a white, hooded cloak over a sky-blue tunic and a pair of dark brown pants. He had the most unusual eyes Jack had ever seen: a rich violet. Jack thought this must be the druid, Aelf Ethelwulf. He certainly looked the part.

The druid restrained Miss Butters by the back of her jacket, preventing her from launching herself off the stoop toward Hob. As Miss Butters dangled in mid-air, her feet still running, she madly swung the rolling pin in the direction of the Faeden. Rather than looking disturbed, Hob had the appearance of someone watching grass grow. Miss Butters continued to shriek.

"Let me at him, I'll pulverise him! Let me at him!"

Jack's heart skipped a beat. Harriett was no longer with him by the door. A surge of fear cut through him. He looked around and saw with alarm that in all the commotion Harriett had moved closer to, rather than further away from, Hob. Jack watched, as if in slow motion, as Harriett took Hob's hand. She had a look of fear on her face, directed not at Hob but at the squalling halfling woman. It was as if she was frightened that the tiny woman would hurt Hob! Typical Harriett, Jack thought, no idea how to look after herself.

Hob looked down at the little girl with undisguised surprise, showing the most emotion Jack had seen on his face since they'd met him. Hob didn't shake Harriett's hand away, allowing her to entwine her fingers with his, as if shocked into inaction by her act of affection.

"Dorothea Butters!" The druid spoke sternly, with a commanding voice that drew all their attention. "What ill manners you're displaying for our guests! Besides, as you well know, Hob can't enter your house without an invitation and so, if you'll just quiet down for a moment, I'll explain everything."

Miss Butters continued to wriggle, trying to escape, until she apparently accepted that the druid was far too strong for her. She let out a sudden, vociferous raspberry, sending a large amount of spittle in Hob's direction. Then she deflated and hung there limply like an old coat.

"Oh, goodness me," the druid said, "how impolite, Dorothea!" The little woman looked only slightly abashed, her dangling feet casting tiny shadows over a pot of nodding violets perched on the stone stoop. She mumbled something in response, her eyes downcast, watching the shadow of her feet swing to-and-fro like river reeds in a breeze.

"Beg pardon, Dorothea?" the druid asked.

"I said," Miss Butters replied dejectedly, "if I can't hit the devil with my rolling pin then I shall give him a ruddy good tongue-wiggling."

"Oh, I see." The druid's lips bent in a tiny smile. Hob, on the other hand, was not smiling at all. The Faeden was now looking at Miss Butters with a face filled with either shock or awed admiration, Jack couldn't tell which. The druid spun the halfling so that she faced him. "Do you promise not to try to attack Hob again, Miss Butters?"

"Are you sure he's not going to throttle us?" she asked.

"Certainly he won't, my dear Dorothea, Hob has no such intentions. Do you, Hob?"

Hob shook his head indicating that he had no murderous intentions, though Jack thought the look on his face indicated otherwise.

"And he can't come inside unless I invite him?" Miss Butters pressed.

"He has not the power to cross your threshold without your very own invitation," the druid assured her.

"To be precise," Hob interjected, "it is not a question of *power*, Ethelwulf—"

"Not now, Hob!" the druid exclaimed before turning back to the dangling halfling. "Be assured, Miss Butters, you are perfectly safe."

"Oh, very well. But if we find ourselves deceased it'll be on your head, Aelf Ethelwulf! And I'm keeping the rolling pin!" At that Aelf gently placed Miss Butters just inside the door, where she took up a fighting stance, ready for any sudden attack from Hob's direction.

"Now that we have that sorted," the druid said, passing a quick glance at Miss Butters before turning to Jack and Harriett, "let me welcome you to the village of Bright. I am Aelf Ethelwulf. It is very nice to meet you!" He beamed at them as he extended his hand. Harriett walked up and shook it immediately.

"You have very twinkly eyes," she said.

"You're very kind and particularly observant." Aelf smiled.

He extended his hand to Jack. Jack, less trusting and less forward than Harriett, hesitated before taking the druid's hand. This was all so strange. To see a three foot tall woman try to brain a faerie with a rolling pin was not something one saw every day. Add to that the fact that Jack had no idea where they were, had been hearing a voice in his ear and had no idea why that skinwearer thing had chased them in Cairnbawn and it all made Jack feel dazed. More to the point, he couldn't ignore the look of terror on the halfling woman's face when she'd recognised Hob. Why was this druid associating with Hob in the first place? Clearly Hob was bad news. Nevertheless, Jack needed help and these were the only people he'd encountered since leaving the graveyard. He shook the man's hand and managed a small smile.

"Welcome to Bright, Jack." The druid was still beaming.

"How do you know my name?"

"Ah, to explain that I will need to tell you a good number of other things. Perhaps Miss Butters will put on the kettle and we can discuss it in the comfort of her kitchen over a cup of tea?"

"I'm not having that demon in my kitchen!" Miss Butters blustered, brandishing the rolling pin at Hob.

"That's *demigod* to you," Hob said, sneering.

"Now, now, let's all try to get along!" Aelf frowned and wagged a finger at Miss Butters and Hob. "Miss Butters, Hob may be one of the Faeden but he really isn't all that bad. In fact, I have often found him to be rather nice." He looked at Hob and smiled. Hob sneered in disgust at being called nice.

"At the moment," the druid continued, "Hob has agreed to help the Order of Druids with certain things, one of them being safely escorting these youngsters here. Does their safe arrival not put him in good stead? Besides, he has assured me that he will be on his best behaviour."

Miss Butters looked like she might waver for a moment but then, as if remembering something, her face set into a determined expression.

"You can't trust the assurance of the Tricksy Ones, everyone knows that! The Tricksy Ones are nasty through and through. They're the natural enemies of all those who are upright and dainty!"

"Dainty? You?" Hob scoffed and rolled his eyes. "You're about as dainty as a mountain troll, and about as attractive as well."

"How dare you!" Miss Butters spluttered, her knuckles whitening around the rolling pin. "Compare me ... troll ... how dare you!"

"Come now," Aelf said uncertainly, looking ready to step between Hob and the halfling if needed. "Can't we at least be civil to one another?"

"Civil? To a tricksy devil? Never!" Miss Butters' voice was shrill. "They say one thing and do another. There is no trusting them at all and I won't have him in my kitchen! I'll eat my own stockings first!"

"Well, I somehow believe you would indeed," Aelf said. He faced Hob. "I'm afraid we shall have to part ways now, my friend."

"Not to worry," Hob replied. "It is of no concern. These *fatlings* are known for their rudeness, after all."

"Rude? Me? How dare you!"

"That is enough!" Aelf scolded. "Goodness, what are things coming to when civilised people can't even be polite for the duration of a cup of tea?"

"She started it," Hob said, to which Miss Butters poked out her tongue and brandished the rolling pin again.

"Well, at the very least, young Jack and Harriett and I are going to act maturely, aren't we?"

"I will," Harriett said. "But Jack has puberty hormones that make him pretty grumpy." She shrugged her shoulders as if to say 'what can you do?' and went straight inside. Jack's face burned with embarrassment. Miss Butters, after a nanosecond of indecision, promptly trotted after Harriett, rolling pin in hand, clearly glad to get out of Hob's presence. Jack and Aelf went to follow her when Hob stopped them.

"Ethelwulf," the Faeden said, "just one *minor* thing. When I brought the children out of the circle, I felt the presence of another being. It was hidden from my perception somehow, but I felt it nevertheless."

"Why didn't you say anything at the time?" Jack asked, remembering that Hob had stopped suddenly when he and Harriett had stepped out of the circle, looking around as if searching for something hidden from view.

"It would only have alarmed you," Hob answered.

"Indeed, a being powerful enough to hide itself from Hob is something that demands attention," Aelf added.

"As I keep telling you, Ethelwulf, it has nothing to do with power, it is far more complex than that. It has to do with the way things were at the beginning, when time was made."

"When *time* was made?" Jack interrupted. "You don't make time. It just is."

"Nothing 'just is' human. Everything was made, even time, even space."

"Such things are beyond me, I'm afraid," Aelf shrugged, winking at Jack. "Needless to say, we don't need to understand the origin of the universe to know we need to be alert to this hidden being who, powerful or not, managed to evade Hob."

"Nothing evaded me, Ethelwulf. I sensed the thing."

"But you didn't locate it, did you, and you can't tell us what it was?" Aelf said, enjoying pointing out that Hob, despite all his ranting about being the sun and the moon and every other darn thing, wasn't all he was cracked up to be.

Hob glared at Aelf but said nothing.

"Never mind," Aelf continued. "Thank you for safely delivering Jack and Harriett. I am most grateful."

"There is one other thing," Hob said with clenched teeth. "As I led the humans here, we were pursued by a herd of bog nags."

"Good gracious!" Aelf said, his eyes wide with surprise. "Bog nags, here, in the dale! In broad daylight! How absolutely extraordinary!"

"It appears that others know of the children's arrival, others who commanded the bog nags to pursue them. But you need not worry, I dealt with the nags. They are no more."

"In that case, Hob," Aelf said, recovering his composure, "my gratitude to you for bringing the youngsters safely here is well deserved indeed."

Hob gave the slightest bow and, without another word, walked into the night. Aelf called after him, "Oh, and Hob, I'll be in touch when we need you again." Hob grunted and vanished into thin air.

"Where'd he go?" Jack asked.

"Off to sulk I should think." Aelf smiled in a satisfied way and then motioned to the front door.

"After you, Jack."

Jack went inside and headed down the hall with the druid following behind. The cottage smelt like a candy store and, given the way it was decorated with frilly, floral chairs and lots of lace, it looked a lot like one too. As they passed through the sitting room Miss Butters emerged from a side room with a large key. She went nervously to the front door and shut and locked it. Not satisfied with that, she pushed a hat stand up against the door for good measure, then joined them.

"I never would have believed it," she muttered to herself as they reached the doorway into the kitchen. "I, Dorothea Butters of Bright, fended off the Hob with nothing more than a rolling pin! And you, Aelf!" She looked up at the druid and chided, "I am very disappointed in you! Inviting that *tricksy demon* to my home!"

"I do apologise, Dorothea, but as I have already assured you, Hob had promised to behave, and I needed him to safely bring the children here."

At that Miss Butters looked at Jack as if seeing him for the first time. "Where are they from, Aelf?" she asked, looking at

Jack's clothing and hair. "They dress most peculiarly, even for Pix-kind."

"They hail from a very distant place, another realm in fact, and they come because they are in need of safe refuge, Dorothea."

"Refuge, you say?" Miss Butters' eyes popped a little. Jack sensed that she was reluctant to accept that he and Harriett were not from Anwynn. Something about the way she looked at him reminded him of the way people in his world looked at those who believed in ghosts or the Loch Ness monster, with a kind of condescending pity.

"Yes, Dorothea, they are in grave peril," Aelf continued. Jack flinched at the word 'peril' but said nothing.

The halfling glanced toward the bolted front door and whispered. "They must be if the Hob's involved."

"I will tell all, my friend, over a hot cup of tea, as I'm sure the children are in need of refreshment, having come so far." The druid's constant talk of tea was getting on Jack's nerves. There was so much he didn't understand. What was happening to him and Harriett was far more important than a cup of tea. But Miss Butters didn't seem to agree. The reference to Jack and Harriett having come a long way, and the blasted cup of tea, pulled her out of herself. She stood tall and sucked in her rather large belly, as though steeling herself for a very difficult task.

"Right, let it not be said that Dorothea Butters of Bright was negligent in her hospitality. A cup of tea we will have, and cake, and I might drag out some googy eggs too and whip up a nice omelette to boot." With that she turned and entered the kitchen.

Jack and Aelf followed her in. The kitchen was a cosy room with well-built, practical-looking timber furniture, all of a honey colour. Hanging from a rack suspended above the stove were all manner and make of frypans and saucepans. There were shelves laden with blue and white striped jars and sacks of flour and sugar and all kinds of other, mostly sweet, things. The table in the centre of the room was crowded with cakes and trays of cookies and fat loaves of freshly-baked bread, all giving off a mouth-watering fragrance. All of this was framed by large windows with potted flowers happily growing in window boxes. In pride of place by the kitchen hearth was an old wing-backed chair, where Harriett was making herself totally at home. She sat on the chair by the fire with her feet crossed at the ankles on a matching pouf. She was just finishing a cupcake and looked perfectly relaxed.

"It's nice here," she said matter-of-factly. Jack shook his head with disbelief.

"This is precisely why I asked Hob to escort you here." Aelf chuckled. "I must say you look very comfortable there, Harriett. I had my eye on that chair just before you arrived but barely had time to say hello to Miss Butters before Hob knocked on the door."

"Never mind, Aelf," Miss Butters said, busying herself by the stove, "we'll have a proper sit down in a tick. I'll just make the omelettes first."

"So gracious of you Dorothea, and might I say you look well. You've put on quite a bit of weight since I saw you last," he said in a flattering voice, winking at Jack and Harriett.

"Now Aelf, you know that's not true, though I wish it were, but I can't have put on more than a pound, if that."

"Oh, don't be modest. I'd say at least five pounds, Dorothea, if not more."

"Hush now." The halfling blushed. "I'll put out your tea as I set to finishing the omelettes and we can have a nice chat." She pulled out a kitchen chair and motioned for him and Jack to take a seat.

"Excellent," Aelf said as he sat down. "This tea will work wonders on our frazzled nerves."

"To hell with the cup of tea!" Jack had finally reached breaking point. He threw his arms in the air. "Are you joking? We've been chased through a graveyard by some monster thing! Then a branch made of silver light appeared and brought us to a stone circle who knows how far away from home. And then this, this, magical Hob dude came along and dragged us here to this crazy midget's house, but not before we were chased by blood-thirsty nags, and you, a total nutter by all accounts, can think of nothing else but having a cup of tea! This is just totally messed up!" He was shaking, his knees weak. He took a step closer to the wall in case he needed to lean against it. "I don't want a stupid cup of tea! I want to know what's going on!"

"Why, I never!" Miss Butters gasped as the room fell quiet amid the tension. Jack's head was pounding. He wanted to yell some more but then that voice, the disembodied voice that sounded like his own, returned: *Shush. Be still. Be calm.* Almost as if against his will, he felt himself instantly calming down. The desire to yell just went away. He found that he didn't want to say anything at all.

"I like cups of tea," Harriett said into the tense silence.

"Me too," echoed Aelf, "and though I do understand you are confused and frightened, Jack, a little touch of normalcy will do us all the world of good. I have things to tell you both that will not be pleasant and you will, I think, be grateful for the warmth and sweetness of that cup of tea before I'm done."

## THE VEIL

Jack managed to calm down enough to take a seat at the kitchen table with everyone else, but only after Harriett relocated herself there to be closer to the cakes and patted the seat next to her invitingly. Miss Butters placed a pot of tea before them, then four individual omelettes still in their pans and cake as well. The halfling was able to make food in the blink of an eye, and eat it even quicker than that. Jack wondered if the table ever got properly cleared, or if Miss Butters had a single meal each day that lasted from dawn to dusk.

"There's your tea," Miss Butters said, handing Aelf a recently poured cup. "Are you sure you won't have one, young man?" she asked Jack. He shook his head.

"Do you have any sarsaparilla?" he asked, not quite sure why. He normally didn't drink it, but for some reason he had a strong craving for it.

"Sarsaparilla? Let me see. Yes, I think I have some sarsaparilla-root cordial I made a little while ago. I'll get you some." She went into the pantry and came back with a bottle of black cordial. She poured him a glass and sat it before him. "Now," she said to Aelf, "let's have our explanation as to what this is all about."

"Very well," Aelf began, "but first I must determine how Jack and Harriett came to be here in Anwynn, or more importantly, which one of them brought them here." He looked at them expectantly, first at Harriett and then at Jack.

"Umm, well I don't really know how we got here," Jack began. "One minute we were back home, and the next we were here."

"Yes, of course, of course, but what I mean to say is, which of you opened the Way?" the druid asked. "Was it you, Harriett? Or you, Jack?"

"It's not likely to be me because I don't even know what

you're talking about," Harriet declared.

"Opened the Way?" Jack asked, remembering the words of the voice in his ear.

"Yes, the Way Between." Aelf looked surprised that they didn't know what he was talking about. "One of you must have summoned the Silver Bough that carries the bearer between the realms. One of you must have parted the Veil for you to have journeyed here," he explained.

"The Veil?" Jack asked, confused.

"The Veil separating our realm from yours, the Veil that keeps the realm of Anwynn hidden."

"I think it was me," Jack said cautiously, thinking of the voice in his ear and how he'd called out and the Silver Bough had appeared. "I think I opened the Way."

"Tell me how you did it, Jack," the druid said, his eyes going to the hollow of Jack's neck. Was the druid looking for the birthmark? How did he know it was there? Jack tugged up the zipper on his leather jacket.

"I sort of just knew what to do. I mean, I had this thought to call for a way to escape from that thing, the skinwearer—"

"How do you know that word, Jack?" The druid looked both surprised and curious, as Hob had done when he'd heard them use that word. On the spot, Jack decided not to tell him about the voice in his head. He didn't want to sound crazy.

"Ah, err, well, Hob explained what it was when we told him we'd been chased by a thing that changed shape, that had green glowing eyes—"

"Green glowing eyes? Do you mean you saw a glint of green in its eyes when it was in human form?" Aelf looked positively astounded now.

"Ah, yes. Why, is that important?"

"Extraordinary is what it is. A skinwearer's disguise is powerfully magical. Only an experienced and powerful druid can detect a skinwearer when it has taken human form, and then only because they sense the sorcery at work or notice it behaving strangely. Not even the most powerful druid can see a trace of the skinwearer's true form beneath its disguise."

Harriett looked at Jack, her eyes wide with surprise and worry. Jack's gut tightened.

"I, I don't know what to say," he said.

"You need not say a thing, Jack. Let's move on. So, you were in the stone circle in Cairnbawn?"

"Yes."

"Of course, that circle is the only Waypoint in your realm that leads to Anwynn. The Veil can only be parted within that circle. On this side there are many circles, but only one of them leads to the human realm, and that is the circle right here in Bright. I haven't been to the Cairnbawn circle myself, is it lovely?"

"It's in a graveyard," Jack said bluntly.

"Delightful!" Aelf laughed. "Graveyards are such charming places, don't you think?"

"Not really," Harriett said, apparently at one with Jack in not believing that anybody could find a cemetery charming. Jack recalled that while they were in the graveyard the voice in his left ear had demanded that they 'stay inside the circle'.

"We hid from the skinwearer inside the circle," he said. "I think that was why it didn't get us."

"Yes, of course. That circle is protected by many wards of magic, including an oak ward."

"Oak ward?" Jack swallowed hard, his throat tight. The voice in his ear had directed him to hide beneath an oak.

"Yes, an oak tree imbued with magic that acts as a shield. Beneath its canopy, no dark magic can penetrate. No evil creature can break the perimeter of an oak ward."

"We hid beneath an oak!" Harriett exclaimed. "Remember, Jack?"

Jack nodded in response, feeling uneasy. The voice in his ear had knowledge of things well beyond his own experience. But how could that be, given that it was his own voice?

"Well, it was quite a turn of good fortune you made it inside the circle safely, all things considered," Aelf said.

"But, but why was that thing, that skinwearer, after us in the first place?" Jack asked.

"Let me beg your patience, Jack. I will answer that and all of your questions, but there is much else that you must know first for you to understand the situation you find yourself in." The druid sighed, hesitating as if he didn't want to tell them something.

Jack had seen that kind of hesitation before, years ago, when the police had come to tell him that their father was dead and their mother missing, presumed drowned. Aelf's eyes showed the same reluctance and pity. "These are not pleasant things to tell," the druid continued, "and, as much of what I have to say will be strange to all of you, it may be best if I get it all out in one go without interruptions and then answer any questions you want to ask later."

"Sounds good to me," Harriett said, interrupting the druid already.

"I shall begin then," Aelf smiled. "To answer your first question, Jack, as to how I knew your names and was awaiting you here. In my Order, the Order of Druids, there are some who have what might be called the Second Sight, the ability to see into the future. We call these people Seers. It was the most powerful of those Seers who predicted that two children would arrive at the circle tonight, pursued by a skinwearer, and that their names would be Harriett and Jack."

"Spooky," Harriett said.

"Not the word I would have chosen," smiled Aelf, "but I see your point. The Seer in question is a most graceful woman by the name of Alva, and her Sight is faultless." At the name Alva a twinkle appeared in the druid's eyes. Jack suspected Aelf's appreciation of Alva went far beyond her powers as a Seer.

"Now, to explain why it was so important for us to bring you safely here, I must explain many other things." Aelf looked at Jack and smiled softly. "The first and most important thing that you must know, Jack, is that you are a Waycaller."

"A what?" Jack asked.

"A Waycaller. There is vast power within you, more power than most druids could ever hope to attain. Most of all, it is only the Waycallers who have the power to part the Veil and travel between the realms."

Jack stared into the druid's eyes looking for some hint that he was joking, but there was only sincerity there. Vast power? Him? Jack was half-way between laughing and shouting. The idea that he had that kind of power was both ludicrous and overwhelming.

"But, what is this Veil?" Harriett asked.

"The Veil," the druid answered, "hides the realm of Anwynn from the human realm. It is an enchantment, a magical barrier. At one time, thousands of years ago, Anwynn was a part of your world, a continent like any other. The Veil was created to hide it, to divide the realms."

"But why? Who created it?" Jack asked.

"Amallayne created the Veil," the druid said. "She is one of the Faeden, known by some as the Great Goddess."

"Blasphemy!" Miss Butters spat, her whole body tense. "There is but one God and that God is Eugene, Lord of the Chimney Brush!"

"Err, well, umm, let's leave religious discussions aside just for now," the druid said carefully. "What is important is that the Veil was created by Amallayne, goddess or not, to separate Anwynn from the human realm."

Miss Butters went to protest again but Aelf silenced her with a stern look.

"Why did this Amallayne want to divide the world?" Jack asked, intrigued.

"She did it to keep your realm safe from monsters and from the Dark Faeden, the Faeden who delight in horror and cruelty."

"Like that tricksy Hob!" Miss Butters said, glancing down the hall towards the barred front door. "Eugene damn him!"

"Well, no," Aelf said. "Hob is not one of the worst of

the Faeden, though he is, admittedly, quite naughty. There are Faeden far worse than he, namely Morrigan."

At the mention of this Faeden's name Jack felt the ground shift beneath him. The room spun. It was as if he was no longer in that warm kitchen but in a deep, dark place, a place suffused with a pale green light. He briefly wondered what had happened, if he'd really arrived someplace else or if this was a hallucination, a symptom of madness.

*You are not mad, Jack,* the voice in his ear whispered soothingly. *The power within you has awoken now that you have crossed the Veil. Now you see visions of things happening far away, maybe even in the future!*

Before he could make any sense of this, a wave of nausea struck him, so strong that he felt he might die from it. He clutched at his stomach and looked around, suspecting that the nausea was caused by something in that place. Coming towards him from out of the darkness was a pale woman, beautiful and yet terrifying, with white hair in long dreadlocks. Her eyes shone in the dark, a luminous emerald green. The nausea increased as Jack was struck by an awful stench. His stomach heaved, but he held it down. The woman opened her mouth, parting lips that were blackened and scarred, as if burned. Out of her ashen mouth came a burst of power that knocked Jack onto the ground, spreadeagled on his back. Then the voice in his ear that was his but not his sang out: *She comes! Morrigan, the Pale Mother!*

"Eugene bless us all!" Miss Butters squeaked, shattering Jack's vision and jarring his senses so that the warm kitchen came back into focus. "Why mention *her* in my house, Aelf?"

Jack sat frozen in his chair, sweating and terrified, the nausea now dissipating but still strong. He'd never experienced anything like that before. What was it? A hallucination? Surely not a vision? He couldn't trust the voice in his ear. Only lunatics heard voices and believed what they said. But part of him did believe the voice. The fear that he was going the way of his mother, losing his mind, rose up stronger than ever and sent a chill down his spine. He didn't dare say a word about this to anyone. They would think he was mad. At the same time, he wished there was someone he *could* tell, someone who would comfort him, someone like a mother or a father. A hazy memory came to him of his mother's arms wrapped around him and of his father's smiling face, but that was all gone. There was no-one like that in his life anymore. He'd been alone from the moment his mother killed his father in the Cairnbawn graveyard.

"Do not speak of the Dark Ones again," Miss Butters warned Aelf in a whisper, looking to the window and the dark garden beyond. "If they hear us they will come and bring doom down on us!"

As if at Miss Butters' words, the oil lamp hanging above them dimmed. Jack was struck by a sudden chill. His knees and elbows ached and he shivered. Beside him, Harriett whimpered, her teeth lightly chattering. The room grew darker and the very air stilled, as though life itself were being sucked out of the cottage by the cold.

"Stay still," Aelf whispered, looking to the window, which was frosting up before their eyes. A shadow passed over the glass and it creaked as the frost on it thickened.

"What is it?" Miss Butters mumbled, her eyes wide.

"Quiet," Aelf hissed, "say not a thing more. It cannot enter, but it can hear us."

The roof above them groaned as the shadow passed overhead, as if bearing a huge weight. Then the windows at the front of the cottage creaked and the oak front door groaned. The oil lamp fluttered and nearly went out. Then, as it quickly as it had come, the shadow was gone. The lamp flickered back to brightness, the warmth returned and the air came alive again. They all breathed in, aware suddenly that they had all been holding their breath.

"What was that?" Jack asked, rubbing his knees.

"A Sending," Aelf said. "A shadow sent forth to do a sorcerer's bidding. A Sending is powerful and dangerous, but it had no hope of touching us while we remained inside." Aelf nodded towards the fireplace, as if the warm flames there explained why the Sending hadn't found its way into the house.

"Lord Eugene be blessed," Miss Butters said, patting Harriett on the shoulder and puffing up proudly. "Without Him the dark things would have us all. But they can't come in, can they? No, thanks to Eugene we are safe inside."

Aelf noticed Jack's look of confusion and explained. "Long, long ago Eugene, one of the Faeden, placed a magical ward over every dwelling where there is a hearth fire. Where a home fire burns, no Faeden may enter uninvited, no dark creatures may enter either, nor any sorcery penetrate the walls. It is a most profound magic, apparently unbreakable. Quite a feat for so small a Faeden." He cast a quick glance at Miss Butters, realising what he'd said. "No offence meant, Dorothea."

"None taken," the halfling said. "Lord knows, the longer the legs, the slower the mind."

Aelf mock winced, feigning offence, but smiled warmly. Miss Butters wagged an accusing finger at him.

"And speaking of slow minds, didn't I tell you not to mention *her*? That's what brought that shadow down on us!"

"I doubt the mere mention of the Pale Mother was enough to do it," Aelf said. "That Sending was no doubt here seeking out Jack and Harriett and was likely sent by the same sorcerer who sent the bog nags, not by Morrigan herself."

Miss Butters squawked and nearly fell off her seat.

"Apologies, Dorothea," Aelf said as he righted the halfling and patted her on the head. "I sometimes forget," he added to Jack, "that halflings are very sensitive about dark creatures, and especially about Morrigan."

Miss Butters squeaked at this next mention of the Dark Goddess and made a strange sign over her heart by wiggling her fingers. Jack watched her chubby fingers waving in the air for a moment, finding the movement strangely calming, like watching seaweed bobbing on the tide.

"Who is, ah, she?" Jack asked once he could speak again, careful not to say the Pale Mother's name. He glanced at Miss

Butters, still wiggling her fingers.

"Goodness," Aelf said, "it seems incredible that you do not know who she is, for she is the ultimate reason why you are here. She is the Queen of Doom, the Mistress of Monsters, one of the Dark Faeden, terrible and cruel, and the most powerful of her kind. She is a goddess to the Vellenor, the Dark Elves, and to the goblins and trolls. They call her the Pale Mother, or the Screaming Queen."

A cold dread spread from Jack's throat down into his gut. The Pale Mother, she was the one in his vision. Was she real? Were Dark Elves, goblins and trolls real as well? From the earnest look on Aelf's face, they were. Jack took hold of the table top to steady himself.

"The Screaming Queen?" Harriett asked.

"Yes, they call her that because most of her power resides in her voice, which can control and kill with the merest sound."

"Eww, she sounds awful!" Harriett said.

"Indeed. It is because of the Pale Mother that Amallayne created the Veil," Aelf continued, not noticing or perhaps ignoring the fact that Jack's skin had paled to a clammy white. "You see, Morrigan was unsatisfied with the worship of the Vellenor and the other dark creatures. She wanted all the beings of this world to worship her as a goddess. To force them to do so, she launched a terrible war, the Doom War. That war nearly destroyed the world, but at the last Morrigan was defeated and imprisoned in her own domain, Uffern, which is a cavern deep under Anwynn. This was many thousands of years ago and Morrigan, immortal, has been striving to break free ever since."

"To prevent anything like the Doom War ever happening again," the druid continued, "Amallayne created the Veil, keeping the continent of Anwynn, and all dark creatures with it, on one side of the Veil, and the human realm on the other—"

"But, that means that everyone else in Anwynn is stuck on the same side as the monsters!" Harriett said, appalled.

"It does," Aelf said with a sad smile. "You see, Anwynn is the oldest continent and original homeland of all the magical races: the elves, the halflings, even the goblins and trolls originated here. Anwynn is the source of all magic in the world, the very ground here is rich with it. The enchantment Amallayne used to create the Veil separates the magical from the non-magical, and so it separates all of Anwynn from the human world."

"I'd move, if I were you," muttered Harriett, clearly thinking of the skinwearer and the bog nags.

Aelf chuckled. "Even if we could leave Anwynn," he said, smiling, "we wouldn't. We could never be separated from our homeland, from all that we love and from the source of magic. Anwynn is our home and ever will be, for good and ill."

"The question is moot though," he continued. "Amallayne made the Veil impenetrable to all but those she empowered as Waycallers. The Waycallers are the only ones who can open a Way between the realms, and even then only at certain points marked by stone circles. Even Amallayne herself cannot travel into the human realm."

"But, why did this Amallayne let other people have the power to open the Way?" Jack asked. "Wouldn't it have been better if only she could do it?"

"The reason why the Waycallers were given the power to open the Way has to do with the nature of the enchantment Amallayne used to create the Veil. It takes immense power to hide the whole continent of Anwynn and sustain the Veil, and to pass through the Veil. The only way to contain that kind of power over millennia is to place it inside living beings, one on each side of the Veil, who act as anchors. These living anchors keep the Veil tethered to its place between the realms. On this side of the Veil, that power is held by the Head of the Druid Order."

"So, are you one?" Harriett asked.

"Goodness no, the Head of the Druid Order is Lady Kashashem. She is far wiser and far more powerful than I am.

She is also far older, being elvish. In the human realm, your world, Jack, the power of the Waycaller is hereditary and much stronger, because with each generation the power intensifies and builds. There is one Waycaller in each generation, the power passing down a female bloodline to this day."

"Female bloodline?" Jack said, confused, for surely he was the Waycaller. After all, hadn't he brought himself and Harriett to Anwynn?

"Yes, but the Waycaller is not always female – it can be a son *or* a daughter of the female bloodline. Your mother was a member of that bloodline and now the power has awakened in you, Jack. Your very presence here proves that. You are the Waycaller of your generation, Jack. You carry the blessing and power of Amallayne within you."

Jack still didn't know what to think about that. He just sat there, dazed, staring at his nearly empty glass of sarsaparilla. How could he have this vast power inside of him and not know it? He didn't feel powerful, quite the opposite. And did this all mean that his mother was not mad at all? That she had been to Anwynn, had actually seen the things she believed in and talked about? But, if she wasn't mad, why had she killed Jack's father, her own husband? Jack wanted to ask the druid about his mother, if he'd known her, but couldn't bring himself to do it. He couldn't handle one more shock. Knowing beyond doubt that his mother was not mad after all would change everything he thought he knew, including what he thought he knew about himself.

"Typical," Harriett said suddenly. "You get all the luck, and now you're magic too." She rolled her eyes at Jack.

"Well," Aelf said, "we should be glad of that. We'll need all the good luck we can find now that Morrigan's influence is growing again."

"The Pale Mother's influence is growing?" Miss Butters stuttered.

"Oh yes, dramatically. We must assume that it was her followers who, somehow, sent the skinwearer across the Veil to hunt Jack and Harriett. The Seer I mentioned before, Alva, had a vision in which she saw clearly that Morrigan wants the human Waycaller killed."

Aelf turned to Jack and Harriett, his whole demeanour grave. "I'm so sorry to have to tell you this, Jack and Harriett, but you are in great danger. There are worse than skinwearers on your trail. Morrigan has many dark sorcerers as disciples who will do anything to see her released and they are quite as monstrous as she is. It must have been one of them who sent the bog nags after you, for it is only the followers of Morrigan who have any control over those beasts."

"But why?" Jack asked, his voice dry. "Why does she want to kill me?"

"The power that sustains the Veil resides within the Waycallers, in their very blood. Morrigan believes that by making the hereditary line of human Waycallers extinct, the enchantment that imprisons her will be broken. We do not know for sure if this is true, but I must confess that it sounds plausible to me."

"Me too," added Harriett in a frightened whisper.

"I also find it worrying that the skinwearer was able to cross the Veil without the aid of a Waycaller. Until Alva saw it in her vision, we thought that was impossible. It might mean that Morrigan, or her dark disciples, have found some sorcery more powerful than the magic of the Veil. This is something we need to discover, which is why I must take you to the home of my master to seek his advice. He knows more about the powers of the Veil than anyone except Amallayne herself."

"But, all I want to do is go home. I don't want to see your druid master," Jack said, aware that he was sweating though his clothes.

"I'm very sorry to have to be so blunt, Jack, but in these times delicacy simply wastes valuable moments. The fact is that you have no choice. None. If we do not discover how the Veil was breached and the skinwearer sent into the human realm, you will not be safe. You are the Waycaller and

Morrigan's followers will pursue you and eventually they will find you. They have ways of seeking you out that are beyond my magical skill to prevent. Once they find you, they will kill you and then Morrigan may be loosed to wreak havoc again. That cannot be allowed. I would die first. I am so terribly sorry, but you cannot go home."

"So much for luck," Jack said bitterly.

Tears formed in Harriett's eyes and leaked down her cheeks. Her head sagged and she drew in on herself as if cold. Jack understood how she felt. His stomach was churning. How could all this be happening? What had they done to deserve it? Jack put his arm around his sister and held her tight.

"What about Harriett?" he asked the druid quietly. "They're not after her, she's not the Waycaller. Can't we send her back, to somewhere she'll be safe?"

"No, Jack!" Harriett wailed. "I want to stay with you!"

"Apart from your sister's wish to remain with you, there are other reasons why she can't be sent back," Aelf said gently. "The Veil has been breached. She would be no safer there than here. Besides, Morrigan does not yet know which of you is the Waycaller. Therefore, I must assume that she seeks you both and that she intends to kill you both."

It was as if a series of doors were closing all around Jack, leaving him with only one choice. If he and Harriett were to survive, they had to stay in Anwynn and do what Aelf suggested. But he wasn't going to stay forever. He would go with Aelf to see this master druid, but as soon as the druids worked out how to stop any more of those monsters crossing into his and Harriett's world, he was out of there, back to Cairnbawn and his nice, quiet life kissing girls by the schoolyard. He wasn't staying anyplace where a Dark Goddess wanted to kill him, Waycaller or not. Who'd want to be a Waycaller when the job description included being hunted by monsters and sorcerers?

"Fine," Jack said quietly, "fine, we'll stay, and we'll come with you to see your master."

"I think that is best," said Aelf, reaching out a hand and patting Jack on the shoulder.

At Aelf's touch the room spun again and Jack found himself in another vision. This time he stood on a vast, blood-soaked battlefield, the sky dark with smoke. A light snow was falling, joined by flakes of cinder and ash. It carpeted the ground, laying a grey blanket over everything. Jack looked up to the sooty sky and knew somehow that this vision was of the near future, of the winter soon to come. Then he looked around. For miles and miles in every direction were bodies, all bloodied and twisted into awful shapes, the bodies of men and women clad in armour and the bodies of what Jack thought must be elves, their long ears stained with soot and blood. Arrows and spears and tattered banners littered the ground, many of them smoking.

He looked down and to his horror saw lying at his feet the unmistakeable form of Harriett, face down and lifeless in a pool of blood. He staggered back and realised he had a sword in his hand, a black sword, dripping with blood. He looked back down at Harriett and then at the sword in his hand. A thought rose instantly in his mind: *I killed her. I've gone mad and I've killed my own sister.* He dropped the sword and staggered back again, tripping over another lifeless form. He looked into its face and saw that it was Aelf. His eyes were closed as if asleep but his skin was the pallor of a corpse. The druid's nose and ears oozed a dark, almost tarry substance. Jack scrambled back from Aelf's body, got up and turned to run.

He froze on the spot. Coming towards him through the smoke, walking barefoot over the field of broken bodies, was Morrigan. Her eyes shone through the haze of the battlefield like emerald beacons. The stench of death struck him, accompanied by a powerful nausea. He wanted to run but couldn't, paralysed by fear and shame. He had killed Harriett, and probably Aelf and who knows who else. It would only be justice if the Pale Mother killed him now.

Now just feet from him, Morrigan opened her arms wide

as if to embrace him, her blackened lips spreading in a terrible smile. She looked down at Harriett's lifeless form and her smile twisted into a gratified leer. Then her voice was in his mind: *Look what you have done, my child, look what you have done!*

# PART 2: FROM THE LOST NIGHT

# PROPHECY

*Rosemond, palace of the King of Pix*

Eloise stopped short of cracking him over the head with her sword. True, it was only a wooden practice sword, but that wouldn't stop it from making him see stars. She shouldn't care if she hurt him. He was cocky, over-confident and called her 'otherworlder' behind her back. He led the palace boys in laughing at her for being different, for her unusual clothes and way of speaking. She was the only girl learning swordcraft at the palace, and the only one who hadn't been born and raised in Pix.

He dodged out of her reach, taking advantage of her hesitation. The smirk on his face made her wish she'd clobbered him good and proper.

"You can smirk all you want," she said, circling him, "because ten seconds from now I'm going to wipe that smirk clean off your face." And so she did. She feinted to the left, tricking him into lurching right, then spun back, bringing the sword down on his back, hard. He fell face first in the dust with a grunt and didn't move.

She straightened up, standing tall, panting only a little. Now it was her turn to smirk. She waited for him to roll over, to stagger to his feet and scowl at her, as he always did when she bested him at sword practice. He just lay there. She nudged him roughly with her toe. He didn't react. She took a step closer, concern rising in her. Had she hurt him badly this time? Was he unconscious? Or worse?

She nudged him again, gently this time. He still didn't move. She dropped the practice sword and knelt beside him, reaching a trembling hand towards his shoulder. The second her fingers touched him he twisted around, grabbed her hand and rolled over, dragging her on top of him. He rolled again, positioning her underneath him. She struggled and kicked and maybe even bit him a little, but he held on tight, laughing.

"Let me go!" She thumped every part of him she could reach.

"No. You may be better with a wooden sword, but I'm twice as big and quite a bit stronger—"

"And uglier!"

He let her go and rolled off of her, a wounded look in his eyes. She shoved him as he went and got to her feet, glaring down at him, furious.

"Ugly?" he said. "That hurts my feelings, Eloise."

It was the first time he'd used her name and it made her blink. He'd always preferred 'otherworlder' before.

"I thought you found me charming," he said, that smirk blooming on his lips again.

"About as charming as a troll, Prince Noble, but only half as smart." The anger in her voice had gone. The sight of the prince's full lips with that half-smirk had chased it away. She had to admit that if it weren't for his over-confidence she might find him attractive. His dark hair and blue eyes were typical of the people of Pix, but he had a playfulness and also a seriousness that were uncommon. She found that appealing, despite herself.

"Are all otherworlders so cruel?" he asked, shaking his head, pretending to be stung. "Or is it just the pretty ones?"

She waited for him to add an insult, to call her names, or to make fun of her clothes. He'd never seen a girl in jeans before. She'd heard him joking with the palace boys that she dressed like a farmhand. No insult came. He just lay there in the dirt, looking up at her, smiling. Smiling at her like he really did think she was pretty.

Someone entered the practice field from behind them and called out.

"Are you done with your practice?"

Eloise recognised the deep yet gentle voice as Kashashem's. The magenta-haired druidess was striding towards them, her night-dark skin a counterpoint to her bright yellow eyes.

"Yes, we're done," she said, quickly stepping away from Noble, who was still smirking at her from his place in the dirt.

"Good." Kashashem nodded her head at the prince in recognition before picking up Eloise's practice sword and handing it back to her.

Noble scrambled to his feet, bowing deeply to Kashashem while hastily dusting himself off.

"My Lady," he said, the awe he felt for Kashashem ringing in his voice. Everyone at the palace, from the maidservants to the highest courtiers, treated the druidess the same way. Partly it was because she was elvish. The people of the city of Pixett rarely, if ever, saw elves. Mostly it was because Kashashem was the greatest druid alive. The maidservants whispered that Kashashem could turn night to day if she pleased. Mostly they adored her, but some were terrified of her too.

"King Mael has asked to see you, Eloise," the druidess said with a sideways glance at Prince Noble. "He awaits us in the audience chamber."

"The king wants to see *me*?"

"You are the Waycaller," Kashashem said as if explaining something very obvious. "And rumour about your skill at swordplay has reached even King Mael's ears. Of course the king wishes to meet you."

"But, we've been here weeks and the king hasn't summoned me before. He's only wanted to see you."

"My uncle, the king, is slow to recognise value," Noble said, his voice cold.

Kashashem waved the comment off with a lazy gesture. "The king has been ill and distracted with other things, but now he has summoned you, as he should."

She gestured for Eloise to follow her and headed towards the high arch that led from the practice grounds into one of the inner courtyards, her magenta dreadlocks swinging with her every step. Eloise nodded goodbye to Noble and hurried after her, stuffing the practice sword into its cloth scabbard as she went. They passed under the arch and into a cobblestoned courtyard. Kashashem turned to speak to her as they went.

"Mael is moody and difficult, but he is still king here in Pix. Try not to say anything to agitate him."

Eloise didn't know what to think of that. What could she say that would annoy a king? She knew that Kashashem was not fond of King Mael. The king was not a great supporter of the druids, nor on friendly terms with the elves. Eloise had learned only a little about King Mael since she'd been at the palace. She knew he'd just had his sixtieth birthday, that he had no direct heir and that he was not popular among the common people of Pix. On one of her occasional trips to the marketplace in the centre of the ancient city, she'd overheard a fishwife call him 'that blond King', with a sneer that spoke volumes.

The common people of Pix were all dark-haired and blue-eyed, like Noble. Prince Noble took after his father. The king's only sibling, his sister and Noble's mother, had shamed the House of Mael by marrying a poor country lord. Noble had told her that himself. The king, whom Eloise had only seen in paintings, had fair hair and green eyes, as did most of the courtiers. Kashashem had explained that the blood of the king and the courtiers was not rooted in Pix, but in the far-off land of Danussan. To the people of Pix, the king was a foreigner, and an unwelcome one at that. The Pixish were suspicious of all foreigners, Eloise had learnt that first-hand, but their dislike of the king went deeper. As they crossed the courtyard towards another archway, Eloise decided it was time to understand that a little better.

"Kashashem, why is the king so unpopular with the people?"

"The Pixish, living so close to the lands of the Dark Elves, are unforgiving by nature. As you know, the House of Mael is not Pixish by descent, which the people resent. Worse, to the Pixish, is the fact that King Mael, and all the kings of the House of Mael before him, have rejected the religion of Pix. The House of Mael has long favoured worship of the young god Danuss over the Great Goddess Amallayne."

Eloise knew little about the religions of Anwynn. She had first crossed the Veil with Kashashem, and the elvish druidess had been her guide to this new world ever since. Like all of her kind, Kashashem did not see the Faeden as gods, but as powerfully magical beings who, though they themselves thought they were superior to all others, were just as fallible as anyone else. Eloise had come to feel the same way about them.

"Is that the only reason?" Eloise asked, thinking there must be something else. Religion seemed like a very poor reason for the Pix to dislike their own king.

"It is the main reason. The veneration of Amallayne has taken deep root in the hearts of all the Pixish. They see her as their saviour, which is the truth. If it were not for their beloved Amallayne, then—"

"Morrigan."

"Yes, Morrigan."

Eloise shuddered. She knew enough about Morrigan to be glad that the Dark Goddess was eternally imprisoned, down in the pit of Uffern. If only all of her followers were down there as well, but the Vellenor, the Dark Elves, still ruled over Fellwood Forest, and the goblins and the trolls were as numerous as ever. She looked to the sky and thanked the stars she hadn't come face-to-face with any of Morrigan's minions. The dreams she'd had of the Pale Mother were bad enough. She glanced at Kashashem, who'd taught her the way to banish those nightmares forever, and felt a rush of affection.

Kashashem's mouth took on a half-smile, as if she knew what Eloise was thinking. She probably did. Eloise knew the druids could do extraordinary things, and Kashashem was the most extraordinary of all the druids.

"Do not speak to the king about the Veil," Kashashem said then. "It will just make him think of Amallayne. That is a sore topic for him, as it is the reason he is so unpopular with his subjects."

"Okay."

"And try not to sound so otherworldly. That also will irk him. He may not be Pixish by blood, but he is Pixish in his prejudices."

"Okay."

They went through another arch and entered a long, colonnaded cloister that encircled yet another courtyard, this one with a small grove of birch trees at its centre. A group of finely dressed, blond courtiers sat on the grass by the birch grove, chatting idly. They went silent at the sight of Kashashem, staring at her until she and Eloise passed through yet another arch, this one low and narrow, that led into a long passageway.

Eloise tried to keep track as they went deeper into the palace, rounding one corner, then another, but soon she had no idea where they were or how to get back to where they'd started. They passed through yet another door and entered a hall with high ceilings and tall windows. Shafts of light angled in and warmed the bare flagstone floor. They walked the full length of the high hall until they came to an oaken door flanked by pairs of heavily armoured guards. Eloise expected to be led straight through that door but instead Kashashem steered her to the side of the hall where a marble bench sat beneath a window.

"Wait here," Kashashem said, indicating the bench. "I will be back to get you in a moment." She went to the door and was immediately admitted by the guards. Once Kashashem had gone through the door, it closed with a thud. Eloise sat down on the bench to wait. The sun coming through the window was warm on her hair. She leant back against the wall and closed her eyes to enjoy it. Long minutes passed as she allowed the sun to heat her scalp, enjoying the contrast of the cold stone wall against her back.

She wasn't sure how she knew, for she hadn't heard a sound, but she suddenly felt that someone had joined her on the bench. She leant forward, opening her eyes. Sitting next to her, engrossed in an old cloth-bound book, was a girl close to her own age, maybe nineteen. Her skin was dark, not as dark as Kashashem's but so dark that she could not be Pixish. She reminded Eloise of the Andanese merchants she'd seen in the marketplace, but her clothes were not the same as theirs and she didn't have the same aloof look about her. The girl's hair was long and black, hanging half the way down her back. It shone softly and smelled of something Eloise found familiar. Was it sandalwood? The girl's eyes were focussed on the yellowing pages of the book, scanning left to right, sliding across the page with a quick and even pace. Eloise slid a little further away from her on the bench. The girl looked up. Her eyes were nothing like Kashashem's, not that striking yellow. They were such a deep, empty black that they took Eloise's breath away.

"It's rude to stare," the girl said, closing her book.

"Sorry, I was just a bit surprised. I didn't hear you sit down."

"I'm very quiet. It's part of my job."

"Are you a chambermaid?"

"Just a servant," she said, casting a nervous glance towards the guards at the oak door. The guards did not appear to notice her. They gazed unblinkingly down the hall, as if in a daze. The girl turned her eyes back to the book but didn't open it again.

"Is it good?" Eloise asked. "The book, I mean. You seemed really into it."

"Into it? You speak in a strange fashion. You are not from Pix."

"No, I'm not." She decided against telling the girl where she was from. In Eloise's experience, people were frightened when they learned that she was an otherworlder.

"I am Laynie."

"I'm Eloise."

"I am glad to meet you, Eloise." She glanced down at the book and stroked it with a finger. "This is a very old book. I have read it many times. But I think I am finished with it now." She laid the book gently on the bench between them and looked into Eloise's eyes. Eloise found it hard to meet that gaze; found herself a little short of breath as well. "Books are magical things," the girl continued. "They change us so that we can never change back. Don't you think?"

"Uh, yes, I suppose."

The oak door swung open. Eloise looked over to see Kashashem gesturing for her. She turned to say goodbye to Laynie but the girl was gone. Eloise's heart thudded in her chest. How could she have walked away so quickly, so quietly? She looked down the hall, expecting to see Laynie somewhere down there, but the high hall was completely empty. The old book was still there on the bench, seemingly heavy on the marble seat.

"Are you coming?" Kashashem asked. Eloise nodded, a little confused. She picked up the book and followed Kashashem through the door. She considered saying something about Laynie but couldn't bring herself to do it. Kashashem, normally so observant, didn't appear to have seen the girl or noticed the book. If she had, she didn't mention it. They walked through a large and ostentatiously decorated room towards another door, this one covered with gold leaf and flanked by another pair of guards. The door opened as they approached and Kashashem led Eloise into the audience chamber of the King of Pix.

King Mael, the twenty-fifth king of his dynasty, didn't look as old as Eloise had expected. He wore his sixty years well. His pale hair was like silk, the colour of chalk and cut to shoulder length. His eyes, a light green that reminded Eloise of spring grass, were distant, troubled. He looked up as they entered but did not smile.

Kashashem led Eloise to a place just in front of the throne, which sat on a raised dais set beneath a domed ceiling. Behind the throne was an arched, stained glass window, featuring the image of a young king. The king in the window had features remarkably similar to King Mael's, blond hair and pale green eyes. In front of the window and directly behind the throne stood a marble pedestal that held a life-sized statue of a young man. At the sight of the statue the word 'beautiful' came unbidden to Eloise's mind. It was the only word that could describe it. The man was shirtless, wearing only a short kilt. His body was muscled and athletic. His eyes, though stone, seemed to burn into Eloise. Her skin prickled with discomfort under that gaze.

Kashashem whispered under her breath, "Danuss, the young god." Then she bowed to the king, gesturing for Eloise to do the same.

"Welcome, Waycaller," the king said, his voice dry. "We greet you and grant you our sovereign protection while you abide in our domain." Eloise recognised that for what it was: a formal greeting with no real warmth or sincerity.

"Thank you," she said, careful not to say anything at all that might be considered controversial.

"Rumour of your daily besting of my nephew on the practice field has brought much merriment to this court. My nephew is overly sure of himself. His father was overly bold as well. Noble takes after him in more than appearance. My nephew greatly benefits from regular humiliation. It is why I brought him to court in the first place. My thanks to you then, Waycaller, for fulfilling my wishes, even if unasked."

Eloise didn't know what to say to that, so she simply smiled politely.

"The Lady Kashashem tells me your training is going well. That is good and as it should be. We regret that your training will soon take you elsewhere, to meet the other Kings of the Four Nations, as is custom, and thence to the heart-place of the druids, I believe, and out of our domain. Know that our care will travel with you and that, as was always true in the past, the House of Mael is ever open to you and your line."

Again, these were formal words that Eloise could tell the king did not mean. If she wasn't mistaken, the king would be pleased to see the back of her. But why? What had she done to upset him? The only sincere thing he'd said was that he'd enjoyed hearing about her beating Noble on the practice field. It almost made her feel sorry for Prince Noble ... almost.

The king watched them mutely for a while, shifting uncomfortably on his throne. Eloise wondered if she should say something. She looked to Kashashem for guidance, only to find the druidess staring to the right of the throne, into the shadows beneath an arch leading to another room. Eloise started a little when she saw what Kashashem was looking at – a very small person, no taller than four feet, concealed in the shadows of the archway. A halfling woman, with hair so white that it reflected the little light that entered the archway from the window above the statue of Danuss. She was wearing a hooded cloak, drawn closely around her stout form. She clearly hadn't wanted to be noticed. Eloise had seen halflings before, in the marketplace where groups of them gathered to buy all the tweed cloth and eagle feathers they could lay their hands on. As she understood it, all the halflings in Pixett were simple traders. What was this one doing here, in the throne room of the King of Pix?

Kashashem glanced at Eloise, raising an eyebrow, before directing her attention back to the king. The king coughed uncomfortably and said, "If you ever journey this way again, the House of Mael will be pleased to welcome you both." He nodded then by way of a dismissal. He waited for them to bow and leave, his eyes dwelling on their feet. Once they had turned to walk out, the king coughed.

"One other small thing," he said, causing them to turn and face him. He paused a minute before looking into Eloise's eyes. "Tell me, Waycaller, have you ... *feelings* for my nephew? For Prince Noble?"

Eloise blinked and stuttered. What a strange thing for the king to ask. A movement in the archway told her that the halfling woman had taken a step closer, perhaps to hear Eloise's answer. She wanted to say no but was too shocked to say much of anything. But would no be the truthful answer? Did she have feelings for Prince Noble? She stuttered a little longer, wondering herself what the answer was.

"Your inability to answer tells me all I need to know." The king looked at her with a new interest, a glint of disgust in his cold eyes. He looked to the ceiling, as if too repulsed to look at her any longer. After a heavy silence he spoke again. "Do you know the story of how the House of Mael came to occupy this throne?" Eloise shook her head.

"It was more than a thousand years ago, when the Pixish capital was still at Amaltor. The dynasty of the House of Senn came to an end at the time of the Doom War. What was left of Pix was then ruled by the queens of the House of Ceyr. The Ceyr queens brought my ancestors to Pix from Danussan, as bed slaves. Over the centuries, those bed slaves were allowed more and more responsibility. First, they were given the task of running the queen's private affairs. They did this so well that they were promoted from slave to consort. Decades went by, each successive consort proving himself to be capable and loyal. Then they were granted authority to govern the palace. A century later, they were granted governorship of the city of Pixett. Soon they were ruling all of Pix on behalf of their queens. By the time the last Ceyr queen passed away, without an heir, it was only natural that her slave consort should assume the throne."

The old king gestured to the image of the young king in the window. "He was Mael the First, the original Slave King of Pix. His kingly descendants are not called slaves anymore, but none of us have forgotten our origins, how high we have risen from so low a beginning."

Eloise didn't know where the king was going with this story, but a tight feeling in her gut told her that it wasn't good.

"The commoners in the marketplace may sneer at us, but it is a *Mael* who sits on this seat. *We* rule Pix. We rose from bed slaves to kings. No other house has ever risen so high from so modest a beginning. No-one but a Mael has ever achieved anything like it; a truly rare accomplishment, unrepeatable. The dynasty of Mael the First has ruled over Pix for a millennium. Tell me, Waycaller, how do you think we accomplished this extraordinary feat?"

Once again, Eloise had no idea. She shrugged, certain that Mael the Twenty-fifth was about to tell her exactly how. He shifted in his seat and looked behind him to the statue of Danuss.

"That is how," he said gravely, his eyes lingering on the bare-chested form of his god. "Through the blessing of Danuss. None are dearer to us than Him. We hold no other god above Him. You may carry the blessing of Amallayne within you, I do not know if those old tales are true, but that does not raise you up in my eyes. The blessing of Amallayne means naught to me. The druids may have fooled you into thinking that you are special, but I am here to tell you that you are not. You are just some bedraggled girl who knows a few tricks with a sword—"

"That is enough!" Kashashem shouted. "Is your mind so enfeebled that you think it right to say these things? Have you lost all ability for reasonable thought?"

"Do not think to command me in my own throne room, she-elf," Mael spat, half rising from his seat. "I am not so weak that I will tolerate being ruled over by one of your arrow-eared kind!"

"Come, Eloise, it's time we left the king to his thoughts, poisonous though they surely are." They turned and headed for the golden door.

"My nephew may be flawed," the king shouted after them, "but he is still my heir. I will not allow him to waste his attention on a boyish girl of no decent house!"

Kashashem stopped in her tracks and spun around, raising her hand. The whole room sparked with energy. Mael shrunk back on his throne, but the burst of energy from Kashashem's hand was not directed at him. It struck the stained glass window behind him. The window and its image of the Slave King shattered with such force that it turned to fine powder and showered down on the throne. Mael jumped to his feet, screeching as though his throat were cut.

Before Eloise left the audience chamber for good, she

glanced back and saw the halfling step out from under the archway, her hood thrown back to fully reveal her white hair, her eyes gleaming with hatred and directed straight at Eloise. The king's wailing snapped her attention back to the throne, where the powder-covered old man had slumped to the floor. Eloise was struck by the idea that the king on the throne of Pix was a ghost; a wailing, lunatic ghost.

Guards rushed passed them towards the sound of the king's wailing as Eloise and Kashashem entered the high hall. Some of the guards considered barring Kashashem's way. Their hands went to their scabbards, half-drawing their swords, but they re-sheathed them and continued towards the throne room, thinking better of trying to apprehend the most powerful druidess alive.

"I take it you noticed the halfling," Kashashem said later, as they passed out of the dark passageway into the courtyard with the birch trees.

"Yes. What was she doing there?"

"I do not know. Halflings are simple folk, only leaving their home in the dells for reasons of trade. It is strange to see one in the company of Mael. They are not known for seeking the attention of the high-born. I am certain of one thing however: Mael's sudden suspicion of you came from her. I sensed her will in his words."

"She was controlling the king?"

"Not controlling, no, but influencing. She is more than just a simple halfling. About that I am certain also."

They took an indirect, less populated route out of the palace. Eloise hadn't realised how tense she'd been until her stomach muscles relaxed when they left the palace by a small side gate. She looked back over her shoulder at the huge maze of buildings with relief. Its beehive-shaped towers had never seemed more threatening to her. She could almost hear the angry hum of the agitated swarm of courtiers and guards inside. She shivered, picturing that swarm streaming out of the palace gates after her, led by their wailing, ghostly king.

"Kashashem, why did the king say those things about me

and … and Prince Noble?"

"That is a question best asked of that halfling, for I am sure it was she who really wanted to know."

"Know what?"

"Whether or not Prince Noble, the heir to the throne of Pix, is in love with you."

Eloise stopped in her tracks. The very idea that Noble might love her, that all his teasing and cockiness might have been hiding other feelings, immobilised her. Could boys, men, be so deceptive?

"Is it so hard to believe," Kashashem began, "that he might have feelings for you?" She reached out her hand and tidied Eloise's unruly hair, pushing a loose strand behind her ears. "You are uncommonly beautiful, very bright and also a Waycaller. The proper question is why *wouldn't* he have feelings for you?"

Eloise stuttered. She wanted to refuse the idea, to say that it was impossible that Noble liked her at all, but a sensation in her chest, a sensation that felt like both hope and dread, stopped her. Could it be true? Could he love her? Then the fighter in her placed that question aside for another one.

"Why does a halfling woman care if Noble has feelings for me?"

"If Noble were just an ordinary lad and you just an ordinary girl, I doubt she would care at all. But you are the Waycaller and Noble is the heir of Pix. A union of those two bloodlines would matter to everyone."

"Why?"

"There is a prophecy. A prophecy about the final defeat of Morrigan and the Dark Powers. The prophecy speaks of a Druid King, an Oracle, descended from the House of Senn, the ancient kings of Pix. The prophecy says that the Oracle will overcome darkness once and for all."

"But what has that got to do with Noble and me?"

"Noble is the last living descendant of the House of Senn. You are the Waycaller, your bloodline is infused with immense magic. With each generation, the power of the Waycaller grows. Your children, Eloise, will cross a certain threshold—"

"What threshold?"

"The threshold between what is human and what is more than human."

"I don't understand."

"You will, one day. All you need to understand now is that any child born of a union between the House of Senn and the bloodline of the Waycaller ... that child could fulfil the prophecy."

Eloise reeled. She took hold of Kashashem's arm to steady herself with one hand, her other hand clutching the old book the servant girl Laynie had left on the bench. She stood there, concentrating hard on breathing, as it had suddenly become the most difficult thing in the world to do. As she breathed, images and memories swirled in her mind. Noble saying she was pretty. The gleam of hate in that halfling's eyes. Kashashem tapping on her bedroom window years before. Noble smiling cockily at her, his eyes trailing over her body. King Mael glaring at her with disgust. Kashashem watching her practice swordcraft with Noble, smiling knowingly. The window with the image of Mael the First shattering to fine powder and then showering down on King Mael, making him look like a ghost.

It was a long time before Eloise could bring herself to speak. When she did, she said what she needed to say with more care than she'd ever said anything before.

"You didn't bring me here to learn to use a sword. You brought me here to meet Noble." Her voice caught in her throat. She swallowed and looked into her friend's face. "You brought me here to fulfil this prophecy, didn't you?"

Kashashem made no response, merely took Eloise's hand and squeezed.

"This prophecy, it says if Noble and I have a child, that our child could defeat Morrigan, once and for all?"

Kashashem still didn't speak but nodded. Eloise looked

up to the sky, barely aware that she was still holding the old book in her free hand. A few white clouds hung motionless over the city, as if waiting for something to happen, some decision to be made. She thought about Noble, how equally irritating and intriguing she found him. An image of him came to her mind – the look on his face as he'd said that his uncle was slow to recognise value. He'd meant that *she* was of value, of value to him. There'd been no cocky grin on his lips then. He'd looked more serious than she'd ever seen him. A warm sensation dawned in her chest, accompanied by the thought that a life with Noble Senn might not be so bad. At least it would be interesting, perhaps even wonderful.

"Alright then," Eloise said, thinking what it would mean for Anwynn to be rid of Morrigan and the Dark Powers forever, "I suppose Noble isn't all that bad."

Kashashem smiled and led Eloise away from the palace, holding tightly onto her hand.

# THE DOOM WAR

*Butters Nob, in the halfling village of Bright*

Jack reeled as the vision of Morrigan, arms open wide to embrace him, dissolved. He found himself back in Miss Butters' kitchen, sitting at the table, his arm still around Harriett. He was so happy to find Harriett alive he thought he might cry out. The vision of her lying at his feet, her blood pooling around her, still hung in his mind, making his heart ache and thump at the same time. He could feel Harriett's lungs expanding and emptying beneath his arm. He wondered if any sensation had ever made him feel so relieved. He doubted it.

It took every bit of his control not to pull her into a tight embrace and never let go. He didn't want to frighten her. Nor did he want to tell anyone what he'd seen. He shivered as Morrigan's voice echoed in his mind: *Look what you have done, my child, look what you have done!*

"Are you not well, Jack?" Aelf asked, taking his hand away from Jack's shoulder and looking into his eyes. Jack shook his head, still unable to speak.

"I'm quite sorry," Miss Butters said loudly, not sounding sorry at all, and making Jack and Harriett jump. "But this is all rather ridiculous! The Pale Mother is down in a deep, dark hole, where she rightly belongs, and can never get out! Everyone knows that! And, even if she could escape, what difference would it make? There are loads of Tricksy Ones afoot already, one of them came to this very cottage this very night! I hardly think we should tangle our stockings just because another one of them might get loose. Eugene will protect us, as he always has!"

"My dear Dorothea, I could not disagree with you more. Have the halflings forgotten how it was before Morrigan was imprisoned?"

"We don't bother ourselves with those old stories," Miss Butters said sniffily.

"How bad is Morrigan really?" Harriett asked, looking sideways at Miss Butters, who hissed at the repeated use of the Pale Mother's name.

Jack's stomach lurched at hearing the name on his sister's lips. If she had seen what he'd seen, she would not have needed to ask and she wouldn't have said the name so easily. Aelf sighed, looking resigned, and settled back into his chair.

"I did not want to go too deeply into this tale," he said, "for it is a dark one. But I knew when I came here to meet you that I might have to tell it. You need to know what it means to be a Waycaller, Jack. You need to truly know why it is that the Veil was created in the first place and why the burden of the Waycaller was placed on your family. It seems that Miss Butters also needs to hear the tale. Like it or not, the halflings have a part to play in all of this."

Miss Butters tutted in protest but was quelled by another stern look from Aelf. She satisfied herself by ripping apart a muffin and squeezing a large chunk of it through gritted teeth into her mouth.

"This all began," Aelf said, looking away from Miss Butters, "some eight thousand years ago at the time of what we now call the Doom War. That was the time when Morrigan grew hungry for conquest, seeking dominion over the hearts and minds of all places and all people."

"As I said before, Morrigan's greatest power is her voice. With mere words she has the power to subdue, seduce and control. Her voice was the source of her might. Using that power, she gathered around her all the foul creatures of the dank and awful places—the monsters, the Vellenor, the goblins and the trolls—and marched against the nations of human-kind."

"She really sounds awful," Harriett interjected.

"That she is, Harriett," Aelf smiled, untroubled by the constant interruptions. "The four nations of human-kind fell quickly. The swords and arrows of their armies were like nothing against the power of Morrigan and her dark horde. The remnants of the Four Nations, under the command of the last great King of Pix, Duan Senn, fled for refuge to the eastern slopes of the Craggy Mountains, within the realm of Elvinidd, the dominion of the Bright Elves. There the elves and the last of Duan's army stood against Morrigan's tide until even that sacred country was aflame. At the last, the surviving elves and humans crossed by the only mountain pass into this very dale where, joined by the halflings, they awaited what they thought was certain destruction." Aelf took a sip of his tea.

"They say that King Duan's despair was great, for he feared that soon all his people would be slaves to Morrigan, and all the worse because his people's prayers for aid had gone unanswered. Duan and his people, who had long worshipped Amallayne above all the Brighter Faeden, began to lose their faith. How could Amallayne abandon them in the face of Morrigan's terror? Duan went to the Bright Elves for counsel. The elves looked to the workings of the stars and planets for some omen—"

"Ooh, I love astrology! I'm an Aquarius!" Harriett interrupted again.

"Congratulations," Aelf smiled. "As I was saying, the elves searched the stars for some hint, some message, as to how they might prevail. They found nothing. The halflings, whose god Eugene had long comforted them, prayed in their Hallowed Hall for him to smite Morrigan and her assembly. Alas, that did not happen. There was no response of any kind. Not from the heavens, not from the Brighter Faeden, and not from the god of the halflings. The stars were silent. No god or goddess stood between the survivors and Morrigan's march of destruction."

"Who did the druids pray to?" Harriett asked, breaking the solemn atmosphere once again.

"Stop interrupting, Harriett!" Jack hissed.

"That's quite alright," Aelf continued. "The Order of Druids did not exist at that time, it was founded a short time later. But, to answer your question, we druids do not pray to any being. In that sense we are like the elves. We have a great appreciation for the forces of nature instead."

"I like nature too," Harriett said.

"Wonderful," Aelf smiled. "Now, to continue the tale. All that stood between Morrigan and the complete enslavement of all the known peoples of the world was the great elvish magician, Kashashem, the very greatest among the first magic-wielders."

"Kashashem's power was very remarkable, even back then, but she was no match for Morrigan who, as one of the Faeden, possessed powers far greater. All the Faeden have power over nature – they can transform one thing into another, they can appear and disappear anywhere at will and they can take on any form, that sort of thing. But some Faeden, the older ones like Morrigan, have power that is practically limitless."

"Wicked tricksies!" Miss Butters spat the words through a mouth full of muffin.

"Actually, most of the Faeden, though they can't be called 'good' by our standards, are not wicked at all. Self-interested, yes indeed, manipulative, certainly, but some have long aided and benefited human-kind. Some of them have aided us out of their own egotistical need for worship but some, like Amallayne, the Great Goddess, have acted simply because, strange as it seems, they care for us."

"Blasphemy!" Miss Butters said. "Eugene bless us!"

"Quite," Aelf said unabashed. "Now, as I was saying, Morrigan's army had arrived at this very village of Bright. The dark horde converged on this place at midnight one moonless eve, taking advantage of the blackness of the night to make their attack." He glanced out the window before continuing. "The foul hordes under Morrigan's control despise sunlight; it blinds and disorients them. What occurred next is of some importance, so I wish you to see it for yourselves, as it actually happened."

The druid took a small sphere out of his pocket, a sphere

that was perfectly round and white. It looked to Jack like a flawless representation of the moon, complete with craters, plains, canyons and mountain ranges.

"Is that the moon?" he asked.

"Yes, Jack, or at least a representation of it. For us the moon is a talisman of memory and knowledge. This is a memory stone. Memory stones give the ability to experience the past as if you had been there yourself. This particular stone has been imbued with the memories of all those who survived the Great Battle of Bright."

"Be warned, much of what you will see will not be pleasant. I regret having to show ones so young such things, but I am afraid there is no other way to alert you to the danger that faces us all."

Aelf reached out the hand holding the memory stone and held it above the middle of the table-top between them. When he removed his hand, the stone hung in mid-air like a tiny planet in a motionless orbit.

"Cool!" Harriett exclaimed, as Miss Butters gasped. Jack couldn't quite believe his eyes. Aelf gave the stone a gentle prod with his finger and set it turning so that it looked like a real-life moon spinning in space. Aelf took a few hurried sips of his tea and, in response to a questioning glance from Jack, said, "We'll be off in a minute and I do hate to waste a good cup of tea."

"Off?" Miss Butters choked, watching the spinning memory stone with taught lips as beads of perspiration pooled on her brow.

"Yes," Aelf whispered, "back thousands of years to the Great Battle of Bright."

He moved his hand over the stone, as someone might pass their fingers over a candle to feel its warmth, and then the room went totally, startlingly black. All was silence. The only thing that Jack could see was the spinning orb. Miss Butters' kitchen was gone, Aelf was gone, Harriett was gone, even his own body was gone. There was just his mind, the pervasive blackness and the little white moon.

The miniature moon spun peacefully in the black for a moment and began to glow. Soon it cast a luminous light that shone out in sharp spears that filled all the space around it. That light filled with vapours and those vapours formed into shapes. First a tree, then a hill, then the distinctive forms of the Craggy Mountains in the distance, then a river cutting left to right in a valley. The vapours then formed into Jack's own body, and that of Harriett, Aelf and Miss Butters. In moments, they all stood beside him looking exactly as they had in the kitchen. Only now they stood on a hill looking down on a wide dale, beautiful and green, where the waters of what appeared to be a very real river sparkled under the moonlight.

"Sweetwater River," Miss Butters whispered, astonished.

"We have arrived at the place," Aelf explained. "We have but a moment before we arrive at the time. Hold steady," he cautioned as he placed an arm around Harriett, "the experience can be somewhat jarring."

As soon as Aelf finished speaking, the world spun, colours blurred, the ground became like sticky liquid beneath Jack's feet. It felt like a kind of earthquake, only the air and space vibrated as well. Just as suddenly as it started, the shaking stopped. As soon as it did so, Jack threw his hands to his ears as they were struck by a deafening roar of noise.

All around them echoed a tumult of howls, screams, shouts, the clang of steel on steel, the blasts of horns and the boom of drums. Jack looked beside him to see Harriett and Miss Butters covering their ears as well. Only Aelf had not acted to shield himself from the deafening din. He motioned for Jack to look down over the valley below.

It was late in an autumn night. The air was frigid on Jack's skin. The beautiful, green dale was neither green nor beautiful anymore. It was scorched and black and much of it aflame. Pillars of black smoke billowed upwards to the sky from every direction. The ground was littered with bodies, many of them burning. The river now ran dark red with blood. To the right of them in the valley below, lined across the horizon as far as the eye could see, was an immense army, a mix of creatures the like of which Jack had never seen before, not even in his worst nightmares.

At the head of the horde were rows of white-haired beings with pale skin and iridescent pink eyes that shone in the dark, like the eyes of supernatural cats. Their ears were long and thin and ended in sharp points. Even from this distance, Jack could see that they had strange circular tattoos on their ear lobes. Many of them carried black banners emblazoned with the image of a snarling white mouth. The banners flapped and snapped in the wind like whips.

"Those are the Vellenor," Aelf shouted above the roar of noise. "They are fearsome to behold for certain, but they cannot harm us, as we are not really here."

Jack was glad to be reminded of that. He had been about to soil his pants and run for his life. Harriett didn't look reassured at all. She clung ever tighter to Aelf like an infant monkey to its mother. Miss Butters stood stock still, her eyes round as saucers, her hands still clamped tightly to her ears.

The left and right flanks of the dark army were made up of shorter, almost man-sized creatures with grey, leathery skin, bat-like ears and needle-sharp teeth. They had beady, black eyes and black hair cropped close to their skulls. They charged into the dale howling like demons from hell.

"Goblins," Aelf said, so calmly that he might have been commenting on the weather. As the goblins spread into the dale they parted to allow another mass of creatures to come forward from the rear. The creatures that loped out from behind the goblins Jack had seen before. Skinwearers, hundreds, if not thousands, of them stampeded forward; huge hyena-like beasts with snake-like faces. Harriett screamed and threw herself behind Aelf, who held her tightly and reassured her once more that they could not be harmed as they were not really there.

A thunderous horn sounded, emitting long earthy and resonant notes. Jack and the others spun left to see what had made the sound. Another army was pushing forward from the opposite side of the dale, smaller by far, but equally awe inspiring.

This army was a vast company of humans and elves. The advance line of human infantry and the goblins crashed into each other on the banks of the river. The force of the impact of bodies sounded out a terrible thud and boom. The goblins squealed awfully, and slashed and cut at the human soldiers, sparks flying as blades struck chainmail and armour. The humans were just as awesome in their attack, but they were steely and determined rather than frenzied.

As the human infantry slowly pushed the goblins back, and hacked down hundreds of skinwearers at a time, a line of cavalry moved forward. The human cavalry was made up of four different groups. The group in the centre were all pale-skinned with black hair. Jack guessed these were the Pix, whom Hob had said he and Harriett resembled. Jack was surprised to see many women among them. They were led by a young man, twenty years old at the most, who was blowing on a long curved horn. A golden crown sat on his head of shaggy black hair. He urged his huge white war horse forward and thrust his sword aloft.

"Duan Senn, the last of the old Kings of Pix," Aelf said sadly.

The Pixish horsemen struck the goblins at full gallop, trampling many of them beneath the hoof. But there were so many goblins that for every one cut down or trampled there came another twenty. Soon the rank of riders to the left of the King of Pix entered the fray. These horsemen controlled their horses with their knees, the reins left hanging as their hands were busy firing a shower of arrows on the goblin horde. They were led by a muscular woman with light brown skin and striking, coal-lined eyes. Her hair, like that of all her companions, was tied in a topknot, but she wore a steel crown. She rode on a freckled grey and black horse and carried a long spear.

"The warriors of Harshan and their queen," Aelf announced.

The cavalry to the right of the King of Pix spurred their horses forward. This group was a mixture of fair and black skinned people. The dark-skinned soldiers far outnumbered the fair. They rode in chariots drawn by muscular black horses with dyed red manes and tails. Their faces were painted white, like skulls. Each chariot contained two warriors: one controlling the horses, the other armed with a longbow, which they fired so swiftly that Jack could barely make out their movements.

"They are the archers of Anda," Aelf shouted.

The fair-skinned men accompanying the horse-archers were mostly blond, though there were not many of them. They wore their hair long beneath helms adorned with silver wings. This group was led by a huge man on the biggest horse Jack had ever seen. He was a block of muscles with fair skin and shoulder-length, blond hair. When he entered the melee, he dispatched dozens of goblins with a single swing of his axe. It was as if he were at harvest, a terrible reaper, only he was harvesting goblin heads, which flew through the air like so many grains of wheat.

"The fearsome King of the North," Aelf declared, a touch of anger to his voice. "Few of his kinfolk are here. The Northmen have long kept themselves to themselves. Their god Danuss is aloof, preferring his own company above all else."

Another horn blast rang out, this one so sweet in sound that Jack's mind stopped for a moment, revelling in its first note. Behind King Duan's cavalry was an army of elves. As they moved forward, the elvish archers lay down a withering rain of flaming arrows that fell on the goblins and skinwearers with devastating impact. The firelight from the arrows made it almost like day. As one, Morrigan's army flinched back from the light. Thousands of the dark horde were slain. The smell of burning goblin flesh nearly made Jack retch.

Another trilling note came from the elvish horn and Jack's mouth fell open with wonder as a line of elvish warriors came up from the rear. These fearsome-looking elves, with black skin and brilliant yellow eyes, marched forward at a measured pace. Their long, black hair, often braided or in dreadlocks, was topped by helms of white metal in the shape of dragon heads breathing flame.

"The Sovereign Guard," Aelf explained in an awed voice, "the protectors of the elvish kings and queens." He gestured to the head of this group of fearsome elves to a tall, dark-skinned man wearing a golden crown in the shape of outspread wings behind an upturned crescent moon. "And there he is," Aelf said, "King Dhudhannan himself."

The elvish king looked to Jack like the most noble and courageous being alive. His winged crown reflected bursts of light from flame and the moon so that his golden eyes seemed to be a source of lightning.

At a thunderous sound above, Jack jerked his attention upwards as dozens of blasts of flame came out of the sky to hit the ground. The flames scorched hundreds of goblins and skinwearers at once. In the dark sky above were about a hundred winged reptiles, dragons, all mounted by a pair of elves. One of the mounted elves commanded the dragon while the other fired burning arrows that hurtled down to slay the goblins and Dark Elves amassed below.

The dragon-riders were different to the other elves. Wearing hooded black cloaks, their coal-black hair was held in place by a circlet of leather.

"The firewyrm riders of the Ehmaara," Aelf shouted over the screams of thousands of dying Vellenor. Jack couldn't help but think these elves looked almost as fierce as the Vellenor. Aelf must have sensed his thought because he said, "The Ehmaara, the night elves, were nocturnal like the Vellenor, though they were never seduced by Morrigan. They stood apart from all other elves, indeed all other races. This is the last of them. They were dying out even before Morrigan's rise. Sadly, the Ehmaarim have not been seen in the world for a thousand years at least."

As the smoke cleared, the Dark Elves drew longbows of

their own and fired at the dragon-riders. But the firewyrm riders were far out of reach. The dragons blasted the ground with even more flame and the Vellenor and goblins were incinerated by the hundreds, their black, snarling-mouth banners turning to smoky cinders that swirled on the wind.

The bombardment of the dragons was enough to allow the human cavalry to break through the goblin ranks and charge down the dale, the goblins fleeing before them. The lines of elvish archers parted and the Sovereign Guard surged forward, easily matching the full gallop of the horses, their longswords levelled to meet the Vellenor lined before them with deadly force.

A cacophony of noise from a narrow gully to Jack's right heralded the charge of a horde of halflings, most of them portly, middle-aged women like Miss Butters. Mounted in chariots hauled by huge muscular boars, they emerged from the gully at an unbelievable pace.

"You really haven't seen anything," Aelf shouted, "until you've witnessed a troop of halflings in their war plumage and armour, mounted on their war boars."

The halflings met the retreating goblins head on. The boars gored and gouged and bit the goblins as the halflings thrust their spears into thighs and buttocks and groins. Jack winced. The halflings fought dirty. The goblins and remaining skinwearers were decimated, the halflings lopping off the heads of the few who remained.

The line of Vellenor parted, and at first Jack expected them to break and run, but then he saw moving to the front of the line a group of Dark Elves who filled Jack with a terrible anxiety, even though he knew they couldn't harm him. There were about a dozen of them, all dressed in long leather coats that covered them from neck to ankle. Their heads were bald. Their eyes were not pink like the other Vellenor, but blood red.

"Dreads," Aelf hissed. "The worst of the Pale Mother's Vellenor sorcerers."

As one, the Dreads attacked. They sent streaks of lightning

against the remaining firewyrms and against the lines of cavalry and footmen. They hurled boulders by magic at the archers. They caused fires to erupt throughout the dale and crushed elves and humans and halflings alike with mere gestures of their fingers.

Jack tensed with panic; all was lost. What could be worse than these Dreads? As if in answer a terrible boom sounded in the distance. Jack looked toward the far end of the dale where a bright green halo of fire floated in mid-air. A female figure appeared in the middle of the halo of pulsing green light. Very white-skinned with hair in long, white dreadlocks, her eyes shone like green stars.

"Morrigan, the Queen of Doom," Aelf whispered. Jack did not need to be told. He had recognised her as soon as she'd appeared. Miss Butters screamed. Harriett closed her eyes. Jack felt another overwhelming urge to grab Harriett and run. But he didn't, he couldn't. The urge to flee was overpowered by the fear invoked by Morrigan. He was frozen in place, trembling. Miss Butters, shaking as much as him, made that strange sign of a wiggly line at her heart and muttered a prayer to Eugene, pleading with all her might. It had no effect.

Morrigan opened her mouth and wailed. The sound rolled forward as a visible thing, a shimmering wave of power. Miss Butters pressed her hands more tightly over her ears, apparently forgetting that she was perfectly safe. When the wave of power met the advancing human and elvish army, hundreds of them simply dropped dead. Others fell into fits on the ground; still others bled from the ears, nose, mouth and eyes and screamed as if in terrible agony. Some exploded into clouds of dust. When the wail struck trees, they ignited in flame and were consumed in seconds, turned to swirling billows of ash that whirled upward like tornadoes. The river boiled to steam and vanished. Jack suddenly understood that Morrigan's voice was death itself.

Morrigan extended her hand and made a strange gesture which sent thousands of sizzling balls of green light flying out amongst the surviving cavalry. On contact with riders and their horses, the green lights burnt away armour and flesh until they were just skeletons; skeleton horsemen on skeleton warhorses that crashed to the ground in a pile of bones.

Next Morrigan sent forth spears of crackling lightning that struck the Sovereign Guard and exploded in a flash of light, heat and noise. In just moments, they were nearly vanquished. Streaks of lightning raced through the sky and connected with dozens of firewyrms at a time. They imploded with a thunderous boom. Nothing was left of the dragons or their riders but clouds of ash that fell to the ground to cover the dale in a blanket of death.

A deafening roar overhead caused Jack to look up so fast that he jarred his neck. Hurtling toward Morrigan was a huge black firewyrm, mounted by two of the Ehmaarim, a man and a woman. As the black dragon carried the elves nearer to Morrigan, she cast a bolt of lightning directly at them. The black dragon veered aside just in time. The lightning sizzled past them and struck a hill, exploding with such force that the ground shook. The top of the hill was reduced to a cloud of debris.

The female elf stood on the dragon's back and drew a black sword that shone with a halo of fire. The she-elf heaved the sword over her head and hurled it with all her might at Morrigan. Somehow, the blade passed through the green nimbus of Morrigan's power and, before the Faeden could deflect it, it grazed her cheek. But the Queen of Doom flicked the sword away and it fell to earth. Still, a small cut on Morrigan's cheek now oozed green light. She wiped at the bloodless wound with her hand and screeched. The force of her screech knocked the swordless she-elf from the dragon's back. The dark-haired elf plummeted downwards. Before she made impact, Morrigan extended her hand and froze her just feet from the ground. She struggled to free herself but was trapped by Morrigan's power. The Pale Mother curled her hand into a fist and the elf howled in pain. The sound of bones snapping echoed throughout the dale. Morrigan was crushing her alive. With a final balling of Morrigan's fist, the she-elf went limp. Only then did Morrigan allow her to finally slump to the ground, dead.

The black firewyrm streaked back toward Morrigan, with the remaining rider bent low against its body. The rider's long, black hair whipped behind him, his eyes seeming to blaze with an inner fire. Morrigan merely sneered and, pointing her long pale hand directly at the dragon, sent another burst of lightning that spiralled through the air faster than the eye could comprehend. The elf dodged sideways, but the lightning struck the dragon and it erupted into flame and smoke. The dragon-rider tumbled toward the ground and Morrigan extended her hand again, stopping him in mid-fall, ready to crush him to death as well.

"By this point," Aelf shouted over the din, "no-one expected anything other than complete annihilation, but look there …"

Another burst of light appeared in the sky. This light was brilliant red. Hovering at its centre was another Faeden, also a woman. Morrigan shrieked with rage. Forgotten, the night elf plummeted to the ground and lay still. The red light emanating from the new Faeden was so bright Jack had to shield his eyes. He had no real sense of what she looked like. All he could tell was that her skin and hair were black and seemed to blaze with fury.

"Amallayne, the Great Goddess," Aelf whispered, his eyes welling with tears.

Without hesitation, Morrigan threw the full horror of her voice at Amallayne. It came in the form of a terrible scream that caused everything in its path to wither and die. The grass turned grey and then black, trees crumbled in on themselves. Elves and people and horses alike turned to wrinkled grey corpses, as if mummified on the spot.

When the wave of noise struck Amallayne the red brightness of her halo dimmed a little, but she did not shrink away. Instead, she focussed her shining gaze even more intensely on Morrigan. The light she cast was greater than a midday sun. Vellenor fell in the thousands, their pink eyes turned white and steaming. Goblins and skinwearers erupted into flames and the company of Dread sorcerers screamed in agony and fell writhing on the ground until most of them were dead.

Morrigan howled with outrage, a blood-curdling sound that caused Jack and his companions to fall to their knees, even though what they were experiencing was not real. The howl turned the moon black and dimmed the stars above so that the dale pitched into a terrible darkness. Horses and boars screamed in terror. When the Queen of Doom's howl reached its highest pitch, raging tornadoes of flame erupted throughout the valley, obliterating the blackness. The flaming tornadoes careened in every direction, whipping out long tendrils of fire to engulf every living thing within reach, like crazed dancers spinning about, obliterating everything and everyone they touched.

Amallayne responded by raising her arms and, making slashing movements as if with an invisible dagger, sending forth blistering waves of light that turned everything in their path to black soot. These razors of energy cut through Morrigan's army as though it were butter. Where the lines of fully armoured and fierce Vellenor had stood before, there remained only long mounds of soot, like the ploughed furrows of a field sown with some terrible crop.

When the razors of heat and energy hit Morrigan, the sword wound on her cheek opened a little further and pulsed with unhealthy-looking green light. She screeched in agony. The wound enabled Amallayne's power entry into Morrigan's body. Without hesitation, Amallayne sent forth more razors of power, cutting such a devastating swathe through the Vellenor and goblin horde that mere handfuls remained alive. Morrigan's wail was now so intense that the sky above the dale trembled and seemed to break, as though life was being sucked out of the very air itself. The surviving Dark Elves broke and fled as four razors of power converged on Morrigan at once. The sound that came from Morrigan then was the most blood-curdling thing Jack had ever heard, the sound of a mad animal in terrible agony.

As Morrigan screamed, another sphere of light appeared in the dale. This one was pearly white, the most beautiful, shimmering, lustrous white imaginable. As soon as it appeared, the moon bloomed from black to white again and the stars blinked back into existence, shining like beacons with the same lustrous light as the halo of the latest Faeden to appear in the dale. This Faeden was male, with golden blond hair and fair skin. His eyes shone a beautiful blue, like sapphires. He was tall, lean and muscular and wore nothing bar a short white kilt.

"The young god, Danuss," Aelf said. "Danuss the Beautiful."

When Morrigan saw Danuss she wailed once more, though her voice sounded weakened. The light from the iridescent moon and stars was muffling its sound and power. Danuss raised a muscled arm and suddenly was holding a huge white raven, made completely of sizzling energy. He released the raven into the air where it divided and multiplied into a glowing flock, thousands strong, that sped through the air towards Morrigan.

Once the ravens reached the Dark Goddess, they pecked and clawed and lunged at her from dozens of different angles. Morrigan seized some and tore them apart, so that they popped and exploded like fireworks, but there were too many. Every time Morrigan tore one into pieces, another dozen were born from the beating mass of wings, beaks and claws that threatened to completely smother her.

Jack soon realised that the white ravens were all focusing on the wound on Morrigan's cheek. They were coordinating their attacks so that every second or so one of them got through to worry the gash. Each bite and slash weakened Morrigan even more. The wound on her cheek soon tore open, leaving her cheek hanging by a mere thread of snow white skin. Beneath the gash was nothing but green fire.

Morrigan redoubled her efforts, casting a wall of green fire that surged toward Amallayne and Danuss like a tidal wave. When it struck, Amallayne faltered for the first time, and the nimbus of white light around Danuss shrunk to barely an inch. Then, with the ringing of a thunderous bell, another burst of light appeared in the sky. This light shone like platinum. Hovering at the centre of this aura was yet another Faeden, this one a dark-skinned girl of just twelve or so. Morrigan howled and increased the power of the wave of fire that threatened to consume Amallayne and Danuss. The new Faeden, whom Aelf said was Erima, did not attack the Pale Mother. She extended a hand each in Danuss and Amallayne's direction and sent streams of energy to them, which renewed their strength. Morrigan howled with a rage that she had not yet displayed. The earth trembled.

"We should go," Aelf said. "What occurs next is far too frightening to watch."

"Now you're worried that we might be frightened!" Harriett moaned. "You might have thought about that when goblin heads were flying through the air like frisbees!"

The druid glanced around at them. Harriett was pale as a ghost and looked like she was about to bring up every meal she'd ever eaten. Miss Butters was paralysed with fear, unmoving and unable to speak. Her eyes were the size of dinner plates and bulged so much that Jack thought they might actually shoot out of her head. Jack himself felt clammy and nauseated, his whole body trembling. He was still on his knees, unable to drag himself up. "Yes, of course," Aelf said apologetically, "I should have, you're quite right, my dear. I forgot that you are only younglings. Perhaps we have lingered too long." The druid passed his hand before them and muttered some strange words. As abruptly as they'd arrived there, they vanished.

# DARKGATE

Back in Miss Butters' warm and safe kitchen, Harriett and Miss Butters were mute with silence. They were all shaking. Jack fought to calm his trembling arms and legs. He could barely pick up the glass of sarsaparilla without spilling it everywhere. Miss Butters clung to the kitchen table, as if to prevent being dragged off again to experience something even more awful. Harriett pulled her knees up to her chest, trying to curl up into a safe little ball.

Aelf plucked the spinning memory stone from mid-air, pocketed it and poured himself another cup of tea, as though they had not just witnessed, only moments before, the most terrifying and catastrophic battle of all time.

"So," Aelf began in a hushed tone, "an awesome battle between Amallayne, Danuss and Morrigan ensued. The very mountains shook and crumbled. The Sweetwater River turned to steam. Then, with Erima's help, Danuss and Amallayne were finally victorious."

"Amallayne and Danuss stripped Morrigan of her voice, making her powerless. The curse that removed Morrigan's power was so fearsome that it burnt her lips and tongue, leaving her mouth blackened and disfigured."

"Afterwards, Amallayne and Danuss cast Morrigan into Uffern, the deep pit in the bowels of the world that is the realm of monsters. Once Morrigan's home, Uffern became her eternal prison. Amallayne blocked the entrance to it with a magical door, known as Darkgate, so that none might come and go from that place. The seal on Darkgate is impenetrable: the most powerful sorcery cannot break it, nor can the power of the Faeden open it. It had to be that strong because Morrigan was, after all, the most powerful of all the Faeden. The power of Darkgate is linked to the Veil; while the Veil remains, Uffern is closed to all and Morrigan cannot escape, which is why she is hell-bent on tearing the Veil by destroying the line of otherworld Waycallers."

"Which means us," Harriett said glumly.

"Yes, which sadly means you." Aelf looked from Harriett to Jack and tried giving them a reassuring smile, but he failed to mask his worry. Clearly Aelf didn't hold out much hope that they would survive. Jack had to admit that he didn't either. The tinkling of china alerted Jack to the fact that Miss Butters had finally calmed herself enough to let go of the table and attempt a sip of tea, though her hands trembled so much that the cup and saucer quaked incessantly and tea sloshed all over the place.

"Oh dear," she said as she wiped up the spillage, "I'm shaking out of my skin."

The mention of skin made Jack think of the skinwearer that had chased them in Cairnbawn; the reason they'd ended up in Anwynn in the first place. If Aelf had thought showing him the battle that led to Morrigan's imprisonment would make him want to stay in Anwynn, he was mistaken. If anything, it made him more determined to go home, especially knowing that a demon goddess on this side of the Veil was determined to kill them. Harriett would never be safe in Anwynn. It was full of monsters. As soon as the druids found out how to stop any more of them from crossing the Veil to Cairnbawn, he was taking Harriett home. A small twinge in his gut forced him to admit that part of him might have liked to stay and explore Anwynn, and discover what it meant to be a Waycaller, but not if it endangered Harriett. Besides, the fight against Morrigan had nothing to do with him. He didn't owe these druids anything. He decided it was time to make his intentions clear.

"All this stuff about dark gates and Faeden battles is very interesting, but what has it got to do with us? All I care about is stopping any more skinwearers or any other horrible thing from turning up in Cairnbawn and trying to eat Harrie or me. So, how long will it take to go meet your master and get this sorted?"

Aelf studied Jack for a moment before answering, as if

weighing him up, assessing his character.

"My master lives not far from here. If we leave first thing in the morning, we will be there before sunset. Is that acceptable to you, Jack?"

Jack nodded in response but said nothing. His mind was still swimming with everything he had seen and all the druid had told them. It was all so completely unbelievable, but undeniable too. His forehead was tight, as though everything he'd learned in the last few hours had filled his skull to its limit and it was about to burst. He'd seen and experienced so much that shouldn't be real, that upturned everything he believed, he was now doubting his own senses. Besides, could someone who heard voices trust his perception? And what of this strange violet-eyed man: should he trust him? As if on cue, he heard the voice at his ear: *Trust him. Aelf Ethelwulf is good.* Jack found that, despite everything, he did trust Aelf and that, yes, he believed that Aelf Ethelwulf was good.

"Do you have any questions?" Aelf asked.

Jack shook his head. He had too much information to absorb already. Harriett on the other hand asked,

"That skinwearer thingy, is it still back home, in Cairnbawn? Or will it follow us here?"

"Having failed to kill you," Aelf answered, "it is likely to have returned from whence it came. It depends on darkness to survive. It cannot survive the full light of day. If it did not manage to return to its dark home, it will have perished."

"So, we're safe here," Harriett pressed. "It's not going to follow us?"

"If it was going to follow you, it would have done so straight away. Do not worry, you are safe here. Now, if you have no other questions, I must insist that you children get some rest. You have been through a terrible ordeal and seen much I wish I could have spared you. You require some time and space to absorb all the strange things I've said. Sadly, I can only allow you this one night, for tomorrow we must seek my master's council. After that, we will know what we need to do to preserve your safety and to keep Morrigan closed up in the pits of darkness where she belongs." The druid turned to Dorothea. "I trust, my friend, that we can take lodgings in your lovely home?"

Miss Butters was taken aback at first but, on looking into the eyes of Jack, and especially Harriett, any reluctance she had to help melted.

"Yes, yes of course, Aelf, you are all welcome to stay."

Miss Butters made beds for them in her back bedroom, which she seemed to think was a great honour. Once she left them alone, Jack helped Harriett into her bed.

"Can you believe all this?" he asked her as he tucked her in.

Harriett simply nodded. She appeared to accept all this magic stuff more easily than he did, but he knew that underneath she must be terrified.

"Don't worry, Harrie, I'll get you home."

"It's not safe at home," she said sleepily. "Besides, we have to do the quest."

"Quest?"

"Uh huh. We have to go on a journey to complete a quest. It's always this way."

"That's just how it is in books, Harrie. Anyway, what quest are we completing? As far as I can tell we're just trying to keep Morrigan from getting us."

Harriett brushed her hair out of her face, closed her eyes and snuggled into her pillow.

"It's not a normal quest," she yawned, "but it's still a quest."

"You can say that again, nothing about this is normal." He pushed her unruly hair behind her ears.

"I always knew that elves and faeries were real," she said, yawning, drifting into the drowsy space before sleep. "And now we know that there are halflings ... and trolls and goblins and dragons—"

"And Aelf," Jack added.

"He's just a person. There are lots of *them* back home." She yawned again.

"But some of the ones here are druids," Jack whispered as Harriett's eyes fluttered closed. "Not many people where we come from are druids."

He didn't think Harriett heard these last words, for her breath had slowed and evened out. She was already asleep. Jack, on the other hand, was wide awake; he doubted he would sleep a wink all night. For starters, he and Harriett were in tiny halfling beds. Harriett fit perfectly into hers, but Jack was forced to lie in a contorted foetal position. The blankets were not much bigger than towels and smelt powerfully of lavender. They quickly got tangled in his legs as he tossed and turned thinking about everything Aelf had said, about the horrors of the Battle of Bright.

His mind raced with thoughts about Morrigan and her dark sorcerers, the Dreads, and about how the skinwearer had crossed into his world. The most distressing thoughts were about how all this would affect Harriett. It wasn't easy being seventeen with a nine year old sister to care for. He sighed and rolled over in the bed once more, looking out into the moonlit night through the small window. Only hours before he'd had no bigger decision to make than if he should let Harriett walk home alone so he could spend some time with a pretty girl. That seemed like another life now; a life before skinwearers and druids and Faeden. A life that, just hours earlier, he would have said was boring. But now ... now he'd give anything to have that boring life back again. He could barely comprehend that in the time it took for the sun to pass behind the moon in that eclipse, his whole life had totally changed.

Thoughts like these agitated Jack and kept him wide awake. The loud snores coming from Miss Butters' bedroom, which sounded like the snorts of a pig with a serious head cold, didn't help either. At one point, around midnight, he contemplated getting out of bed and going to sit in the kitchen with Aelf. He knew that Aelf would be awake. The druid had elected to forgo sleep in order to keep watch over the cottage. Not wanting to be told any more horror stories about goblins and evil sorcerers, Jack stayed put. He remained agitated and awake right up until just before dawn, when he finally nodded off from sheer exhaustion.

# HATTER

Jack's sleep did not last long, and was troubled by dreams of goblins and skinwearers and other frightening things. In one lingering, unnerving dream a figure lurked at the edge of his consciousness. Although he couldn't see clearly who it was, Jack knew that it was a woman. It was as if she had taken up residence in the dark shadows at the edges of his mind. She emanated a cold, sinister menace. Jack felt that she was trying, by sheer force of will, to get him to climb out of bed and go to where she waited for him, in some cold, dark place. She called out to Jack in his mind and he felt a kind of sickening vibration. It was then he realised it was Morrigan.

Jack struggled to wake from the dream. He tried to call out to Aelf but couldn't, his whole body paralysed with fear. The dream only faded when he became aware of an odd sound: a soft whistling. The whistling dissolved the bad dream and slowly eased Jack awake. When he opened his eyes, it was daylight, although still early, and he realised that the whistling sound had not just been in his dream, for he still heard it. Once completely awake, he judged that the whistling was coming from outside. After disentangling himself from the tiny blankets, he staggered to the window. When he peered out, he was met with a peculiar scene.

In Miss Butters' back garden, which positively overflowed with flowers and bushes of every colour, but mainly pink, there was a circular paved area with a wooden outdoor setting. The table and four chairs were ornately carved and were occupied by Miss Butters and a nervous looking Harriett. The table was laden with food. Jack made out at least five separate dishes – scrambled eggs, beans, jam on toast and some kind of cheesy dumplings. The ever-present pot of tea was there as well, covered by a flowery knitted tea-cosy topped with a bobble in the shape of a gaudy, pink rose.

Looking around for the source of the whistling, he spotted

Aelf. The druid was not seated at the table but sitting astride the shaggy cow they'd seen in the garden the night before. As Aelf whistled to himself, he wiggled his bare toes in the sun. He was holding a dainty tea cup and saucer in his hand, from which he was sedately sipping. The cow had its four very fluffy white hooves spread wide so it could lap tea out of a second cup on the ground in front of it. Miss Butters was pointedly not looking at the cow, but with each messy lap she visibly shuddered.

"Even the animals in this place are crackers," Jack muttered to himself. As he exited the back door into the warm sunlight a few minutes later, he realised that he was famished. All he'd had for dinner the night before was a glass of sarsaparilla cordial. He joined Harriett and Miss Butters at the table and, as the smell of food hit his nose, his mouth started to water.

"Good morning, my boy!" Miss Butters said, as she popped a plate in front of him and started piling food on it.

"Thanks," Jack replied, his eyes popping at the sight of all the food.

"Start with the toast, dear, and a little whistleberry jam. I made the jam myself last week."

"Whistleberry?" Jack asked.

"Whistleberries are a staple in halfling diets," Aelf explained from the cow's back. They make a rather sticky jam and, when fermented, make a powerful and very sweet wine. Most halflings are very fond of drunkenness and so the whistleberry occupies a place of affection in their hearts."

"Goodness, Aelf," Miss Butters reprimanded, "you'll have the boy believing that all halflings are drunkards! But," she said turning to Jack, "it's true that all halflings love whistleberry jam, myself included."

Jack spread a small bit of the dark jam onto the corner of his toast and tried it. It was good, very sweet, and so he shovelled some more on.

"Tea, my boy?" Miss Butters asked, lifting the tea pot.

"Yes, please."

"Oh, goodness gracious," Miss Butters started, scanning the table top. "I've not brought out a cup for Jack. How silly of me. I don't know what's wrong with me today! I'm all out of sorts ... I'll just go and get one. Won't be but a jiffy."

As she heaved herself out of the chair she cast a slightly irritated look in the direction of the cow, who was now slurping up tea with relish. "That ruddy bovine's got my nerves all a-jingle," she muttered. "It's got the extra cup hasn't it, wretched rump roast ..."

Once Miss Butters had gone indoors, Harriett turned to Jack, her face tight and her eyes wide with alarm.

"Save me, Jack! I think she's trying to feed me to death!"

"Don't be stupid, Harrie, she's just being hospitable." He dived into his breakfast.

"Oh no, she's not! She's trying to do me in! She practically stuffed three whole pieces of toast in my mouth!"

"Come off it, Harrie, I'm not in the mood."

"Jack! I swear she's trying to stuff me to death!"

Jack was about to lose his temper and tell Harriett to pipe down and let him enjoy his breakfast. Before he did, the clip clop of hooves alerted him to the approach of the shaggy cow.

"Actually," Aelf said, perched atop the shaggy bovine, "Harriett is not exaggerating. Halflings are well known for force-feeding their guests. They tend to think that anyone who isn't as round as them is malnourished. Harriett here, being a little on the thin side, appears to Miss Butters like she is positively starving."

"I told you, Jack," Harriett snapped.

"But she's not trying to hurt you. She's just trying to fatten you up a bit," Jack said reasonably.

"Indeed," Aelf began, "but Miss Butters did in fact push a good three pieces of toast right into Harriett's mouth. She seemed to think Harriett wasn't eating quite quickly enough."

"Oh ... sorry Harrie. Why didn't you just tell her you'd had enough?"

"I couldn't say anything as every time I opened my mouth

she kept shovelling food into it! It was all I could do to breathe!"

"Halflings respond to firmness, Harriett," Aelf said. "You have to stand up to her and tell her not to be so pushy." He took a sip of his tea. "Halflings are kind and generous but they are *very* narrow-minded. They can't accept that obesity isn't for everyone."

"Well, I don't mind at all," Jack said. "I *am* starving. She can fatten me up all she likes."

"I'd be careful not to say that to Miss Butters if I were you, Jack," Aelf warned. "You might find yourself outmatched. No-one can eat more than a halfling, except perhaps for a firewyrm, which can eat thrice its weight in one sitting. Absolute gluttons! The really naughty ones have been known to eat whole herds of cows in half a morning." At that the cow made a nervous sound of disapproval and stamped one of her front hooves on the ground. "Soxy doesn't like firewyrms," Aelf offered by way of explanation.

"Soxy?" Jack asked.

"Yes, my cow. Her name is Soxy."

"Because of her white hooves, Jack," Harriett explained. "Isn't she just gorgeous?"

Jack smiled noncommittedly. "Are there any firewyrms around here?" He glanced upwards to the sky, the memory of the firewyrms' bone-chilling roar from the battle Aelf had showed them with the memory stone all too present in his mind.

"Not in the Halfling Dells, no. But there are firewyrms beyond the Craggy Mountains." The druid pointed in the direction of the row of massive, snow-topped peaks in the distance. "Not to worry though. For the most part the firewyrms are kept under control by the elves of the mountains. Like the Ehmaara of old, the mountain elves domesticate them and ride on their backs."

"Cool," Harriett said.

"Do you think so, my dear? I'm feeling rather warm myself," Aelf said, not understanding Harriett's otherworldly turn of phrase.

Miss Butters returned with another cup and saucer *and* a pile of pancakes dripping with syrup. At her return, Harriett surreptitiously sucked in a number of mouthfuls of air, apparently hoping to build up a store of oxygen before Miss Butters filled her mouth with any more food.

"I thought while I was indoors," Miss Butters said as she made room on the table for the plate of pancakes, "that I'd whip up a batch of pancakes. Nothing like pancakes to sweeten up your morning." She smiled and, without asking, piled three pancakes on each of their plates. Harriett made a small retching sound, but Jack sighed in appreciation and hoed straight in.

"I lubb maple sywupp," he mumbled through a mouthful of the most delicious syrupy pancakes he'd ever tasted.

"Maple syrup, dear? What maple syrup?" asked Miss Butters, looking perplexed. Jack pointed to the sticky syrup dripping down his pancakes as he stuffed in another mouthful.

"Oh, no dear, that's Sweet Stoat Syrup. It came from the teat of a rare, black stoat."

Jack nearly gagged and spat out the bit of pancake left in his mouth. He looked to Harriett for sympathy but none was forthcoming. She gave him a look that said 'you got what you deserved'. He dropped his fork and watched Miss Butters eat her way through her pancakes, growing queasy as she used her fork to push every last syrupy morsel into her mouth. He looked away rather than watch any longer, glancing down the lane towards the centre of the village.

He wasn't sure what he was seeing at first. Bobbing along the hedge that separated Miss Butters' back garden from the lane into Bright was a black shape topped by long feathers. Jack thought it might be some kind of bird until the shape came close enough for him to see that it was a hat; a large felt hat adorned with plumes of feathers at least two feet long. The hedge was only about chest height on Jack, but clearly higher than most halflings' heads. When the hat-wearer came to the gap in the hedge where the side gate was, Jack saw that it was a stout halfling woman all dressed in black. She looked to Jack like a vicar; stern and primly dressed from neck to ankle in a black dress that fitted like a robe. The broad brim of the hat cast most of her face in shadow. The rest was obscured by a lace veil. The minute Jack laid eyes on her, he felt a sudden and overwhelming loathing. It took him aback. He'd never felt anything like it before.

The woman rapped on the fence with her chubby hand, causing Miss Butters, whose back was to the gate, to jump up from her seat.

"Oh, good grief," she said under her breath, "what is Hephaestia Hatter doing here?" She trotted over to the gate, wiping her hands on her apron as she went.

"How do, Hephaestia," she said in a voice that sounded less than friendly. "What brings you to my gate this morning?"

"You have strangers here," the woman said in a hostile, croaky voice that reminded Jack of a crow that'd been taught to speak.

"Guests," Miss Butters said firmly, "I have guests here. I can't see what business it is of yours, Hephaestia?"

"As a member of the Council of Florid Spinsters it is my business to know who comes and goes in Bright. We can't allow *unwholesome* types to just enter as they please."

"Unwholesome types?" Miss Butters' voice was cold. "Hephaestia Hatter, I'll have you know that no guest of mine is unwholesome. You will apologise, if you don't mind, for making such a suggestion."

"I do not apologise for doing my duty. I suppose next you will want to bring these guests of yours into the Hallowed Hall, before the very effigy of Eugene?"

"And why not?"

"That one there, perched on the cow, that one is a druid." Hephaestia pointed a chubby white finger accusingly at Aelf. He waved back sheepishly. "Druids consort with elves and are friends with heathens," she said in a tense whisper. The more venomous she got, the quieter she became. "Worse, they are godless and fiddlers with magic."

"I will not have my guests insulted at my own gate," Miss Butters snapped. "Good day to you, Hephaestia. I will be very pleased if you never darken my gate again." She stomped back towards the garden setting, her lips drawn tight and her eyes sparkling with anger.

Hephaestia did not move. Although Jack could not see her eyes, he could tell that she was staring straight at him and Harriett. He stared right back at her, refusing to let her intimidate him. Somehow he knew that her visit here was not about Aelf being a druid, but about Harriett and him. Hephaestia Hatter was very curious about them and he doubted it was merely because they were not from Bright.

Jack felt a sudden churning in his belly, a now familiar nausea that made him think that Morrigan was somewhere nearby. His skin prickled with alarm and the hair on his arms stood on end. As soon as he thought of Morrigan, Hephaestia Hatter stepped away from the gate and headed back towards town. The nausea, and the sense of Morrigan's presence, did not abate until she was well out of sight.

"How dare she tell me who I can have as guests?" Miss Butters was still mumbling minutes later, turning her rage on an unsuspecting piece of toast that she buttered fiercely and ate in one gulp. Jack wondered if he should tell Aelf what had passed between him and the Florid Spinster, but what would he say? That he had a *feeling* that she was connected with Morrigan somehow, that his skin had prickled and he'd felt sick in his belly? It sounded ridiculous even to him. Besides, he was probably just imagining things because of everything he'd been through in the last twenty-four hours. No, he wouldn't say anything.

"What are Florid Spinsters?" Harriett asked. Miss Butters was too busy murdering another piece of toast to answer, so Aelf answered instead.

"They are in charge of the halfling church. The church dedicated to Eugene. They govern almost every part of halfling society."

"Oh," Harriett said, looking off in the direction Hephaestia had headed and then back at Miss Butters. "They don't seem very nice."

"Don't judge the Florid Spinsters by Hephaestia Hatter," Miss Butters said. "She is in a league of her own, that one. How she got on the council I will never understand. The woman is positively hateful. I daresay pastries changed hands. Pastries and jams, no doubt. Yes, she must have paid a very sweet bribe to get herself on the council. It makes me furious, and famished. Pass that stoat syrup, Jack. I need some sweetness to wash the taste of that awful encounter out of my mouth."

Jack passed Miss Butters the syrup and looked the other way while she poured a huge amount of it on the last stack of pancakes before attacking them as though she were a half-starved skinwearer.

# SETTING OFF

After Miss Butters finally finished her breakfast, Aelf asked Jack and Harriett to gather their things and get ready to leave. Jack stood and waited while Harriett heaved herself out of her seat, rubbing her belly and looking balefully at Miss Butters.

"Where does your master live?" Harriett asked, suppressing a burp. "Is it far?"

"My master lives at the foot of the Craggy Mountains," he answered. "It's a long walk but a pleasant one. If we leave soon we should be there before dusk."

"Your master lives near this dale?" Miss Butters asked, surprised.

"Yes, always has done, my dear friend."

"Why, I never. I had no idea there were druids so close to Bright. I'd like to meet the fine fellow someday."

"That day has come, my dear Dorothea. My master expects you today."

"Wha ... what? Oh, no, I really couldn't, Aelf. I have so much to do today."

"Such a shame, Dorothea. As I said, he is expecting you. He will be very disappointed if you don't come." Jack suspected that Aelf was playing on Miss Butters' sense of etiquette and decency. Judging by the torment on her face, Jack figured that halflings hated to disappoint anyone, especially when it came to such things as visits.

"But I—"

"I expect he has already boiled the spuds and drawn down the ale," Aelf added matter-of-factly.

"Ale, you say?" Miss Butters asked, her interest piqued. "Spuds?"

"Yes, my master brews the most delicious ale. A shame you won't get to taste it."

"Oh, well, I'm sure a short visit won't hurt. But ... but I

couldn't be travelling back in the dark—"

"We shall all stay the night, Dorothea, and see you safely on your way in the morning."

"Well, if you're sure he's expecting me."

"Most sure, Dorothea. He'd be positively devastated if you didn't come."

Jack couldn't help but feel uneasy at the way Aelf so clearly manipulated Miss Butters with the offer of ale and boiled spuds. He also couldn't understand why it was so important for her to come along. After all, it was he who was the Waycaller, and he and Harriett who were in mortal danger. What had Miss Butters to do with it? Not that he wasn't grateful that she'd put them up for the night. But surely it was only endangering her to involve her any further? A little later, while Miss Butters was inside packing for the journey, Jack voiced his concerns to Aelf directly.

"It was not my intention to manipulate our friend," Aelf explained, "but Dorothea would not have come without some enticement and my master has made it clear that she must accompany us. I can't tell you why. Let me just say that my master can be trusted in all things. As soon as I can, when my master deems it permissible, I will inform you as well. I know this is all very strange and difficult for you, Jack. I hope that you can try and trust me a little. I will never allow you to be harmed and will do anything I can to protect you and Harriett, and Miss Butters for that matter."

Jack felt instinctively that Aelf was telling the truth. So he left Aelf in the yard, mounted on his highland cow, and joined Harriett in the kitchen where they waited as Miss Butters finished packing a ridiculously huge picnic hamper. The halfling apparently believed that if she forgot to bring a sample of every foodstuff in existence disaster would befall them. Jack felt a pang of empathy for her. Clearly, she was not used to travelling outside her village. She certainly wasn't in the habit of visiting a druid master she'd never met, in the company of two children from another world.

Jack and Harriett watched with growing alarm as Miss

Butters' stuffed her hamper to overflowing. Harriett reached her limit of tolerance when the halfling tried to pack a long, fat sausage, angling the sausage this way and that to fit it in. Harriett pushed in front of Miss Butters and snapped the sausage in two to get it into the basket. In an irritated voice she said, "There, that's the sausage in. Now, what else can I do to help?"

Jack knew that Harriett would regret that immediately. Miss Butters stared at the dismembered sausage in disbelief.

"My nut-mince sausage," she stammered. "You've *throttled* my nut-mince sausage." She turned a cold eye on Harriett. Harriett backed away, reaching out for Jack's hand but finding that he had both hands shoved firmly in his pockets. Jack expected an explosion of shouting and gesticulating but Miss Butters merely smiled. It soon became clear to Jack that Miss Butters' revenge, unlike her meals, was not to be served promptly.

"Help, dear?" she said in a flinty voice. "Why, yes, my sweet, you can certainly help. Let me think what use I might put you to." She paused for effect, smoothing her tweed skirt with her plump hands. "Ah, yes, I think I've found just the task for you, dear. We will be needing the wagon to cart this lot." She indicated the bulging hamper. "You can come out to the barn with me to collect Piggy-poo and help me hitch him to the wagon."

"Piggy-poo?" Harriett asked nervously, looking to Jack for support. Jack shrugged. Now was as good a time as any for Harriett to learn that irritating Miss Butters came with a price.

"Yes, dear, he's my pig," the halfling explained. "We'll need to bribe him with some nice cake or something to get him to let us hitch him to the wagon. He can be a wee bit ornery." Miss Butters smiled in a triumphant way. Harriett's knees were visibly trembling. Before she could ask Jack to intervene he walked out of the kitchen and rejoined Aelf outside.

Hitching a pig to a wagon took longer than Jack expected. When Miss Butters and Harriett finally came out of the thatched barn they were leading a large black pig wearing a gaudy pink bonnet. The pig was hitched to a halfling-sized wagon. Miss Butters led the huge porker up to the front of the cottage, leaving Harriett to follow behind with a distinct limp. When the wagon reached Jack, Aelf and Soxy by the front gate, Harriett went immediately to her brother's side, her face flushed with anger.

"It sat on my foot!" she said. "That tub of bacon deliberately sat on my foot!"

Miss Butters chuckled, saying, "He is a bit stubborn, my little Piggy-poo."

Harriett's face reddened with anger. "That pig's not just stubborn, he's mental! And he's not little, he's ridiculously fat!"

"Why, thank you, young lady." Miss Butters beamed, patting her pig proudly.

Harriett flushed even further and gaped at Miss Butters, utterly bemused, as the halfling bent over so that she was cheek to jowl with Piggy-poo.

"He's my little fat Piggy-poo, yes, my lovely, porky Piggy-poo. My fatty-watty piggy-poodle." She kissed the great beast on the snout and Piggy-poo, with eyes full of love and adoration, snuffled up to Miss Butters in delight.

Jack didn't think he'd ever seen a more sickening sight, especially as from where he was standing, behind Miss Butters as she bent over to kiss her pig, he noticed a distinct similarity in Miss Butters and Piggy-poo's rear ends. The main difference being that one had a curly tail that was wiggling furiously as Miss Butters smooched its owner all over its piggy face.

Following that disturbing scene, Jack lifted Harriett and the picnic hamper into the back of the wagon and then assisted Miss Butters to climb into the driver's seat. Jack climbed into the wagon beside her. Aelf moved off astride Soxy, heading towards the snow-capped peaks of the Craggy Mountains, and Miss Butters urged Piggy-poo forward.

After just a few minutes progress they turned down a lane

that struck directly eastwards toward the mountains. Aelf scanned each side of the lane as they went, seemingly worried about being seen or followed. Jack agreed that the fewer who knew they were passing by, and what direction they were heading, the better. He didn't want to come face-to-face with another skinwearer, or one of those strange, shadowy Sendings that passed over Miss Butters' house the night before.

After a short time they were beyond sight of the village, and even Miss Butters' brightly painted cottage was no longer in view. The countryside around Bright was lush and green; grassy river flats with large leafy trees, oak and birch and cherry. Every few hundred yards, the path crossed little stone bridges over a stream banked by willows, where lilies grew in the shade at the water's edge. Either side of the trail were meadows, sometimes occupied by more shaggy highland cows, but mostly wide, empty spaces filled with little more than clover and the droning of bumble bees.

Jack listened silently to Harriett as she chattered about how beautiful it all was. She pointed out every tree, every stream and every meadow and wildflower as if describing them to a blind person. This irritated Jack but he didn't tell her to pipe down. He knew this was how she behaved when she was nervous or out of her comfort zone. Besides, he was too busy worrying about their future to tell her off.

What would Aelf's druid master tell them? Where would they go after seeing him? Would they go straight home, or would they have to stay longer in this strange place? What if the druids couldn't guarantee that no more monsters would cross the Veil and come after them? Where would they live then? What if they could never go back to their own world? And what if Morrigan somehow escaped Uffern and got hold of them? Jack knew that would be the end of him and of Harriett. The question that lay just as heavily on him had to do with his mother. The events of the last day suggested she hadn't been insane, which made Jack wonder what had really happened to their father.

Time flew by as Jack pondered these things. Soon they stopped in a wide, sunny meadow to rest and have lunch. They unloaded the wagon under a large oak tree near a stream that ran between avenues of flowering cherry trees. The cherry blossoms were all white and perfect, like perfumed stars. Miss Butters set about making a fire and boiling a kettle. She laid out a large pink blanket and unpacked the picnic hamper. Piggy-poo swiftly took up position on the picnic blanket, like a weird dog, drooling at the sight of the cookies and other goodies that Miss Butters was unpacking. His curly tail wiggled at a dizzying speed.

Harriett strolled in the grass nearby, picking wildflowers. Aelf wiggled his toes in the stream. Jack took up a position near Aelf, hoping the druid might provide some answers to his questions. Part of him also feared what he would be told. He decided to ease into it.

"How much farther is it to your master's house?"

"About the same distance again. My master lives in the foothills at the edge of the Halfling Dells, near Narrownotch Pass, which cuts through the Craggy Mountains and is the only way in and out of the Halfling Dells. We will be there before sunset, if we can get Piggy-poo to pick up the pace a bit, that is." He smiled, wiggling his toes naughtily.

"What do you think he'll say, your master? Will he let us go home?" Jack looked at his anxious reflection in the stream and wondered if its water had run red with blood during the Battle of Bright.

"I do not know, Jack. Our goal, and by 'our' I mean the Order of Druids, is to protect existence as we know it from the wickedness that lurks in the dark pits of Uffern. But equal to that is to protect you, not only because you are the Waycaller, but because you are an innocent in all this, as is Harriett. We have long fought hard to protect innocence, on both sides of the Veil, and you could say that though we must at all costs stop Morrigan, we would rather do that without risking any further loss of innocence. That is to say, without risking you. Sadly, as Morrigan cares naught for anything but her own desires, loss of some kind may be inevitable. When we reach my master's home we will know what our course of action will be. Let us worry about it then. For now, let us enjoy this lovely place, for there is a kind of blessing in its beauty."

"Blessing?"

"Yes, this place was remade by Amallayne herself, after the Battle of Bright. You saw the destruction that Morrigan's dark sorcery wrought. Every blade of grass withered, every tree burned, the soil itself turned to ash. Nature cannot recover from that kind of destruction. The dells would have remained desolate for all time if Amallayne hadn't used her power to remake this place, to make the soil rich again, to make the grass sprout and the trees grow strong. This place is filled with her intention, her power. To merely touch the grass here with one's toes, to sip at the sweet water, to let the warm sun heat the skin, to be caressed by the shade beneath the trees, is to know in some small way Amallayne's heart, to feel her grace. There is magic in the very air here."

"I thought druids didn't worship the Faeden," Jack said, trying not to make it sound like an accusation.

"We don't, but we know goodness when we see it and value it very highly."

Jack didn't know what to think of all this. He wasn't a religious person at all, but he knew that what Aelf was describing was a spiritual experience of the kind he had never known. He looked away from Aelf, down into the clear water, not sure what to say. He'd always thought that kind of thing was a bit crazy. On the other hand, he had felt surprisingly well since they'd been in the dells. With everything that had happened, not the least hearing voices, he'd half expected to turn into a gibbering idiot. Instead, he felt calm, sort of level-headed. He hadn't heard the voice in his ear all morning. Maybe it was Amallayne's blessing that was keeping him from losing his mind?

Perhaps it was the warmth of the sun, or the sweet scent of the cherry blossoms, or the tinkle of the stream over its pebbly bottom that eased his mind and made him feel that Aelf was right. He wasn't sure what it was. But he was certain that there was no point worrying about what would befall them until they knew what they were really facing. They'd know that after they'd spoken with Aelf's master, who apparently knew a lot more than Aelf did and would also know what to do about it all. Perhaps he would also know more about their mother? Jack decided, as he sat there watching Aelf dangle his bare feet in the stream, that he would trust Aelf. He would put worry away for a while.

He looked up to watch Harriett walking in the meadow. She was following a trail of bluebells away from their little picnic group. She bent to pick a few and put them to her nose before heading towards another cluster of the vivid flowers at the edge of a stand of trees nearby. Jack was about to call out to tell her not to go too far when she stopped dead in her tracks. Her body tensed and she stared into the shadows of the trees. Jack stood up. Something about her posture told him she was afraid. He looked from his sister to the stand of trees, searching the shade for whatever had caught Harriett's attention. At first he couldn't see anything, but then a small movement, a shift in the shadows of a tall oak tree, set him in motion. He paced towards Harriett, hoping that whatever had moved was just a squirrel. A knot rose in his stomach at the thought that it was something much larger and more dangerous. He knew Harriett wouldn't have frozen in her tracks because of a squirrel. He started to jog.

When he got to Harriett, she reached out for his hand and he took it. They both squinted into the shadows to try and make out whatever was concealed there.

"What is it, Jack?"

"Quiet, and stay still." He squeezed her hand in caution.

It moved again. It was far too big to be a squirrel. Was it a bear, or something worse? He slowly moved Harriett behind him, trying to remember what you were supposed to do when faced with a wild bear. Never run and don't make any sudden moves or loud noises. He stood as still as a statue, the only part of him moving being a few beads of sweat that rolled down his brow. The bear or whatever it was moved again. This time it came swiftly through the trees, closer to where they were standing, stopping just inside the edge of the tree shade, remaining hidden. Whatever it was, it was smart.

Jack could see the outline of it now. Definitely not a squirrel, but not a bear either. It was about as big as Harriett. It grunted and took another small step forward, stopping short of coming out of the protection of the trees. It really didn't want to be seen. It was so close now that Jack could see the glint of its eyes peering at them through the dark. They were fierce and red. Jack wanted to call out to Aelf but was terrified that if he did, it would charge.

As the thing continued to watch them, Jack realised it was glaring only at Harriett. It grunted again, its eyes fixed on his little sister, and then blinked. Jack was pretty sure bears did not blink. The thing looked from Harriett to where the others were sitting preparing for lunch, its eyes darting back and forward a number of times. Jack got the strong impression that it was weighing up whether or not it could make a dash across the open ground and reach Harriett before anyone came to their aid.

"Harriett, dear, and Jack," Miss Butters called out, "come for lunch. Eugene knows you need the nourishment." They both turned in the direction of Miss Butters' voice. When Jack looked back to where the red eyes had been, they were gone. Jack let Harriett out from behind him and she ran straight back to the group. Jack followed, looking over his shoulder to ensure the thing didn't come out of the trees after them.

"I think I saw a bear!" Harriett said as soon as they re-joined the group, flicking her dark hair out of her face with a shaking hand.

"A bear?" Aelf asked, standing and looking towards the trees. "Are there bears in these parts, Miss Butters?"

"No bears," Miss Butters said disinterestedly as she cut

into one of the many cakes she'd laid out, "but we have some real nasty badgers, some of them as big as cows." Jack hoped she was exaggerating for effect, but if that thing was a badger then maybe she wasn't.

"It must have been a badger then," Harriett said, looking relieved and taking a seat on the picnic blanket.

"I don't think it was a badger," Jack said, looking meaningfully at Aelf. He wondered if he should tell Aelf about the blinking red eyes and the sense that it had been weighing up whether or not it could get to Harriett before anyone could stop it. He decided against saying anything more. He didn't want Aelf thinking he was so afraid of shadows that he was seeing things. Besides, maybe he had been imagining things. Hearing unexplained voices made him doubt himself even more than he usually did.

"Perhaps we should lunch quickly," Aelf said, responding to the worry in Jack's eyes, "and then be on our way."

# ANARRA

Piggy-poo thoroughly disgraced himself over lunch, eating his way through a dozen cookies. Once they could all eat no more, they packed up the wagon and headed off again. Harriett, nervous due to her encounter with the red-eyed animal, insisted on squeezing onto the driver's seat with Jack and Miss Butters. Not wanting to sit directly beside Dorothea, she made Jack shuffle along so that he was uncomfortably pressed against Miss Butters' fleshy thighs. Aelf ambled along beside them, astride Soxy once more.

The path towards the mountains now closely followed the stream, which gurgled over pebbles and fallen logs as it made its way past them and westwards into the heart of the dale. They moved through the shade of willow and cherry trees that banked the stream as, on each side of them, the meadows grew larger and wilder, changing from well-tended pasture-land to fields of wildflowers. Harriett resumed her chattering as they moved through this green countryside, buzzing with nervous energy. She'd eaten more sugar over lunch than was healthy for so small a girl, much of it at the point of Miss Butters' threatening fork. She soon started peppering Aelf with questions.

"So, where do the elves live?" she asked, scratching her ear absentmindedly and looking around as if one might step out from behind a nearby cherry tree.

"The dominion of the elves, Elvinnid, is to the east of here, on the other side of the mountains. There are three great elvish cities. The oldest one, Songarielle, is in an alpine valley high among the peaks of the Craggy Mountains. Then there is Tessarelle, the city among the treetops, in the Great North Woods. The elves of Tessarelle are also known as woodland elves. The palace of Merielle is on the Misty Isle far to the north, where the sea elves dwell. Merielle is the home of the Elven Sovereign, King Dhudhannan."

"Cool," Harriett said distractedly, casting an eye back along the path in the direction they'd just come. Jack wondered if she was still thinking of the meadow where they'd seen the red eyed creature.

"Separate from the Dominion of Elvinnid," Aelf continued, smiling at Harriett as she twirled her short fringe with nervous fingers, "are the Vellenor, the Dark Elves. They live in Fellwood Forest and at Bonemound. Bonemound is in the Swampmere, the vast shallow swamplands to the south."

"Tell me about Bonemound," Harriett said bluntly, still buzzing.

"Very well," Aelf said patiently. "Bonemound is the temple of the Dread sorcerers. It is a place of terror."

"Eugene protect us," Miss Butters murmured, making that strange, wiggling handsign in front of her heart again.

Harriett was quiet a moment. Jack knew she was thinking about Bonemound and Morrigan. Though unmentioned, the threat of Morrigan hung in the air, tarnishing the beauty of the sunny woodland they were passing through. Just as Harriett opened her mouth to ask another question, a terrible howl rent the air. The baying of a massive wolf, it sent shivers down Jack's spine. Harriett stiffened on the seat beside him. In moments the howl was answered by others, many others. The howls were growing louder and louder. With a lurch of dread Jack realised the wolves were moving swiftly in their direction.

A whole heap of things then happened all at once. Aelf instantly leapt off Soxy's back, faster than Jack thought possible for a human being. He dashed in front of the cart and stretched out his hand like a weapon at the ready. Soxy's normally placid demeanour changed in a second to that of a fierce beast, her nostrils flaring. She stamped her hooves and lowered her horns in the direction of the baying wolves. The howling of the wolves had the opposite effect on Piggy-poo. He dropped to his knees, shaking like a big black mound of jelly, and tried to hide himself among the leaf litter on the ground, but there were only enough leaves to cover a part of his snout. He closed his little black eyes, apparently hoping that this made him invisible. Miss Butters leapt out of her seat and, with one hand grabbing hold of Harriett's shoulder and the other Jack's, dragged both of them into the back of the cart, shoving them down so that they were lying flat. She faced the direction of the oncoming wolves, planting herself firmly between them and the wolves like a pint-sized human shield.

Seconds later another sound reached their ears, the pounding of feet. Someone was running towards them, maybe more than one someone. At this sound Jack raised his head to see what was happening. A voice shouting in the distance made Harriett poke her head up too. It sounded like someone was being chased by the wolves.

Two figures emerged from the trees well ahead of them, running so fast they seemed to almost be flying. At first Jack could only make out their shapes. But as they neared and came out of the shade of the woods and into a patch of sunlight, he could tell that one was a man, tall and muscularly built with shoulder-length black hair. The other was an incredibly beautiful girl; so beautiful that Jack's breath caught in his throat.

The girl was tall and thin, though clearly strong and fast. She was no more than sixteen or seventeen years old. Her long hair was so black it looked like a halo of darkest midnight. Her skin was pale, luminous and smooth, and her eyes were a brilliant shining blue, like twinkling blue stars. Both the runners were dressed in black leather jerkins over black shirts and black leather trousers, all beneath hooded black cloaks. They were armed with swords and they were clearly running for their lives.

"Impossible," Aelf said to himself when he saw them, loud enough for Jack to hear. "Impossible—"

"Who are they?" Jack asked. Before Aelf could answer, a huge wolf, silvery-grey like a ghost, loomed out of the gloom behind the runners. It was gaining on them fast. Following closely on the grey wolf's heels were about a dozen other wolves, all silvery-grey, smaller than the leader but still bigger than normal wolves.

"Run!" Jack shouted, making Harriett jump. He was echoed by Aelf.

"Run, Ehmaarim, run!" Aelf's voice did not merely urge them to run faster, it commanded them to. It was as if his voice had transferred some of his own power to the runners and given them a much needed boost. They picked up speed, but it wasn't enough. The huge silver wolf was almost on them.

Aelf leapt forward, sprinting to meet the runners. As he ran, he waved his hand towards the huge wolf and let loose a wild cry. It sounded to Jack part shout, part incantation. There was a flash of white light and a huge crack. The silver wolf flinched and howled furiously, as though stung by a whip, but it didn't slow down. Aelf shouted again, sending forth another burst of light and sound that caused half of the wolf pack to turn tail and flee. Undeterred, the pack leader increased his speed and, to Jack's horror, leapt into the air towards the girl. Jack was certain that the wolf's powerful jaws were about to close around the girl's throat. He couldn't look away, his eyes glued to the horrific scene before him.

At the last second, as the giant wolf's claws caught the girl's cloak, the male runner threw himself at the massive beast, grasping it around the neck and shoving it away from her. The wolf landed on top of him. The man stabbed and stabbed at it with his sword, but the wolf was undaunted. With one awful snap of its jaws, it took hold of the man's throat and shook. The man went limp, his sword falling beside him. The wolf released him and sprang after the girl with barely a pause.

The girl had put some distance between her and the silver wolf but the rest of the pack was now on her heels. She looked back to see where her companion was and saw him lying still in the grass. She shrieked with rage and stopped to face the pack that was now just yards from where she stood.

"No!" Jack and Aelf shouted together. But it was too late,

the wolves had reached her, circling, snarling and hemming her in. The huge silver wolf was bearing down on her as well.

She did not flinch or cower. She drew her sword and stood against the pack. Jack had never seen anything so brave and incredible. Her black cloak billowed around her as she launched herself at the wolves. In moves so precise and fast that they were like a whirring dance, she lunged and stabbed and swung her sword so that first one wolf, then two, then another and another fell dead. Those left alive bolted. But the worst was not over. The pack leader had now caught up and sprang at her with a blood-curdling growl.

Just seconds before the giant wolf landed on top of the girl, there came a blinding flash and a terrible boom. The wolf was thrown backwards and landed in a heap, feet away. Aelf had reached the girl at last. The wolf leapt to its feet and launched itself back towards them. Aelf raised his hand and shouted another incantation. The wolf was thrown backwards again. Snapping and snarling furiously, it scrambled to its feet and went at them once more. Again, Aelf waved his hand and hurled the wolf away. It staggered to its feet and shook its head, growling, but this time it did not come at them. It glared at them, head lowered, snarling.

"Be gone, hollow-wolf," Aelf commanded. "You are outmatched!" The wolf snarled, baring its massive fangs. Even from where Jack was, he could see the pure hatred in its eyes. He saw something else too, a flash of rage at Aelf's words, as though the wolf understood what Aelf was saying. "Be gone! Or you will feel more than just a sting from me!" The wolf growled even more viciously, and though it was clearly reluctant to leave its prey behind, it turned and pelted away.

The minute the wolf had gone, the girl crumpled to the ground. Jack leapt out of the cart and raced towards where Aelf was kneeling beside the girl, checking her for injuries.

"Jack, me boy," Miss Butters shouted, "come back this minute! Those howlers might still be out there!" Harriett leapt after Jack, narrowly evading Miss Butters' grasping fingers.

When they reached where the girl lay, Aelf had her head propped up in his lap. Jack looked into her face, shaking his head with mingled awe and fascination. Up close, she was so slight, even more beautiful, and yet she had been so brave, so fierce and tough. All around the girl lay the bodies of slain wolves. Jack heard Harriett moan with sadness for them. She was staring at the nearest one, its fur covered in blood, with tears in her eyes.

"Do not pity them, Harriett," Aelf said, "for they are not what they appear. These wolves were dead long before this girl's blade touched them. They have been brought back from death by dark magic. They are soulless, mere puppets possessed by the will of a sorcerer, a Dread sorcerer most likely. That is why they are called hollow-wolves. They are empty of any life of their own."

The tears in Harriett's eyes continued to well despite what Aelf said. She gazed around her at all the wolves and muttered, "It's even worse that they've been brought back from the dead. I hope they go to some nice wolf heaven now."

Aelf smiled gently, before turning his attention back to the unconscious girl.

"She is not seriously wounded," he said after a moment. "But she is exhausted."

"Who is she?" Jack asked, his voice a near whisper, unable to tear his eyes away from the unconscious girl's face.

"That I cannot say, though I can tell that, though it seems impossible, she is one of the Ehmaara, one of the Night Elves, as was her fallen companion." Jack looked to where the dark-haired man lay, utterly and awfully still. When he looked back, his breath caught in his throat again as the unconscious girl moaned quietly without waking.

"I thought you said the Ehmaara were all gone, that none had been seen for thousands of years," Harriett said.

"That I did, Harriett. That I did. It seems I will have to admit an error in my telling. For this girl clearly carries the blood of the Ehmaarim. Though I think she carries some human blood also, for her skin is not cold as is the norm for Night Elves." He brushed away the hair from her face and tested the temperature of her brow. As he did so, he uncovered her ears which, though elvish in shape, were not nearly as long and pointy as the ears of the elves Jack had seen in the vision of the Battle of Bright.

"She doesn't have the markings," he muttered.

"No, she doesn't," Aelf agreed. "Well spotted, Jack. I am impressed by your powers of observation. Despite all the tumult and horror of the vision I showed you, you managed to take in and retain that small detail. Well, once we wake our friend here I'm sure we will know the answer to that and many other questions."

Aelf bent low to the girl and whispered some strange words into her ear. With the sound of the words, the light in the wood pulsed brighter and a beautifully scented breeze passed among the trees. As Aelf whispered, the girl's eyes flickered and opened. She tried to sit up but Aelf restrained her. "Do not move just yet, my friend. You have been through much and need to remain still for a while."

"Who are you?" she demanded, looking from Aelf to Harriett and Jack and then to Miss Butters, who had finally waddled over.

"We might ask you the same thing, girly," Miss Butters said. "Running at us with wolves at your heel! Here in the dells! What were you thinking, girl! Though, judging by your ears you're half-elvish, and if my grandmammy Belladonna taught me one thing about the half-elvish it's that they're not great thinkers. They inherit the worst of both breeds, the mischief of the elves and the hot-headedness of humans—"

"Dorothea!" scolded Aelf. "Have you no kindness? Did you not see what this girl just endured?" Miss Butters looked abashed but not enough to still her tongue.

"Kind? Why, of course I'm kind! Eugene only knows that truth is the greatest kindness. I was just saying that elf and human-kind aren't a good mix. And if that's not the truth, and therefore a kindness, then I don't know what is."

"Well, we can agree on one thing at least," Aelf said. "You don't know what kindness is." It was the harshest thing Jack had heard Aelf say. It clearly stung Miss Butters for she said no more. Jack looked away rather than see the red blush of mortification on the halfling's cheeks.

"To answer your question, my friend," Aelf said to the girl, whose pale skin had regained some of its luminosity since she woke, "I am Aelf. These are my companions, Harriett, Jack and Miss Dorothea Butters of Bright." He indicated each in turn. "Might I ask your name?"

"I am Anarra Settonett."

"Impossible," Aelf whispered, as if to himself, his eyes wide with shock and his mouth forming a small 'O' of surprise.

"Ah, what's impossible?" Harriett asked. Jack put his hand on his sister's shoulder and squeezed it for her to be quiet. Her limitless curiosity was out of place given there was a very weak half-elvish girl lying on the ground before them amidst the bodies of slain hollow-wolves and another elf lying dead in the grass just a few feet away.

"I am Ehmaarim of the House of Sett," the girl said to Harriet. Harriett took a step back, surprised that the girl was answering her directly and looking straight into her eyes. "We Ehmaarim have not moved openly in the world for millennia. We have hidden ourselves from all, even the druids. It must seem impossible to Master Aelf Ethelwulf that I exist, especially as I carry the family name of the House of Sett."

"Yes, that is exactly why I am surprised. I hope you will forgive my disbelief," Aelf said courteously. "And I see that you know more about me than I do about you. You know my full name—"

"And that you are a druid, a member of the High Council of the Order."

"Goodness," Aelf smiled. "You *are* well-informed for one so young. But I suppose, if you really are a member of the House of Sett?"

"I am. My father was the last Thane, the Throneholder, of

the house."

"Was he indeed?" Aelf said quietly. "That explains much."

Jack didn't think it explained much at all.

"My father raised me on his own. My mother, a half-human woman, died when I was just a babe. So you see, little lady," she said coldly to Miss Butters, "I am more than *half* an elf."

"Three quarters at least," Harriett said, smiling.

Jack shook his head. Aelf chuckled. Miss Butters fiddled self-consciously with the buttons on her tweed jacket and pretended she hadn't heard anything.

"I was raised apart," Anarra continued, "as is the custom of the Ehmaara. I wear not the marks, as I'm sure you have noticed, because I am in grieving. My father was captured and killed by a troop of Vellenor less than a year ago."

"I am sorry for your loss," Aelf said before asking: "Tell me, my Lady, how did you come to be here?"

"Please, do not call me 'Lady'. I bear no title. I bear only a sword. My companion, my father's dearest friend, and I were captured by four skinwearers disguised as travelling traders and carried from the Empty Lands to the foot of the mountains, where the skinwearers met the hollow-wolves. The hollow-wolves led the skinwearers to a place just east of here. I overheard the skinwearers talking of their sorcerer master, who abides here and to whom we were being taken."

"Now I'll be the one to say *impossible*," Miss Butters interrupted. "A sorcerer in the Dells! There are none, my girl, none!"

"Once we entered this dale, the sorcerer communicated with the skinwearers through a Sending. The Sending led them to a glade of beech trees and a pond where there were many willows. There was a single standing stone on an island in the midst of the pond, where an apple tree also grew," Anarra said defiantly.

"Dale Delving," Miss Butters gasped.

"You know of this place?" Aelf asked.

"Yes, it is the spring that is the source of the Sweetwater

River. It is an isolated place, few know of it, and all of them Brightlings."

"The skinwearers must have an ally in the Dells," Aelf began. "Only someone who knows the area well could have led them to this Dale Delving place. Also, why would the skinwearers bring their captives here if not to deliver them to their sorcerer master?"

Miss Butters moaned. It was clear that her sense of the dells as safe from the evils of the world beyond the huge Craggy Mountains was slipping away. The image of the red eyes flashed into Jack's mind. He had the disturbing feeling that the red eyes and Anarra's kidnapping by skinwearers were connected.

"At dawn this morning we broke our bonds, slew the skinwearers and escaped," Anarra continued. "We have been pursued by the hollow-wolf pack ever since." She paused, as if remembering everything that happened to her in the intervening hours. "I need to understand why this has happened to me, why my companion lies there dead. Will you help me? I seek the aid of the Council of Druids."

"Of course I will help you," Aelf said. "We travel now to my own master's home. We will need his wisdom to understand what has happened to you." He helped Anarra to her feet.

Once she was standing, Jack saw that she was almost as tall as him. They were standing side by side now. Jack stepped away, uncomfortable to be in such close quarters to such a beautiful girl. He kept sneaking glances at her as she straightened her hair and readjusted her cloak.

He was struck by how similar they were in colouring. Both black-haired and pale, both blue-eyed, though Anarra's eyes shone with an almost supernatural radiance. She was also far too good looking, kind of unnaturally good looking. Jack couldn't remember seeing anyone so stunningly attractive. Judging by the positively mesmerised look on Harriett's face, she also thought Anarra was incredibly beautiful. Anarra glanced over and caught them staring at her and turned away, as if embarrassed or annoyed. Jack couldn't tell which. Aelf chose that moment to bend and pick up Anarra's sword. He handed it back to her and, with a sidewise glance at Jack, said, "You are not friendless, Anarra Settonett, not anymore."

Aelf buried Anarra's fallen companion beneath an oak tree. The half-elvish girl watched unflinchingly and without a word. The druid placed a stone as a memorial at the base of the tree and magically carved the symbol of a wildflower on the stone with his finger. Anarra didn't watch this, looking away until the task was done.

After the burial, Aelf hastened them on their journey. Once they'd set off, he made sure that they travelled much more quickly than before. As the afternoon wore on, the little wagon moved through wide meadows and then up a series of small hills. Aelf rode beside the wagon on Soxy, his eyes and ears alert for any more trouble. Harriett sat in the back of the wagon with their new companion, who sat with her hood drawn up and her head drooping. Jack couldn't tell if Anarra was actually sleeping or feigning it to avoid talking. Jack shared the wagon seat with Miss Butters, though his eyes were rarely on the trail ahead of them. His gaze repeatedly went to the corner of the wagon where Anarra sat slumped. Miss Butters' eyes were also frequently drawn to their new companion, her distrust clear on her face. Her amber eyes practically shone with it.

Soon the rise of each hill was a little larger than the previous one. Piggy-poo heaved and panted with the increased effort but Aelf did not allow the pace to slow. As they crested each hill, they were met with ever more spectacular views of the snow-capped Craggy Mountains, which appeared to grow larger and larger as they proceeded.

As the sun dipped low in the sky, they crested yet another rise and saw before them a vista of undulating hills and ridges that reached all the way to the feet of the mountains. The hills had about them a purplish hue, covered by a kind of heather with purplish seed heads. In the dips between hills and ridges, there grew sunny glades of large trees, overhanging pebbly brooks. Some of the trees were among the biggest Jack had ever seen.

As they moved down into one of these glades, Miss Butters described the large trees as Notchward Oaks. According to her, they were the largest type of oak in the Halfling Dells and were only found in the Purple Hills through which they now moved.

"Why are they called Notchward Oaks?" Harriett asked from the back of the wagon.

"A bit of old superstition," Miss Butters answered. "It's said that these oaks guard Narrownotch Pass. Ridiculous of course, how could an old tree guard anything?" At that Aelf cleared his throat, as if he disagreed, but he held his tongue. "Before the founding of the Congregation of Florid Spinsters, all kinds of superstitions were common in these parts. But, Eugene be praised, no longer. The Spinsters have stamped out that rubbish well and truly."

As Miss Butters spoke, Jack considered the idea that these oaks protected the dells, much as the oak in Cairnbawn had protected the stone circle there. He wondered what the oaks were meant to be protecting the dells against. An image of the red eyes he'd seen back where they'd had lunch came instantly to his mind. He considered the idea that those red eyes were connected to the hollow-wolves and Anarra's capture somehow. The longer he thought about it, the more uneasy he became, so much so that he started to feel as though those eyes were boring into his back, that they were being watched and followed.

Every now and then he looked over his shoulder to reassure himself that nothing was following them. He saw only purple heather and Notchward Oaks and rolling hills. Each time he looked back and found nothing, he convinced himself, for a time, that it was just his imagination. Then the feeling that they were being followed would return so that he was compelled to look over his shoulder once more.

After a while, he decided that he couldn't keep doing this. If nothing else, he was going to get a crick in his neck. So he decided on a new strategy. He would look one last time and if he didn't see anything, he would accept that this was because there was nothing there. He determined to be clever about it this time though. He would look back over his shoulder once, turn around to face the trail ahead and then quickly look behind again. If there was anything following them it would think, after he'd looked back the first time, that it was safe for it to move again and he would catch it.

After the first look behind them there was nothing, just gentle beams of sunlight filtering through the open woods and a bluebird flitting among the trees. Maybe there wasn't anything there? He felt reassured until he turned around the second time and saw a shadowy figure dash behind a tree. It was in the very periphery of his vision, but he was sure it was a small figure running upright on two legs! His heart hammered in his chest. He stared at where he thought it had been but couldn't see it at all now.

He tried to convince himself it was just his imagination. At least that was what he was afraid Aelf would say if he told him about it. So he didn't tell him, he just tried to put it out of his mind. After all, it probably was just a big badger. Miss Butters had said they were huge, and maybe the badgers in Anwynn ran on their hind legs? If he'd learnt anything recently, it was that anything was possible.

A while later, as the sun turned golden and touched its toes to the peaks of the Craggy Mountains, causing shadows to lengthen and the air to cool, they found themselves atop a ridge looking down into a perfectly circular glade. The glade was like a large, natural bowl, rich in purple heather and dominated by one massive oak at the centre. At four points around the glade's circumference were large megaliths shaped a bit like elongated eggs. Jack could tell that this was a place of great power; it almost hummed with magic. Even Miss Butters was thrown into silence at the sight of it.

Jack, Harriett and Anarra climbed out of the wagon to get a better look. For the first time since Anarra joined them, she threw back her hood. She looked down into the glade with wide blue eyes that brightened with both wonder and relief. Her shoulders visibly relaxed. She was almost smiling. Then she saw Jack watching her and the smile faded. She avoided his gaze by directing her eyes back to the glade below. Jack couldn't decide if Anarra was shy, still shaken by her ordeal, or just didn't like him.

With her gaze fixed on the glade, Jack could watch her without being noticed. Her skin, though pale, looked soft and smooth. The urge to reach out and touch her was strong. He put his hands in his pockets and balled them up. If he were her, he wouldn't want some stranger touching him. Especially after what she'd been through, with the skinwearers and the wolves and losing her friend. He wondered what she was feeling, or if she felt very much at all. She had barely reacted when her friend died, nor cried when they buried him, just averted her eyes as though it was something she needn't witness.

A slight wind picked up, carrying a leaf from a nearby tree so that it landed in Anarra's hair. She gently untangled it and pulled it loose, casting it back onto the wind. It rose up for a moment, hovering over them as though about to soar off into the sky, but the wind died down and it fell, landing on Jack's shoulder. He brushed it off. In the moment of touching it a flood of images flashed through his mind. Among those images, a number of scenes stood out:

Anarra as a very young girl, about three years old, sitting on a log in front of a campfire. She is so small that her feet dangle just above the ground. It is a dark night, no moon. Her father sits beside her, feeding her tiny morsels of food. Both of their faces are impassive, but Jack feels waves of emotion coming from them both: contentment, affection, happiness, love.

Another night. Anarra, perhaps eight or nine years old now, is crouched behind a rocky outcrop high on a ridge with her father. Down below in the valley a troop of elves moves by silently. A boy about the same age as Anarra, with blond hair and pointy ears, runs to-and-fro among the adults, joy written all over his face. The boy stops, looks up to the rocky outcrop where Anarra and her father are hidden and stares right at them. Anarra whispers to her father: *How does he know we're here? No one has ever sensed us before.* Her voice is steady, seemingly unconcerned, but she is filled with surprise and wonder. Her father whispers back: *He is special, that one.* Then the boy's mother calls to him out of the night: "Ellisenn, come!" The boy makes a slight nod towards Anarra and her father and runs off toward his mother.

A fourteen year old Anarra, sitting by a slow-moving river, the wind causing tiny waves on its surface. She watches these waves with a powerful focus, delighting in their silent movement. Her father sleeps nearby with his back against a tree. A shape surfaces in the water, surprising her, causing her to jump up and draw her sword. Her father jumps up as well, hitting his head on a low hanging branch. Anarra realises that the shape in the water is an otter and not a bloodthirsty goblin. She puts her sword away and laughs at herself. Her father laughs then as well, rubbing his sore head. Anarra laughs until she is hoarse, until the otter, perhaps deciding she is mad, swims away.

Anarra jogging through the night, running for miles and miles with no destination in mind. Her eyes are emotionless, fixed on the setting moon on the distant horizon. Her hair flies behind her on the wind. In her heart there is a terrible, aching pain over the loss of her father. Far off in the distance a wolf bays at the moon. Anarra thinks it is her heart that is howling.

Anarra bound beside her companion, captive to three traders who are really skinwearers. She struggles with her bindings, but they are too tight. Her face shows nothing of the emotions inside her: defiance, humiliation, fear, but mostly anger. So much anger, every bit of it directed at the skinwearers. It is a wonder that they cannot feel it, that they do not run for their lives.

Jack had to steady himself against the wagon so that he didn't fall over. Luckily no-one noticed. All their eyes were still on the glade below. What had just happened to him? Was this part of the power that came with being a Waycaller, the ability to read people's minds? Out of the corner of his eye Jack glanced back at Anarra. Now he did not see her as emotionless at all. Her skin glowed with feeling, her whole body thrummed with emotion.

She felt his gaze and looked into his eyes. At first defensive, her face quickly softened for, Jack knew, she had seen in his eyes that he could see who she really was, what she'd been through, and that he admired and respected her for it. She looked away, a blush forming on her cheeks.

That's when Jack knew. He had never felt for any other girl what he felt for Anarra Settonett. Though he'd barely spoken to her and had known her only a few hours, he had seen into her heart. How could he ever be the same after that? Just being close to her filled him with a skin-prickling mix of excitement and nerves.

He shook his head, surprised at himself. How much more was Anwynn going to change him? The visions were transforming him. He had changed so much already, after only a day in Anwynn. But what was he changing into? A Waycaller? Or something else, something that led to his hurting Harriett? The image of his little sister bleeding to death on some future battlefield flashed into his mind. He shivered, looking out over the grassy dell, with its oak tree in the centre that seemed to hum with a soothing power. The image of the battlefield dissolved.

Aelf was right, there was magic everywhere here. And it was turning him into someone he didn't recognise. He hoped all of these changes would be good ones. The part of him that Anwynn hadn't affected yet, where his feelings of self-doubt and grief about his parents were kept locked away, worried that they wouldn't be. With the worry came the echo of Morrigan's voice speaking to him as though he was hers: *Look what you have done, my child, look what you have done!*

# PART 3: THE DARK PRINCE

# ASSASSIN

*Cairnbawn Village, Scottish Highlands*

Eloise feared it was a trap the minute she realised that Kashashem wasn't coming. Unease spread through her like a cold fever, but she said nothing to Noble. They were waiting for Kashashem just outside the boundary of the ancient stone circle on the edge of the village of Cairnbawn. The stones stood, tall and dark, like frozen silhouettes, casting long moon shadows over the cemetery and church. Eloise and Noble stood in one of these shadows, peering into the fog that shrouded the village and the loch below.

An owl hooted far off in the distance, making Eloise jump despite herself. She caught Noble watching her for signs of unease. He knew she hated nights like these, dark, foggy and claustrophobic. She'd hated them since she was a little girl, when nights like this one were often accompanied by nightmares, nightmares of Morrigan. She quelled the rising smirk on Noble's lips with a firm glare and pushed her anxiety aside, telling herself her unease was just left-over silliness from her childhood. She was twenty-eight years old and shouldn't be frightened of such things any more, especially not after everything she'd experienced, both the wondrous and the terrifying. To distract herself, she tied her long black hair in a ponytail and blew on her cold fingers. In the gloomy light, her pale hands almost shone. Noble took a step closer and took hold of her hands.

"I've always said your skin is like moonlight," he whispered with a smirk, pressing her hands between his to warm them.

"Oh, good lord, Noble." She sighed with mock exasperation. "You're such a cornball."

"But you're happy to be married to this corny romantic, admit it." He smirked more broadly. The familiar sound of his voice helped ease Eloise's worry.

"I'll admit no such thing," she said, trying hard not to smile.

She looked up into his blue eyes, where the cold was drawing out tears, and saw her own eyes reflected there. She wiped away the dampness at his eyes and caressed his cheek, patting it playfully. Glancing up at the cloudy sky, she wished she could see the stars she knew were up there somewhere. The same stars that shone over Anwynn. The fact of the stars being the same on both sides of the Veil often confused her, though comforted her as well.

A soft sound of rustling in the trees at the edge of the cemetery made her peer in that direction, looking for Kashashem, but the fog obscured any movement. It was only minutes past the midnight meeting time, but Kashashem had never been late before. She looked back at Noble, who was still watching her carefully, wondering if she perceived some danger he couldn't. Her senses were much more acute than his.

"You're worried because Lady Kashashem is late," he said. It wasn't a question. He knew her well and could tell that she was concerned. Before she could say anything, he smiled. That same roguish smile he always used to put her at ease.

"As far as I know," she whispered, "the elvish are never, ever late, not even by a second. Especially not Kashashem." She rubbed her arms against the cold and stood behind a huge megalith to protect herself from the damp wind. She tried to reassure herself that, as the Head of the Order of Druids and a she-elf of extraordinary power, Kashashem had many responsibilities. Perhaps it was one of those that had delayed her? But then a sudden chill ran down her spine. She recognised it as a warning.

Something was wrong. Her pale skin tingled with dread, and not just because of the gloomy night. She scanned the shadows for the slightest sign—a small movement, a dark shape—that would reveal that something, or someone, was concealed there.

"What is it?" Noble whispered. Eloise didn't answer, but swiftly raised a hand to silence him. The air was heavy and still. A creeping mist rose from the damp earth to enfold them in a blanket of gloom. Eloise strained her ears for the slightest unusual sound. A slow but bitter wind moaned across the loch, buffeting the megaliths and making an eerie song as it funnelled between the stones. Eloise knew that the elves believed that such songs, the wailings of stones, were harbingers of doom.

She decided to get out of there as quickly as possible. She grabbed Noble by the hand and took one step towards the gate leading to Cairnbawn and her father's cottage. At that precise moment, the soft sound of stealthy footfall behind them alerted her to another's presence. She spun around just in time to see him coming. At first, she couldn't believe her eyes.

"One of the Vellenor!" Noble spat, his voice trembling. "I thought it was impossible for the Dark Elves to cross between the worlds?"

"As did I," Eloise hissed. "The Order must know of this!" Until that moment, Eloise believed there were only two beings alive who could cross the Veil between Anwynn and the human world: the Head of the Order of Druids, Kashashem, and herself. But here a Dark Elf was, striding towards them, sneering with murderous loathing. With a jolt to her stomach, she realised that the midnight meeting was a trap after all. Kashashem probably hadn't even sent the message that drew her here. Without thinking, she shoved Noble behind her to protect him.

Her Vellenor stalker saw the disturbing realisation that she'd been led into a trap dawn on her face. He smirked with cold pleasure. Like all elves, even the dark ones, this one was mesmerizingly beautiful. The magic of his elvish blood made sure of that. His long ice-white hair danced over his shoulders and his pale pink-hued eyes shone in the night with a malevolent fire.

"Full of his own prettiness this one, isn't he?" Noble

joked. A slight shake in his voice undermined his attempt at bravado, but Eloise nodded her agreement to his point. This Dark Elf was exceptionally handsome and thus likely to be exceptionally cruel. Eloise had learned that the more beautiful or handsome the Dark Elves were, the crueller they were likely to be. One of the few things that Eloise knew for certain was that the Vellenor were all brutal and sadistic. She had come to that knowledge the hard way, for they had attempted to kill her many times. The first attempt had come soon after the revelation that she was a Waycaller.

But why was she remembering all this now, as the Vellenor rushed towards them, leering? She'd not been the same since her second child, her daughter, was born. Something had changed in her, and in the world, as the result of her daughter's birth. Her reflexes had slowed and her mind often wandered into the past. The world seemed to be holding its breath, as if waiting for some calamity to fall. It was this change that Eloise had thought was the reason for Kashashem's summons. She shook her head, banishing all thought of the past, and drew herself up to her full height. Kashashem hadn't summoned her at all. The Vellenor had sent a false message. Her eyes raked over the advancing elf for some hint as to who he was.

His long black coat billowed behind him. Eloise shuddered, remembering that the Vellenor's trademark coats were made from human skin. He wore the sword of one highly born and a dagger at his thigh that marked him as an assassin. The wind and the elf's rapid movement towards them whipped his hair away from his ears, revealing their sharp elongated shape and the tattooed circular marks that indicated the rank he held among his kind. This one's tattoos showed that he was not only a warrior assassin but an accomplished sorcerer as well.

This is it, Eloise thought, Noble and I are going to die. Her only chance, and it was a slim one, was if she could provoke the Vellenor into pursuing her inside the circle of stones. She steeled herself, adopting a defensive fighting stance, and faced her advancing attacker. Noble stepped out from behind her and did the same, retrieving the long thin dagger concealed in his boot.

The Vellenor assassin lifted his hand, contorting his fingers into the shape necessary to cast a fatal spell. Eloise anticipated him. Rather than trying to run, which would have been futile anyway, she lunged straight at him. If she was going to die, she was going to die fighting, and maybe take the wretched Vellenor with her before he could harm Noble.

Her unexpected move surprised the assassin enough that he faltered and miscast the spell. Eloise seized the advantage and drew her dagger from its sheath hidden beneath her overcoat. She swung it in the direction of the Dark Elf's handsome skull. He easily dodged her attack, but his eyes flared with surprise. Eloise knew that the Dark Elves, especially the truly powerful ones, were not accustomed to their victims fighting back. Their prey usually cowered in terror.

Eloise lunged again, this time aiming for the soft spot beneath the Vellenor's arm that gave direct access to the heart. The elf suddenly vaulted into the air, as if weightless, and somersaulted out of her reach. He landed in a crouch a few feet further away from where he'd been moments before. Noble darted forward, his dagger at the ready, and lunged at the Vellenor's throat, aiming for the jugular vein. But he had misjudged. The assassin spun away from Noble's lunge. In a move so fast and terrible that Eloise barely saw it happen, the Vellenor grabbed hold of Noble's head and, with a sinister pirouette, broke his neck. Noble fell to the ground and did not move again. Eloise screamed and nearly fell to the ground herself. How could this be happening? How could Noble be dead, so suddenly and irreversibly dead?

The Vellenor seized his advantage and made a swift magical gesture that threw Eloise backwards. Now it was her turn to vault through the air, but she didn't stumble when she hit the ground. She landed firmly on her feet and, screaming with fury, immediately launched herself towards her attacker once more. She was so filled with hate and rage that she did not know herself. The Vellenor's eyes widened further, this time showing more than surprise, perhaps even a little respect.

"You are bold, Waycaller," he sneered, before snapping his fingers together to ignite a ball of fire, "but that will not prevent me from killing you, as I killed your sweetling."

Eloise leapt aside as the flaming sphere burst from his hands, but the sphere collided with her anyway. It blasted her backwards into one of the outer standing stones. On impact, a number of her ribs shattered with a sickening crunch. Eloise thudded to the ground, her head smashing against a boulder. Dazed and unable to move, she lay there, panting, hurting and screaming inside about Noble.

The Vellenor's sneering words echoed in her throbbing skull. *As I killed your sweetling.* Something stirred in her then, a determination, an unstoppable, furious drive to punish the Vellenor for what he'd done. But she couldn't move, not yet. The rage had not built to the point where it overcame the pain and concussion. But that moment was coming fast, she could feel it.

Clearly believing that Eloise was close to death, the Vellenor raised his hand to finish her off. He formed his fingers into the killing gesture and jabbed them towards her. She was utterly defenceless as a flash of brilliant green energy hurtled through the air and struck her torso. She convulsed and howled in agony.

The elvish assassin stopped motionless where he was. Fury and confusion transformed his face into a frightening mask. Eloise, though slipping into a fog of pain, knew why. How could she still be alive? Anyone subjected to that kind of power should be dead. The shock of her survival thrummed through her body, bringing back some of her strength. The Vellenor's eyes narrowed as he used his sorcerer's skill to reach out with his mind to examine her.

Eloise felt him penetrate her own mind and knew that he would detect that her life force was still strong. She could feel that herself. She didn't know exactly how or why, but knew that some magic was blocking the assassin's power. The Vellenor came to the same conclusion. He snarled so vehemently with enraged disbelief and frustration that the sound of it reverberated around the stones and echoed throughout the valley. That echoing sound broke through the pain encasing Eloise's mind. She knew the assassin had discovered that she was far from the brink of death, and that no magic of his could tip her into the abyss. She also knew that, like many of his kind, he knew perfectly well how to kill without magic. Eloise had seen the gruesome evidence of that. As though inspired by Eloise's own thought, the assassin drew the dagger from its sheath on his thigh.

She had to pull herself together. She had to get back up and fight. The Vellenor charged toward her and reached her just as she struggled to her feet, screaming against the pain. The Dark Elf thrust the dagger toward her heart. Eloise twisted and dodged to the side so that his blade struck empty air. She heaved her own dagger above her head, shouting in pain with every movement, and swung it down toward the assassin's skull with everything she had left. He blocked her blow with a powerful up-thrust and their blades glanced off each other with a reverberating clang.

The rebounding force of the blow pushed them apart, giving the Vellenor just enough room to cast another spell. He clicked his fingers and Eloise's left ankle broke with a sickening snap. She teetered and fell down, her head hitting the ground again, this time striking a stone that cut a wide gash across her forehead. Struggling to drag herself back up and gasping for breath, her whole body wracked with pain, she was sure that the moment of her death had finally arrived. The Vellenor laughed. He was certain that he'd won, that Eloise was going to perish by his hand.

She desperately brought her dagger to bear against the ground, trying to use it to leverage herself up, but the pain in her ankle and head were too strong. She couldn't stand. She looked up with horror as her attacker took the few steps required to bring him to where she lay, still struggling to get up, just within the ring of standing stones. With a final, terrible effort, Eloise crawled a few more feet away from him, further into the circle, and then collapsed. She could go no further. There was not an ounce of fight left in her. If the Vellenor would only cross the perimeter of the circle after her, then she might have a slither of a hope.

The assassin stepped forward once more, to the very edge of the circle, kicking her dagger away with a smirk of awful triumph. "Once I have finished you," he taunted, his voice sounding like a terrible hymn, "I am going to kill each of your children, the little boy and, very, very slowly, the baby girl." With an evil grin he raised his dagger and lunged.

"No! Not my children!" The words came out of Eloise like a primal scream as, by some miracle, she managed to roll away and pull herself back into a standing position. The Vellenor's dagger cut into her shoulder as she lurched upwards, but it was not a fatal wound. Her head pounded and blood poured over her face and down her arm, but she was on her feet. She was going to fight to the very end. The Vellenor swiped at her again with his dagger. Eloise pitched backwards at the last moment and he missed. The force of his stab at Eloise unbalanced him and he staggered forward, just inside the circle.

He actually looked stunned, but he had no time to react. Consumed with a desperate need to protect her children, Eloise stretched her left hand toward the Vellenor and yelled with all her might, "Be damned to Uffern, foul Vellenor!"

The sorcerer shrieked with shock and fury and vanished in a burst of blinding silver light. When the light dimmed, Eloise was alone in the circle again. The wind sang quietly among the stones as if pleased by Eloise's victory. The Dark Elf should never have followed her within the boundary of the stones; that mistake had been his undoing. Within the stones, Eloise had powers that even the most adept assassin could not overcome. Her heart leapt with relief. She'd done it, she'd avenged Noble. The assassin, forever sealed in Uffern, could not harm her children now. He had learned first-hand why his kind hated and feared the Waycaller.

Eloise fell to her knees, exhausted by the effort it took to banish the Vellenor to the dominion of monsters, and trembling with pain from her battered body. As she knelt there on the ground, her forehead throbbing and bleeding, her ankle aching, she felt herself losing consciousness.

She desperately tried to hang on. She needed to return to her children and take them to safety, to the protection of Kashashem and the Order of Druids. The assassin had made it clear that he'd set this trap not just to kill her, but to dispose of her so that he could then murder her children. With her children gone, the human line of the Waycallers would be extinct.

What would happen then? With the bloodline of the Waycallers cut, would the Veil between the worlds be cut as well? Would the Veil tear apart, making it possible for all the dark beings of Anwynn to cross freely into the human world? Worst of all, would the death of the last Waycaller allow Morrigan to break out of her eternal prison?

She was losing the struggle to stay conscious. She toppled sideways onto the dew-soaked earth. Her eyesight darkened and her body lost much of its warmth to the midnight cold. Her blood was feeding the grass. Her eyes closed against her will and she saw a vision of her little baby girl, Harriett, cradled in the arms of her brother Jack, both of them smiling and safe, oblivious to the fate of their parents. It was how she'd left them that evening, in the care of a babysitter. That comforting image was then replaced by one in which a Vellenor assassin crept through the shadows to the house where her children slept. She saw it like a nightmare in her mind – the Vellenor effortlessly disposing of the sitter and then turning his vicious powers on the children. If one Vellenor could somehow cross the veil, then more could. Her children were not safe.

"No," she moaned, "please, don't harm them." She addressed her plea to the night, to any higher power that might hear and help, but she held little hope that her plea would be heard, let alone answered. Tears rolled down her face. Even if she'd wanted to, she couldn't have held the tears back. Her heart was breaking. "Please, no, don't take my children from me as well."

Then Eloise heard a familiar sound, footfall on damp grass. With every bit of her remaining strength she forced her eyes open. Through a veil of tears, she saw a young man walking towards her, outlined against the creeping mist by a halo of power. He appeared barely nineteen years old and was very handsome, far more handsome than any of the elves she'd ever seen, dark or bright. But he wasn't elvish, even in her weakened state she could tell that. He was far more magical than any of the elves. She could feel the power emanating from him in waves. His long blue-black hair and pale skin glowed with their own light. His eyes sparkled like vivid blue stars. Strikingly, he was dressed from head to toe in old-fashioned blue velvet finery, like a prince from some fairy tale. This being was Faeden. She didn't know how she knew this, but she knew it with an undeniable certainty. He was Faeden and his magic had protected her from the assassin's sorcery. As he reached her, she saw that he was smiling. That smile was the last thing Eloise saw before she surrendered to the pain and fatigue and all went dark.

# OAKHOLME

*Oakholme, residence of Wadget*

As Jack and the others watched, the sun dipped lower behind the peaks of the Craggy Mountains, turning its golden rays to a deeper orange touched with crimson. Still standing by the wagon atop the ridge with Harriett and Anarra, Jack looked down into the circular glade, taking in the purple heather, the four standing stones shaped like elongated eggs and the huge oak tree in the glade's centre. The sky above was cloudless and clear except for the streaks of orange light cast by the setting sun. Even so, a very light sun shower began to fall; so light that it was barely enough to dampen their clothes. It carried with it a sweet scent that reminded Jack of sandalwood. Piggy-poo raised his head to the sky, delightedly catching raindrops in his open mouth.

"Ah," Aelf said from Soxy's back, "my master has dissolved the protective wards so that we may enter." At that Soxy bellowed excitedly and headed at full tilt straight down the ridge. Aelf, teetering dangerously as the cow picked up speed, grabbed two handfuls of shag to steady himself. When cow and rider reached the bottom of the hill, Soxy stopped suddenly, dropping her head to graze on the grass. Aelf lurched forward on Soxy's back, then tipped clear over her horns, doing a strange somersault in mid-air and landing flat on his backside.

"So it's true," Miss Butters exclaimed from the driver's seat of her little wagon. "Druids, like cats, always fall the right way up!" She told Piggy-poo to giddy up and the wagon trundled on down the ridge. When they all reached the bottom of the slope and met up with Soxy, who was still happily grazing, Jack saw that Aelf was nursing a grazed knee.

"Nearly made it!" he said. "She does that every time. I really should learn to dismount before the glade comes into view. Such an enthusiastic cow, she can barely contain herself. The grass here is so sweet, you see." He stood up and dusted himself off. "Let's unhitch Piggy-poo and leave the animals here to graze. They'll be perfectly safe." Once unhitched, Piggy-poo flopped to the ground and immediately went to sleep.

"Poor dear," Miss Butters sighed, "he's utterly exhausted."

"And full to the brim with cake," Aelf chuckled. "Let's press on, shall we?"

As they approached the tree in the heart of the glade, Anarra straggling at the back of the group, Aelf turned to them all and said, "Welcome to Oakholme, the abode of my master, Wadget."

"Wadget? That's another funny name," Harriett observed. "Is it a faerie name?"

"Not quite," Aelf answered. "My master is of another kind."

"What kind is that, exactly?" asked Miss Butters, her hand twitching, readying to make the wiggling sign at the first hint of blasphemy.

"My master is an Oakling," Aelf said, "which, Jack and Harriett, means he is quite small, has green skin and very long ears that he likes to waggle." The word 'waggle' set off Miss Butters' hand a-wiggling like crazy.

"Oh cute!" Harriett beamed.

"Cute!" Miss Butters gasped. "Oaklings are far from cute, young Miss. I've never heard of an Oakling that could be described in that fashion."

"So, what exactly are Oaklings then?" Jack asked, steeling himself for the answer. Based on the frenzied wiggling of Miss Butters' fingers, Oaklings must be bad.

"An Oakling is a magical being," Aelf said calmly. "Their appearance is somewhat like ours, apart from the green skin and pointy ears that is, but they are quite small, smaller even than Miss Butters. Their size, however, is no indication of their strength of will or magical prowess. Oaklings are formidable."

"They sound cool." Harriett smiled and looked towards the oak, straining to catch sight of the Oakling.

"Yes, quite cool," Aelf chuckled, trying out Harriett's otherworldly phrase. "My master is one of only a very few of his kind, and he is one of the oldest and most powerful. He is also a member of the Order of Druids and has mastered the arts of magic like practically no other, except perhaps for Kashashem herself."

"Fiddlesticks!" Miss Butters hissed so that they all jumped. "Oaklings are nasty things, every halfling with any sense will tell you that! They live in holes in trees, of all unseemly places, and what's more they are the minions of the Tricksy Ones! Some of them," she whispered as if scared of being overheard, "even do the bidding of the Pale Mother. They can't be trusted and shouldn't be put up with at all! If I'd known I was travelling all this way to visit an Oakling, I'd never have come! I certainly wouldn't have packed such a fine basket!"

For the first time, Jack sort of agreed with Miss Butters. If some Oaklings were followers of the Faeden, then why would Aelf have anything to do with one?

"So, are Oaklings like goblins then?" he asked, casting his eyes around for any sudden movement, half expecting some horrible thing to leap out from behind one of the standing stones.

"Oh, Jack," Harriett said rolling her eyes. "Stop being such a worry-wort."

"Harriett is quite right, Jack, you have no cause for concern," Aelf said firmly, disagreeing with Miss Butters with a cold look from his lavender eyes. "Oaklings are most certainly not like goblins! Goblins are all wicked, like their dark mistress, Morrigan."

Miss Butters squeaked.

Aelf continued unperturbed. "Oaklings, on the other hand, are just like you and me. Some are very good, and some not so good, like any other being."

"See, Jack," Harriett said. "Wadget is a nice Oakling, isn't he Aelf?"

"Nice is not a word I would use to describe Master Wadget." The Druid smirked. "But he's most definitely good."

"But Oaklings *are* known for consorting with the Tricksy Ones, you can't deny that, Aelf," Miss Butters insisted.

"I suppose I cannot deny that," Aelf answered cautiously. "It is true that some Oaklings, being older even than the elves, have had a long relationship with the Faeden. Some have formed close bonds with them."

Miss Butters made a sound of triumph.

"But that does not make the Oaklings wicked," Aelf added in response.

"So you may say, Aelf," Miss Butters said testily, "but as my grandmammy Belladonna always said, it is far smarter to judge a hound by the pack it runs with than by the wag of its tail. I'll bet my stockings this Wadget is no good. None that ever treated with tricksy devils can be of any account."

Aelf stopped in his tracks so suddenly that Harriett walked straight into his behind. He said nothing to her however, because his full gaze was on Miss Butters.

"I will say this but the once, Dorothea. You will not disparage Master Wadget in my presence ever again. Apart from the fact that much that you hold dear only survives because of Master Wadget's protection, he is my master, my teacher and my greatest friend. Never, ever, speak ill of him again." Aelf's voice was so cold that it chilled the air around them. The tension between Aelf and Dorothea was as taught as a trampoline. Jack wasn't surprised to see that Miss Butters showed no inclination whatsoever of continuing to slander Oaklings.

"Now come along," Aelf said, with a total change of tone. Gone was the cold, severe druid and in his place was smiling, friendly old Aelf. "I believe Master Wadget has the kettle on the stove for us." He smiled as he gently untangled Harriett from his cloak and continued on. At that very moment, Jack heard the soft whistling of a kettle. He took this as another sign of the strange prescience of druids.

The kettle sound was coming from the centre of the glade, where the huge tree sat, casting its shadow to the very edge of the circle to touch the easternmost standing stone. As they got nearer, Jack saw that there was more to the massive oak than there first seemed. At the base of its huge, buttress-like roots there was a door and the trunk had windows in it. The windows were round like portholes, as was the door which was painted a deep green. It looked to Jack like there could be more than one floor. The highest window was up among the boughs of the oak, which was a good distance from the ground. A chimney, a small green L-shaped thing that looked like a young branch, puffed wisps of white smoke up through the leaves to the sky.

"It's a tree house, Jack!" Harriett whooped.

"That is sadly evident," said Miss Butters with a rather worried look on her face. "I don't like the look of those upper windows," she added. "They are far too high to be safe. And that chimney looks positively un-sweepable. The Spinsters would never have approved this house's construction. Positively risky those windows look."

"Well, Spinster approved or not," Aelf said, "it has one of the comfiest armchairs in all of the known world. Very springy and right by the hearth. Very good for toasting one's toes after a long tramp." He smiled at Harriett. "Ah, and here comes the master himself."

Jack couldn't believe his eyes. Emerging from the round door at the base of the massive tree trunk was a small being at least half the size of Miss Butters, about two feet tall. He had long pointy ears that adorned a bald head, big round brown eyes and a stout little button nose. He had a very stern looking mouth and skin the exact shade of the oak leaves on the tree above: a kind of dark, luminous green. He didn't resemble a human very much at all and didn't look like an elf either. He was wearing a nut-brown tunic over darker brown pants of a heavy, woven cloth. Around his waist was a belt of rough rope. A wand-like stick was stuffed in the belt on the right side. He was unshod, having tiny, fat feet with claw-like toes wholly unsuited to shoes. His hands had claw-like fingers too. Jack realised his mouth was open and closed it quickly.

"Oh my goodness, Jack," Harriett whispered, bouncing on her feet with uncontained excitement. "It's Yoda!"

"Shush, Harrie, it's not Yoda," Jack scolded.

"Don't shush me, Jack! I'm sick of being shushed!"

"What's this shushin'?" the little Oakling said in a surprisingly deep voice. "Whatever it is, I don't like the sound o' it. Sounds like whooshin' an' I don't like whooshin' one bit. Whooshin' rustles the leaves and I don't like me leaves rustlin'."

"Master Wadget," Aelf said with a little bow, "may I introduce Jack and Harriett Gordon. Jack is the human Waycaller and Harriett is his sister." Jack noticed that at the word 'Waycaller', Anarra stared at him in surprise. But when he looked over to her, she turned away. He was quite used to her turning away from him now, but it still stung.

"This," Aelf continued, "is Miss Butters, a halfling of Bright, and this," he paused as if for dramatic effect, "this is—"

"One o' the lost Ehmaarim," Wadget interrupted, sizing up Anarra with his big brown eyes. "O' the House o' Sett, if I'm not mistaken, and 'alf-Pixish too by her bearin'."

Aelf looked terribly deflated that Wadget had guessed so much about Anarra.

"Yes, yes, Ethelwulf, I can tell one o' the Ehmaarim when I see one. My eyes still work as good as they always did." The Oakling chuckled in a way that was far friendlier than Jack thought possible for a little green thing with such big claws. He was still chuckling when Anarra suddenly dropped to one knee. At first Jack thought she'd finally succumbed to the trauma of her ordeal but then she spoke. Her voice was not weak but strong, with a tone of awe.

"Master Wadget, Forest Friend, Deepwood Dweller, Oak Lord, long have I heard tales of your deeds. I am humbled to meet you. I am Anarra Settonett, daughter of the ancient

House of Sett. I am at your service, My Lord."

"Lord? What's this Lord?" Wadget grumbled. "I'm just Wadget, plain ol' Wadget. More oak *son* than oak *lord*. Oh, that's fer certain. Fancy titles are fer the likes o' yer kin, me girl, an' fer those that lives behind high walls. I'll 'ave none o' that nonsense 'ere."

Anarra looked a little taken aback but simply bowed her head obediently and said no more. Jack couldn't quite reconcile the different sides of Anarra he'd seen so far: the fierce one that slew half a pack of hollow-wolves, the brooding silent one that said not a word on their journey, and now this formal, pliant one. Why were pretty girls so complicated, he wondered to himself. He also wondered what tales about Wadget she had heard. He looked at Wadget with much more interest now. Maybe there was more to the little Oakling than his tiny green body let on.

"So," Wadget said suddenly, turning his attention to Jack, "a *boy* Waycaller, eh? Bit funny if yeh ask me. The otherworld Waycallers have mostly been girls. Are yeh sure he's the one, Aelf?"

"Yes, Master Wadget," Aelf answered. "He called out for a Way to open and it opened."

"Hmmph. Funny looking boy, aren't yeh?" Master Wadget said accusingly.

"You can talk," Jack shot back.

"I *can* indeed talk, young otherworlder," Wadget grumped. "Many bein's *can*, though few *should*." His long ears waggled with irritation. "His tongue is unhinged and I don't like the look o' him," he concluded, speaking as if Jack weren't right there in front of him. The group stood silently for a moment, not sure how to respond to this statement. Then Harriett chimed in.

"It's his hormones. He's growing all over the place. It makes him look funny, and makes him cranky as a bee."

Jack thought he might die of embarrassment right there on the grass. He didn't dare look in Anarra's direction. Out of the corner of his eye he thought he saw the hint of a smirk on her lips.

"Hormones, yeh say," Wadget pondered. "I s'pose we can't blame him fer that." The Oakling headed back toward the oak house. As he did so, he removed the stick from inside his belt and, making the most rudimentary flick with it, sent a tiny green spark up into the sky where it sizzled and disappeared with a tiny pop. Apparently the stick was a wand after all.

"The protective ward is back in place," Aelf explained.

"That's all it takes?" Jack asked.

"That is all it takes for Master Wadget. Such understatement! He is a genius!" Aelf beamed.

"Well, come on then," Wadget said. "Hormones or no hormones, the tea'll go cold if yeh don't move yer butts."

"Why, I never ..." Miss Butters huffed.

"I wouldn't dawdle if I were you, halflin'," Wadget called back. "There's ale an' spuds an' acorn dumplin's ter be had fer those that want 'em."

"Acorn dumplings ... ooh, I haven't had one of those for years!" Miss Butters headed toward the open door without a backward glance.

Beyond the green door of Oakholme, Jack found a pleasant surprise. It was much nicer than any tree house he'd ever seen. The interior walls were plastered white and framed by natural timbers of weathered oak. A rustic spiral staircase of a honey coloured timber corkscrewed upwards to another two floors and downwards to a below-ground level.

The ground floor room they passed through was furnished with a desk by a large window and a number of tables covered in huge maps, charts, weird instruments and lots of jars of things with labels like: 'For Warts', 'To Behead an Ogre', 'To Ward off Nasty Sprites' and 'To Have with Jam and Toast'. These were described by Wadget, in passing as he led them downstairs, as his unguents and concoctions that were "Not ter be fooled around with!"

The underground room was a perfect circle. The walls were made up of curving bookshelves that reached from the floor to just below the ceiling. At regular intervals around the room, between the top of the bookshelves and the roof, there were small portholes that, being at ground level, had views mainly of tufts of grass. At the back of the room was a large hearth, made of river stones. This room was furnished with comfy armchairs, benches and a circular table, where Wadget encouraged them to take a seat. What illumination there was came from the fire and from a large brass candelabra hanging in the centre of the room. The chamber was ninety percent library and ten percent kitchen.

As Wadget took the kettle off the stove, Aelf positioned himself in the much-lauded springy armchair by the fire. Jack and Harriett took seats at the round table while Miss Butters hovered by the staircase looking nervous. Anarra, apparently still wishing to stay apart from the others, sat on the floor by the fire, clearly craving its comfort. She sat warming herself for just moments before she promptly fell asleep. It was, Jack thought, probably the first time in ages she'd felt safe enough to let down her guard and close her eyes.

Jack watched her sleep for a while, a strange feeling growing in his stomach. It was like the butterflies you get before an exam, or the anticipation you feel leading up to your birthday, but mixed with other things. There was a kind of gnawing feeling, like hunger, and a kind of fear. But fear of what? Jack didn't have time to work out these strange feelings; his attention was caught by something Wadget was saying.

"This Anarra's got 'erself some grit," the Oakling said somewhat admiringly. "Not too high an' mighty to sleep afore an Oakling's fire. That's a mark in her favour in my book, an' I ain't normally fond o' the high-born elves. Most of 'em are so full of 'emselves they don't see nothin' beyond their own shadows."

"Well, that is not true of Anarra," Aelf said. "I saw her slay four hollow-wolves as quick as it'd take Miss Butters to eat a cupcake."

Miss Butters looked as though she ought to take offence at

that but couldn't quite work out how being called a fast eater could ever be an insult. Unsure how to react, she just smiled as if in thanks for a compliment.

As the tea brewed and Anarra slept, Aelf explained to Jack, Harriett and Miss Butters that the room above them was Wadget's workshop. What was worked there he did not explain. He did explain however that the whole glade was a magic circle that completely prevented any being from entering uninvited. "Most wards work either against ill-will or react against the powers within those trying to enter, but the wards protecting Oakholme are the most sophisticated I've ever seen. Nothing can pass them without Wadget's permission. Goblins, trolls and other wicked things, as well as sorcerers, are stopped in their tracks. If they linger too long they sicken and eventually perish. Halflings and human-kind who stumble on this place find themselves feeling very confused and just wander away. If the outer circle is breached, which has never happened, this tree is an Oak Ward. It protects those within from sorcery and other forms of harm. Its power extends above with the canopy and below with the roots, forming a three-dimensional barrier. This oak is the parent of the Notchward Oaks that defend the road into the Dale."

Miss Butters started to object but Aelf silenced her with a look and kept speaking.

"It was Wadget who planted and tends the Notchward Oaks, to help keep the Halfling Dells safe."

Miss Butters' eyes bulged with indignation and surprise at this, but she said nothing.

"This glade, Oakholme, is one of the most defended places in all of Anwynn," Aelf added. "Wadget likes to be left alone."

Jack thought back to when he and Harriett were hiding beneath the boughs of an old oak in the Cairnbawn graveyard. The voice in his ear had said that the boughs and roots were withering and that therefore the skinwearer might be able to reach them. He shuddered at what might have happened if the oak hadn't been there at all. He wondered who planted it and filed the question away as one more thing he had to find out.

Aelf then explained that above the workshop were two floors consisting of living quarters and that the room they were currently in used to be the kitchen but, as Wadget fancied books more than anything else, it had long ago been taken over by the overflow from above.

"It is all I can do to keep him from filling his bedroom up with books as well," Aelf said. "He'd have them instead of pillows if he had his way."

"He's not very nice, is he?" Jack said, watching as Wadget grumbled away by the stove.

"Not all beings who are good are also nice. In fact, some of the purest beings in the world are quite fantastically grumpy," Aelf explained.

"You're not kidding," Jack said as Wadget swore at the fire to hurry up and get burning.

Miss Butters stood nearby, reluctant to sit on any of the furniture, mumbling that it looked ill-made and not altogether structurally sound. She was eyeing the oak supporting beam above her head with severe disapproval. Jack thought he heard her mutter 'should be condemned, not Spinster approved' but he couldn't be sure. None of this stopped her from taking a seat once the acorn dumplings were brought out.

"Halflings hate to eat standing up," Aelf whispered to Jack as Miss Butters sat herself down.

The dumplings were made with a very delicious donut-like batter with sweet acorn meal as a filling. Jack was surprised to find that he liked them. At least they weren't smothered in stoat syrup. After tea and dumplings, Miss Butters and Aelf were served flagons of ale whilst Harriett was given a green juice she eyed anxiously but did not touch. Strangely, Wadget placed a glass of deep black sarsaparilla in front of Jack. Jack wondered how Wadget knew about his new taste for sarsaparilla but didn't ask. Another question he wasn't sure he wanted to hear the answer to.

"Drink up, younglin's, those drinks'll curl yer tails," Wadget demanded.

"I don't have a tail," Harriett said.

"Well, it'll curl yer ears then, just bloody well drink up." Wadget's ears twitched threateningly as he sat back down again.

Despite the fact that Wadget was abrupt and not very accommodating, Jack felt very safe in this place, knowing that the little Oakling was a very powerful druid. By Aelf's description, Wadget was one of the most powerful beings in all Anwynn. Even so, part of Jack wanted to get out of there as soon as possible. It was all too strange. He wanted to be back in his cramped but familiar room in Cairnbawn with all of his things around him. He wanted this to be just another uneventful evening listening to music in his room, imagining quiet afternoons spent with girls behind the churchyard. He glanced over at Anarra, whose breathing was barely perceptible, and took a deep breath of his own.

Once Wadget was settled as well, he asked Aelf to tell him all that had happened to date. Aelf carefully related how a skinwearer had been in Jack and Harriett's world and how Jack had called for a way for them to escape and suddenly the Way had opened. He also related that Hob had met them at the stone circle and escorted them to Miss Butters' cottage.

"That mincin' popinjay," Wadget said at the mention of Hob's name. "Miracle he could drag 'imself away from his endless primpin' an' prancin' about ter help anyone with anythin'."

Jack thought maybe this Wadget wasn't so bad after all. Anyone one who disliked Hob was fine in his books.

"That's a little harsh, master. Hob, for reasons I have yet to fathom, always comes when we call. He has often given the druids extraordinary aid."

"No myst'ry there, Aelf, Hob likes three things: ter brag about how superior he is, ter show off and ter complain. Helpin' us gives him opportunity ter do all o' 'em at once. But glad I am he brought the younglin's from the circle; skinwearers an' bog nags are no match fer a Faeden an' without him the younglin's would've been killed afore they arrived in Bright."

"But why are all these monsters after us?" Harriett asked. "Aelf said that maybe Morrigan wants us dead because of the Veil, because …" Harriett couldn't finish the sentence.

"Because the magic that keeps her imprisoned and the magic of the Veil are connected," Aelf said. "But, master, would the enchantment break, would Darkgate be weakened, if the line of human Waycallers were extinguished?"

"The power that anchors the Veil is *within* the Waycallers, in their meat, their blood. If they're killed, I reckon the Veil will tear fer good. If the Veil tears, Darkgate will surely open. Morrigan knows as much about Faeden magic as Amallayne, an' if she wants the Waycaller dead, then it must mean it will help her ter break free."

"I was afraid of that," Aelf whispered.

"Me too," Harriett echoed.

After that Jack didn't listen very carefully to Aelf and Wadget's conversation about the journey from Bright to Oakholme and their encounter with the hollow-wolves. He was so consumed with dread he didn't hear anything they were saying. It was true. Morrigan wanted them dead. She had been imprisoned behind Darkgate for thousands of years, surely she would do whatever it took to escape. She wouldn't stop her monsters from hunting them until they were caught and killed. What could he do in the face of that? How could he protect Harriett from a dark goddess who commanded legions of monsters? His stomach tightened and churned. A ringing sound started in his ears. His mouth went dry. It was over. He could not fight this.

Out of the blue, the voice in his ear was back again. *Listen,* it said. *All is not lost yet. Listen to Master Wadget.* Jack nearly fell off his chair.

Wadget growled. "Watch it, younglin', those chairs don't grow on trees, yeh know!"

"But," Harriett said, "they're wood and wood *does* grow on trees."

"The girl child's got a pinch o' nous but her tongue is even more unhinged than the boy's," Wadget muttered before continuing. "A skinwearer being in the otherworld is the worryin' thing. It couldn't have opened the Way itself."

"So someone else opened the Way for it?" Jack asked.

"The skinwearer barely has a mind, an' hardly no power. It couldn't pass through the Veil unless the Way were opened fer it, o' that I'm certain. Even then, it would be a mighty feat to weaken the Veil enough to let even that base creature pass. Power like that is beyond any Dread sorcerer, an' even most o' the Faeden. Tell me, boy," he turned to Jack, "did yeh notice anythin' out o' the ordinary the night yeh was attacked?"

"You mean, apart from a slobbering zombie hyena chasing us around?"

"Now, Jack," Aelf said, "Wadget is trying to help you, there's no need to be defensive."

"It's his hormones" Harriett said.

"It's not bloody hormones!" Jack yelled.

Miss Butters, Aelf and Harriett all stared at him, shocked by his outburst. Aelf even seemed a little disappointed. Almost immediately, Jack felt ashamed. It must have shown on his face because Harriett stopped glaring at him more quickly than normal, apparently glad to see that Jack was suitably disgusted with himself.

"Apart from the eclipse, there wasn't anything," he mumbled, hanging his head.

"Eclipse?" Aelf asked.

"What kind o' eclipse?" Wadget pressed.

"Umm, a solar eclipse. Everything went black. It was so dark I could barely see a foot ahead of me."

Aelf and Wadget exchanged knowing glances.

"Were there any other phenomena accompanying the eclipse?" Aelf questioned.

"No," Jack said, "it was just really dark."

"What about the lights?" Harriett said. "The lights didn't go on."

"Lights?" asked Wadget. "What kind o' lights?"

"The streetlights," Jack explained, "they're electric, they should've come on automatically but they didn't. I think there was a power outage. There weren't any lights on in anyone's house and it was really quiet."

"It's a rare eclipse that drains light an' sound in that fashion," Wadget surmised. "Only very dark powers can bring such a thing about. There only one bein' who could've done that."

"Who?" Aelf asked.

"The only bein' who has the power ter do somethin' like that, ter create an eclipse that drains all energy, ter drain so much energy that even the Veil was weakened, is Thullu."

Harriett gasped.

"No, surely not," Aelf said with disbelief, his voice a near whisper.

Jack stared at Wadget, waiting for him to continue.

"Only Thullu's power could've done it, Aelf," Wadget said. The Oakling stared into the fire, thinking, orange flames reflected in his big brown eyes.

"I suppose this means we're in really bad trouble?" Miss Butters asked, noisily swallowing another dumpling.

Jack was surprised at Miss Butters' seeming lack of concern. For someone who went into a near fit at the mere mention of Faeden, she was strangely unconcerned by the idea that Thullu might have been behind sending the skinwearer across the veil to kill Jack and Harriett. When she spoke again he understood.

"Who is this Thullu anyway, some no-good, good-for-nothing sorcerer?"

"Thullu, the Lord of Chaos, is the Faeden's very own god, Dorothea." Aelf said. "One of the most powerful beings in the universe. This is the worst possible news, and yes, it does mean that we are in very bad trouble."

Miss Butters stared at Aelf, trembling. Though she had not

known Thullu's name, she knew what it meant that a being more powerful than the Faeden had a hand in the events that had led Jack and Harriett to her door. She downed her ale in one gulp and filled the cup again.

"Yes, trouble it'd mean if Thullu were involved," Wadget said, taking his eyes off the fire. "That'd mean that Thullu seeks Morrigan's release. But there may be another explanation." He scratched his green button nose, his brow furrowed, thinking deeply. "Perhaps ... perhaps one o' the Pale Mother's minions has found Thullu's Gift."

"But, Master," Aelf said, his eyes wide, "Thullu's Gift is lost, lost since a thousand years before the Doom War!"

"That's the thing about things that's lost, they often gets found."

"I probably shouldn't ask," Jack said, "but what is it, this Thullu's Gift thing?"

"Yeh explain, Aelf," Wadget said, still scratching his nose. "I need ter think."

"No-one really knows what Thullu's Gift is," Aelf began. "Some think it is a magical object of some kind. That is what we druids believe. Thullu gave this magical gift to his followers, who called it Thullu's Gift. The power of it is practically limitless. With it any sorcerer would become immensely powerful."

"But, didn't you say this gift thing was lost?" Harriett asked.

"Yes, most believe that Thullu's Gift is lost," Aelf answered. "Long, long ago, at the dawn of time, Thullu gave it to the Tiqq. The Tiqq are a parasitic race of dark sprites, the most despised beings in all of Anwynn, rejected even by Morrigan herself. They are devoted to Thullu, who they call the Lord of Chaos. The Tiqq live in hives, in disused burial mounds usually. But there is a rumour that there was once a vast Tiqq city in an ancient elvish necropolis, abandoned thousands of years ago, the location now long forgotten. It is believed Thullu's Gift is hidden somewhere in that lost necropolis."

"Let me get this straight," said Miss Butters, suppressing a hiccup. "Either this Chaos Lord whatsit, or a sorcerer using this gift thingamajig, has broken the wards separating the worlds? Not that I really believe in this otherworld place or this awful dark god, Thullu thingamabob, but a lot of very bad things have happened since the younglings turned up and, well, Jack and Harriett *are* a bit odd. I mean, *unusual*," she corrected at the hurt look on Harriett's face and the indignant one on Jack's. "I mean, unlike any human children I've ever met."

"I think we gather your meaning," Aelf smiled.

"The wards on the Veil aren't *broken*," Wadget said. "Either Thullu, or someone usin' the gift, created the eclipse ter send a skinwearer across ter seek young Jack 'ere. But, as the beast failed ter kill Jack, I see this as a victory."

"Some victory," Jack said, thinking that he and Harriett would be lucky to survive another day in Anwynn.

"It *is* a victory, laddie! By escapin' the beast yeh've thwarted whoever is behin' this. An' who stands to benefit most from yer death no matter who's behin' it? Morrigan! Morrigan can't abide bein' thwarted, 'specially when so much is at stake! This'll enrage her!" The Oakling actually laughed.

"And why is that funny?" Jack asked, dismayed.

"Morrigan is a thing o' pure emotion. She lets her rage get the better o' her. When riled up she acts rashly an' makes mistakes. That, my younglin' friend, gives us the upper hand. Despite using their mighty Thullu's special gift, they've failed. Fer this we should be thankful."

"You're forgetting," Jack said angrily, "Morrigan and her monsters are still after Harriett and me. Why should I be thankful about that?"

"I've not forgotten that!" Wadget yelled, thumping his clawed fist on the table. "I'm sorry fer the danger yeh face younglin', but I *am* thankful that yeh aren't already lost. Thankful too I am that through yeh Morrigan hasn't escaped her prison an' begun anew her reign o' darkness."

They all sat quietly for a few minutes, the only noise

accompanying the tension being Miss Butters chewing on acorn dumplings and slurping down ale. Jack wanted to say something; something about how all this was more than he could comprehend, something about how confused he was and how frightened he was for Harriett.

"Sorry," he finally said, unable to form any of that into a full sentence.

"No need fer sorries," Wadget grumbled. "Yeh've been through much, but allow an ol' Oaklin' his little victories. The fact that Morrigan failed ter seize yeh is enough reason fer me ter feel glad."

"But will Morrigan get us anyway?" Harriett asked out of the blue, tears in her eyes. Before Aelf or Wadget could answer, Miss Butters threw her arm around her and squeezed tightly.

"Not if I have anything to do with it, my dear," she said. "I don't care if the White Demoness herself hears me – Eugene smite her I say! Let her be damned in her soggy pit! Don't you worry yourselves about it any further! Miss Dorothea Butters will let no harm befall you. Now, young lady, eat another dumpling, you're practically emaciated." She shoved another dumpling into Harriett's mouth. Harriett, apparently moved by Miss Butters' outburst, did not resist this time. Jack felt a rush of warmth for the halfling, even though she appeared to be choking his sister to death with an acorn dumpling.

"Well said, Dorothea!" Aelf smiled. "And might I say that Master Wadget and I will also do whatever we can to protect you both."

"I think we've had enough talk fer one night," Wadget added. "An' enough ale." He glanced at Miss Butters. "Aelf an' I have much ter discuss an' little time ter spare. I'd be grateful to yeh, Miss Butters, if yeh'd take the younglin's upstairs an' put 'em ter bed, an' get some rest yerself."

"But, what are we going to do? Morrigan's still after us," Jack said.

"That is precisely what we must discuss, Jack," Aelf said.

"We have things that must be decided tonight. Master Wadget will tell you of our plan in the morning."

"I don't want to go to bed," Harriett said.

"Don't make me turn yeh into a ferret," Wadget threatened. "If yeh don't go ter bed that's exactly what I'll do."

"Can you really do that?" Harriett asked, disbelieving. Jack was wondering that himself.

"Indeed he can," Aelf said. "Once, when I was a boy and still Wadget's apprentice, he turned me into a rabbit, to teach me a lesson for not studying hard enough. He left me that way for a month. To this day I can't abide the taste of carrots."

"Now off ter bed!" Wadget growled.

"But—" Jack started to complain.

"No buts young man!" Miss Butters asserted with a slur. "Off to bed you go!"

He reluctantly got out of his chair but then, seeing Anarra slumped asleep by the hearth, turned toward Wadget rather than the stairs.

"What about Anarra? She can't sleep on the floor all night."

"The Ehmaarim must stay where she is fer now," Wadget said. "I've got questions fer her. I'll send her ter bed later."

Jack wanted to argue but Miss Butters tottered over and started dragging him away by the arm. Jack thought being dragged along by Miss Butters was a bit like being swept away by a small, rotund tsunami. The unnaturally strong halfling herded them up the spiral staircase to the ground level and then on up to the first floor. As they ascended the staircase, she got behind Jack and held tightly onto his waist. She claimed this was due to her fear of falling but Jack suspected it was because she was drunk.

When they got to the first floor they found four bedrooms, each with their names on the doors. Jack's and Harriett's rooms were next to each other and had windows looking south. Miss Butters' and Aelf's rooms had windows looking north. Jack noted there was no room for Anarra. Clearly Wadget hadn't been expecting her. For a brief moment, Jack half-believed she might be sharing a room with him. But then he knew with a disappointed certainty that she would be sharing with Harriett, or more likely have a room all to herself. She had been through a terrible ordeal, after all.

Jack and Harriett followed Miss Butters into her room, wanting to check it out. Everything in the room, apart from the wooden furniture, was green. Green curtains, green shaggy rug, green quilts on the bed with leaf patterns. Harriett opened the window and looked out. Jack caught a whiff of night air, which was warm and sweet. He joined her at the window and looked out as well.

"Look," Harriett said, smiling, pointing down to the base of the tree. Jack looked down and saw Piggy-poo and Soxy asleep by the front door, beneath blankets provided by Wadget, on beds of heather. For once Piggy-poo's face was free of its usual complaining expression. "Aren't they cute?" Harriett cooed. They stood there at the window a while, taking in the night air and looking out over the glade, until Harriett gasped and stepped back.

"What?" Jack demanded.

"I ... I thought I saw a shape just beyond the stones."

"At the edge of the circle?" he asked. She nodded, still peering in that direction. He followed her eyes to the edge of the glade. As a cloud moved away from the moon, filling the glade with its silvery beams, Harriett gasped again.

"There," she said, pointing. "I thought I saw two little red eyes." Jack stared in the direction she was pointing but saw nothing.

"Are you sure?" he asked her.

"No, not really. I thought I saw something, but whatever it was has gone."

"What are you younglings looking at?" Miss Butters asked.

"Nothing," Harriett answered unsurely. "I think I just saw another badger." Jack heard the fear in her voice. Whatever Harriett had seen, she didn't really believe it was a badger and nor did Jack. He was sure now he hadn't been imagining it when he'd seen something, or someone, dash behind that tree as they travelled towards Oakholme. He was also sure that who or whatever it was had followed them all the way from Bright.

"Lots of badgers 'round here, dear. Now, come away from the window," Miss Butters hiccupped. "It's not safe."

Miss Butters closed the window and pulled the curtains tight, not wanting to be reminded of how high up in the air she was. "Halfling houses are always one story," she sighed, before catching her toe on the shaggy rug and toppling backwards onto her bed. "Whoopsy!" she laughed. "Oh well, now that I'm down, there's no point getting back up again! Off to bed you go!" she commanded. Then she immediately fell fast asleep and started snoring.

Jack and Harriett dropped to the floor giggling, covering their mouths to muffle the noise so they didn't wake the halfling up. After a moment, Jack had an idea. The idea must have shown on his face as an odd expression because Harriett looked into his eyes enquiringly. The idea quickly coalesced into a plan. His face must have now shown the determination he was feeling. Harriett sighed, apparently recognising the mischievous look on his face.

"Shall we?" Jack said immediately.

"No, Jack, we shouldn't."

"I'm not going to bed, Harrie. I want to know what they're planning, it's about us after all. Don't you want to know?"

"Yes, but I don't want to get in trouble. She might feed me again," she whispered, jabbing a finger in Miss Butters' direction.

"I wouldn't be scared of her. It's Wadget I'd be worried about. Did you see those claws?"

"Yeah, but he's cute."

"Just because he's little doesn't mean he's not tough, Harrie."

"I know that, I'm not dumb."

"Well, claws or not, I have to find out what they're planning. You coming?"

"Oh, alright. But if we get caught, I'm blaming you."

"So what's new?"

# A THICKNESS OF PLOTS

As they crept down the spiral staircase, Jack heard the soft mumblings of a conversation occurring in the library below. Jack's heart pounded in his chest. What if they got caught? What would Wadget do to punish them? Would he really turn them into ferrets? He tried to look unworried, to avoid spooking Harriett, but couldn't help imagining what his life as a ferret would be like.

At first the voices from the library were indistinct, but as they descended to the workshop level, and the light from the underground room touched their feet, Jack could discern three distinct voices, those of Wadget, Aelf and Anarra. Jack motioned for Harriett to stay back and crouched down so that he could hear better without descending any further and risking being seen. Harriett, apparently wanting a more prime position and totally ignoring his gestures, alighted from the staircase and sat on the floor by a shelf of dusty jars and books. Jack let her stay there when it was clear she wasn't about to do what she was told. He couldn't do anything about it without making noise and being discovered. The voice of the two druids and Anarra drifted up the corkscrew staircase, amplified slightly as the sound was funnelled upwards.

"I am sorry, Oak Lord," Anarra said. "I know nothing more about my kidnappers. I know only that they ambushed us on the Empty Plains and took us to the Halfling Dells, where the hollow-wolves awaited us."

"An' the Sendin'; the Sendin' led the skinwearers an' the wolves ter this Dale Delvin' place?" Wadget asked.

"Yes, where we awaited the sorcerer who conjured it. But we escaped before the sorcerer arrived."

"Can you tell us what the sorcerer sounded like?" Aelf asked. "Did the Sending ever use a voice?"

"No, Master Ethelwulf, it merely led them with

gestures."

"This is ill news," Wadget growled. "A sorcerer in the Halflin' Dells, an' a powerful one at that."

"I wouldn't have thought it possible," Aelf said.

"Anythin' is possible, Aelf, as the presence o' Sendin's, bog nags and hollow-wolves in the dells makes awful clear."

A soft sigh in Anarra's voice told Jack that the half-elvish girl was both troubled and very tired. He pictured her, still sitting on the floor by the fire, her hood thrown back, her dark blue eyes clouded with fatigue.

"Yeh better go up ter bed now, me girl," Wadget said in an uncharacteristically kind voice. "We won't unravel the secret behind yer kidnappin' by talkin' about it anymore tonight. We'll need the help o' the Druid High Council ter unravel this myst'ry. Go up ter bed. Aelf an' I will think on what ter do. We'll share our thoughts with yeh in the mornin'."

The sound of feet on the stairs caused Harriett to look up into Jack's face, her eyes wide with alarm. Jack jumped up, searching for somewhere to hide. Before they could scramble away, Anarra emerged from below. Stopping still in her tracks, she looked from Harriett to Jack, a frown forming on her face as she realised they'd been eavesdropping.

"Are you sure you are the Waycaller, Jack Gordon?" Anarra whispered. "Or is your right title *Hallcreeper*?"

"Jack made me do it," Harriett said, batting her eyelids in order to look more innocent.

"We just wanted to hear what they were saying about us," Jack said defensively, glaring at his sister.

"In your world it may be different, but here *children* do not eavesdrop, especially not on their betters."

Children? Betters? Jack felt his face flush and was glad it was too dark for Anarra to see that she'd wounded his pride. He looked away from her and held out his hand for Harriett to lead her back upstairs, but Harriett did not take his hand.

"Who are you calling *children*?" Harriett hissed, her eyes steely and her lips drawn into a tight line. "You're not much older than me, and about the same age as Jack, so don't go calling us children!"

"I am elvish, Harriett, we do not age as human-kind do. If I were a thousand years old I would still look much the same."

"*Are* you a thousand years old, then?" Jack asked, his voice dry. He'd heard other boys in the village loud-mouthing about older women but didn't think this was what they had in mind.

"Well, no," Anarra admitted, looking back down the corkscrew stairs to avoid Jack's gaze.

"Spit it out, how old are you?" Harriett demanded.

"I am seventeen. Today. Today marks the turning of my seventeenth year."

"It's your birthday?" Jack took a step closer to her, thinking about all that Anarra had been through that day: fleeing from kidnappers, being hunted and nearly torn apart by hollow-wolves, the death of her companion. "And I thought I've had some rubbish birthdays."

Harriett tiptoed over, reached into her pocket and pulled out a small, slightly wilted flower: a tiny blue columbine. She must have picked it from Miss Butters' garden and carried it in her pocket ever since. She handed it to Anarra.

"Happy birthday," she said. "I know it's a little crushed, but it's the same colour as your eyes."

Anarra looked at the flower a long while, as if amazed, and then whispered a barely audible thank you. She stood looking at Harriett a long moment, then drew out of her pocket a small bracelet woven from what Jack guessed to be black silk. Anarra tied this around Harriett's wrist, whispering: "Among my people, the Ehmaarim, gifts of great beauty or kindness must be reciprocated. This bracelet is woven from the silk of a very rare moth, one that lives a long but solitary life high in the mountains of my people's island home. The bracelet was my father's. It is very dear to me."

"Oh, no, I can't accept it! Not for a little flower!" Harriett was clearly thinking what Jack was, that this bracelet must be the most precious thing Anarra owned, especially as her father had been killed not long ago. Harriett didn't know how very close Anarra was to her father, but Jack did. He had seen it in his visions. Jack's heart lurched for Anarra Settonett, for her dignity and generosity. He wanted to give her something as well, but his pockets were empty, except maybe for a little lint. He was pretty sure she wouldn't want that, even if it was lint all the way from the otherworld. Then he thought of something. It wasn't much and he wasn't sure if he could do it.

"I want to show you something," he said as he stepped even closer to her and reached his hand toward her cheek. She stiffened and stopped him by pushing her palm against his chest. As soon as her hand was on him he knew he could do it. Images were flooding through his mind, and, with the images, waves of emotion, many he couldn't name, emotions so intense he rocked on his feet. "Please," he said, "I want to show you something, for your birthday."

"Do not try to trick me, Jack Gordon, I am Ehmaarim. We are not fooled easily."

"I'm not trying to trick you. Trust me …"

She dropped her hand and let him touch her cheek. He looked into her eyes, seeing the uncertainty there, and then closed his eyes and thought of the thing he wanted to give her. He focussed on it with all his energy until it bloomed in his mind. Anarra gasped with surprise and he knew she could see it too. It was one of the images that had passed through his mind when they'd arrived at Oakholme, triggered by touching the leaf that had been in Anarra's hair. It was an image of Anarra's father laughing, laughing so hard tears were rolling down his cheeks. The image pulsed with emotion, with love and joy. Jack couldn't help but smile, the joy infectious.

Anarra stepped back, breaking the connection. The image of her father faded. Jack wondered why she'd moved away. When he opened his eyes he couldn't interpret the feeling playing on her face. Was it fear? Shock? Had he done the wrong thing? Had showing Anarra her father upset her, rather than remind her of how much he loved her?

"I'm sorry," Jack whispered, his hand reaching out to her automatically.

"Do not apologise, Waycaller," she said, her tone warm but controlled. "You have given me a great gift. I thank you."

Jack smiled. He knew he didn't have to say anything, Anarra understood why he'd done it, but he wanted to make it clear. "He loved you very, very much."

"He did," she whispered, her voice a little less controlled now. "I fear forgetting how much."

"What are you two talking about?" Harriett asked, irritated. They both smiled at her, unsure how to explain. While they were all silent Aelf's voice floated up the stairs as clear as if they were in the room with him.

"It is too much to ask of them, Master," Aelf was saying. "It is too dangerous a journey. They are only children."

"Yes, younglin's they are, but one is the Waycaller and the other might as well be. Morrigan will assume it's the girl who has the power. It's almost always been that way. Yeh well know, Aelf, we can't risk the Dark Ones gettin' hold o' 'em. It'd mean their deaths, an' the end o' this world an' theirs. Hark the words o' the prophecy, 'cause Morrigan will fer certain!"

"Born to the House of Senn will be the Druid King, the Oracle returned," Aelf intoned. "Only then will Amaltor be rebuilt as of old and Pix become great again. The fruit of the Line of Senn will be as a new dawn, turning back the night; and the Oracle, returned from time and from death, will be as the sun against all shadows, banishing darkness forever."

"Nice ter see, Aelf, that yer month as a bunny rabbit helped yeh learn how ter memorise word for word." A deep chuckle preceded the sound of tea pouring into a cup.

"Should we tell them, Master?" Aelf asked. "Should we tell Jack and Harriett about the prophecy?"

"Yes, they deserve ter know, but not yet. They've had ter deal with a lot already. The burden o' the prophecy might scare 'em so bad they never stop shakin'. Besides, their mam sacrificed much ter see the prophecy made real. If we tell 'em too soon an' Jack turns away from his destiny, then where will we all be, eh? In a pile of pig muck, that's where!"

"I'm surprised they've said so little of their mother. Surely they must wonder about her?"

"Much pain I see in 'em, most o' it comin' from the loss o' their mam. Younglin's are easily broken, maybe losin' their mam has tied their tongues about such things."

Listening in the stairwell, Jack felt a shiver of anxiety and guilt. What had this prophecy to do with them? With their mother? It was true, it had become an ingrained habit for him and Harriett to avoid talking about their mother, mostly because of the shame about what she'd done. What kid wanted to talk about their mother when the mere mention of her frightened people, made them cringe and look at you like you were a freak, the offspring of a lunatic killer? He reached out and drew Harriett in close to him, putting his arm around her as he continued to listen.

"Eloise Gordon was a fierce an' brave Waycaller. I'm proud ter have known her," Wadget said. "She wouldn't thank us ter scare Jack away from his path by tellin' him too much too soon. She knew the prophecy as well as yeh do, Aelf. She knew the danger an' she didn't shrink from it."

"But to take the children on such a perilous journey seems ... unwise. Beyond Narrownotch Pass every dark beast in the Empty Lands will come after them. Can they not stay here where they are safe? I will make the journey alone and bring what I find back to you here."

"We don't have time. The younglin's must go ter the temple an' seek Amallayne's counsel themselves. The Faeden are secretive an' keep much hidden. They're not fond o' the Order o' Druids. We don't worship 'em and 'cause o' that they've told us little o' the things they've created, includin' the Veil an' the magic that keeps Morrigan imprisoned. Anyways, I fear it may already be too late, the dark powers are moving in the world once again. Surely yeh feel it?"

"Yes, I feel it also."

"There's more, Aelf. We face a thickness o' plots. Morrigan's fell fiends are amassin' in the Swampmere ter the south: trolls an' goblins an' a vast Vellenor army. They gather on the border ter the Kingdom o' Pix."

"The Vellenor have often sent war upon Pix. They have always been defeated."

"But this time somethin' is diff'rent. I feel it."

"What is it?"

"I don't know, yet. Even afore Anarra turned up like a ghost out o' the lost night o' eight thousand years ago, with her story o' a sorcerer in the Halflin' Dells, I felt a great darkness buildin', swellin' up like a storm on the horizon. I felt it afore we learned o' the breachin' o' the Veil. It was confirmed tonight when Jack told us about the eclipse. The storm must be very near, the darkness very strong already, if Thullu's power is movin' in the world. If we're not careful, that storm'll overcome us all."

"What can we do about all this?" Aelf whispered so that Jack barely heard him.

"The Order would have its hands full dealin' with just one o' these things, let alone the lot o' it. For the first time in thousands of years we're facin' things beyond our power ter counter. Amallayne must be beseeched ter deal with the threat on the Waycaller, our knowledge in that realm is poor anyhow. That will leave the Order free ter meet the dark armies amassing in the south an' solve the myst'ry of the sorcerer who kidnapped Anarra. There's no other way."

"Very well, Jack must go to the temple, but why should Harriett go? She is not the Waycaller, surely it is wiser for her to stay here, or perhaps even with Miss Butters?" At that Harriett flinched against Jack's side and went still. Jack knew she would rather eat her own leg than stay with Miss Butters while he went somewhere else.

"I reckon the younglin's'll want ter stay together," Wadget continued. "Besides, I can't keep the girl 'ere now. I'll have ter come with yeh. Anarra will have ter come along as well. We can't leave her alone with a sorcerer after her, no matter how handy she is with a blade. Harriett can't stay with Miss Butters neither. Dorothea's a stout halflin', but if Morrigan sends the Dreads from Bonemound after 'em, they won't last long. In the end, the Dreads'd have Harriett, at the cost o' perhaps all of Bright. We don't want that. No, the younglin's must go to Songarielle, with us. Only fully trained druids have the skill ter protect 'em against whatever Morrigan sends."

"Surely Morrigan would not send the Dreads themselves to capture a little girl?"

"Don't forget, Aelf, that ter Morrigan this girl may be a Waycaller, the one an' only means ter her escape from Uffern. These younglin's are all that stands between her freedom an' eternity in her prison. Thousands of years she's been down there. I reckon by now she's itchin' for more room ter move."

"Very well, they will both come with us to Amallayne's temple. I only hope we make it and that Amallayne intervenes. Since the making of the Veil, the Great Goddess has ignored the pleas of the faithful and has gone unseen. Some say she is asleep to the woes of the world."

"She's not asleep," Wadget said quietly. "Why she remains withdrawn I don't know, but the otherworld Waycallers have a special bond with Amallayne. I reckon she'll show herself fer Jack."

"What if she doesn't?" Aelf asked. "What if Amallayne doesn't intervene?"

"Then we're all doomed," Wadget sighed. "Doomed."

There was a moment's silence, in which both Jack and Harriett craned to hear what would come next. Anarra made a little cough beside them, making them jump. She raised her eyebrow and motioned that they should all go upstairs to bed. Jack shook his head and so Anarra, frowning, went upstairs alone. Jack was in half a mind to follow her, but then Harriett stepped away from him towards the stairwell. Her shoulder brushed against a bookshelf. At her slight touch, a very old book fell to pieces on the shelf, making the tiny sound of pages slumping apart. They both stood motionless, terrified that the sound had exposed them. Jack glared at his sister. They waited, listening to the silence below. But then Wadget resumed talking and offered Aelf more tea. They hadn't been discovered. Jack sighed with relief and glared at Harriett some more. She poked her tongue out at him. Jack ignored her and resumed listening.

"What o' the halflin'?" Wadget asked. "Does she suspect anythin'?"

"No, Master. She has no idea why we've brought her here."

"Good," said Wadget. "She'd rather die than know the truth."

"How will we tell her?" Aelf asked.

"We won't. If we can, we'll simply let her discover it fer 'erself. If she's only half as stubborn as she looks it may take a while. If she fails ter come ter it 'erself, we may have ter take things into our own hands."

Jack bristled with this further evidence that Miss Butters was being manipulated. He couldn't understand what the druids might want of Miss Butters, or why they were secretly plotting against her. His train of thought was interrupted when the druid's conversation continued.

"How the halflin' responds when she finds out the truth is even more important now that there may be a sorcerer loose in the dells," Wadget said. "Does Miss Butters understand what it means that Anarra's kidnappers took her there?"

Aelf replied quietly. "I doubt it. If she does, she is in denial about it, and will probably continue to deny it for some time,"

"Shame," Wadget growled. "Halflin's are ruddy useful when yeh can drag 'em away from their table."

There was a pause and then Aelf cleared his throat and spoke in a near whisper.

"Master, there is something about Jack you should know. When the skinwearer attacked them in Cairnbawn, Jack saw a glint of green in its eyes when it was still in human form."

"He saw a trace o' the skinwearer's true form beneath its disguise?" Wadget's voice was higher than usual. Jack guessed that's how he sounded when surprised.

"Yes. I thought that was impossible."

"Not impossible, but ruddy rare. Only the Faeden can see through powerful sorcery like that."

"What does it mean?"

"It means we have ter get Jack to Songarielle, quick as we can. The prophecy is rushin' ter fulfilment, nothin' else could give the boy such power."

Jack couldn't hear what was said next, so he leaned forward. Just as he was considering moving closer, his skin prickled with a sudden, biting chill. A cold mist blew in under the front door. Jack looked around and saw that Harriett was shivering. A strange silence descended on Wadget's house, a silence that didn't feel natural.

Next minute Wadget and Aelf were bounding up the stairs. Jack grabbed Harriett and dragged her aside. They just managed to scuttle behind a bench and hide as Aelf and Wadget dashed out from the staircase and headed for the front door. Wadget already had his wand out. When the druids opened the door, Piggy-poo tumbled in. He seemed to have been cringing up against the door in terror. Wadget climbed over the pig deftly and Aelf simply leapt over him, landing silently on the ground outside. Soxy stood just outside the door, facing the edge of the glade, her horns lowered and her hooves stamping the dewy ground in anger.

Jack and Harriett rushed to a window to look out. The temperature dropped even further. Judging by the frost forming on the window before Jack's eyes, it was below zero outside.

Wadget and Aelf bounded to the edge of the oak canopy and stopped, looking determinedly south. Wadget's wand and Aelf's hand were raised and at the ready. Jack peered down toward the southernmost megalith and squinted to see what was there. He didn't see anything until, out of the mist, a streak of blue lightning illuminated the sky. But this lightning was not natural. It was travelling from the ground up into the air. Though it sizzled and crackled as it moved, the lightning made no thunder. It threw the whole glade under an eerie blueish glow. Under that odd illumination, a lone figure was revealed, standing at the perimeter of the circle. The sight of him made both Jack and Harriett flinch.

The lightning flashed again, illuminating the figure further, whose long white hair, pale skin and terrible, hollow pink eyes marked him as one of the Vellenor, the Dark Elves. The Vellenor was tall, easily as tall and thin as Aelf, though young-looking, about nineteen. He had long slender ears that curved upwards to a point and was dressed all in black, with a long cloak that fluttered eerily as if moved by some power emanating from his body. As Jack and Harriett watched from the window, more lightning strikes erupted from the being's hands and flashed across the sky. The silent flashes became swifter and brighter.

"Is he a Dread?" Harriett asked, her voice shaking.

"I don't think so, but maybe," Jack answered. "All the Dreads we saw in the vision of the battle were bald, and their eyes were different, darker. But he's definitely bad news."

"Be gone, Prince Serza o' Fellwood," Wadget shouted, his voice resonating throughout the glade, amplified by some magic. "Yeh have no business 'ere."

A vibrating voice boomed back, deep and melancholy and seemingly accompanied by dozens of other whispering voices. It was as if the Dark Elf were speaking through a barrel of snakes.

"My business is with the otherworlders, Oakling. Surrender them and I will let you keep your life."

The voice sent a wave of fear through Jack so strong that he nearly blacked out. Harriett swayed on her feet so Jack put his arm on her back to steady and comfort her. She was very pale and clammy, her eyes glassy with fear.

"Give them to me!" the Prince of Fellwood commanded.

Jack instinctively cupped Harriett's hands to her ears and

then used his own to cover his mouth to stop himself from retching. The sorcerer's voice had so terrified Piggy-poo that he scuttled inside and took up a hiding position behind a wooden bench. The pig's huge behind made hiding pointless, and he knocked a lot of stuff over in his attempt to make himself less conspicuous.

"Yeh alone have not the power ter break this circle, Dark Prince. Be gone an' *I* will spare *yer* life," Wadget threatened. The prince laughed. His laughter echoed off the ridges of the glade and sent a chill down Jack's spine.

The lightning resumed and soon it was almost constant. In the blueish light, Jack saw that the stones at the circle's edge were shimmering, as if the power the prince sorcerer was using threatened to make them disappear. Wadget responded, using his wand to send tiny green sparks that moved like butterflies to all of the stones. The megaliths absorbed the sparks and became solid again. But this didn't last. All too soon the stones were shimmering once more. At that Aelf added his own power to the defence. He raised his hand and sent waves of white light to arch over the circle. Aelf's white light was joined by another burst of green lights from Wadget's wand. Together, Aelf and Wadget's magic caused the lightning to dim. The elvish sorcerer screamed with rage but didn't give in. He let out a bloodcurdling wail, beckoning to unseen allies. What followed caused Jack and his sister to gasp with horror.

Swarming over the ridge above Oakholme were hundreds of hideous, screeching creatures that looked like evil versions of elves. Their dark grey skin, pointy ears and jagged drooling teeth gave the impression of creatures given over to total madness. As the creatures hurled themselves down the ridge, Harriett screamed.

"Goblins!"

# MOG OF FELLWOOD FOREST

Goblin howls filled the night. Illuminated by the constant flash of blue lightning, Jack could see that the seething mass of screeching creatures was heavily armed, with swords and clubs and spears. They wore metal breast-plates over their leather doublets that bore an awful emblem of a kind of six-armed cross made out of bones. Unlike the goblins at the Battle of Bright, these goblins had eyes that glowed with an awful green colour. Their teeth glowed green as well. They reminded Jack instantly of the skinwearer that had chased them in Cairnbawn.

The goblins hit the edge of the glade at a full run. Some of them exploded the minute they reached the perimeter. Some fell down writhing in agony. Still more turned and attacked their brethren as if confused. But others hurled themselves repeatedly at the thin air of the stone circle and bounced back only to hurl themselves at it once more. The protective wards Wadget had placed over his glade were powerful. More and more goblins poured down the slope. The dark prince launched his lightning assault once again and this time, perhaps because of the charge of the goblins, the stones began to shimmer more swiftly than before. Nothing Wadget and Aelf did was preventing it. Amidst all the noise of goblins shrieking and howling Jack heard Aelf shout to his master.

"Prince Serza is using more than simple sorcery!"

"Yes, somehow he wields power beyond what is normal."

"What could it be, Master?"

"I sense somethin' I have not sensed fer thousands o' years." Wadget paused for just a second then leapt into the air. The Oakling spun like a top, sending blast after blast of green light to hurtle like bullets at the dark prince. This sudden action caught the Vellenor momentarily off-guard so that some of the green blasts struck him square in the chest. The blasts blew open his shirt, revealing strange patterns of blue energy pulsing just under the skin. The patterns looked like snakes slithering through the Dark Elf's veins and arteries. Wadget landed back on his feet and gazed at the dancing patterns, his eyes widening in recognition and concern.

"No!" Wadget yelled. "He draws on the power o' Thullu! The circle will not hold!"

How can that be? Jack thought. Aelf had told them that this circle had never been broken! Then there was a voice in Jack's ear. *Open a Way! The dark prince will soon be through! Open a Way!* Jack felt that same incredible compulsion to obey. He resisted. If he opened a Way, they might end up somewhere worse, far from Wadget and Aelf's protection. *Open a Way! Open a Way now!* He couldn't resist any longer. Deep within himself the desire to escape the sorcerer and the goblins surged to an irresistible crescendo. Then the voice convinced him. *If you go, the sorcerer will follow you and the others will be safe.* Somehow, he knew this was true. He closed his eyes and called out in his mind: Open a Way. Open a Way for me to escape! Then the voice was back again, *Use your voice! Use your voice now!* And Jack instantly opened his mouth and called out:

"Open a Way now!"

A sound like cracking glass caused him to look at the porthole window. There, in the centre of the window was a small crack which widened as he watched. Before long, a small white light broke out from the crack and, instead of the Silver Bough, it gave form to a small orb. Once it reached the size of a tennis ball, Jack went to press his palm against it and, by passing through to another place, lead the dark prince away from Harriett and the others.

"What are you doing, Jack?" Harriett demanded.

"I'm going to lead the sorcerer away. If you stay here, you'll be safe. He will follow me."

"No, Jack!"

Harriett screamed as he stretched out his hand to touch the orb. At the same time, Jack was stopped by a sharp pain at his waist. He spun and saw a groggy Miss Butters latching onto his shirt and a fold of skin along with it, trying to pull him away from the window.

"Eugene save us!" she squealed. "What are you doing, boy, get away from the window! There are goblins out there!"

Jack pulled away and touched the orb, just in time to see Harriett lunge forward and grab hold of Miss Butters' arm. Waves of pleasure filled Jack. He felt as if he was out of time. All of his fear and worry dissolved. In one corner of his mind he was aware that Wadget and Aelf were dashing back toward the house to stop him. But he knew they'd be too late. He was also aware of a terrible shriek, the cry of the dark prince who had already turned on his heels and bolted. Jack knew that the Vellenor was using all the powers of his mind to sense where Jack was going so that he could pursue him.

For a split second the power of the orb enabled Jack to see into the sorcerer's mind. He saw the image of a cave leading down to a pit and a huge metal door, and behind that door ... an awful menace. Then he saw a vast, tangled forest and a huge old tree. In the shadow of the tree was a small dark shape that filled Jack with trepidation and fear. Jack closed out the sorcerer's thoughts.

Just before the waves of bliss overcame him, Anarra came running down the stairs from above. She froze at the bottom of the stairs, immobilised by the sight of the shining orb pulsating against Jack's palm. Jack thought she looked more beautiful than ever. The power of the orb somehow revealed the magic of her elvish blood. Her eyes shone with that magic and her skin glowed with its pearly light. For one brief moment they looked into each other's eyes. For the first time, Anarra didn't look away. Jack felt that he was adrift in the deep blue of her eyes. Then the bliss swept him away. He closed his eyes and there was nothing but the pleasure and the light.

❧ ❧

When Jack reopened his eyes, the image of Anarra revealed in all her shining beauty still burning in his mind, he thought he hadn't gone anywhere. He was still in a round room filled with dusty books, jars of weird things and odd-looking instruments. There was also a round door painted green, but this one was a darker, mossier green. Unlike Wadget's workroom, this room was a filthy mess. There were chairs turned over and stuff smashed everywhere. It looked like it had either been empty for ages or it had been ransacked.

Jack also realised he wasn't alone. Standing beside him were Miss Butters and Harriett. Miss Butters still had hold of his shirt. Harriett had hold of Miss Butters' arm. Miss Butters' eyes were closed but Harriett was looking at him as if to say 'Ha, you can't get away from me'.

"Harrie! What are you doing here! Don't you realise you won't be safe with me!"

"I'm not going to let you leave me, Jack! Besides, Morrigan thinks I'm the Waycaller because I'm the girl. That nasty elf's after me as much as you."

"But when I opened the Way he knew that I was the one. I could feel his mind reaching out to me. He's searching for me right now!"

"Where is he?" Harriett asked nervously.

"I don't know. I don't even know where we are." He looked around the room.

"This looks like Wadget's house," Harriett observed. "It's a treehouse, almost exactly the same, only there's no upstairs."

"There are stairs leading down though," Jack pointed out. He dislodged Miss Butters' fingers from his shirt. She let out a little moan but stayed put, as if frozen, eyes closed. Jack went over to a rickety staircase leading down underground. He crouched down and tried to see anything below. It was very dark. He couldn't make anything out.

"I don't think anyone's home," Jack surmised. He stood up and went to a window to look out. When he did he saw that they were definitely not in Wadget's glade any longer. Outside was a thick, dark forest filled with huge trees, all equally as big as the one they were inside. The trees were all ancient looking, gnarled and covered with long tendrils of some kind of moss that glowed a faint green in the dark. The colour of the glowing moss was exactly the same green as the eyes of the skinwearer who'd chased them in Cairnbawn and the goblins who'd just attacked them at Oakholme. A layer of mist sat ankle deep on the ground. The forest was completely silent. Jack shivered.

"I have no idea where we are," he said.

Harriett came to the window and looked out as well. "It looks like Halloween out there." Her voice was anxious. "Maybe Miss Butters will know where we are." They turned to Miss Butters, who was standing with her eyes closed, her hand clutching air as if still hanging onto Jack's shirt. "What's wrong with her?" Harriett asked.

"I don't know," Jack said, "maybe she's scared?" They went over to her and saw that a wide smile had broken out across her face. She was swaying gently on the spot as if dancing to some strange, internal music.

"Maybe she's still drunk," Harriett whispered as she tugged on the halfling's tweed jacket sleeve. "Miss Butters, Miss Butters are you alright?" Dorothea slowly opened her amber eyes, the kooky smile still lingering on her lips.

"Oh, there you are, dears. Wasn't that just the most *delicious* experience? I've never known such loveliness." She paused and sighed, as if realising something for the first time. "It was so very good it was probably very, very naughty. Do you think it's made me a heathen?"

"It's just what happens when I open a Way," Jack said. "How could that make you a heathen?"

"You'd be surprised how many things can make you a heathen, my boy."

"Well, I don't think this is one of them. Miss Butters, we

need you to take a look outside and tell us if you know where we are."

"You mean, you didn't bring us here on purpose?"

"No, I just called for a Way and this was where we ended up."

"I don't know much about this Waycalling business but it seems to me you're very inefficient at it. Surely you should know where you're going before you get started. That's rudimentary, my boy."

"Could you just look outside please? We can go over my inadequacies later."

Miss Butters went over to the window and looked out. She had barely looked out when she gasped.

"What?" Jack asked. "Where are we?"

"Eugene save us!" Miss Butters stuttered, making that wiggly sign at her heart again.

"Where were we?" Jack demanded again.

"Only one place in the world could look this … miserable … and that's Fellwood Forest."

"Fellwood?" Harriett asked. "Didn't Aelf say the Dark Elves live here?"

"Dark Elves, goblins and fiends," Miss Butters said. "Of all the places to bring us, boy, you've brought us to one of the worst! Out of the frying pan and straight into the fire!"

Jack bristled. "It's not my fault. I just touched the light and we ended up here."

"Well you'd better get us out of here quick smart!" Miss Butters demanded. "Those green-eyed Fellwood goblins will sniff us out lickety-split! They'd like nothing better than to have a nice, fat halfling and some juicy younglings to eat in place of all that moss!"

"That's why their eyes glow green, because they eat that glow-in-the-dark moss?" Jack thought this was a perfectly reasonable question. Miss Butters apparently did not.

"My dear boy, the most important part of what I just said was *not* that Fellwood goblins eat moss, but that they'd much prefer to eat *us*! Now get your wits about you and get us out of here!"

"Okay, okay, but there's no point me opening a Way if we can't choose where we're going. We could end up somewhere worse."

"Certainly, but how are you going to learn how to do it properly without the druids to help you?" the halfling asked curtly.

"Maybe one of these books will help?" Harriett suggested, indicating the piles of old books.

"Good idea, Harrie!" Jack patted his sister on the back. "Quick, let's see if we can find something before whoever lives here gets home."

"But maybe the person who lives here will help us." Harriett looked around. "This looks like an Oakling house to me."

"Oaklings are not all to be trusted," warned Miss Butters. "I don't profess to know very much about these heathen subjects but I know that. Some Oaklings are very nasty indeed."

"Ok, let's get a move on then," Jack said.

They all went to a different part of the room and started searching through books. It didn't take them long to realise that Miss Butters was right. If this was an Oakling's house, it was a very nasty Oakling. Many of the books described horrible sorcery such as magical disembowelling, turning people into toads, slugs and other slimy things, and how to make poisons that kill with a single drop. Periodically Miss Butters gasped with either horror, disgust or fear and made her little wiggly sign again. One book was so awful that it caused Harriett to burst into tears. After that Jack let her take a rest from the search. She went to a small chair and sat down, pulling her knees up to her chest and looking rather disturbed.

After about an hour Miss Butters gasped again and staggered back, her hands covering her eyes.

"Such terrible things, such terrible things," she moaned. "I can't look at these awful books anymore. I just can't."

"What's in it?" Jack asked warily.

"Halflings … Dark Elves torturing halflings …"

At that Jack was ready to give up. He was just going to have to open a Way and hope they ended up somewhere better. After all, it was a fifty-fifty chance they'd land somewhere okay. But that meant there was an equal chance they'd land somewhere worse.

*Harriett's jacket pocket, the book in Harriett's pocket,* the voice in his head said. It startled him so that he jumped. The others looked at him like he was crazy. He covered his odd reaction by pretending to suppress a sneeze. He went over to Harriett and felt her jacket pocket and was glad to feel the hard shape of the book there.

"Do you mind, Jack!"

"You numbskull, Harrie, you've got the book about Thullu in your pocket! That's bound to have something in it!"

"Oh, I forgot, but you didn't have to start feeling me like I was a bit of fruit you wanted to check was ripe!" She pulled out the book and handed it over. For the first time, Jack had a close look at it. He'd forgotten how old it was. Bound in some kind of stiff leather, it still had dust caked on the cover, partially obscuring the title. Jack cleared the dust away so that the title was easier to read: *The Word of Thullu.* He flicked through the pages but none of it looked useful. As he flicked, the book kept falling open at the same page, as if the book wanted to show him what was written there. He scanned this page until his eyes fell on a passage that looked promising.

"Yes! I think I'm onto something."

"I've found something too," Miss Butters said, looking paler than ever. She came over holding an ugly looking, fur-covered tome. Without saying a word she opened the book to the first page and there, in an untidy, handwritten scrawl was an inscription.

*This book belongs to Mog. Keep out! Don't touch it!*

"Mog," Miss Butters groaned. "Mog! She is the meanest of all the old Oaklings. We have to leave this place! We have to leave now!"

"We will," Jack assured her. "Just as soon as I find out how to do it without ending up somewhere worse."

Jack turned back to *The Word of Thullu* and read intently, running down the page with shaking fingers. While Jack read, Miss Butters, terrified that Mog might return any minute, took up watch by the door. She made a constant stream of prayers to Eugene for protection so that her wiggling fingers reminded Jack of the frenetic tentacles of a sea anemone. Harriett circled the room, trying to keep her mind off the horrific things she'd seen in the books. As she paced, she determinedly avoided looking at all the creepy jars that had labels like 'Blood Drawn at Dawn from a Red Oxen' and 'Fingers of Elves'. One cupboard, made of a dark, sticky wood with a door hanging off its hinges, was filled with hundreds of bells. They were of all shapes and sizes, some made of silver or gold, but most made of a dark, ugly looking metal.

"What's with all the bells," Harriett asked, as if to herself.

"Morrigan is drawn to the sound of bells," Miss Butters moaned. "Some say terrible bells announce her arrival. There are legends that she rides into battle on a ghoulish mount, an eyeless stallion, with strings of eerie bells adorning its harness and bridle. Go to any halfling house in the Dells and you will find they all have one thing in common – no doorbells. We have knockers instead, for fear of a doorbell summoning the Queen of Doom."

"So this Mog, she's definitely one of Morrigan's followers then?" Jack asked, distracted from his reading.

"Yes," Miss Butters whispered. "Mog is one of Morrigan's most vicious disciples."

"Well, if this is really Mog's house then we better hurry!" Harriett said direly.

"Oh, thank you for that warning, Harriett. I hadn't quite realised how urgent this situation was."

Jack rolled his eyes and resumed reading his mother's old book. He didn't get very far before a long, guttural moan came up from downstairs and froze him in his tracks. Jack turned to Harriett, who had heard it too. Miss Butters' fingers were frozen in mid wriggle, her head cocked to listen to the sound coming from below.

"Hurry, Jack!" Harriett whispered.

Jack hurriedly scanned the page the book kept presenting, desperately looking for the information he needed. He raced through half a dozen or so paragraphs and then, at the bottom of the page, there was one line that told him what he needed to know:

*With the Way in mind the Waycaller calls out for the Orb.*

He just had to have a destination in mind. It couldn't be simpler! It also explained how they'd ended up in Mog's house. He'd seen this place in the Vellenor sorcerer's mind. It was the last image he saw when he was in Wadget's workshop, before he allowed the light to engulf him. He now knew who must be moaning in the darkness below, the same shadowy figure Jack had glimpsed in the Vellenor sorcerer's mind that had filled him with fear. They had to get out of there and they had to do it now!

"I've got it," he said. "Quick, come here." Harriett rushed to his side, clearly alarmed that the moaning below had grown audibly louder. Jack closed the book and stuffed it back inside Harriett's jacket pocket and waited for Miss Butters to reach them.

As the halfling crossed the floor from the door to Jack and Harriett, her wide hips collided with what looked like a dusty old stone perched on the edge of a shelf. The stone, shaped like a flattened-out oval, was dislodged from its place and fell, in what seemed like interminable slow motion, toward the floor. They all drew in a startled breath, waiting for it to hit the floor with a clatter and rouse who or whatever was below, but it never hit the floor. Miss Butters, with reflexes so fast they were imperceptible to the eye, somehow caught the stone just inches from the floor.

"She's fast for a fat old thing, isn't she!" Harriett whispered.

"How ... how did I do that?" Miss Butters whispered

back, frightened by her own actions.

"We can work that out later," Jack said. "Just come over here, quickly." Miss Butters waddled over, her attention fixed on the flat stone that was somehow in her hand.

"All I have to do is think of where we want to go." Jack shuffled Harriett closer to him.

"But where is that?" Harriett asked.

"To Amallayne's temple," Jack answered, recalling Wadget and Aelf's conversation.

"Where's the temple?" asked Harriett.

"I don't know. Miss Butters ... Miss Butters, can you please tear your attention away from that stone for one second and help us?" Jack demanded.

"Oh, sorry dear, what did you say?"

"Do you know where Amallayne's temple is?"

"I should hope not," Miss Butters stated. "I make a point of remaining ignorant about heathen doings."

"Great." Jack flinched as the moan below turned into a growling, semi-coherent voice.

"The secret ... my secret gift," the voice moaned. "Wretched Serza! He wanted my secret gift but I say no and so he knocks me on my noggin' and tooks it!"

There was a pause in which Miss Butters tiptoed to Jack and Harriett's side. Despite being obviously terrified herself, she drew them to her in a protective embrace. The voice resumed.

"How long has Mog lain here hurting? Days maybe ... I lets him in, silly Mog! I lets him in my circle, traitor! Morrigan slay him! Traitor who dares beat on old Mog! Wanted me to give the Secret to him, but I didn't! No, Mog stays loyal to the Great Terrible One. Mog stays true to the Queen of Doom! Morrigan slay all traitors that knock Mog on her noggin' and takes secrets that aren't theirs!"

The voice growled and there was a huffing like someone dragging themselves to their feet. "But he tooks it anyway! Vile elf that betrays the Dark Queen! Traitor! He tooks the Secret Gift! Morrigan slay him! Villain! Let Morrigan slay the traitor and give him to old Mog to eat him. Yes, Mog bets Serza's tasty to these old teeth!" The voice trailed off into a mad cackle and then a dry, rasping cough.

Jack didn't know what to do. If he didn't open a Way soon, Mog would discover them. By the sound of things, she was already angry and not only that but a cannibal as well! He whispered to Miss Butters, "Don't you have any idea where Amallayne's temple is?"

"I shouldn't say—"

"Miss Butters, please!" Jack pleaded.

"Eugene forgive me," she whispered. "I believe there was a temple for Amallayne in the Empty Lands at Amaltor. That is all I know, but I don't know if it's even there anymore."

"It will have to do," Jack said. "Now, let's get out of this house."

"You mean out into the forest?" Miss Butters squeaked.

"It's either that, or we stay here and wait for Mog to eat us."

"Let's go." Miss Butters headed straight for the door. Jack and Harriett crept after her and, as quietly as they could, opened the door and slipped outside. Miss Butters went first, then Harriett and then Jack. Just as Jack was closing the door, he heard the sound of laboured steps coming up the staircase. It sounded like more than one person, the pad of not two but four feet. The footfall stopped and Mog growled and hissed.

"What is that I smell?" she spat. "Is it warm skin? Is it stupid Serza, still lurking?" The feet resumed at a much more rapid pace and Jack shut the door behind him and bolted.

"Run!" he hissed and all three ran for their lives. At least Jack and Harriett ran. Miss Butters, unaccustomed to running, sort of wobbled forward like a lump of jelly rolling down a hill. From inside the house, the sound of a sudden shriek of rage spurred them on even faster.

"Morrigan slay all burglars and sneaks!"

They ran as fast as they could, slowed only by the tangle of tree roots, branches and hanging moss.

*Pass beyond the stone,* the voice urged.

"What stone?" Jack yelled out loud. The other two looked at him like he was crazy again. He didn't bother explaining. He just kept running. After just a few more yards, Jack saw a tall, weathered, needle-like stone covered in strange markings. It was on a bit of a lean and was so overgrown by moss that it almost looked like an old tree trunk. It was nothing like the pristine, neat stones at Oakholme. It looked kind of diseased. They ran past it and the voice rang in his ear again, *Mount a tree!* Jack selected a big tree off to the right a bit and urged the others up it. Getting Miss Butters up the tree, given her irrational fear of heights, was no easy task. But with Harriett pulling and Jack pushing they managed to get her up. Miss Butters took up position in a secure-looking nook of a large bough and, though visibly terrified, didn't complain one bit about the height. The possibility of being eaten apparently motivated Miss Butters even more than acorn dumplings.

Just as Jack and Harriett settled into one of the large mossy boughs beside Miss Butters, they heard the door of Mog's house swing open and the distinct patter of what sounded like an animal running toward them.

"Is that a dog?" Harriett asked, puffing.

"Shush, Harrie, quiet," Jack whispered.

Little more than a second later, a thing on all fours came running into view. It was green with pointed ears, a buttony nose all plugged up with mucus and big round yellow eyes with cloudy patches of white. It moved like a cross between a monkey and a small dog. It was clearly an Oakling, only it couldn't be more different from Wadget. This thing was filthy, wearing a very soiled dress cinched around its waist with a leather strap. Its talon-like fingers and toes dug into the ground and threw up clumps of mud as it ran. Though frightening, it looked a bit decrepit.

"Mog," Miss Butters sighed almost silently.

When Mog reached the standing stone, she stopped and sniffed the air. There was so much mucus in her nose that Jack doubted she could smell anything, but she had managed to detect their presence in her house. She looked like some kind of demon dog. She took a few cautious steps forward and sniffed again. *Her senses wane,* the voice in Jack's ear said reassuringly. Jack could have worked that out for himself. Or did he? Wasn't the voice his?

Mog growled again. Her eyes were so cloudy she must've been practically blind. Jack doubted she could've seen them if they were right in front of her. Her ears, however, looked perfectly functional. They twitched this way and that searching for even the smallest sound. Jack and the others stayed deathly still. For long moments they didn't dare breathe. Mog moved the slightest distance forward, to the very perimeter of what must be the circle that surrounded her house. But she went no further. She sniffed the air some more.

"Don't know who's out there. Mog shouldn't go out," she hissed to herself. "Not with the traitor Serza out there. Who knows what else is with him … goblins, trolls. Mog could kill them all and eat them! But he has the Gift. No, Mog mustn't, Mog mustn't go out. Mog must go back. Mog must build her wards again. Then they can't get in. Mog won't let them in this time! No! Mog will be safe inside, like always, always safe inside. Mog has many powers and many tricks! Mog can keep them out. Yes, then when I gets the chance I will kill Serza and eat him. Yes! Mog will eat Serza down to his bones!"

At that Mog hissed toward the dark trees and stood upright. She pulled a short stubby stick out of her filthy dress and, with the slightest flick of her wrist, caused a tree to explode into flame. It splintered and smoked, its boughs falling to the ground as red embers. She cackled and used her wand to detonate another tree just yards away from where Jack, Harriett and Miss Butters were hiding. Satisfied with that, and with a grunt and growl, Mog loped back toward her house. Soon they heard the door slam shut behind her.

"Let's get out of here," Jack said.

"Shouldn't we climb down out of the tree first?" asked Miss Butters.

"Do you think that matters?" Jack couldn't see how it

would matter, but what did he know?

"Little that is good happens off-ground," Miss Butters chanted, sharing with them what was apparently a sacred halfling saying. "Besides, I believe we are outside the circle."

"Okay, we'll only go just inside the circle and I'll call out there."

"Will we be able to get in?" Harriett asked. "Remember what happened to those goblins when they tried to cross Wadget's circle."

"I think this circle isn't working," Jack said. "Didn't you hear Mog talking to herself about it?"

"She was talking to herself a lot. She's nuts," Harriett said.

"She is that, but she's also powerful." Jack motioned to the burning trees. "I think we should hurry before she puts the wards back up."

They climbed down and headed to the edge of the circle. Just in front of the leaning stone, they halted. They were all reluctant to cross the threshold just in case Mog had already put her defences back in place. Jack went to step his toe just over the perimeter but Miss Butters grabbed him by the shoulder and stopped him. She then took a deep breath, steeled herself and crossed the threshold herself. As she stepped inside, nothing happened.

"I think I'm not dead," she said, relieved, motioning the children over the line.

"What's the name of the place again?" Jack asked, looking over his shoulder in the direction of Mog's house.

"Amaltor," Miss Butters whispered.

"Okay," he said, "here goes: Open a Way, Open a Way to Amaltor!"

Jack put all his will into it and, even though this time he was not being compelled by the voice, he felt the same determination rising in his belly. The sound of timber splitting drew his attention to a notch in the trunk of a tree just above them, where a crack grew and soon emitted thin shafts of white light. The crack grew wider and a white orb of light emerged and hovered just above them. "Okay, hang onto me and think of Amaltor."

He waited for his sister and Miss Butters to take hold of him and then placed his hand to the orb. As the wave of pleasure raced up his arm, he heard a terrible yowl emanating from Mog's house. The yowl was followed by the sound of a door flying open and the animal-like patter of clawed hands and feet as they thumped through the mud. But she wouldn't come anywhere near them before they were gone. Jack had become confident that his passage from place to place was almost instantaneous. He relaxed and enjoyed the pulsing bliss.

# AMALTOR IN THE EMPTY LANDS

They were no longer in Fellwood Forest, but where they were didn't seem very much better – a pitch black grassy plain buffeted by cold winds. The night sky was obscured by clouds and there was no moon. For a moment Jack even wished for some of the strange green light given off by the hanging moss of Fellwood Forest, but when he thought of Mog he came to his senses. He looked around but couldn't see a single structure anywhere, not that he could see very far due to the darkness.

"Where's the temple?" asked Harriett.

"I don't know. It should be here," Jack answered.

Jack shook Miss Butters, who was doing her strange blissed out, on-the-spot dance again.

"Oh, hello again, dears." She opened her eyes and blinked dreamily at them. "Wasn't that just as delicious as the first time?"

"Yes, very delicious." Jack gestured to the vast flatness. "But we don't seem to be at Amallayne's temple. There's nothing here at all."

Miss Butters looked around. "I don't understand. I thought you could only travel between circles?"

"So did I," Jack answered.

"But there's no circle here, dear," Miss Butters pointed out. "At least I don't think so. I have quite good eyesight, more so in the day, but even in the dark I can see clearly for at least a mile and there are no stones in sight."

"Do you have any idea where we are?" he asked

"None at all."

"Great." Jack kicked the ground. "I've got us completely lost."

"Not to worry, dear. We shall bunk down here and see what rises with the dawn," she said with uncharacteristic positivity. "At least we're not going to be eaten by Mog,

215

which is something, isn't it? And if you have to open a Way again in the morning, or a dozen times in a row if need be, well, that won't be bad will it? Actually, it'll be quite lovely."

Jack was starting to think that Miss Butters was becoming addicted to the bliss accompanying the white orb. He suspected that her current light attitude would quickly darken when she realised not only were they totally lost but there was no chance for even a cup of tea for breakfast in the morning.

Despite his reservations, he acquiesced and allowed Miss Butters to make them a nest of soft grass behind a tussock big enough to offer them slight protection from the wind. Miss Butters pulled them into a tight cuddle, one on either side, which made Jack decidedly uncomfortable. He found however that her round body was surprisingly warm. Harriett snuggled into Miss Butters' side and soon managed to fall asleep. As Jack listened to his sister's breathing slow and deepen, he thought that, despite their indulgent natures, halflings must be very hardy creatures, able to withstand severe cold at least. It took Jack longer to nod off but, despite his anxiety about where they were and what might be lurking out in the dark, he finally fell asleep as well.

When Jack woke it was well after dawn. He felt surprisingly refreshed. The wind had gone and the sky cleared and, although peppered with clouds, the sun was shining and warming the ground. He was quite surprised by the vista that met him when he looked around. Stretching for miles and miles in every direction was a vast grassy plain with not a hill, not even a slight rise in sight. It was a great, grey, withered and empty land. Harriett was sitting by a small fire, Miss Butters a short distance away searching the ground for little twigs and bits of dried tussock.

"How'd you make a fire?" Jack asked.

"Apparently all halflings know how to start fires by rubbing twigs together. She's really rather smart despite being horribly fat and bossy." Harriett smirked.

"Now, Harriett," Miss Butters said as she came over and put more kindling onto the fire, "you'll turn my head with all that flattery." Miss Butters used one of her sticks to stoke the flames. It was a rather tiny fire but it added a sense of comfort to the otherwise bleak scene. "Now, come for breakfast, Jack."

"Breakfast?" Jack asked. "What are we going to have? Grass?"

"Don't be ridiculous!" Miss Butters wagged a scolding finger. "We're having toasted marshmallows, brown sugar cookies and a bit of fruitcake."

"I think she's hallucinating," Harriett said to Jack.

"I'm not hallucinating, dear. All well-bred halflings carry four things in their jacket pockets whenever they go on a journey, in case of emergency: half a dozen marshmallows, a few brown sugar cookies, a piece of fruitcake and an image of the Almighty Eugene." She pulled out of her inner pocket the aforementioned provisions and a small locket-sized portrait. As she impaled the marshmallows on some sticks, readying them for toasting, she passed the portrait to Harriett. "Feast your little blue eyes on Him, Miss Harriett, and tell me he's not the most glorious thing you've ever seen."

Harriett looked at the image and smirked, passing it to Jack. The portrait showed a very puffed up and important looking halfling wearing lederhosen, a bright orange shirt, bright orange, checked socks that went all the way to the knees and a fedora adorned with a giant golden feather. He had in his hand a chimney brush that emitted flames and was riding through the sky in a golden cart harnessed to two massive gold boars. Overall, he looked a bit ridiculous.

"What did I tell you? Eugene is most splendid, isn't he?" Miss Butters' bosom inflated with pride.

"Yes," Harriett said politely, "really splendid."

After they ate their unconventional breakfast, Jack pondered the events of the last few days. Things had unfolded so quickly that he'd barely had time to think. It was hard to believe it had only been two nights since everything had been normal and he and Harriett knew nothing about Veils or Morrigan or skinwearers or dark sorcerers. If he had his way he'd just go home and forget about it all. But we can't go home, Jack thought. The Veil was breached once and could be again. It was clear to Jack now that the Vellenor sorcerer, the one Wadget called Prince Serza, was who'd sent the skinwearer after them. Jack had seen the strange blue energy pulsing through Serza's veins with his own eyes. From what Aelf had said about Thullu's Gift, that power made Serza almost invincible. If they went home, the dark prince could send a whole troop of goblins back to Cairnbawn after them. If the goblins failed, and Jack doubted an attempt on his life would fail another time, nothing could stop Serza from crossing the Veil himself. Jack was sure Morrigan would reward her disciple richly for killing Jack personally and thus freeing her. The thought of Serza in the human world made Jack cringe. That couldn't be allowed to happen. He waited for Miss Butters to get up to find more kindling for the fire before taking his opportunity to talk to Harriett.

"Harrie, I think it's time we accept that we won't be going home anytime soon."

"I know." Harriett looked off into the distance. "I've known that since the minute we arrived at the circle in Bright."

"How could you have known that?"

"It's hard to explain. As soon as we set foot in Anwynn I just knew. I've been having this strange feeling that I've been here before, seen this all before." Her eyes passed over the landscape as though trying to figure out why it was all so familiar. "When I first saw Hob, it was as if I'd known him all my life."

Jack found that statement disturbing and completely impossible. "It's just the stress, Harrie, messing with your head, giving you déjà vu."

Harriett didn't answer, her eyes still on the horizon. A melodic sound behind them made them both look around. Miss Butters was humming some halfling tune as she gathered sticks and twigs. Harriett watched her work, her eyes glassy with tears.

"What's going to happen to them, Jack?"

"To who?"

"Miss Butters and Aelf, all of them."

"They'll be okay."

"No, they won't. None of them are safe."

"What do you mean?"

"All those goblins that were at Wadget's, there were so many of them. There are probably lots more. What if one day they attacked Bright or caught Aelf or Wadget?"

"We can't do anything about that, Harrie. Besides, what do you care about Miss Butters?"

"I do care, now. She's weird and force feeds me, but she honestly has been trying to help us."

"How, by toasting some marshmallows?"

"She let us stay at her house when she didn't even know us. She put herself between us and the hollow-wolves, she dragged you away from the window at Wadget's—"

"But I didn't need her help then!"

"It doesn't matter, she thought you were in danger. And she tested the circle at Mog's. That could've killed her, Jack. And she kept us warm all night. She also shared her emergency food with us, which is a pretty big thing for her. And Aelf and Wadget, they risked their lives to protect us from Serza and those goblins."

"What do you want me to do?"

"You're the Waycaller, Jack. You have to help keep them safe."

"I don't have to do anything. They'd be facing danger even if we'd never come here. Their safety is not my problem." As he said this he watched Miss Butters gathering twigs and clumps of dried grass, still humming the cheerful tune and oblivious to their conversation. She saw him looking and smiled. He felt a small twinge of guilt at suggesting her safety wasn't his problem. But was he really responsible for Miss Butters? For Aelf and Wadget? He had to think of Harriett first and foremost. Anything else was too much. He couldn't be expected to protect all of Anwynn. What seventeen year old kid could deal with that kind of responsibility?

Harriett looked straight into his eyes. "Well, I think it is our problem, Jack. We have to help fight Morrigan."

"Harriett, you're nine years old, what can you do to help? As soon as I'm sure nothing awful can follow us across the Veil, I'm taking you back to Cairnbawn. Let the druids deal with Morrigan and Serza."

"What about Mum?" she asked.

"What about her?"

"Wadget said she was a brave Waycaller, that she'd sacrificed a lot—"

"She was a lunatic who killed our father."

"Look around, Jack. She wasn't crazy. It's all real: elves and dragons and magic, all real."

"She still killed our father."

"No, I don't believe that anymore, a Waycaller would never—"

"You don't know what you're talking about." The image of Harriett lying at his feet, dead or dying from wounds inflicted by a bloody sword in his own hands, filled his mind. "She killed our father and then herself, Harrie. She was crazy, Waycaller or not, and now she's dead and we're all alone. We have to look out for ourselves."

Tears pooled in the corner of Harriett's eyes, but there remained a defiant glint to them. Jack could tell she didn't accept what he was saying. She wiped away her tears as Miss Butters returned to the campfire. Dorothea stoked the fire and sat down beside them, noticing the remnants of tears on Harriett's cheek.

"You poor dear," she said, dragging Harriett into a bear hug. "Crying from hunger no doubt, you're practically as thin as the kindling I've been gathering."

"I'm not crying from hunger!"

"Such a brave girl! Faced with starvation and still got the fighting spirit!" Miss Butters squeezed Harriett so tightly she practically lost her breath. "Well, if you can be brave, I can be brave. Though I must confess I'm not feeling well at all. I think I've begun to self-digest."

"To what?" Jack asked.

"To self-digest, dear. My stomach's so ravenous it has started to eat me from the inside out. I fear I shan't last long—"

"We ate less than twenty minutes ago! Besides, I don't think your own stomach can digest you." Jack shook his head. Halflings were nuts. At least this one was anyway.

"Well, that's a lot you know, young man. It's well known in Bright that Pansy Wainwright, who got herself trapped in her own root cellar, completely self-digested after just one week! And she was plumper than a pregnant sow. All that was left of her was hair and nails! I'm afraid I shall suffer the same fate. I shall perish here in this heathen circle."

"Circle? What circle?" Jack decided that though she was not self-digesting, perhaps she was getting a little confused by hunger.

"The circle of Amaltor! Oh, I've been so dizzy from famishment I forgot to tell you. You didn't get us lost at all. We're right where we should be."

"I don't understand. I don't see a circle anywhere."

"Of course you don't, Jack. But I'm a halfling and I can see perfectly well, even though my night vision isn't as good as I'd thought it was. I didn't see them last night, but in the daylight I can see for miles, far enough to see the stones."

"What stones?" Harriett asked, still caught in Miss Butters' tight embrace.

"Those stones." Miss Butters pointed off to the horizon.

Jack looked to the horizon but couldn't see anything and said so. Miss Butters told him to look more carefully and pointed out a particular spot to the south of them. He stared and stared and then finally could make something out. It was so far away that it was just a small dark mark on the horizon.

"Is that a standing stone?" he asked. "It must be miles away."

"Yes, quite a few miles I'd say." Miss Butters one-handedly loaded more twigs on the fire as Harriett struggled under her other arm. "Legend says this was the biggest circle ever made. For once the legends don't seem to be an exaggeration."

"Why would they build such a big circle?" Harriett's voice was muffled through a mouthful of Miss Butters' lapel.

"To encircle the great temple of Amallayne and the whole city of Amaltor, which was once the capital of the Kingdom of Pix, before the Doom War."

"But," Jack said, "where's the temple now? There's nothing here."

"Long gone is my guess. The temple, and the Pixish capital along with it, were probably destroyed by Morrigan's horde eight thousand years ago. There's nothing but grass here now."

"But there has to be a temple to Amallayne somewhere," Jack said, struggling to keep his voice calm. "I heard Wadget telling Aelf we had to go there to get Amallayne's help."

"I'm not surprised," said Miss Butters. "Oaklings are up to their ears in tricksy business. Nothing but trouble can come of it. The Pixish were known heathens, worshippers of Amallayne and fiddlers with magic to boot. The Florid Spinsters are very clear on their iniquity." She lowered her voice to a whisper. "There are even rumours that the Pixish have elvish blood. Totally indecent, the lot of them, and look what happened to them!" She gestured out over the grassy plains which once held a great city but was now empty, silent and desolate.

"So, where did the Pixish go?" Harriett asked.

"To Pixett, in the north of what remains of their kingdom. This deserted place is now known as the Empty Lands. It's been desolate since the Doom War. Only goblin hunting parties cross it now."

"Was the temple rebuilt there, at this Pixett place?" Jack tried but failed to sound calm.

"I have no idea," Miss Butters answered. "But I do recall an old trader from Bright telling tales about a temple somewhere. That might have been a temple for Amallayne, but I tend to close my ears when such heathen topics are raised."

"It's worth a try," Harriett said.

"Is there a stone circle at Pixett?" Jack asked.

"No, that I know for sure. The traders all say the King of Pix isn't fond of stone circles, which is the only sensible thing about him."

"It might be sensible, but I can't open a Way if there's no stone circle. We'll have to walk there. How far is it?"

"It's a long way from here, a very long way. There's not a bakery or inn or anything for hundreds of miles between here and Pixett." Miss Butters looked rather desperate about that.

"Well, don't worry, Miss Butters, I'm sure we'll get there before you fully self-digest." Jack knew that was mean of him to say, but he was a bit annoyed at Miss Butters.

"Do you think we can get started straight away, my dear? I'm positively weak with famishment and the sooner we leave the sooner we can find sustenance."

"Sure," Jack said. "We can go whenever you're ready."

With a surprising degree of dexterity Miss Butters hopped up to put out their little campfire. Jack and Harriett watched her, both shaking their heads. Dorothea Butters was as close to self-digestion as they were to the moon.

Miss Butters had left her portrait of Eugene beside the fire, along with the oval stone she'd stopped from falling to the floor at Mog's house. Harriett picked up the grimy stone, which fit neatly into the palm of her hand, and wiped it clear of dust. Beneath the dust and grime the stone was a luminous blue with veins of pink and white, like an opal.

"Oh, Jack, look, it's so pretty." She wiped it again, getting it to really shine. When she wiped the stone a third time, the surface of the now gleaming stone looked like shimmering water.

"What is that?" Jack asked, leaning in for a closer look. Harriett wiped the surface of the stone again, buffing it with the edges of her sleeve. As she buffed, the surface of the stone changed, became more reflective, like rippling quicksilver. Jack peered more closely. He got the impression of being in the bottom of a bucket looking up. Harriett gasped. The shimmering surface of the stone was now like a window that looked into a small, cupboard-sized room. Somehow, the stone was letting them see some kind of vision, a vision of a small closet.

"Miss Butters," Jack said, "come and look at this!"

"A magic seeing stone!" Miss Butters gasped. "Perhaps that's how I came to catch it before it hit the floor? It's magic."

"Here," Harriett said, attempting to pass the seeing stone to Miss Butters.

"Oh no, dear," the halfling said, "best you keep it. The Florid Spinsters forbid halflings to even touch magical objects." Harriett took it back and held it so that they could all see the image it reflected.

"What is that? Is it a cupboard?" Jack peered into the stone.

"I don't know," said Harriett. "I was just wiping the dust off it, thinking about Wadget and Aelf, and it went all kind of watery and then I could see this little room."

"It's a pokey little room, isn't it?" Miss Butters said, prodding the stone. "It couldn't be a cupboard as there aren't any shelves or rails."

As they all peered into the seeing stone, taking in the featureless little room, a shape loomed before them in the vision. The shape shimmered and rippled as if they were looking up at it from underwater. They all gasped. Miss Butters started to flee but then Harriett recognised what, or rather who, it was.

"That's Wadget!" she said. At first Jack wasn't so sure. The perspective was disorienting and made him feel a bit odd.

"What's he doing?" he asked, as Wadget came into focus, really looming over them now, and started to unfasten his belt.

"Good gracious!" Miss Butters shrieked. "Cover your eyes

children!" She slapped her chubby hands over their eyes just in case they didn't do it themselves. "Master Wadget, there are women and children present!" she yelled.

Jack heard Wadget shout with surprise. He couldn't see through Miss Butters' tightly clasped fingers but heard a kind of a thump followed by a thud that sounded like Wadget had fallen backwards into a wall.

"Great stars!" Wadget's voice boomed "What're yeh three doin' in my privy! An Oaklin's toiletin' is a private affair!"

"What are *we* doing? What are *you* doing practically exposing yourself to a woman and children!" Miss Butters scolded.

"Well, how was I ter know yeh were lurkin' in my privy bucket! It's not somethin' that happens every day! Where in blazes are yeh, and how're yeh sendin' yer image into my privy water?"

Harriett broke free of Miss Butters' blindfolding fingers. "We're at Amaltor and we're using some kind of stone." Once Harriett was free, and Wadget appeared to be remaining completely clothed, Miss Butters released Jack as well.

"A seein' stone eh?" Wadget scratched his ear. "Well, well, well." He chuckled and stepped out of view. There was the sound of a door opening and Wadget calling out. "Ethelwulf, come take a look what's in me privy."

"I'd rather not, if you didn't mind," came Aelf's voice from a bit of a distance.

"It's not what yeh think, come an' look."

After a moment Aelf's face came into view, looking apprehensive about what he might see when he glanced into the privy. When he looked down and spotted Jack, Harriett and Miss Butters, his face immediately transformed into one of delight.

"I don't believe it!" he said. "Of all the things one normally expects to see in a water closet this is the very last, and perhaps the only one I'm actually happy to see!"

"They're at the ruins o' Amaltor," Wadget explained.

"Usin' some kind o' seein' stone."

"Really?" Aelf looked delighted. "And where might I ask did you acquire a seeing stone? Such things are very rare."

"Miss Butters took it from Mog," Harriett said.

"Mog!" Both Aelf and Wadget shouted at once.

"Yes," Miss Butters explained, "when we first left Oakholme we found ourselves in Mog's house—"

"Goodness!" Aelf said.

"Yes, I can tell you it was rather a shock, but Jack here managed to get us out of there before she ate us."

"Thank grace for that! Mog has a notorious appetite." Aelf adopted a matter-of-fact tone. "She ate my good friend Adelard you know."

Miss Butters gulped. "How horrendous! Nothing good can ever come of being eaten!"

"Indeed, the only good that came of it was that Mog got a rather horrendous stomach ache. Put her out of action for weeks. Serves her right. She's a terrible glutton."

"It's lucky that we found yeh in my privy and not in ol' Mog's belly," Wadget said with a chuckle. "Few have ever bested her. How is the ol' thing?"

"Hideous," said Miss Butters.

"Very snotty," Harriett added.

"She ran around on all fours like a monkey." Jack grimaced at the memory. "And I think she's going blind."

"The practice of dark sorcery has ill effects on the body," Aelf explained. "Even an immortal being like Mog can't avoid those ill effects forever."

"It was smart o' yeh ter take the seein' stone," Wadget said. "Without it much time would've been wasted findin' yeh."

"Thank you," said Miss Butters, choosing not to explain that the taking of the seeing stone happened completely by accident. "But, how does the seeing stone work?"

"It is simple," Aelf began. "It sends an image of the holder to a reflective surface in the vicinity of the person you are calling. You simply think of the person and the seeing stone does the rest. It's a very handy object to have."

"I'm so glad you're alright," Harriett said with a sigh. "I thought the goblins might have got you."

"No, once yeh three left, Serza ran off." Wadget sneered and spat in the privy, causing ripples to obscure their view. "With him gone it was easy enough ter dispatch the goblins."

"Dispatch?" Miss Butters asked uneasily.

"Yes, a stroke of genius it was too," Aelf explained. "Master Wadget summoned an artificial sun. Roasted them all on the spot. The place still smells a little of barbeque."

"Gross." Harriett made a gagging sound.

"Very," said Aelf.

"Gross or not it did the trick," Wadget grunted. "An' fertilised me grass in the process. Now, ter more important matters. What yeh did was foolish, boy. We can't protect yeh if yeh take off whenever yeh please. Yeh not only risk yerself but all o' us."

"But, if I hadn't left, that sorcerer would have broken the circle and we'd have been done for." Jack wasn't going to feel bad about escaping Oakholme, no matter what Wadget said.

"The fact that things turned out fer the good this time don't forgive that yeh acted foolishly," Wadget grumbled. "Besides, what if the dark prince had managed ter follow yeh? Then yeh would've been in real trouble!"

"Well, what's done is done," Aelf said, trying to smooth things over. "Now that we know where you are, we'll send someone to collect you."

"Couldn't Jack just open a Way?" Miss Butters refused to look at Jack and Harrie and adopted an innocent voice. "Wouldn't that be nicer ... I mean, quicker?"

"It is best if Jack uses his power as little as possible. Just in case by using it he can be tracked by Prince Serza," asserted Aelf.

"Serza is rank with the power o' Thullu," Wadget added. "He has learned many dark secrets. How I don't know, but frightenin' it is if Thullu is involved in this."

"Mog's Secret Gift!" Harriett shouted.

"What did yeh say?" Wadget's brown eyes narrowed intently.

"Mog, she was talking to herself about some Secret Gift that Serza stole from her," answered Harriett.

"Then it's as I feared," Wadget grumbled. "That must be how the Veil were breached, how Serza has become so powerful." The Oakling looked at Aelf with undisguised concern on his face. Even the rippling effect of the seeing stone couldn't disguise how alarmed Wadget was.

"Is it definitely Thullu's Gift then, that Mog was talking about?" Jack asked, preferring to ask that than ask why Serza was after him and Harriett. He just couldn't deal with all that right now.

"Almost certainly," Aelf said gravely.

"Looks like it," Wadget said.

"It is astounding that Mog had it all this time," Aelf said to his master. "Clearly she did not know what it was, or she would have used it."

"Doubt it," Wadget said. "Mog belongs ter Morrigan, she's the Pale Mother's puppet through an' through. She'd never use any power other than Morrigan's. Mog's as crazy as a rabid bat, but she's utterly loyal."

"Yeah, I noticed that." Harriett said. "She was furious because Serza has betrayed Morrigan."

"Betrayed Morrigan?" Wadget grunted. "A prince of Fellwood betrayin' the Queen o' Doom? That's one fer the books!"

"If the dark prince of Fellwood is not acting on Morrigan's orders, but for his own purposes, well, that quite complicates things." Aelf looked just as worried as Wadget now. "It begs the question why Serza is hunting Jack and Harriett, if not on Morrigan's orders."

"That it does," Wadget grumbled. "That it does. So many damn secrets! If I hate anythin', it's damn secrets!"

"So, will the dark prince use Thullu's Gift to break Morrigan out?" asked Harriett, her eyes wide.

"Not if he's betrayed her as Mog seems ter think," Wadget

answered. "He'll want her ter stay right where she is. But with the Gift, Prince Serza could bring down a darkness even worse than the Doom War."

"Oh no," Harriett moaned.

"Oh no indeed," echoed Aelf.

"With Thullu's Gift Serza has the power ter do almost anythin'," Wadget explained, "maybe even shatter the Veil fer good. Serza havin' it is bad, but if Morrigan's minions get hold of it they'll use it ter destroy Darkgate, releasin' the White Demoness from her prison. An' there's still a chance that Thullu himself is involved in this somehow. It's now more important than ever that we go ter Amallayne fer help. Perhaps she knows a way ter counter the Gift—"

"I've always said," Miss Butters began, "that nothing good comes of associating with Tricksy Ones or elves. All of this Secret Gift business just proves me right. I think it's best we just stay out of it. Who cares if this dark prince has betrayed Morrigan? Let the prince and the Pale Mother's minions fight it out amongst themselves and let us go home to a nice cup of tea."

"What do yeh think Serza an' Morrigan's disciples will do once they've finished fightin' it out?" Wadget growled. "The winner'll turn on us, that's what. Whichever one wins is the one we'll have ter deal with. Frankly, I don't know which is worse, the White Demoness loosed or the Prince o' Fellwood with unimaginable power. No, Amallayne must be asked fer aid, an' the Waycaller is the best person ter do the askin'."

"Terrific," Jack said, his head practically spinning. "So, it won't be safe for us to go home unless Amallayne deals with Serza and makes sure Morrigan's followers don't get hold of this Secret Gift?" Jack thought the likelihood of any of that working out in their favour was next to none.

"Unfortunately not," Aelf said. "I'm so sorry, Jack."

Jack's heart plummeted into the bottom of his belly. The small glimmer of hope that he and Harriett might be able to go home soon was crushed. He felt the hope fade from his face, along with all its colour. The reality that there was no easy way out of confronting Morrigan, Prince Serza and all their hordes hit him like a kick in the heart. Miss Butters reached out and rubbed his shoulder.

"I'm so sorry, dear boy. I truly am." Her little hand was warm and insistent.

"If only we could have a nice cup of tea," Miss Butters continued, "that'd make you feel so much better."

Jack flushed, suddenly very angry. Tea! All these people thought about was tea! Though they were all saying they were sorry they weren't really. They didn't really care about Harriett or him at all! They didn't care that Morrigan wanted him dead, just that she never got loose. They didn't care why Serza was after them as well, only that a way was found to counter Thullu's Gift. All they cared about was saving their own necks and defeating Morrigan. The druids were just using them!

*That is not true!* The voice in Jack's ear was back, with more power behind it than he had felt before.

"Shut up!" Jack shouted this out loud, cupping his ears as if to block out a deafening noise.

"Why, I never," Miss Butters started.

"Not you!" Jack shook his head, as if trying to get water out of his ear.

"Eugene spare us! I think you're ear-whipped, my boy!" Miss Butters backed away with alarm. "Talking to yourself, acting odd, those are the two prime symptoms of ear-whipping."

At these words Jack's anger vanished to be replaced by a cold dread.

"What's ear-whipping?" he asked.

"It's an infestation," Miss Butters explained. "An earwisp, a tiny Tiqq sprite, crawls into the ear and uses its magical voice to take over the mind. Earwisps are wicked, sneaky, horrible little things that possess you and make you commit all kinds of debauchery against your will. It is a very *indecent* sort of infection."

Jack's skin paled and went cold. Each word of Miss

Butters' description caused his stomach to twist. Aelf had said the Tiqq were devoted to Thullu, the worst of all the Faeden, and were despised by all other beings in Anwynn. Could he be possessed by one? Could that be the source of the voice in his ear?

Wadget growled, drawing their attention. "The lad's not ear-whipped! Just upset. Leave him be an' he'll come good. Fer right now, we got ter send someone ter collect yeh."

"Who?" Harriett asked.

"Yes, *who*?" Miss Butters nervously echoed.

"Daniselle, one of the mountain elves," Wadget answered.

"An elf! Cool!" Harriett actually clapped her hands. "Where are we going?"

"To Songarielle, in the Craggy Mountains," Aelf explained. "These new events require us to meet with the Druid Council. If we are to thwart both Serza and Morrigan we are going to need their aid to do it. Also, that is where Amallayne's temple has been rebuilt. We will meet you there."

"But," Miss Butters said, "won't it take a very long time for an elf to come all the way from Songarielle?"

Jack knew Miss Butters was fearful of spending another night out in the open at Amaltor, given the fact that an evil sorcerer was searching for them, but suspected she was also angling for him to open a Way so she could experience the bliss again and get to Songarielle in time for morning tea.

"Not this elf," Wadget smirked. "Now, get out o' me privy! I'm ruddy bustin'!"

As Miss Butters and Harriett said goodbye to Wadget and Aelf through the seeing stone, Jack picked a direction and just walked. As he walked, he wondered what he'd done to deserve all this. What had Harriett done? He kicked at a tuft of grass in his path and squealed with pain. His foot had connected with something much more solid than grass. He angrily tore at the tussock to see what it was concealing and found the corner of a fallen pillar.

The pillar had intricate carvings of interwoven spirals. Its beauty disarmed him for a moment. He knelt down and moved more grass and dirt away from its surface. Apart from the interwoven spirals there were carvings of some kind of procession, people dressed in medieval kind of gear, tunics and the like, and what were clearly elves, tall and thin with ears that curled up to a pointy tip. At the head of the procession was a group of druids; he could tell they were druids by their cloaks. As he removed more grass and dirt to reveal more of the carving, he found the focus of the procession – a beautiful girl encircled by rays of light. She looked about sixteen years old. Jack knew she could be a lot older; look at Hob. Like Hob, she looked human. The way she was rendered however, with the halo and all the other figures kneeling before her, told Jack she was more than just a beautiful girl. *Amallayne*, the voice in his ear whispered, *Amallayne the Conqueror.*

Jack stared at the image and at the stone, and then looked out to the horizon. What was it that Miss Butters had said – that once a great city had stood here, Amaltor, the capital of the Kingdom of Pix? A whole city reduced to just a few fallen stones. He uncovered more of the pillar and found what he assumed was a likeness of Amaltor as it once was, a large city of grand buildings, palaces and temples, with long avenues of trees, all surrounded by a vast stone circle. Jack looked around at the unending emptiness.

"There's nothing left," he said to himself. *Nothing,* the voice echoed in reply. Jack's heart sank. Morrigan's armies had destroyed this place. He would have liked to have seen it. But it was a ruin thousands of years before he was born. Nothing could be done about it now. *Fight Morrigan,* the voice whispered. *Avenge the Kingdom of Pix.*

"Get out of my head," Jack mumbled. "There's nothing I can do."

*You are the Waycaller,* the voice said, *not some snivelling boy. Live up to your destiny.*

"Snivelling? Who are you accusing of snivelling?"

"Jack?" Harriett's voice came from behind him. He spun around and saw her just feet away, stuffing the seeing stone in her pocket as she walked toward him. "Who were you talking to, Jack?"

"Nobody," he said defensively. "What do you want?"

"Just to see how you are." This softened him. His nine year old sister was faring better with all of this than he was and was showing more concern for him than he was for her.

"I'm fine, Harrie. Are you okay?"

"Yes," she said. "So, were you talking to yourself, Jack? Because if you were, I wouldn't let on to Miss Butters that you were."

"Why, what business is it of hers?"

"She makes everything her business, Jack. She already thinks you're ear-whipped and, from what she said, earwisps are not very nice."

"Yeah, well, Miss Butters makes everything sound awful, except for Piggy-poo, of course."

"So, you're not possessed then?" Harriett searched his eyes. What was she looking for? Some evidence that a monster lurked inside him?

"No, of course not." He didn't sound very convincing. He was not convinced himself.

"Okay," Harriett said, "but you know you're far too old for that sort of thing."

"What sort of thing?"

"Invisible friends." Her voice took on a superior tone. "I gave mine up years ago."

"I'm not talking to an imaginary friend. But, if I were, it wouldn't be something you should tell anyone else. They wouldn't understand."

"It's okay, Jack, your secret's safe with me."

"Thanks, Harrie, you're a real pal."

"You're welcome." She smiled. "So, I know you're bummed we can't go home, but at least we have a proper quest now. We have to ask Amallayne what to do about this Secret Gift thingy and how to defeat Serza and Morrigan."

"Is that all?" Jack said sarcastically.

"Yes, that's all," Harriett confirmed without irony.

"You're the Waycaller, Jack. Wadget thinks that you're the only one Amallayne will listen to. Besides, we have to do something. We can't just wait for them to get us."

He knew she was right. He looked into her eyes and, though he saw fear there, she clearly wasn't as frightened as he thought she would be. She had already accepted that there was nowhere else for them to go, nothing else for them to do. He supposed he had to accept that too. If she could accept it, and so bravely, he thought he'd better be brave about it as well.

Besides, on top of everything else, he now had to find out more about this earwisp thing and, if he did have one in his ear, how to get rid of it. He certainly couldn't do that in Cairnbawn.

Harriett looked west toward the setting sun. "I wonder how long it will take for this mountain elf to get here?"

"Who knows?" Jack answered.

"I hope we don't have to spend another night here." She looked a little worried.

"I hope so too," said Miss Butters, coming up beside them. "Eugene knows what's lurking out there. And I am now officially self-digesting. I can feel my body dissolving away. Do I look drawn, Harriett, dear? Am I ... am I *thin?*" She said the word 'thin' the way others might say 'grotesque' or 'leprous', as if being thin were a shameful disease.

Harriett looked at her sympathetically and said, perfectly honestly, "No, you look pretty fat to me."

"Oh, you're such a dear, but I know you're just trying to be nice. You can tell me the truth. I am thinning, aren't I?"

"You're not self-digesting," Jack said grumpily. "There were probably enough calories in the sugary breakfast we ate to last us at least another couple of days. Just relax and stop panicking."

Miss Butters' nostrils flared and her lip trembled. "Panicking? Panicking! Why shouldn't I panic when all I've had to eat is a third of my emergency rations? No morning tea, no lunch, no afternoon tea! And there'll be no dinner or supper. As the Florid Spinsters rightly say: A meal every two hours and a halfling flowers! Well I can tell you I am certainly *not* flowering, I'm positively wilting! *Wilting!*"

# DANISELLE

Jack feared for Miss Butters' sanity. She was wild-eyed and had developed a nervous tick. Every few minutes she went through her pockets looking for any morsel of food she might have overlooked. Each time she came up empty handed, she moaned and complained of self-digestion all over again. As the last of the sun dipped below the horizon, her hysteria peaked and she began pulling out clumps of grass and eating it.

"Not so bad," she muttered as she chewed on a particularly long stalk of grass, "not so bad at all. Probably very nutritious. Yes, probably lots of minerals and such."

Jack was half glad for Miss Butters' hysteria. It kept his mind occupied. As the three of them sat by their little campfire watching the day wane, his mind constantly returned to Morrigan, Serza and this new threat, the earwisp that may have taken up home in his left ear.

He couldn't imagine how it got there. He knew one thing for certain: it wasn't there before the eclipse. He hadn't heard its voice before then. It probably came from the other side of the Veil around the same time as the skinwearer. That thought made Jack shudder. What if the earwisp was in league with Serza or Morrigan? His stomach churned, from anxiety rather than hunger this time.

Then he thought of something that made his stomach churn all the more. The earwisp mimicked his own voice. It was possible it had been there for years without him noticing, getting him to do things and making him think they were his own idea. If it hadn't started talking about stuff he couldn't have possibly known about, such as how to open the Way Between, he might never have noticed anything was wrong. He felt violated. This thing could have been controlling him for years and spying on his most private thoughts.

Out of fear and indignation he spontaneously jabbed his

236

finger into his left ear, trying to dig the thing out. *Get out of my head*, he silently snarled, half-hoping that there wasn't actually anything there. He jabbed his finger in as deep as he could. *Do you hear me*, he demanded internally, *get out of my ear!*

As he poked his finger in for one final deep lunge he heard, as clear as day, a loud and resonant hiss. This time it was not his own voice, but an eerie female voice. He ceased digging in his ear instantly. Something about the hiss compelled him to stop. He removed his finger, his whole body shaking with terror. It was true. He was possessed.

"What are you doing, Jack?" Harriett whispered by his side. He looked into her face but couldn't bring himself to tell her. She'd had enough bad news already. She didn't need to know that her brother was possessed by some nasty Tiqq sprite.

"Nothing." His voice trembled a little. "My ear was itchy, that's all."

Harriett looked at him quizzically but before she had a chance to interrogate him, Miss Butters doused the fire with her feet, grabbed them and dragged them behind a tussock of grass, all in one rapid movement.

Jack struggled free of her clutches. "What are you doing?"

"Quiet!" Miss Butters whispered. "I can see goblins."

Jack's heart immediately began to batter against his chest. He looked in the direction where Miss Butters was staring but, partially because the sky was now darkening, he couldn't see a thing.

"Where?" He closed his eyes a moment and opened them again, hoping to improve his vision.

"About three miles out." Miss Butters pointed with a trembling finger. "They are coming up out of a goblin hide. I don't know if they saw the fire."

"Goblin hide?" Harriett asked.

"A kind of burrow the goblins dig to sleep through the daylight. They can't survive for long in the sunshine," she explained.

"If they didn't see the fire we'll be alright, won't we?" Jack asked.

"The wind was blowing in their direction. They'll whiff us out for sure," Miss Butters whispered, all the hysteria suddenly gone from her voice.

Jack knew now that Miss Butters, though pampered and self-obsessed in her resting state, was very alert and level-headed when faced with danger. She had demonstrated that many times over the last couple of days. It was as if being out of her natural environment had caused her to draw on reserves that even she did not know were there.

"What should we do?" he asked.

"Stay put. If they start to come this way, I'll see them well before they see us and then, well, then my boy, Eugene spare us if we were not going to have to run for our lives."

"Can't you pray to Eugene for help?" asked Harriett, perhaps remembering that Amallayne had intervened on behalf of those threatened by Morrigan's armies.

"I am already, dear girl, but without the direct intercession of the Florid Spinsters I'm afraid my prayers are weak."

Jack thought perhaps Eugene was not as powerful as the halflings believed. In fact, he thought Eugene might even be a figment of the Florid Spinster's imagination.

"Will we be able to outrun them?" he asked, remembering Miss Butters' rolling jelly waddle.

"Goblins are fast but my eyesight will give us a good head start ... but, if you open a Way, Jack, then we'd be out of here instantly."

"No," Harriett said. "Wadget told us that might tip off Serza about where we are."

"It's either alert the dark prince or be eaten by goblins, my dear," Miss Butters said sternly.

"But what about the elf Wadget sent for us? If we go, won't we be harder to find?" Harriett's voice was sounding increasingly anxious.

"We won't need to be found if Jack opens a Way," Miss Butters said. "We'll go straight to Songarielle."

Jack didn't have much time to think this through before

Miss Butters shrieked

"They're coming! They've sniffed us out! Quickly, Jack, either open a Way or we have to run!"

Jack had never been very good at making decisions on the spot, but it seemed Miss Butters was right. The only way to escape the goblins was to open a Way. He opened his mouth to call out but was stopped by a ringing voice in his ear: *Silence!* The force of the voice made him feel totally winded, as if he'd been punched in the stomach. Now the voice was showing its true colours, Jack thought. Though it had helped him before, now it was preventing him from escaping these goblins.

As he desperately tried to force a sound out of his throat, it suddenly all made sense to him. The earwisp, the Tiqq sprite, helped him to cross the Veil to Anwynn, escaping the skinwearer sent by Serza. It also helped him escape Serza at Oakholme. The earwisp could not be in league with Serza. The dark prince had betrayed Morrigan and so it made sense that the earwisp was one of the Pale Mother's minions. But why did the Tiqq help him escape from Mog, Morrigan's fiercest disciple? He couldn't answer that question for sure but thought it might be because it wanted to deliver Jack to Morrigan itself. Yes, he was sure of it now. The earwisp was a servant of Morrigan and it wanted to deliver him to her.

He had to resist the earwisp, he had to. He pushed every last bit of air out of his lungs to try and form a word. But would it be enough to open a Way?

"Open ..." he stammered, "a W—"

*SILENCE!* The voice screamed in his ear. He nearly passed out from the force of it.

"Jack, Jack are you alright?" Harriett asked.

"Don't feel well ..." he managed to say.

"You chose a fine time to sicken on us, dear boy!" Miss Butters scolded. "Well, we'll just have to run. Come on, run!" She dragged them both up with a strength Jack wouldn't have thought she possessed and urged them onwards. After about ten minutes of running, Jack got his breath and strength back and tried to pick up the pace. He quickly realised that Miss Butters and Harriett couldn't run much faster anyway. Harriett's legs were too short and Miss Butters' bottom far too wide.

He glanced over his shoulder to see how far behind them the goblin hunting party was. As soon as he did, he wished he hadn't. He didn't have to squint to see them at all. They were less than a few hundred yards behind them and gaining fast. They were ugly beyond measure – the same grey, leathery skin, pointy ears and jagged teeth as the ones who'd attacked Oakholme. Their eyes weren't green though, they were sickly red orbs glowing in the dark. Their teeth shone red too, as if stained with luminous blood. Jack faced ahead and kept running.

"Their eyes and teeth are glowing red," he grunted as he ran alongside Miss Butters.

"Pitmouth beasts," Miss Butters panted, "from the Black Fortress above the Pale Mother's tomb. Their eyes and teeth glow red from the filthy cave fungus they eat when they don't have such as you and me for dinner."

Pitmouth goblins loyal to Morrigan, not Fellwood goblins whose eyes and teeth were glow-in-the-dark green. Jack's suspicions about the earwisp's motives must be right. He grabbed hold of Harriett and forced her to run faster still.

It wasn't long before it was obvious that the goblins were going to overtake them. Jack could hear their growls and jeers in the dark just behind them. He looked back over his shoulder again and saw that the goblin pack was less than twenty yards back. Miss Butters turned and looked as well and emitted a strangled, defeated cry. But then she did something totally unexpected. She stopped, faced the oncoming mob, put up her fists and adopted that same fighting position she'd taken in the face of Hob.

"Keep running," she shouted at the children. "I'll give these foul beasts something to whet their appetite. It'll take them till dawn to eat every morsel of my fine girth! Now run! Run!"

Jack hesitated for a moment but, seeing the goblins charging forward, bolted, dragging Harriett after him by the sleeve.

"No!" Harriett cried. "Miss Butters!" But Jack heaved her up over his shoulder and ran as fast as he could. Even carrying Harriett's weight he made a better pace than with her running under her own steam. He took one last fleeting glance back and saw the mob of goblins bearing down on Miss Butters, who had already started swinging her fists. He turned back around and gave it everything he had, running like he had never run before. He ran so hard his side ached with a stitch and his lungs burned, but he didn't stop. He pushed and pushed himself, giving it every last ounce of his strength. Otherwise, Miss Butters' sacrifice would be for nothing.

Harriett screamed. Jack stopped, looking behind them to see what had alarmed her. In the sky above where they last saw Miss Butters was a huge creature, a silver-winged dragon emitting shafts of blue flame. Its silver scales reflected every skerrick of light in the night sky. It was about the size of a bus. Jack stood still, gaping upwards, stunned into immobility.

The dragon blasted the ground with its flame and emitted a deafening roar. The night air was filled with the squeal of goblins in agony as they were instantly incinerated. Goblins, some aflame, dashed in every direction to escape the dragon. It was no use, the winged beast burned some of the fleeing goblins with blasts from its mouth and grabbed others with its claws and tore them apart. Then a tall figure in a long billowing coat leapt from the back of the dragon, landing on the ground in the midst of the goblin pack. In moves so impossibly fast they were practically a blur, the figure drew a sword and summarily chased down and beheaded one, then three, then eight goblins in a row. If any goblins were left alive they had bolted. The fierce figure sheathed its sword.

"Serza?" Jack thought out loud. Who else could it be? The dragon landed on the ground with a boom and folded its wings, emitting one last blast of flame in the direction of some decapitated goblins, apparently just for good measure. Jack turned to continue running but stopped when he heard a familiar voice.

"Jack, Harriett dear? Are you alright?" It was Miss Butters' voice. "It's alright, come back. The dragon-rider was sent by Wadget."

Jack hesitated. The dragon and its rider were sent by Wadget? He put Harriett down and they cautiously headed back toward Miss Butters' voice. When they saw her, amidst the smoke and burning goblin carcasses, they ran to her and she enfolded them in a tight embrace. Her cap was askew and her nose covered with soot. Apart from that she appeared unscathed.

"Thank goodness you're alright!" Harriett cried.

"I'm fine, dear, I only got one punch in before our friend here arrived."

"A strong blow it was too, halfling," the figure said in a melodic, feminine voice. "It knocked that fell creature out cold." A very beautiful elvish woman stepped forward into the light cast by the burning goblins. Like the mountain elves Aelf had shown them in the memory stone, she was tall and slender with caramel skin, dark brown hair and almond-shaped eyes.

"I do my best," Miss Butters said proudly.

"Indeed." The she-elf smiled approvingly. She wore a tight-fitting jacket, equally snug trousers and a long overcoat all of some kind of brown leather. Her feet were encased in heavy-duty boots that came up to the middle of her shins. Jack thought she was positively stunning. As soon as he thought this, Anarra's brooding face loomed in his mind and he felt, for no reason he could fathom, somewhat guilty. He shook the image and the feeling aside and gave the beautiful elf his full attention. Her eyes widened when they fell on Jack

"The light is surely within you," she said with awe. "You do glow as a star in the night." She bowed reverently to Jack. Jack shifted uneasily on his feet.

"Sorry, I what?"

The she-elf shook her head, indicating that Jack should ignore her comment. "May I introduce myself?" she asked formally. Jack, Harriett and Miss Butters all nodded. "I am Daniselle, of Songarielle. I come at the urging of Wadget and the Druid Council. I am to carry you to my home, or at least Jossa will carry you." She gestured toward the huge silver dragon. "In Songarielle you will be granted an audience with the Council, including Kashashem, the Head of the Order of Druids, herself."

"I'm Harriett, this is Miss Butters and this is my brother, Jack."

"Hel … hello," Jack stuttered, "nice to meet you."

"The pleasure is mine. We must not tarry long however, for there is more than one goblin hunting party in the Empty Lands, and they will be drawn to the smell of burning flesh."

"I don't doubt they will." Miss Butters licked her lips. "I'm so delirious from famishment myself that these burning goblins smell rather appetising."

"Miss Butters!" Harriett gasped in disgust.

"I can't help it, my dear, I'm mad with hunger! If we don't go right now I fear I shall start chewing on a goblin ear!"

"We shall go then. Have any of you ridden firewyrm before?" Daniselle gestured toward the dragon.

"Firewyrm?" Miss Butters stuttered. "Surely you jest? You can't expect us to ride up in the air on that, that thing!" At that the huge dragon looked at Miss Butters with distaste.

"How did you think we were to reach Songarielle?" Daniselle asked.

"Why, I don't know, I thought we'd walk."

"Firewyrms do not walk, except into their coops to sleep," Daniselle explained. "Besides," she continued, "the swiftest, and safest, way to Songarielle is on dragon-wing."

"I absolutely refuse!" Miss Butters shouted. "You will have to knock me out before I go up in the air on the back of that beast!"

"Very well." Daniselle's hand shot out and jabbed a finger

into the base of Miss Butters' neck, close to where it joined her shoulder. Miss Butters went instantly limp, her eyes rolling back into her head as she fell to the ground.

"Miss Butters!" Harriett bent to check that Dorothea was alright.

"You didn't have to knock her out!" Jack exclaimed, torn between defending Miss Butters and not wishing to offend the stunning she-elf.

"You heard her yourselves," Daniselle said coldly. "It was the only option. This way she will not worry over the journey. By the time she wakes, she will be safely back on solid ground, in Songarielle."

Jack looked down at the halfling's crumpled form. "But still, that was a bit rough."

"Halflings are a lot tougher than you think," Daniselle said, "especially this one."

"What do you mean?"

"Never mind." The she-elf stooped and swept Miss Butters up into her arms. "Come, we must alight."

Daniselle carried Miss Butters to the dragon and slung her over its back just behind its neck. The dragon, hissing at the weight, went to bite Miss Butters on the backside. "No, Jossa!" the elf commanded. "No biting!"

"She *is* very heavy," Harriett snapped, staying well clear of the dragon's head as she checked that Miss Butters was safely on its back. "But that's no reason to bite her! She's very brave, you know!"

"Indeed," Daniselle said. "She is at that. My apologies, youngling, Jossa meant no offence to your companion."

Daniselle mounted the dragon directly behind Miss Butters and extended her hand to help them get up behind her. Jack stepped forward eagerly, even though getting on the back of a dragon was not something he'd normally be eager to do. Daniselle's presence made it quite appealing. The she-elf took Harriett's hand instead, placing her directly behind her. "Hold tight to my waist," she said, before reaching out to Jack and helping him climb up behind Harriett. "You must hold onto Jossa with hands and legs, lest you fall to your death."

"You're very blunt, aren't you?" Harriett said. "Is that normal for elves?"

"Just ignore her," Jack said to Daniselle. "She doesn't mean to be rude."

"If you tell one more person to ignore me I'll push you right off this dragon!" Harriett jabbed Jack with an elbow.

"Go ahead," Jack snarled, "I dare you to try."

"Don't think I won't, Jack!" Harriett jabbed him again. "Don't think I won't push you right off!"

"If you do not still your tongues I shall push you both off," Daniselle said coldly, "and leave you to be a meal for goblins."

Jack believed that she probably would too, given how she'd dealt with Miss Butters, so he quietened down immediately, as did Harriett, after furtively poking her tongue out at him.

"Very well, let us alight." The she-elf made a trilling whistle that commanded Jossa to spread his wings and lurch into the sky. Jack's stomach lurched as well, hit by the sudden force of the firewyrm's rapid upswing, and so must have Harriett's for she squealed as they sped upwards.

They soared high up into the night sky, the dragon shooting miles into the air with every thrust of its wings. With another trilling whistle Daniselle directed the firewyrm northwards and they hurtled off at an unbelievable speed. Below them there was just blackness as the night was very dark, but Jack knew that they were passing over miles and miles of grassy plain, the Empty Lands that were once part of the Kingdom of Pix. It was bitterly cold and the wind brought tears to his eyes. Harriett was holding on to Daniselle's waist for dear life and Jack was squeezing so hard with his thighs, in order to cling to Jossa's back, that his legs started to ache.

What seemed like an hour or two passed. Just as Jack was thinking he would black out from the pain in his legs and the strain of holding on, he discerned huge shapes below them – the immensely tall, snowy peaks of the Craggy Mountains, shining in the moonlight. The mountain range stretched for miles to the north and south, all the way to the curved horizon. It was a breathtaking sight, even in the darkness, and for a moment Jack forgot about the pain in his thighs.

"Are you alright?" he shouted over the wind at Harriett.

"Yes," she answered back, but Jack could tell that she was very fatigued.

He tightened his grip on the dragon's back with his thighs, causing them to burn all the more, and put one arm around Harriett to make sure she didn't fall. With his arm around Harriett he could feel how thin she was, how small and vulnerable. He held on a little tighter, pressing her protectively against his chest. As he held her, his fingers brushed against the silk bracelet around her wrist, tied there by Anarra. He caressed the soft fibre, picturing Anarra's long, dark hair, imagining that it would feel much the same in his fingers.

A flash of light blinded him. He cringed away from it, closing his eyes until the light died down. When he opened his eyes again he was in an unfamiliar place, not on the back of Jossa the dragon anymore. Harriett, Miss Butters and the mountain elf Daniselle were gone. He was standing alone in a dark forest. Another flash of light caused him to flinch again. This time the light illuminated a group of figures. A half dozen Vellenor, their swords drawn, circled a single dark-haired elvish man. The light flashed again, causing the dark-haired elf to howl in pain.

Jack could see the source of the light now: a bald, blood-eyed Dread sorceress standing just outside the ring of fighters. Her hand raised, she directed another pulse of light at the dark-haired elf under siege by her Vellenor companions. The flash caused him to stagger a little but he continued to fend off his attackers with fierce thrusts of his sword. The Dread twitched her fingers again and another, much stronger flash of light burst forth, harmless to her and her companions but making the besieged elf drop to his knees. The troop of Vellenor surged forward as one, their swords plunging into the stricken elf's body. Jack averted his eyes, unable to watch. The sorceress shrieked with glee as her victim moaned his final word: *Anarra*.

Jack's eyes shot back to the fallen elf, lying face down on the forest floor, the arm holding the sword adorned with a silk bracelet. Anarra's father. This was how he'd died, outnumbered seven to one, the victim of a Dread sorceress. Tears welled up in Jack's eyes as he thought of Anarra, of what she'd lost, at how much pain she would suffer if she knew this was how it happened.

The Dark Elves sheathed their swords and kneeled before the Dread sorceress, their white-haired heads bowed. She dipped her head to them, showing her approval for their vicious work, and made eye contact with each one. Her eyes were hateful, lightless, the colour of coagulated blood. Jack didn't know how the Vellenor could stand that gaze; it made him want to flee.

"My Lady, Dread Hect," one of the Vellenor said, still breathless from exertion. "What will you have us do now? What other task does the Pale Mother require of us?"

"Our Pale Mother's desires are limitless, ever unsatisfied," the sorceress purred. "Of you, for now, she demands just this: travel to the edge of the Halfling Dells. Do not enter the dells, for they are watched. One of the Dread abides there secretly and will seek you out. Deliver to the Dread this message: 'Now is the time. The father is dead. Take the daughter.'"

"Now is the time. The father is dead. Take the daughter." The breathless Vellenor repeated the message as though it were a sacred mantra.

Jack reeled. Aelf and Wadget's suspicions were correct, there was a sorcerer in the Halfling Dells. Not just any sorcerer but a Dread in league with this sorceress, this Hect. Anarra's father's death was not a random act. It was planned by the Dread under Morrigan's orders, to make it easier for

Anarra to be kidnapped. How did the half-elvish girl fit into all this? Why was Morrigan after Anarra? Why did she want her captured rather than killed? Morrigan, despite being sealed in her prison behind Darkgate, seemed able to reach out and hurt whoever she wanted, whenever she wanted. How could Jack ever withstand her?

Jack's head ached with the weight of it all. He rubbed his forehead to ease the tightness there, then rubbed his eyes. When he took his hands away he was no longer in the forest but in a dark, cavernous place. The shock of it took his breath away. A hand touched his shoulder and he lurched away, his heart instantly kicking into a thunderous beat. He spun around to see Morrigan standing right behind him. The reek of death struck him and he clenched his stomach to avoid throwing up. Morrigan smiled at him, as though it were perfectly normal for Jack to find himself in this wretched place with her.

"Where am I?" Jack scanned the reeking darkness.

"You are not really here, my child. Not fully here, anyway. But this is Uffern, my home, my prison." Morrigan's blackened lips cracked a little as she spoke. Jack couldn't take his eyes away from them, his gaze frozen with horror.

"Why, why did you bring me here?"

"I didn't, my child. Your own power brings you here, Waycaller."

That was it then; she knew he was the Waycaller and not Harriett. Even there with Morrigan so close he couldn't help but feel relieved to know that Morrigan was not focussed on his sister, only on him.

"Your mind ever dwells on me, Jack, and because you cannot control yourself, you find yourself by my side, in spirit at least." She smiled more broadly, her blackened lips forming a terrible leer.

"But, how ... Darkgate ..."

"The gate seals me here. But it has no power over you, my child. In fact, quite the opposite. You are special. That is why I bless you with my presence."

"No, no, you want me dead. You want me dead so that you can break free."

"Silence!" Morrigan's shriek echoed throughout the cavern, filling Jack's ears with dozens of versions of her voice. "Do not presume to tell me of my own wants. What I want, my child, is for you to come here to me in the flesh. I can show you pleasures beyond your wildest imaginings. I can show you how to use and control your powers. I can make you even more powerful than you are now, my child. I can give you the world. I can give you *both* worlds. Come to me, come to me in the flesh. And bring your little sister too. Come!"

"No." It took every inch of Jack's strength to refuse her. Though he knew she could not fully control him, Amallayne and Danuss had stripped her of that power, her voice was still difficult to resist.

"I said come to me!" The cavern shook with her scream, her breath filling it with the stench of carrion.

"No!" He shouted it as loud as he could. At the same time he thought of Harriett and Miss Butters, of Daniselle and Jossa, of those silver dragon-wings beating in the dark sky. A shadow passed over him, which for a second he thought was Morrigan coming closer. When he looked up he saw not the dark hollows of a cavern but a vast starry sky, and the shadow was Jossa's mighty wing.

The vision had gone, dissolved into the night. Jack teetered on Jossa's back, his head swimming. He clenched his thighs at the last minute, bearing down on the dragon's scaly hide, just barely stopping himself from toppling off and dragging Harriett with him. He still had one arm around his sister, his fingers still holding Anarra's bracelet. He looked down, his vision still spinning, and tried to steady himself by focussing on the dark ground hundreds of feet below.

Twenty minutes that felt like twenty hours later, his vision had cleared, but now he was certain he couldn't hold on any longer. Not only were his thighs dead tired but the arm he was using to hang on to Harriett was numb as well. He would have to shout to Daniselle that he needed rest. He opened his mouth to call out but closed it again when he saw twinkling lights ahead. The lights peppered an oval-shaped plateau high among the peaks of the mountains. As they got closer, Jack saw that it was a kind of basin nestled between the uppermost reach of a circle of immense peaks, one of which towered twice as high as the others, its white slopes glistening like quartz in the moonlight.

In the centre of the plateau Jack made out structures, streets, houses and bigger buildings. It was a large and very beautiful town, filled with light, all encircled by a wall of shining white stone. At the centre of the town was a square overlooked by two huge buildings. One of the buildings was a complex of square structures with a series of courtyards. The other was shaped unlike anything else in the citadel, resembling a huge beehive made with natural stone.

"That building," Daniselle shouted over the wind indicating the beehive structure, "is the House of Amallayne, elf-friend and protector. The other is the palace of the Songarielle Senate with its courtyard gardens. It also houses the Council Chambers of the Order of Druids."

As they came nearer to the citadel, the dragon pitched downwards and headed straight for the lights. They all lurched forward but managed to hang on.

Jack tightened his grip on his sister. "It won't be long now, Harrie. Just hang on for a little longer." He needed the encouragement as much as she did, his legs were now totally numb. The ground rushed toward them and Jack feared the dragon was out of control; that they would crash into the earth and be killed. Just as it seemed too late, Jossa beat his wings downwards to slow them almost to a stop. They landed in an open area, near large stone buildings that looked a bit like elongated barns. A burst of blue flame from within one of these buildings told Jack that these were the firewyrm coops. There must have been at least a hundred of them. When the dragon's feet touched the ground there was a muffled boom and a powerful jolt that caused Harriett and

Jack, weakened by their journey, to topple off. They landed on their backs, gasping, exhausted, bruised, but firmly on the ground at last.

Daniselle gracefully slid off her mount and took Miss Butters into her arms, who snuggled into the elf's coat and snored lightly. The she-elf stood over Jack and Harriett, clearly waiting for them to get back onto their feet. They got up, staggering around a bit, not having got their land legs back yet. Jack's thighs were burning too much for him to remain standing. He fell back down onto his backside. He was so thoroughly exhausted he felt he could go to sleep right there on the ground. He looked up at Harriett and saw that, in just the few seconds since she stood up, her eyelids had started to droop. She was literally falling asleep on her feet. Jack was so tired he couldn't raise the energy to rouse her. The flight on Jossa's back and the encounter with Morrigan had drained him of every bit of energy he had.

"You flew well," Daniselle said, apparently by way of a compliment, "the dismount aside." She extended her arm in a very formal manner, encouraging them to take in the surrounding buildings which, in his fatigued state, appeared to Jack like a hazy mirage. "The pleasure falls upon me," she intoned solemnly, "to welcome you to the citadel of Songarielle, my home, and home to all mountain elves." After that, Jack couldn't fight the fatigue any longer. He slipped sideways and passed out.

Adrift in the dark, as if bobbing on a gentle wave, Jack couldn't push his eyelids open to see how he was being carried along. His whole body, his bones and even his mind, ached with exhaustion. The bobbing motion had only brought him part of the way out of sleep. Was he on the dragon's back again, hurtling through the air? No, this motion was too gentle, like floating on his back in a slow-moving stream. And what was that sound? Footsteps on cobblestones, and something else ... the thudding of a muffled drum? No, no, a heartbeat. A beating heart and echoing footsteps.

He listened a long while, his whole world nothing but the heartbeat and the footsteps in the dark. The sound and the motion together took Jack back to his childhood – to a memory of being carried to bed by his father after falling asleep on the rug in front of the fireplace. He had snuggled into his father's chest, the even thump thump of his father's heart like a percussive lullaby. He'd taken comfort in that sound, and in the feeling of his father's arms around him. Forgetting that he wasn't a little boy anymore, Jack took comfort in those sensations now; in the firm chest under his cheek, in the song of a muscular heart, in the strong arms that bore him along in the darkness.

He felt full unconsciousness coming for him again, but an anxious feeling rose up out of the darkness and held it at bay. Whose heartbeat was it? Who was carrying him? Where was he being taken? He struggled to wake further, but it was no good, fatigue held him in a crushing grip. As the darkness of sleep overwhelmed him once more, he hoped that the arms around him belonged to someone as strong and good as they felt.

A mocking giggle sounded in his ear, not his own voice this time, some other voice, tiny and tinny. He rubbed at it without waking, trying to chase the voice away. It just giggled all the more and said, *Sleep, Jack, go to sleep.* Obediently, he turned his face into that warm body until its strong heartbeat sang him into a deep slumber.

# PART 4: NIGHT OF FALLING LEAVES

# BELOVED OF THE BRIGHT CHILD

*Tessarelle, forest home of the woodland elves*

Ellisenn touched the rocky bottom of the pond just moments after diving in. Looking up to the surface far above, shimmering with light and reflecting the green leaves of the forest canopy, he started to count. He had no reason to test himself like this, holding his breath as long as he could, other than his own amusement. This constant testing was a not uncommon trait among woodland elves, he knew, because the Lady Kashashem had commented on it often. Kashashem tolerated this trait in him, even found it amusing, but she had asked him more than once what the point of it was. Ellisenn had never been able to answer her. It was just something he was driven to do, to push himself and discover the depths of his strength and endurance.

A school of small silver fish darted through a beam of sunlight that penetrated into the heart of the pond. Their scales shone with the light a moment before going dark again as they moved down into the green gloom of the deeper water. Ellisenn wished he could swim here every morning, but lately he enjoyed the Sacred Pools of Tessarelle only occasionally. His life had taken an unexpected turn the day, two years ago, when Kashashem had visited his mother, telling her that her sixteen year old son, and only child, was destined to be a magic-wielder, a druid. Few elves joined the Order of Druids. Amongst the woodland elves it was rare indeed. His mother was reluctant at first, but finally agreed to let him go. Since then, he had lived at the citadel of Songarielle in the high mountains, far away from his home in the Great North Wood. His days were now spent training in druidry, under Kashashem herself, not frolicking in pools.

A pain in his lungs forced him upwards, shooting to the surface with just a few kicks. He broke the surface and took a breath, smiling, pleased that despite so long out of the water he was still a strong swimmer. All the sounds of the forest and the pool reached his elvish ears at once – the cascading rush of the waterfall that fed the pool, the rustle of leaves under a light breeze, the song of birds, the laughter of children splashing in the shallows. He swam to the edge of the pool and climbed the rough-hewn steps out of the water, the breeze triggering goose-pimples all over his naked body. His skin also tingled because he felt many eyes on him.

A soft titter alerted him to a group of equally naked she-elves standing waist deep in the water at the other end of the pool. He glanced at them long enough to see that their eyes were all on his bare back, except for one brazen girl whose eyes, bright green with heat, lingered on his rear end. He flushed and looked away, increasing his stride to the mossy bench where he'd left his clothes.

Reaching the bench, he glanced back again. The girls' eyes were still on him, their wet hair and the soft skin of their breasts glistening like pale flowers heavy with dew. Flushing even more, he grabbed his clothes and sat on the bench to let the sun dry his skin. As he shook out his wet hair, a familiar voice sounded behind him.

"Naked again, Ellisenn? Away from Songarielle only a week and you've already abandoned your clothes."

He jumped up to see Kashashem approaching, a warm smile playing on her lips. "My Lady." He bowed. "What brings you all the way to Tessarelle?"

"You do, Ellisenn."

She embraced him gingerly, partly because he was still wet but partly, he was sure, because of his nakedness. As one of the sea elves of Merielle her sense of modesty was much more acute than his.

"I'm sorry to follow you here, Ellisenn, but I need to speak to you."

"My Lady?" He gestured for her to sit with him on the bench.

"Are you not going to dress?"

"I am still wet, my Lady."

She avoided looking at his body, casting her eyes out over the pool instead. When she spotted the huddle of naked she-elves, whose eyes were unashamedly all over Ellisenn's body, her gaze went upwards to the trees.

"Please, Ellisenn, before I tell you why I have come here, put on your breeches at least. Unlike those girls out there, I have no interest in your muscles or in seeing your manhood."

"And for that, my Lady, I am most thankful." He stood and pulled on his breeches. "I am weary of the attention paid of late to my … my person."

"Have you rejected them all then?"

"Yes. The mother of each of those girls, and quite a number more, have called on my own mother this last week to seek my agreement to a coupling. If I'd known my coming of age would be so wearisome I would have stayed in Songarielle and ignored it."

"Have they been so persistent?" She glanced back at the group of girls, then into Ellisenn's green eyes.

"Yes, quite persistent. Most of them are from houses that would greatly benefit from a union with my own."

"Is that why you have rejected them, because you suspect they hunger after status rather than desire you for yourself?"

"Yes, that, and … other things."

"Whatever those other things are, they, and your forest maidens there, will have to wait." She hesitated, looking into the reflective waters of the pool rather than into his face. Ellisenn had never seen Kashashem so reluctant to speak before.

"What is it, my Lady?"

"Since you left Songarielle much has happened, most of it dire, so dire that, though you are only young, the Council must ask you to perform a very dangerous task."

"I will do anything for the Order, for you, my Lady."

"I told the Council as much, though I argued against sending you at all. You are too young, barely trained, and the sole child of an ancient and great house, the greatest house of

Tessarelle. To lose one such as you is unthinkable, to your people, to your mother and to me."

Ellisenn looked into her eyes, seeing in their rich yellow much worry and ... fear? What could frighten Kashashem so, with all her power?

"What has happened, my Lady?"

"The Way Between, the Veil, has been breached and an attempt made on the otherworld Waycaller's life."

Ellisenn's breath caught in his throat. As Kashashem's closest pupil he knew more about the Veil than most. He had thought such a thing impossible.

"How was this done, my Lady?"

"There is only one who is powerful enough to do such a thing: the Lord of Chaos. Or one who has acquired Thullu's Gift. Master Wadget suspects the latter to be the case."

At the mention of Thullu's name, Ellisenn's heart stopped a moment, his lungs contracting with fear. The Lord of Chaos alone inspired such anxiety among the elves, because they understood the havoc that limitless power could wreak. If it was true, if Thullu's Gift had been found ...

"We have one advantage in this," Kashashem said. "The breach was foreseen by the Seeress Alva. She foretold that the Veil would be breached and that the otherworld Waycaller, a human boy, would cross the Way Between, fleeing from a skinwearer. As soon as Alva warned the Council, Aelf Ethelwulf went to Bright to protect the boy from any further threat. He took the Waycaller to Master Wadget."

Ellisenn had many questions. He didn't know which to voice first. He thought a while then asked: "Has there been a male Waycaller before?"

"Not for a very long time, thousands of years befor you were born. We do not know if it will make a difference, if his powers will be different. We will have to wait and see. There is much we do not know, which brings me to you."

"What does the Council seek of me, my Lady?"

"Much. Too much. Master Wadget has sent us more dire news. Last night a party of Fellwood goblins attacked

Oakholme. They were led by Prince Serza himself, in pursuit of the Waycaller."

"Serza is no match for Master Wadget. Surely he is no longer alive?"

"He yet lives. Serza has grown strong in dark sorcery, so strong that he nearly breached Oakholme's defences."

Ellisenn hissed, unable to control himself.

"How? By what dark means does Serza grow so strong?"

"Wadget believes it is he who found the Secret Gift and used it to breach the Veil. If this is proved true, we face a terrible, terrible threat. We must know for certain the source of Serza's new-found strength and, most importantly, what his intentions are. We must know what he will do next, otherwise we cannot defend against it."

"Which brings you to me."

"You see our plan?"

"Yes. You wish me to journey to Vellenhive, to visit my secret friend, to see if she knows anything of Prince's Serza's intentions." His heart thudded against his bare chest. He was going to see her again. That filled him with both excitement and dread.

"You are the only one who can do this, Ellisenn. No-one else has any contact with the Vellenor, and certainly not with a member of the Prince's royal court, so close to Serza himself."

"She is not likely to be pleased to see me. She may kill me on sight, or worse, hand me over to the Dread."

"We know it is dangerous. If you choose not to go, the Council will understand. But rumour has it she still pines over you, and your abilities are not small. You can protect yourself. I will not say I am not afraid for you, but I have confidence in your skills. You are a great magic-wielder, Ellisenn, very great."

"I will leave for Fellwood Forest as soon as I can." Ellisenn stood, as if to emphasise his point. He noticed his heart thumping again, belying his outer calm.

"Your courage honours you, Ellisenn." Kashashem stood

as well, sighing heavily, her face showing even more worry. Then she smiled. "It might be wise to finish getting dressed before you depart. Fellwood is a cold place."

"Yes, my Lady." He pulled his shirt over his head and slipped on his jacket. "Where will you go now, Lady Kashashem?"

"I will open a Way from the stone circle here to the standing stones at Merielle, and then travel overland with our king and his retinue back to Songarielle."

"The Sovereign travels to Songarielle?"

"Yes, there is much about recent events to worry King Dhudhannan. The Sovereign seeks the advice of the Druid Council before he takes action."

"King Dhudhannan will act well and for the good," Ellisenn said, echoing an old elvish saying. "Ever has it been so."

"Well said, Ellisenn, and may your own actions bring you safely back to Songarielle. Be most, most careful."

"I will."

"On your return, come with haste to the council chambers to share with me anything you discover."

"Yes, my Lady, of course."

"Travel well, Ellisenn, travel well."

The dragon soared low over the treetops of Fellwood Forest, its deep blue scales camouflaging it against the twilight sky. The dragon's rider, Tellan, signalled to his passenger that they were nearing their destination. Ellisenn nodded to Tellan that he understood, smirking at the serious look on the handsome mountain elf's face. Unlike Ellisenn's own kin, the people of the North Wood, the elves of Songarielle found even a nightime flight on a dragon a sombre thing. Ellisenn stood, found his balance and walked carefully along the dragon's spine to the base of its tail. He needed to be clear of its wings and talons for the jump. As soon as the landmark they were aiming for came into view, a small clearing overlooked by a lightning-struck oak tree, the dragon swooped down to just above the tree tops. Ellisenn took a deep breath and leapt off the dragon's back, somersaulting through the forest canopy to the ground.

He landed on his feet in a crouching position, his spine thrumming with the impact. After getting his bearing, he dashed into the shadow of the trees at a full run. He didn't stop running until, an hour or more later, he came to the standing stone that marked the northernmost boundary of Vellenhive, the hidden fortress of the Dark Elves. The stone, about twelve feet tall and covered in the wicked-looking glyphs of the Vellenor language, was shaped like a flint knife, its sharp edge scratching at the sky. A narrow trail began just beyond the stone, disappearing into the gloomy tangle of trees with their moss-heavy boughs and knotted roots. From here, stealth would be needed to avoid capture. He crossed the boundary and jogged quietly into this deeper part of the forest.

He had travelled this way only once before; even so the path was etched clearly in his mind. That time he had been seeking the same person he sought now. He had been just fifteen years old then and had not yet learned any magic. He was amazed he hadn't been captured and killed, but luck was on his side on that journey. On this one he would rely on skill, not that a little luck wouldn't be welcome this time as well.

He jogged parallel to the trail, from tree shadow to tree shadow, keeping close enough to the path that he didn't lose his way but always far enough from it to avoid running into any Vellenor patrols. Three times Ellisenn had to take cover behind trees or boulders as long columns of Vellenor warriors or troops of Fellwood goblins marched northwards, in the opposite direction to him. These were not normal patrols, which usually numbered just a dozen or so. Thousands of the Dark Ones, all heavily armed, were moving towards the border with Pix. Ellisenn hoped the Pixish were ready for war, because it was coming to them, whether they were ready or not. This news, when he delivered it, would surely deepen Kashashem's worry.

The moon had reached its zenith in the sky before he saw the dark outline of Vellenhive, just barely visible through gaps in the trees – a huge dome-like shape of solid rock. Legend had it that this massive rock fell to earth from the sky at the beginning of days. Long, long ago, the Dark Elves dug and tunnelled into the stone to such a degree that it was now a honeycomb of caverns and passages. Closer to the top of the dome were streets and squares open to the sky, and palaces so intricately carved that they could have been cut from paper. The fortress walls enclosing the city were shaped out of the solid, unscaleable stone, polished to a gleaming black. When Ellisenn had first seen the home of the Vellenor, on that last journey, he'd been surprised by the lack of light. There were no lamps or candles at all, just the eerie luminescence of the moss that hung everywhere in the trees. The Vellenor had clearly not changed in their habits in the intervening years, for the fortress was just as dark as ever.

He left the trail behind him as he veered to the right, heading for an ancient stormwater drain, long forgotten by the inhabitants. Overgrown by vines and weeds, its iron grate had rusted to dust a thousand years ago. It was the only unguarded way into Vellenhive. He had entered the fortress that way last time. He would never have found it himself, it was too well hidden. His secret friend, the one he sought out now, had told him its location. More curious than normal for one of the Vellenor, she'd found it and used it to sneak out of the fortress as a child. For years she used it to explore the forest, until one night she got lost. After wandering for days, she ended up so far from home that she was found by a troop of warriors from Tessarelle who were pursuing a goblin raiding party on the edge of Fellwood Forest. Ellisenn knew how unlucky that was, that she should be captured by the first Bright Elves to enter her people's forest in a thousand years. She had fumed about it often over the two years she lived as a hostage in Ellisenn's own house, until her father agreed to the conditions of her return.

The grate was even more overgrown than when last he used it. It took him so long to find it he was sure he was going to be seen by guards patrolling high up on the walls. He worked as quickly and silently as he could, cutting away the thorny undergrowth until there was room enough for him to crawl through the grate. The drain was thankfully dry, as it had been last time, which made Ellisenn wonder if it no longer functioned as a drain, if its connection to the gutters of Vellenhive had been sealed off centuries ago.

Ellisenn followed the intricate pattern of twists and turns whispered to him by his secret friend. They'd had many rambling conversations during her time as a hostage in his home. He'd never treated her as a prisoner and she, well, she didn't have it in her to behave like anything but what she was, a high-ranking member of the royal court of Fellwood. She'd told him about this hidden way into the fortress to prove how adventurous she was. He was sure she hadn't expected him to remember it, and never intended for him to use the information to sneak into Vellenhive. She'd certainly been shocked when he did just that. He smirked in the darkness of the tunnel, remembering the look of surprise on her face when he'd stepped out of the shadows in her bedroom. The smirk vanished when he remembered how badly that visit had gone, how it'd ended with her threatening him with imprisonment, torture and worse.

"She's such a bad host," Ellisenn grumbled to himself, thinking he'd better stay close to a window this time in case she decided to make good on her threats. He made his final turn and crept quietly along the next passage, having to stoop a little as the drains were narrower here. He came to the overhead grate he was looking for and pressed gently upwards to make sure it was still loose. It moved easily. So she hadn't had it sealed in place? Perhaps she still used it? Or perhaps she hoped he would use it again one day?

He waited and listened, making sure no-one was nearby,

before pushing the grate aside and climbing up out of the drain into an arched passageway. He gently slid the grate back into place and made a dash for the shadows of the nearest wall. He kept to the shadows as he sped through the halls, passages and stairwells that led to his destination. The moon had travelled far when Ellisenn finally emerged into a small courtyard. He crept along the nearest wall to the first arched window. The window was unlocked so he opened it and slipped inside. The first room he crept through was lit somewhat by moonlight seeping in from the courtyard. The room beyond that was dark, but he could sense it was empty. He waited in the doorway until his eyes adjusted. Furnished with an oval-shaped divan in the centre and a series of low cushions around the walls, he knew this room's purpose had not changed. It was where she received visitors, who sat on the low cushions as she lorded it over them from the divan. He half-snorted at the pretentiousness of it. In Tessarelle such pomposity would be mocked. Here in Vellenhive it was the norm. He crossed this room and passed through another door concealed behind curtains. This next room was darker still, he could only just make out the bed against the far wall. The bed was empty. Where was she? He stared into the blackness of the room, looking for some sign to tell him if this room was still hers, and when she'd last been there. His search of the room revealed the tip of an overturned slipper poking out from beneath the bed. No, not an overturned slipper, a slippered foot. As he stared at it, the foot twitched under the bed and out of view.

"You are terrible at hiding," Ellisenn said. "Is it any wonder you were so easily taken hostage?"

An uncertain voice came from beneath the bed. "Ellisenn? Ellisenn, is that you?"

"It is, Sarritt."

A silver-haired head poked out from under the bed. Sarritt's dark pink eyes stared at him uncomprehendingly a moment before she slithered out and stood up. She had not changed. Her waist-length silver hair still shone like the moon itself, her skin, paler than the white nightdress she wore, still looked as soft as silk, her pale pink lips were just as full.

"Is it really you?" she whispered.

Ellisenn smiled despite himself. She may have threatened him with torture the last time they met, but he was still very fond of her.

"It is, Sarritt. What horrors were you expecting to visit your bedchamber in the dead of night that you dragged yourself under there?"

"No horror greater than you, woodland elf. What are you doing here? Answer quickly before I call the guards."

"I have come to speak with you, as I did before."

"But why, Ellisenn? Why do you torture me?"

"Me, torture you? Last time I was here you threatened to string my intestines up in a Banewood tree."

"That is nothing compared to what you are doing to me. Can you not understand that to see you pains me? Just to hear your voice cuts me deep, to smell the scent of your hair sets a fire burning in my lungs."

"Melodramatic as always, Sarritt—"

"Please, Ellisenn," she interrupted desperately, "please just go, and never come back."

"What have I done to hurt you so?"

"You made me love you and then you rejected me."

"I have neither rejected you nor made you do anything, Sarritt. All I have done is be your friend."

"*Friend.*" She practically growled the word. "What use have I for friends? I am Sarritt, Princess of Fellwood, Daughter of Jah-Setis, Granddaughter of Holy Sar-Mokna!"

"And sister of Serza."

"Ah, I see. You are *not* here to speak with me because we are *friends*, as you claimed the last time you crawled through the sewers to my bedchamber like a *filthy rat*, but to question me about my brother! Admit it, Ellisenn, so that I can call the guards and finally have your innards on a pike as I have yearned for so long!"

"I will not lie to you, Sarritt. You are like a sister to me—"

"*Sister!* I was a hostage in your mother's house for two years. That does not make us kin!"

"I know it was hard for you—"

"Hard! It was *humiliating!*"

"Stop interrupting me, please, Sarritt. Your capture was not my doing. Negotiations for your return began the day you arrived in Tessarelle, mediated by the Druid Order—"

"Druids! Vile, meddling, vindictive, godless weasels!"

"Please, Sarritt, listen to me. I knew nothing about any of it then, and I still don't know why it took so long for your father to agree to the terms of your release. I haven't dared ask Kashashem."

Sarritt hissed and stepped back. The mere mention of the most powerful druid of all setting her pink eyes alight with hate.

"Do not mention that name in my home, ever. Not ever."

"Look, Sarritt, I wouldn't have come here unless it was important—"

"Important to who, the druids?" Her pretty face was transformed by an ugly sneer.

"Will you please stop interrupting me! Yes, important to the druids. I am a druid now—"

"You are just a boy, a *pretty*, blond one, but just a boy all the same."

He flinched at that, but hid his hurt. In the past, when Sarritt was in one of her rages, and they were not rare, he had always got through to her by calling her bluff. "So you will not help me, Sarritt? Shall I just go then and never return, just as you've asked?"

"You might as well," she said quietly. "To help you is to betray myself, to commit treason against my brother. I would never be safe here again if I helped you, though I have not been safe here for a long time." She glanced at her hiding place under the bed.

"Don't tell me you *always* sleep under the bed? Are you in danger here?"

"My brother and I are not as close as we once were."

"Are you afraid he will hurt you?"

"Hurt me? Oh no, I am not afraid of being hurt. But killed, that scares me a little."

"Would Prince Serza kill his own sister?"

"Oh yes," she said, without a second's pause. "I believe it is just a matter of time."

"Why? Why would he do that?"

"To explain that, I must tell you things I have told no other." She paused, looking into Ellisenn's face as if reminding herself how close they'd been, how much she'd trusted him in the past. "My brother has long chafed under Morrigan's yoke. Ever since he was a boy he held a secret hope that one day the Vellenor would be free from the Pale Mother's limitless hunger, her unquenchable desires. It is a hope that he and I shared."

She looked at Ellisenn, knowing, he supposed, how shocking he would find that statement. The Royal House of Fellwood turning against the Pale Mother! He couldn't disguise his surprise. He whistled and leant against the wall.

"For years my brother and I sought a way to rid ourselves of the oppression of the Dread sorcerers, to crawl out from under the Pale Mother's fist. We hoped to do it together, but we argued and parted ways some time ago. My brother sought to free our people by making himself more powerful, powerful enough to defy the Pale Mother, to challenge the Faeden themselves. I sought another way, the most ancient way of my people."

At first Ellisenn didn't know what she meant by that, 'the most ancient way', then, slowly, it dawned on him. "But, Sarritt, that way is lost."

"Nothing is ever lost forever, Ellisenn."

He took her to mean not only her hope that the Vellenor might be free of Morrigan, but also a more personal hope – her hope that he might one day return her love.

"But the Bright Child's power is lost to the world," he said. "The effigy is destroyed, smashed and the pieces taken to Bonemound."

"That is true. The effigy was smashed by the Dread and the remains taken to their temple at Bonemound, where it was ground into dust, mostly."

"Mostly?"

"One small piece remains intact." She reached down the front of her nightdress and drew out a long chain; at the end of that chain hung a small black shape – a little ear, slender and pointed like that of an elvish child. About the size of a three year old's ear. Made of meteorite, it had about it a presence, a sense of being alive and listening. Ellisenn blinked and bowed his head without thinking, filled with an automatic reverence.

"The Bright Child's ear?" he asked, staring at the perfectly formed ear Sarritt held in her hands.

"Yes, this is the only surviving piece of the effigy of the Bright Child gifted to the Vellenor by the Child himself in the beginning of days. Through it the Bright Child's power still flows, surely you can feel it?"

He nodded, unable to speak. Sarritt was right, the little ear emanated so much power he could feel it gently pushing against his skin. "Where, how?"

"I found it at Bonemound and took it, right under Dread Hect's nose."

"If the Dread discover the theft, they will—"

"Tear me to pieces, yes."

"Why then? Why take such a risk?"

Sarritt's eyes filled with tears before she answered. "At first, I only sought to weaken the Pale Mother's hold over my people, but now, now my heart aches with love for the Bright Child. I have dedicated myself to him. I am his now, until the end of my days. I am his one and only beloved. My most secret dream is to wrest my people from the Pale Mother and the Dread sorcerers and return them to worship of the Bright Child."

"Does your brother know this?"

"Not yet, but I cannot hide it from him for long. He is not what he was. He grows strong in dark sorcery and is driven mad by it."

"How has he become so powerful?" He held his breath, wondering if she would answer him.

She looked him over, clearly weighing up if she should tell him more. She shrugged, apparently deciding she might as well after what she had already revealed.

"Serza no longer wishes only to overthrow the Dread and free the Vellenor from Morrigan's grip. He plans to be Lord over all of the Dark Ones, and then over all of Anwynn. To do so he must ensure that Morrigan never leaves Uffern. He would destroy the Pale Mother if he could, but he is not yet that powerful and I hope he never will be."

"He started on this path nine or so years ago when his spies came to him with a strange tale: a mysterious sorceress had come to their attention. This sorceress was consumed with a single obsession − to find the one thing that would release Morrigan from her prison: Thullu's Secret Gift. The sorceress journeyed far in her search, to places un-walked for millennia, until she finally found the thing she sought. The spies could not tell my brother if she found the gift on her own, or if the Lord of Chaos led her to it. The sorceress used Thullu's Gift to send an assassin across the Veil to extinguish the line of otherworld Waycallers, in an attempt to break the power of the Veil once and for all and set the Queen of Doom free. The assassin failed, and somehow the Secret Gift passed to Mog. The spies were not sure how. Mog, hating any source of power other than Morrigan, hid Thullu's Gift somewhere in her house and never used it. From the moment Serza heard that tale and realised the power of Thullu's Gift would help him cast off the control of the Dread, he plotted to steal it for himself. I don't know how he did it, but did it he did. He took the Word from Mog two days ago and used it to breach the Veil again and send a skinwearer across to kidnap the human Waycaller. Serza wants the Waycaller alive, you see, to bend the power of the Waycaller to his own advantage, to ensure that Morrigan is never released. I think he also hopes the power of the Waycaller might help him destroy Morrigan once and for all. Why he thinks that I do not know. He does not share his thoughts with me any longer. He is quite mad now."

Stunned, Ellisenn reeled with everything Sarritt had told him. Things were a lot more serious than he realised, perhaps more serious than even the Druid Council knew. He must take all this information straight back to Kashashem.

"Thank you for telling me all this, Sarritt," he said once he found his voice.

"It pains me to betray my brother, but as he will surely kill me once he learns of my devotion to the Bright Child, I suppose it is only fair." She smiled weakly and Ellisenn's heart ached for her.

"Come with me, come with me to Songarielle. Serza will never be able to reach you there, you will be safe."

"No. I could never live in that place. Vellenhive is my home. It is sacred, plucked from the stars and given to my people by the Bright Child himself. I will not leave it willingly."

"Please, I could not bear it if you were harmed, or if you were—"

"Now who's being melodramatic? No, I will not waver. I am staying here. Go now, Ellisenn, and do not come back again. Your pretty face is too much for *me* to bear." She smiled, then turned her back on him. "Please go, please."

Ellisenn reached the clearing with the lightning-struck oak just on midnight, as he'd arranged with Tellan. He climbed the oak quickly, despite aching thigh muscles from having run without stopping all the way from Vellenhive. He found a strong bough close to the top of the tree and waited. As the minutes passed he went over everything Sarritt had said about her brother. Combined with the masses of warriors he'd witnessed moving north, it all boded ill: for the Kingdom of Pix, for Elvinidd and his own people and for all of Anwynn.

Even so, he didn't feel despair. His confidence in the ability of Kashashem and the Order of Druids to deal with Serza, no matter how strong he'd grown, was great. He also had no doubt that King Dhudhannan and the Sovereign Guard would send the armies of Fellwood packing. King Dhudhannan had only been defeated in battle once in all his long life of over eight thousand years, and that was at the time of the Doom War when Morrigan herself had joined the fray.

The leathery beat of wings alerted Ellisenn to the approach of Tellan and his dragon. Moving in fast from the north, the blue-scaled dragon flew so close to the treetops that their leaves rustled and many were shaken loose. The dragon circled overhead once, then on its next turn Tellan dropped a long rope. Ellisenn took hold of the rope and was instantly dragged out of the tree. Tightening his hold on the rope as he swung out over the clearing, he started to climb. Tellan whistled to his dragon to return north and the dragon picked up height and speed fast. By the time Ellisenn had scaled the rope and climbed onto the dragon's back, the dark green mass of Fellwood that stretched from horizon to horizon was far, far below them.

Ellisenn spent much of the journey to Songarielle thinking about Sarritt. Would she be safe? If either Serza or the Dread discovered her return to the old faith of the Vellenor, her life would be forfeit. Even though he did not return Sarritt's feelings for him, he had been honest when he said he loved her as a sister, as a friend. Her time in his house had been brief but memorable. As an only child whose days were spent mostly with adults, Ellisenn had found Sarritt completely fascinating, despite her being a hostage and a princess of Fellwood. If anything, those things made her all the more intriguing to him. It had taken her months to warm to him but in the end a deep friendship had grown between them. Then she'd told him she loved him, on the eve of her return to Vellenhive, and that had soured everything. He didn't know how to stop her from hurting over that. He couldn't pretend to love her just to ease her pain. Was that what she expected of him? In truth he didn't know what she expected and didn't know what he was supposed to do to make it better. He did know, however, that if Serza hurt her he would bury the dark prince so deep in the ground that his bones would not see the light of day for an eternity.

The twinkling lights of Songarielle brought him out of his ponderings. Even after two years, he still found the sight of the citadel breathtaking. Nestled in an alpine plateau in the middle of a circle of high, snow-capped mountains, Songarielle's white walls shone as if with a light of their own. At the centre of the citadel, overlooking the central square where he had whiled away many hours beneath the shade of the ever-flowering Alder trees, was the complex of buildings and courtyards that made up the Songarielle senate, where the Druid Chambers were housed. That was where he must go as soon as they landed, carrying the worst of news to his master, the Lady Kashashem.

Tellan landed his dragon smoothly and then Ellisenn helped him to wrangle the beast into its coop. Despite being tired, it resisted being put to bed, spouting a burst of flame at the sky to show its displeasure. Once it was safely away in its stall however, it quickly fell asleep, purring so loudly the stone walls of the coop vibrated. Ellisenn left the coop at a jog, shouting a farewell and thank you to Tellan over his shoulder.

As he jogged across the field he was met with a strange scene: Daniselle, dragon-rider and warrior of Songarielle, standing by her great silver dragon, Jossa, with a halfling strung over her shoulder and two humans, a little girl and a youth about Ellisenn's own age, swaying on their feet in front of her. To Ellisenn's elvish eyes the youth appeared to glow with a strange light from within. Before he reached them, the youth had fallen to the ground and passed out.

"Hail, Daniselle, do you need aid?" Ellisenn rushed over and stooped to check that the youth was alright.

"He passed out," the little girl said, looking close to doing so herself. "He'll be okay, won't he?"

"He is only fatigued, Harriett," Daniselle said. "He will recover after rest." She turned to Ellisenn then, readjusting the halfling on her shoulders as she did so. "We have journeyed a long way, Ellisenn. I can carry the halfling and the girl. If you could aid me by carrying the Waycaller to my home, I would be thankful."

Ellisenn's eyes shot to the boy on the ground. So this was the otherworld Waycaller? The one who had survived an attack by a skinwearer and then a host of goblins and Prince Serza. This explained the strange light: it was the blessing of Amallayne.

"Of course, Daniselle." He bent and lifted the Waycaller into his arms. The Waycaller's eyes, though closed, fluttered, as if he knew he was being lifted and struggled to wake. Ellisenn felt an instant recognition and was struck by the fairness of the boy's face, how full his lips were, how pale his glowing skin and how contrastingly black his hair. And there in the hollow of the boy's neck was the mark, the mark of two concentric circles, the mark of Amallayne's blessing. He had to take a breath to steady himself. Was this an effect of the power of the otherworld Waycallers? Ellisenn had never been in one's presence before. If so, he found the experience unnerving.

"I can walk by myself, thank you very much," the girl, Harriett, said, despite swaying on her feet.

"Of course you can," Daniselle replied, "but we must make haste. If you allow me to carry you, we will get there all the faster."

"I suppose if I don't say yes, you'll just bop me like you bopped Miss Butters?"

Ellisenn did not recognise the word 'bop' and was not sure what the girl's meaning was, but he liked her fighting spirit. It reminded him of Sarritt.

"Please, Harriett, this is not the time for squabbling—"

"I can squabble if I want," Harriett said. "You're not the boss of me, Daniselle."

"I do not even know what that means," Daniselle said,

sighing.

"If I may, Daniselle," Ellisenn interrupted, thinking he probably had more experience with obstinate teenage girls than the solitary and stern Daniselle. "You are clearly very tired," he said to Harriett. "Surely you would rather not walk *all* the way to Daniselle's home?"

"How far is it?" The girl's determination was wavering already.

"Quite far," Ellisenn said.

"Well, I am pretty tired. I suppose it will be alright. But why can't *you* carry me?" She looked Ellisenn up and down. "You look *really* strong. I'm sure you can carry both me and Jack."

"I would be happy to," Ellisenn said with a little bow.

"No," Daniselle said firmly. "Jack is in urgent need of rest and must be carried gently. I will carry you, Harriett. I am just as strong as Ellisenn."

"Fine," Harriett said, pouting. "Fine, you can carry me."

With that they set out, Daniselle carrying the halfling and Harriett while Ellisenn carefully carried the Waycaller. They moved swiftly through the dark, cobbled streets of Songarielle. When they came to Daniselle's house, Jack was still unconscious and Harriett was drowsing. Daniselle led Ellisenn up the stairs and directed him to a moonlit bedroom where Jack was to sleep. While Daniselle took care of Miss Butters and Harriette, Ellisenn deposited Jack in the large bed, placing his head gently on the pillows and then covering him with blankets. As soon as he'd done it, he was surprised by his tender action. There was something about this human Waycaller that made Ellisenn want to take care of him, protect him. He backed out of the bedroom, unnerved again, closed the door and went downstairs to make his way to the Druid Chambers.

As he crossed the square towards the Songarielle senate, Ellisenn's mind was preoccupied, still dwelling on the Waycaller, Jack, asleep in that moonlit bed in Daniselle's house. A strange but not unpleasant sensation coursed through him. What was wrong with him? His mind should be focussed on one thing. He had to tell Kashashem everything he'd learned about the armies of Vellenor warriors and goblins marching north toward Pix and about Prince Serza and the Secret Gift. He shook his head and mounted the steps to the senate, determined not to think about the Waycaller again. At least not tonight.

# SONGARIELLE

*Citadel of the mountain elves*

Jack dreamt of a shadow lurking at the edge of his vision. The shadow whispered to him with lips that were black and cracked, bending all the force of its will to compel him to go to it, to do its bidding. The intensity of the near silent command turned Jack's stomach. No, he moaned in his sleep, no, no. When he woke in a very comfortable bed some hours after dawn he'd forgotten about the dream completely.

He stayed in the bed, stretching out each of his sore limbs in turn. Images of their flight by dragon to Songarielle flashed through his mind. Just days ago, if someone had suggested he would be hurtling through the sky on the back of a dragon, he would've thought they were crazy. As crazy as his mother. He put his mother out of his mind and rolled over, looking around the room. Large windows curtained with a sheer blue material let in the morning light but obscured any view. The floors were polished wood, the walls plastered and decorated with a mural of beautiful birds flitting among fluffy white clouds. The room was large and furnished with intricately carved wooden furniture. Opposite the bed in which he was lying, an ornate silver mirror hung above an open fireplace, catching and reflecting the sunlight. He couldn't remember coming here, into this room or this house, and only vaguely remembered being carried from the firewyrm coops through the cobblestone streets. But carried by whom? The idea of being carried at all made him uneasy.

He climbed out of bed, went to the window and pulled back the curtains. Jack blinked at the breathtaking vista outside. The bedroom was on the upper floor of a large house that looked out directly to the rim of mountains surrounding the citadel. Centred in the frame of the window was the tallest of the huge peaks. Capped with snow, this peak was tall, angular, almost like a natural pyramid. Its white cap glistened in the sun. Below him, a cobbled street curved by the house in a wide arc. Jack figured the street must circle the city, echoing the white wall that enclosed Songarielle.

The street was lined with grand looking houses, all of similar structure: river stone foundations with plastered walls, ornate timber window frames and flat rooves with elaborately carved timber eaves, smaller echoes of the palace of the Songarielle Senate. Strings of multi-coloured flags were strung over the street, criss-crossing between the houses, fluttering and snapping in the breeze.

Across the way, at the doorway of a large house, two elvish women—tall, caramel-skinned, dark-haired and dressed in flowing tunics of brilliant blue—emerged and meandered down the street. Like Daniselle, they were dignified and solemn, but unlike her they didn't have a marshal air, the air of a fighter. They were just as beautiful as Daniselle however, and Jack wondered if he hadn't died and gone to heaven. Jack watched the elves disappear around a corner, passing a young elvish man coming from the opposite direction. This elvish man had a different appearance to Daniselle and these others. His shoulder-length hair was a sandy blond and he was of a more solid build. He was dressed in a long black frock-coat over dark, raven green trousers. He looked seventeen or eighteen years old, just a little older than Jack, but where Jack was lean and self-conscious, this elf was muscled and uncommonly graceful. Some of his features were similar to those of Daniselle and the other elves, such as his high cheek bones and the same slender ears that curved upwards to a point, however his skin was fair, and then there was his blond hair and green eyes.

Jack was surprised at how good-looking this young elf was. Good-looking was not really the right word. He was more than just good-looking. He was beautiful. The fact that Jack had noticed that at all made him flush. He justified it to himself by deciding that the elves were not human at all, but supernatural, kind of alien. It wasn't as if he'd thought an ordinary guy was beautiful. The elves were in a category all of their own. When the elf passed out of sight Jack drew the curtain and went to find Harriett and Miss Butters.

Outside his bedroom, Jack found a landing with a number of doors leading to other bedrooms and an oak staircase descending to the ground floor. At each end of the landing shuttered doors led out to balconies. Jack assumed one overlooked the street and the other a back garden. The doors out to the back balcony were open, letting in a gentle breeze that made a rustic candelabra hanging in the stairwell swing a little. The breeze carried a scent Jack didn't recognise. It made him think of high meadows and wildflowers.

Curious to see the garden, he stepped out onto the balcony, and then froze. Someone else was there. Standing with her back to him, dressed in her black leather jerkin and trousers, Anarra Settonett gazed out over the garden below. Straight away Jack knew that the scent on the breeze was not from some plant in the garden but from her black hair, which moved on the breeze like silk ribbons hung out to dry in the sun. He reached out to touch her, to let her know he was there, but thought better of it. He stepped up to the bannister beside her instead, looking into her face and smiling.

Anarra started a little at his appearance beside her and then, for the first time, smiled, right at him. Somehow he had forgotten how beautiful she was, how stunningly, achingly beautiful. Talk about good-looking elves!

"Jack," she said, and he tingled at the sound of his name on her lips. "Jack, I am glad to see you."

"I'm glad to see you too. How did you get here?"

"On dragon-wing." For the first time Anarra sounded mildly excited. "After Master Wadget spoke with you through the seeing stone he sent a message here, to Daniselle, and asked that dragon-riders be sent to find you in the Empty Lands and also to collect us from Oakholme and carry us here. I have not been on dragon-back since I was a child. I would have enjoyed it so much more if I had not been so worried about ..."

"About me?"

Though she wasn't wearing her cloak she drew her arms around herself as though pulling it close to her skin. Jack could tell she wished she could recede beneath its black hood. Instead, she stared out over the garden.

"About Harriett, Miss Butters and, yes, about you."

"I wouldn't have thought you'd worry about me. Until just now I don't think you've ever looked me straight in the face, let alone smiled."

"I am unused to the company of others. Apart from my father, I have spent most of my life alone."

An image of Anarra's father, dead on the ground at the feet of the Dread sorceress, Hect, flashed in his mind. Should he tell Anarra what he'd seen? Would it only hurt her more? No, he wouldn't tell her now. They were just starting to get along. He didn't want that awful revelation coming between them. Besides, he reasoned, Anarra already knew that her father was killed by the Vellenor. But, she didn't know it'd been planned and was part of the plot to kidnap her. Jack decided the best person to tell these things was Aelf, or Wadget. They'd know what to do about it. They could tell Anarra what had happened to her father and be the ones to break her heart.

"I often feel self-conscious," Anarra continued, "unsure how to react, so that I ..." She paused, her eyes searching the sky, as if for the right words.

"Don't know what to say," Jack offered.

"Yes." She glanced at him and smiled again. "It was very brave of you, Jack, to lure the dark prince away from Oakholme. If he had penetrated the protective wards—"

"I couldn't let that happen, not with Harrie there and, and ..."

"Me?"

He didn't answer, just looked out over the garden, aware that his face was a little hot and possibly red. They watched the garden together a while, in complete but comfortable silence, until Jack decided he should find his sister.

"Have you seen Harrie?" he asked, his face still a little warm.

"Yes, downstairs with Miss Butters. Your sister seems quite unaffected by your ordeal. It's as though she faced goblins and dark sorcerers every day."

"Yeah, she's not worried about goblins, but lord help me if I don't hold her hand when she wants."

๛ ๖

Not surprisingly, Jack found his sister and Miss Butters in the kitchen. Miss Butters, muttering to herself as usual, was bent over at the waist, rummaging around in the bottom of a cupboard full of cooking utensils. Her rear end wiggled at Jack as he entered the room.

"Not a pancake pan among the lot!" she said from deep inside the cupboard. "How can these people get along without as much as the rudimentary conveniences? What do they use to make pancakes – a skillet?" She scoffed, her bottom taking on a more furious waggle as she plunged deeper into the cupboard. "Not a teapot in sight either, barbarians!" Clearly Miss Butters didn't appreciate elvish furnishings nearly as much as Jack did.

"She's been doing this all morning," Harriett said wearily on spotting Jack. "She doesn't like elves very much."

"I gathered," Jack said, at which Miss Butters popped her head out of the cupboard to greet him.

"Why good morning, master Jack. Finally decided to join us?" She said this in the same condescending tone his maths teacher used when Jack fell asleep in class.

"It's alright for you," Jack said, "you slept the whole way here. I had to hold on for my life the entire trip and hang on to Harrie as well. My legs and arms are killing me."

"Killing you! I'll tell you what is *killing* someone," Miss Butters retorted. "What's killing someone is my backside! Very sore it is, can't understand why for the life of me."

Jack remembered Jossa's gleaming white fangs bared at

280

Miss Butters' rear end while she was unconscious. Maybe the dragon got a nip in while nobody was looking?

"And my shoulder! My shoulder is throbbing! I'm going to make a complaint against that, that *vile* elf. I'll have her job, I will."

"She was a bit rough," Jack said half-heartedly. "But I don't think she has a job to get sacked from."

"Rough! She was positively *murderous* was what she was! I'll have her job! Just you wait and see!"

"Let's not worry about it now," Harriett said, "let's just have some breakfast. I'm ... I'm starving."

Jack's eyebrow shot up. He never thought he'd see Harriett volunteer to be fed by Miss Butters. His sister had clearly worked out that it was the quickest way to distract the halfling from her rants. It worked like a charm. The mere mention of Harriett being hungry sent Miss Butters into action. She pulled out the skillet and then flour, eggs and milk from a large walk-in pantry and set to making pancakes.

"Hold on dear! I'm a-cooking, it won't be too long now." The halfling mixed the pancake batter in a flash and moved over to an ornate wood-burning stove in the corner. "Poor child," she said to herself, "she's as thin as a hat-stand. She'll never make friends till she puts on at least six pounds."

"I don't suppose there's any bacon in that pantry?" Jack asked, his stomach rumbling.

Miss Butters' spine stiffened. She turned slowly to face Jack, her eyes wide.

"Bacon?" she said quietly. "Bacon comes from pigs, dear."

"Yeah, I know." Jack wondered why Harriett was vigorously shaking her head at him, as if in warning.

"How could you?" Miss Butters' voice was a strained whisper. "How could you even *suggest*, even *say* such a thing ..."

"Halflings don't eat pork, Jack," Harriett said with a sigh. "They love pigs."

"Oh, right," Jack said, realising his mistake. "Sorry, Miss Butters, I forgot."

"I suppose you can't be blamed." Miss Butters turned back to the stove. "You were raised among flesh-eaters after all."

"Flesh-eaters?" Jack didn't like how evil that sounded.

"Yes, dear. Flesh-eaters. Humans, goblins and trolls. They're the only creatures barbarous enough to eat flesh."

"So, halflings, elves and Oaklings don't eat meat at all?"

"Good gracious Eugene, no. Why would we do such a monstrous thing?"

Jack didn't know what to say to that. He shrugged, feeling uncomfortable that humans were in the same category as goblins and trolls, and crossed the room to sit next to Harriett, determined to end that line of discussion. As he sat he noticed that Harriett looked a bit frazzled.

"How are you, Harrie?"

"Okay," she said. "I like it here. It's very nice. All the murals and everything."

Jack took in the kitchen, which had large windows overlooking the back garden. "Yeah, it's cool. Any idea whose house this is?"

"It's Daniselle's house. I woke up just after we got here last night." Harriett yawned. "And she told me all about it."

"Where is she now?"

"She went out early this morning, to the Council Chambers. She said that she'll come and take us to see the druids a bit later."

"Does she live here by herself?" Jack asked.

"She grew up here, with her parents. She's an only child. Apparently elves usually only have one child. She lives alone now because her parents were murdered."

"Really?"

"Yep, really."

"Who killed them?" Jack feared he already knew the answer.

"Accursed Hect, The Witch of Bonemound," Miss Butters answered from the stove, mixing the batter with more violence than was necessary.

"You're kidding?" Jack couldn't believe he was hearing that name so soon after seeing what she'd done to Anarra's father. He pictured the Dread's bald head and blood red eyes and shuddered. He really had to tell Aelf what he'd seen in the vision. Hect had to be stopped.

"I am not kidding," Miss Butters said. "I would never jest about such heathen matters. If I've said it once, I've said it a hundred times, nothing good comes of messing with magic."

"Daniselle's parents were members of the Order of Druids," Harriett explained, rolling her eyes at Dorothea. "They were killed by this wretched Hect or whatever her name is, in a battle against the Dark Elves. But get this, Daniselle said she was only a little girl when it happened, about my age, and that was a thousand years ago! She's like, ancient!"

"No way." Jack couldn't accept that the beautiful, seemingly young she-elf he'd met the night before could be not just old but literally ancient.

"Yes way," Harriett said. "Anarra was telling the truth when she said that elves don't age much. Daniselle told me that Kashashem, who's like the oldest elf there is, doesn't even look as old as Miss Butters."

"Who looks old?" Miss Butters demanded. "I'm in the peak of my prime. Two hundred years old and I barely look one-fifty!"

"You're two hundred years old?" Harriett blinked in disbelief.

"If I'm a day," Miss Butters said proudly. "I know it's hard to fathom. Being as well preserved as I am often leads folks to think I'm just a spring chicken."

"Good lord!" Harriett said. "The way you eat, I'd have thought you'd have died at forty!"

"I beg your pardon, missy?" Miss Butters sounded more confused than offended.

"It's just that humans don't live very long if they put on too much weight," Jack explained. "Being fat is bad for the human heart."

"Eugene bless you!" she sighed, her voice full of shock and sympathy. "What kind of terrible curse has been placed on your poor souls?"

Jack thought he saw a tear well up in one of her eyes.

"Was it the *elves*?" She asked accusatorially. "Was it the *nasty* elves that cursed your breed?"

"Ah, I don't think we're cursed." Jack doubted Miss Butters would accept what he was going to say next. "It's just that humans are different. We live longer if we're thin."

At that Miss Butters dropped the skillet with a clang and emitted a disbelieving squeak. "What an accursed existence," she declared. "You poor things. Any wonder you're so miserable! But there must be a cure. Yes, a cure. I promise you this, little ones, I will not rest until I find a cure for this accursed affliction. Yes, believe you me, you *will* be *fat* if I have anything to say about it!"

"But, but Miss Butters—"

"Don't thank me, Jack! There's no need for thanks among friends." At that she returned to the stove and continued frying pancakes, with a renewed vigour and almost missionary zeal.

"We're just going to have to accept it, Jack," Harriet said, "we're doomed to be as porky as Piggy-poo."

Anarra came down after breakfast and she, Jack and Harriett decided to explore the house while they waited for Daniselle to return and take them to meet with the Druid Council. Miss Butters chose to retire to her room in order to, in her words, 'paste an unction' on her sore behind. The unction looked to Jack more like donut batter than anything else and was made from things found in the pantry.

"You'd be surprised the cures that can be mixed from everyday ingredients," Miss Butters said edifyingly. "Why, I can think of at least fifty medicinal uses for sow's milk alone, but only a few of them are as tasty as this blister-batter." She winked as she dipped her finger in the pot of unction and sucked it blissfully before heading upstairs.

Harriett led Jack and Anarra on a tour through the house, showing them the things she found most interesting, namely all the wall murals. Jack liked Daniselle's house a lot, with all its oak and wildly colourful murals, but had trouble imagining stern, warrior-like Daniselle living there. It was too fine, too subtle. Perhaps the house reflected the taste of Daniselle's mother, who'd died at the hands of Hect. Daniselle was an orphan, like he and Harriett. After a thousand years she still lived in her parents' house. Looking around the parlour with all its ornately carved furniture, Jack thought it probably looked exactly as it had when Daniselle's parents were alive. A rush of sadness coursed through him at that idea and he walked out into the hallway.

Jack paced the length of the hallway a few times, trying to rein in his sense of sorrow for Daniselle, and noticed a pair of double doors directly opposite the parlour that were pushed to but still a little ajar. He peered through the crack between them and, intrigued by what he saw, went in. On a large desk in the centre of the room was what appeared to be a map of the world, but not any world that Jack recognised. The map showed all of Anwynn, the largest feature being the Craggy Mountains that ran north to south like a massive wall. In-between two great arms of the mountain range Jack spotted the Halfling Dells, where the tiny village of Bright was clearly marked.

Harriett walked in behind him and began perusing the map as well.

"Look, Jack, that's where we are." She pointed to Songarielle, marked in the centre of a high alpine valley in the Craggy Mountains. "Oh, and this is Fellwood Forest." Her finger circled a vast forest in the south. Jack's eyes followed the path south through Fellwood, to the Swampmere and the temple of Dread sorcerers at Bonemound. Then his eyes landed on a string of words written at the foot of the Spinepeak Mountains: *Pitmouth, The Goblin Caverns above Uffern.*

"Is that where …?" Harriett whispered.

"Where Morrigan is imprisoned? It must be." Jack was unable to pull his eyes away from that small mark where, miles beneath the ground, Morrigan lurked, plotting to free herself and destroy the world.

After some time poring over the map, Harriett grew bored and looked around the rest of the study. Jack watched her circle the room, wondering what she was going to poke her nose into next. Unlike the Oaklings, like Wadget and Mog, the elves appeared to have scrolls rather than books. Daniselle clearly wasn't anywhere near as fond of reading as Wadget, as there was only one shelf of scrolls, and many of them looked like they'd never been opened.

"I don't think Daniselle reads very much," Harriett said, noticing this herself.

"I think she's more an active, outdoorsy type," Jack replied, referring to the fact that she rode dragons, slew goblins and such. Then Harriett grabbed a scroll, pulled it out and unrolled it.

"Don't break anything, Harrie," Jack warned, coming over to supervise.

"Look at this, Jack, it's got descriptions of halflings and elves and things." The scroll was labelled *The Nine Races*. As Harriett unrolled it, rich illustrations and descriptions of many strange beings were revealed. Apart from the detailed drawings of halflings, elves and Oaklings, there were pictures of Vellenor, goblins and skinwearers. Harriett groaned and said, "I don't fancy being the poor sod who had to get these skinwearers to stay still long enough to draw them."

"Poor sod?" Jack smirked. "Sometimes you sound so old fashioned, like an English professor from Oxford or somewhere."

"Whatever, Jack." Harriett unfurled the scroll further. Here they found pictures of otherworlders, in this case medieval humans, which, Jack noted, were described as 'descendants of the human-kind who are violent, bloody and foolish'. He thought that was a bit much. Harriett continued to unroll the parchment, revealing a drawing and description of a Pitten—a half piglet, half kitten creature that fascinated Harriett no end—and a drawing and description of an earwisp. It showed a tiny, elf-like creature with thin, pointy ears, shaggy red hair and vivid green eyes. This one was female and wore black tights, a fitted black shirt-dress and tiny pointy black shoes. The earwisp had a nasty sneer on its lips and a devilish look about it. At the sight of it Jack felt queasy. Could a thing like that really be in his ear? The description of the earwisp did little to allay his anxiety:

> *Earwisps, otherwise known as the Tiqq, are wicked and evil and detested by all. They are acolytes of Thullu, the much-feared Lord of Chaos. The earwisp is a foul sprite, a magical parasite that tricks and deceives its host. Its original form is that of a mist, or wisp, and in that form it enters the left ear of its prey and whispers instructions to its unfortunate victim in the host's own voice, thus avoiding detection. Its voice has the power to control and subdue and thus earwisp infection is a form of possession. The worst of the earwisp's powers is its ability to animate corpses to do their bidding. The Bright Elves, who abhor death and loathe nothing more than being dominated by another, are the earwisps' mortal enemies.*
>
> *The earwisp feeds on the thoughts and feelings of its host and thereby grows strong. The longer it remains, the weaker the host becomes. Apart from thought and emotion, the earwisp seeks only one other form of sustenance – the root of the sarsaparilla plant that to the ear sprite is akin to liquor.*

Jack inwardly gasped. Earwisps liked sarsaparilla. That was why he was suddenly craving it. It was the earwisp that had been making him want it all along. With a sick feeling in his stomach, he continued reading.

> *The earwisps are ruled by the Tiqq Empress. Almost*

*all earwisps are female. The role the rare male earwisps play is unknown. Legend tells of The Imperial Hive, where the Empress dwells, said to be in a great abandoned necropolis, protected by an army of the walking dead. The whereabouts of the necropolis is long forgotten.*

*No being is immune to the earwisp's voice and so once infected the host is likely to perish. The earwisp lingers by the remains of its previous host until another unwitting victim passes by. Thus, earwisp infections often occur in or near the places of the dead. There is no known remedy for earwisp possession.*

The words 'no known remedy' echoed in Jack's mind. So the damn thing was eventually going to kill him and once dead it could turn him into a zombie! Jack felt the urge to vomit, but pushed it down. He feared the earwisp was slowly taking him over. Soon he would have no say over what he did, whatsoever. The day before, at Amaltor, he hadn't been able to defy the voice at all. It wouldn't be long before he was little more than a puppet. Jack was sure that meant that the earwisp would make him go to Pitmouth, to Morrigan. Jack couldn't let that happen.

But what could he do? He couldn't just wait around until he became a monster. Then Jack remembered Wadget and Aelf, how they'd pledged to protect him. He was just going to have to tell them about the earwisp and hope they could help. Surely they would know some way to get the thing out of his ear? They probably knew a lot more than this old scroll anyway. For all Jack knew, the scroll was really outdated. In his world new remedies and treatments were being discovered all the time. Who said the same wasn't true here? Surely Wadget would know of something. He was one of the wisest and most powerful druids around!

The sound of the double doors springing open caused him and Harriett to turn toward the noise. When they did so, they saw Daniselle striding into the room, Anarra following behind her. Daniselle was still dressed in her flying gear, the tight leather pants and shirt and the long coat. Even though she clearly hadn't slept or changed, Jack thought she looked even more beautiful than she had the night before, perhaps because in the daylight the smooth, faultlessness of her skin was evident, as was the richness of her brown eyes.

"I see you have found my study," she said, neither annoyed nor approving. In fact, Jack couldn't quite make out what her mood was at all.

"Hope you don't mind," Harriett said, jumping in, "but we had some time to kill so we thought we'd just look around."

"Have you killed enough time to satisfy you?" Daniselle asked.

"Ah, yes," Harriett answered, also not sure what to make of Daniselle's seeming detached coldness.

"We were just reading about, um, about Pittens and things," Jack mumbled. Daniselle walked over and took the scroll from them, looking at it only briefly.

"Pittens and earwisps," Daniselle read, noting the section of the scroll they'd been reading. "Have you an interest in such things?"

"Sure." Harriett shrugged. "The Pittens are cute anyway."

"Pittens are venomous. Their poisonous bite causes unbearable pain and sends the victim into madness and then an agonising death." Daniselle sounded as though she'd just said something completely ordinary like 'kittens have whiskers and like to play with string'.

"Oh, I mustn't have read that bit yet," Harriett stuttered.

"The earwisp is also a foul thing, one of the foulest things of our world. So foul that those infected with one are destroyed."

"Destroyed?" Jack asked, suddenly terrified.

"Yes," Daniselle asserted. "There is no cure. An ear-whipped being cannot be trusted. They are completely under the sway of the foul sprite hiding in their ear. The only resolution is to destroy the host. With the host dead, the earwisp flees."

Harriett gasped, echoing the silent gasp in Jack's mind. "That's, that's terrible."

"Indeed," Daniselle said, without emotion. "Now, have you learnt enough of the wicked monsters of this world?"

"Yes," Harriett said firmly as Jack just nodded in shock.

"Good." Daniselle rolled up the scroll. "For the Druid Council, and Kashashem herself, await you."

# THE DRUIDS' COUNCIL

As they wended their way through the cobbled streets of Songarielle, heading toward the Druid Chambers, they attracted a fair bit of attention. Apparently the reserved mountain elves were not accustomed to seeing halflings. Jack and Harriett's otherworldly garb wasn't helping matters either; their manner of dress must have seemed strange to the tunic-wearing elves. Anarra, furtive and hooded as usual, crept along like a thief yet drew only passing attention.

At first the streets they travelled through were lined with large, splendid houses, all festooned with brightly coloured flags and banners, but soon these buildings gave way to more commercial premises, shops and warehouses of various descriptions. The shops mainly sold elvish-made furniture, silverware and clothing, except for the occasional stall selling vegetables and heady spices. Some of the premises however sold much more interesting things, such as swords, beautifully wrought archers' bows, silver breastplates, armour and other elvish weapons. One place, a large square building with a wooden sign hanging out the front depicting a red dragon soaring through a blue sky, appeared to be the firewyrm-riders equivalent of a saddlery, selling harnesses, reins, dragon armour and those sleek leather outfits that Daniselle wore with such perfection.

Amongst all the shops and wares Jack noticed that there were no places to eat, no restaurants, certainly no bars or other such establishments where one might loosen that stern mountain elf disposition with a bit of wine or spirits. Harriett noticed this at the same time and asked, "Where do you elves have fun?"

"Fun?" Daniselle asked, as if never having heard of it. "What do you mean?"

"Like, where do you go out to eat or to hang out?"

"Mountain elves do not eat or drink together *in public*."

Daniselle's tone said that the mere idea of shared dining was ludicrous. "As for this 'hanging out', I do not know to what you refer."

"You know, like getting together and talking and socialising," said Harriett.

"We prefer solitary undertakings," Daniselle said. Harriett was evidently disappointed, her brow creasing with a slight frown. Jack was well aware that to Harriett there was nothing worse than a solitary undertaking. "But perhaps," Daniselle offered, "you will be pleased to hear that the woodland elves are very fond of such things, talking and dancing and singing. They are ... quite unreserved." There was a trace of disapproval in her voice.

"They sound much more fun!" Harriett beamed. "Are there any woodland elves on the Council?"

"Only one," Daniselle answered dryly, "but he is more reserved than most of their kind."

"Bummer," sighed Harriett.

As they made their way down a particularly crowded street, they continued to catch the attention of the local elves. This was partly because Miss Butters was muttering angrily under her breath at the indignity of having to go anywhere with Daniselle. The talk about mountain elves' disapproval of public eating and drinking, which was practically a religion for halflings, angered Miss Butters all the more. Jack half expected her to turn on her heels and head home, all the way back to Bright.

Outside a shop selling the vibrant blue tunics popular among mountain elves, a small cluster of unbelievably youthful and good-looking elves stopped to watch the strange procession pass by, mesmerised by the sight of what appeared to them to be two strangely dressed Pixish children, a firewyrm rider and a deranged, or drunk, halfling. Jack blushed as Harriett smiled and waved at them as if she were the queen of a parade. Anarra drew her hood over her head and hid in Daniselle's shadow. Jack, well, Jack just felt terribly miserable and self-conscious. He half imagined that the elvish onlookers could tell that he had a nasty sprite in his ear. A sprite that would either turn him into some kind of zombie or, if discovered, would lead to his being 'destroyed' like some rabid dog. He was so acutely mindful of his ears that they flushed a beetroot red. Thankfully, Daniselle soon turned into a long avenue flanked by tall, verdant trees where there were fewer people.

"Ooh, those trees are lovely." Harriett pointed to hanging threads of white flowers. She did it so dramatically that Jack flinched. He wished she had an off switch but after nine years living with her he knew she only had two settings: *on* and *full on*.

"Those are the sacred Alder of Songarielle," Daniselle explained. Their life-force is linked to the life-force of King Dhudhannan, the Elven Sovereign. Unlike other trees of their kind, they are evergreen. Even in the height of winter their leaves and flowers remain. No snow touches them nor falls at their base. It is said that while King Dhudhannan endures these trees will flower and Songarielle will be protected from the creatures of doom."

"Even from Morrigan?" Jack asked, remembering that Aelf had said that even this, the oldest city of the elves, had once fallen before Morrigan's armies.

"Against the Faeden there is no protection." Daniselle's voice was cold. "Thankfully the Faeden rarely concern themselves with us."

"But they are still tricksy devils," said Miss Butters from behind, apparently unable to contain herself despite her dislike for Daniselle.

Daniselle nodded. "Indeed, the Faeden are often unpredictable and mysterious."

Miss Butters' face turned sour as if sucking on a bitter lemon. It was evident she found being agreed with by an elf completely disagreeable. Jack suppressed a smirk and followed Daniselle and Anarra as the avenue grew shady beneath the ever-green leaves of the sacred Alder trees. This ancient cobbled avenue had even grander houses, so big they were really palaces. Harriett peered up at them with her mouth partly open. Jack popped it closed for her with a smirk. Every now and then narrow laneways crossed the avenue, curving in from one side and curving out again on the other, laid across the avenue like large wheels that encircled the central square.

As Jack looked down one of these lanes, he saw a hooded shape lurking in the shadow of a large building. As they crossed the intersection with the lane, he looked back again and was certain he saw the glint of two small red eyes. As he stared at the shape, he realised its eyes were fixed on Harriett. A second later it moved back into the darkness and was gone. His skin tingled and goose-pimpled. A wave of familiar nausea rose in his gut.

Jack was now certain that this creature had followed them all the way from Bright. But how did it know where to find them and how had it managed to keep up with them? He had opened a Way to journey to Mog's house, and then to Amaltor, and they'd flown by dragon to Songarielle. No ordinary being could follow them so quickly, only a sorcerer. Then a worrying idea struck him – the hooded figure had a distinctively halfling shape, being about four feet tall and almost as round. Could it be a halfling trailing them, hunting Harriett for some reason? And was this halfling the sorcerer who'd sent skinwearers to kidnap Anarra and have her taken to the Halfling Dells? His skin goose-pimpled even more, so much that his skin actually ached. He looked to Daniselle to see if she'd noticed anything, but her attention was firmly on their destination. He determined to tell Aelf about this strange figure as soon as he got the chance. The things he had to tell the druids were mounting up, each new thing adding an extra dose of anxiety.

He caught up with Daniselle and Harriett and took his sister's hand. She looked curiously up at him and he smiled back to reassure her. They followed Daniselle as she turned right, off the main avenue heading toward the square, and struck down one of the narrow cobbled lanes toward the edge of town. The snow-capped mountains loomed ahead of them.

"Where are we going?" Jack asked. "Aren't the Druid Chambers the other way?"

"Yes," Daniselle answered. "But I wish to take you to the firewyrm coops first. There is something I want you to see. I hope it will improve Miss Butters' mood."

After a few minutes the lane opened out to a large area within the citadel walls where the firewyrm coops stood. In the light of day Jack could see that the hundred or so coops were also made of river stone. They were basically elongated barns, open at one end so that they were a kind of artificial cave. The field was very quiet and Jack assumed that this was because the dragons were either asleep or out flying.

As they came to the closest barn Daniselle whistled a strange trilling tune. The tune was answered from within the dark coop by a baritone purring sound. A bit like what a crocodile might do if it were part cat. The next minute, the silver dragon, Jossa, emerged from the coop at a brisk canter, trotting like an oversized feline toward his master. For a brief moment Jack thought they would all be crushed and closed his eyes ready for the impact, but Jossa slowed and stopped as he reached them, towering above them so that they were all cast in shadow. The dragon, still purring, dropped his head and Daniselle patted him on the snout, a faint smile on her lips. If she weren't one of the mountain elves, Jack might think she was only vaguely fond of Jossa, but for an inhabitant of Songarielle this slight show of affection was positively over-the-top.

"What are we doing here?" Miss Butters demanded, eyeing Jossa suspiciously. "This is not the Druid Chambers!"

"If you look to the east," Daniselle said, still stroking Jossa's snout, "you will soon see something of interest to you. A firewyrm rider comes from that direction today, due any minute now."

"Do I look like I care to learn your ruddy firewyrm timetable?" Miss Butters stubbornly looked in the opposite direction. "I couldn't care less how many ruddy reptiles you've got coming and going."

"Look!" Harriett shouted. They all looked to where she was pointing. In the eastern sky the distinctive shape of a large, blue dragon mounted by an elf approached. As the dragon came closer they saw that it was carrying some kind of harness. Even from this distance they could see shapes in the harness, and that the harness was kind of wriggling, as if it contained something that wanted to get out.

As the blue dragon's shadow threw them into even darker shade they saw that hanging in the harness were Soxy and Piggy-poo. Soxy was contentedly chewing on a bunch of grass. Piggy-poo, on the other hand, was quivering in terror, his little pink bonnet askew.

"My Piggy-poo!" Miss Butters shouted in dismay. "What are you doing to my pig you wretched elf! I demand you set him free this minute!"

"That could be done, halfling," Daniselle asserted, "but if he were loosed now he would surely fall to his death."

"You know what I meant you vexatious elf! I want my Piggy-poo safe and sound!"

Miss Butters didn't have to wait long. Within minutes the dragon had lowered the harness to the ground and swooped off to land nearby. Miss Butters ran to the harness and, with that swiftness that she sometimes showed, most often at meal times, untied the harness and set the black, bonnet-wearing pig free. Soxy stepped out of the harness and trotted over to Jack and Harriett, nudging them with his head until they gave him a pat. Miss Butters threw herself on Piggy-poo and practically strangled him in an embrace. Piggy-poo responded with a series of enthusiastic oinks and a mad wiggling of his corkscrew tail. Jossa, whose black eyes seemed unable to comprehend Piggy-poo and his bonnet, snorted in a derisory way before trotting off to greet the blue dragon that had just landed nearby. As Miss Butters and Piggy-poo reacquainted themselves, Jack and Harriett patted Soxy, who was behaving as though being carried around in the sky by a firewyrm was no big deal at all. Soon they were joined by the blue dragon's elvish rider, a male version of Daniselle, handsome and almond-eyed, wearing the same brown leather outfit.

"Greetings, Tellan," Daniselle said.

"That barrow is the most despoiled creature I have ever encountered," Tellan said quietly to Daniselle, looking at Miss Butters and Piggy-poo in their frenzy of affection with distaste.

"What's a barrow?" Harriett asked. Jack was glad she did because he had no idea what the word meant either.

"A barrow," Daniselle explained, "is a male pig that will never sire piglets because he has been … neutered."

"Oh," Harriett said, "I see."

"That would explain the bonnet then." Jack winked and smirked.

Miss Butters re-joined them. "I don't understand. Why is Piggy-poo here?"

"We respect the bond between rider and mount," Daniselle explained. "When we heard from Master Wadget that you had left your mount at Oakholme, we felt we must reunite you."

"Why I … why, why thank you." Miss Butters' face showed considerable confusion; apparently she was thinking that, though not completely forgiven, perhaps Daniselle wasn't a total fiend.

After the reunion with Piggy-poo and Soxy, and many assurances from the male dragon-rider that both animals would be well cared for and housed in one of the large barns, Miss Butters allowed Daniselle to lead them back toward the druid headquarters. Soon after they re-entered the tree-lined avenue, it opened into the broad square at the centre of Songarielle that Jack had seen from above. In front of them stood the huge senate building that housed the Druid Chambers. To the right loomed the tall beehive-shaped stone temple of Amallayne, where Jack was surprised to see a large group of humans, their heads bowed as they entered the temple through its arched doorway. As they passed in the shadow of the temple Jack remembered what Wadget had said, that he had to beseech Amallayne to help the druids defeat Morrigan and Serza. Jack's stomach did a somersault. He'd never spoken to as much as a school principal before, let alone a goddess. How did one beseech a goddess anyway? And what if Amallayne just ignored him? Would they be doomed to stay on this side of the Veil forever? Not that they'd last long. Morrigan's followers would find them eventually and then the whole world, *both* the worlds, would be doomed.

"Is the temple of Amallayne open to anyone?" Jack asked, wondering if he should just go in now and get it over with. At least then he'd have something to say to the Druid Council.

"We do not call the House of Amallayne a temple. The elves submit themselves to no other being, Faeden or not. Amallayne is our friend and once our protector. We offered this house to her after Amaltor was desecrated, in thanks for her aid in the Doom War. And yes, it is open to all."

"Why wasn't Amaltor rebuilt?" Jack asked, thinking about the huge stone circle and the fallen pillar with its ornate carvings of a once great city.

"The Pixish, whose capital Amaltor was, dared not defy the prophesy."

"What prophesy?" asked Jack, remembering that Wadget had also mentioned a prophecy and that somehow it concerned him.

"Among other things the prophesy predicts a second Doom War, a war worse than the first, and warns that Amaltor should only be rebuilt if Morrigan can be vanquished once and for all."

"Eugene save us," Miss Butters sighed, "a second Doom War?"

"Sadly, yes. We elves consider that war to be upon us now," Daniselle said, as they neared the senate building that housed the chambers of the Druid Council. "The stars speak of its coming, and of the calamity that will soon descend."

"Good lord." Miss Butters' hand wiggled weakly before

her heart.

Daniselle mounted the wide stairs of the senate, with Jack and the others following. Jack climbed the stairs feeling apprehensive. There was so much he didn't understand, so many threats. He silently wished the druids or Amallayne or anyone really would just deal with it all so that he and Harriett could finally go home to their normal lives. He glanced at Anarra, hoping he didn't look as pathetic as he felt and that she couldn't sense how scared he was.

The chambers of the Druid's Council were deep in the senate complex. Daniselle led them all through many passageways and three courtyards before they came to a building that, unlike all the other whitewashed ones, was painted red. They entered this building to find something like a huge, ramshackle library. There were books and scrolls piled up everywhere. Those bits of the walls not covered by shelves were adorned with tapestries that were, from what Jack could tell, maps and illustrations of the mountains, forests, towns and cities of Anwynn.

Off from the entranceway, there radiated four hallways, and off those hallways there were many doors. As they passed by some of these doors, Jack saw they opened into offices and sitting rooms occupied by druids, sometimes just one, sometimes up to a dozen. They all looked very studious, focussed on studying books and scrolls, or prodding at steamy potions simmering away in cauldrons hung in fireplaces. One of these potions, around which four or five druids hovered eagerly, may have actually been onion soup, as it smelt rather appetising as its vapours hit Jack's nose. The druids were mostly, like Aelf, human, but some were elvish.

Daniselle led them all the way down one of the hallways until they came to a large pair of oak doors. Carved into the door was the sign of a pentagram. Jack blinked on seeing it. He'd only ever seen it on the t-shirts of heavy-metal fans and in horror films.

"Why is that mark on the door?" he asked at once.

"That is the mark of Seren, the prophet star that guides

my people, the elves, and communicates the will of the universe. The Star of Seren is a ward against goblins, Dark Elves and evil sorcerers. It is a very powerful mark."

"Really?" Jack said incredulously. "In our world it means witchcraft or something."

"It has power only to rebuff the dark ones. You need not fear it," Daniselle explained, before knocking on the door.

The door opened almost immediately. As they walked through it Jack wondered if the pentagram would stop him from entering, since after all he had a dark being in his ear! But he wasn't stopped. He was able to walk straight through. This made Jack think that a lot of what the druids and elves did to protect themselves was just hogwash. Look how easily the Veil had been breached and how Serza had nearly overthrown the defences of Oakholme. The apparent ineffectiveness of druid magic made Jack feel less and less safe by the minute.

On the other side of the doors Jack found not a room but a large square space, a courtyard with pairs of oak doors in the centre of each of its four walls. This must be the heart of the Druid Chambers. In the centre of the courtyard was a circle of benches, by which were standing a group of druids. Most of these druids were also human, but here too there were some elves. They were a formidable looking bunch, and all wearing white cloaks similar to Aelf. Daniselle walked them to the centre of the room and, extending her arm in the direction of the group in that formal way she was so fond of, said, "The Druid Council." Then, without another word, she turned and left. Jack was sad to see her go, especially as the druids were now all staring at them intently.

"Hi, I'm Harriett."

"Welcome, Harriett," one of the elvish druids said, a beautiful woman with dark hair and soft brown eyes. "Please, won't you all be seated?"

Anarra, Jack noticed, remained hooded when she took her seat, apparently more nervous about this meeting than he was. After all, once the druids realised she was Ehmaarim their attention would swing to her. Her people were believed to be extinct. Jack wished he was extinct. Well, maybe not extinct, but at the very least able to hide under a cloak as well.

Once they'd all settled in their seats, Jack counted ten druids, six humans and four elves. Three of the elvish councillors were women as was one of the humans. The elvish male was blond with green eyes and looked barely old enough to drive. But Jack knew he was probably a lot older than he looked. Beneath his white druid's cloak, the young elf was wearing a black frock-coat and dark green trousers. After a second look at him, Jack realised with surprise that it was the same elf he'd seen in the street outside Daniselle's house. All of the human druid councillors were elderly, bar the woman who was about fifty, like Aelf. She had black hair that extended down to her waist and very alert blue eyes. It was she who spoke next.

"I'm glad you have arrived safely," she said warmly. "My name is Alva."

Jack smiled, recognising that Alva was the Seer who had foretold their arrival at Bright. Oblivious, Miss Butters looked around nervously, her feet dangling far from the floor.

"Nice to meet you." Harriett smiled openly at the Seer. "This is my brother Jack, and these are our friends, Anarra and Miss Butters."

"We have been awaiting you all," Alva said. She turned to Miss Butters. "How are things in Bright?"

"You, you know of my little village?" Miss Butters sounded impressed.

"Yes, I had the good fortune to visit Bright once when I was a child. I thought it delightful."

"Well, thank you for saying so." Miss Butters beamed, taking credit for all of Bright's assets. "And, as you ask, I can inform you that things there are just as they have always been … up until the other night when these poor children arrived on my doorstep."

"The last few days have been a challenge for us all," Alva agreed. "This Council has not slept since all this began."

Miss Butters seemed satisfied by that; at least she knew that someone was on the job.

"What of the children? How are you both faring?" Alva asked.

"We're fine," said Harriett quickly, as if it was nothing to cross into another world and be confronted with Dark Elves and goblins and the rest.

"And you, Waycaller?" the young elvish man asked Jack. "How do you fare?" Something about his voice was very familiar to Jack.

"I'm okay," Jack said sheepishly. "But I'd rather be home."

"I too miss my home," the blond elf said. "My home is at Tessarelle in the Great North Wood. But if Morrigan is loosed, there will be nothing to return to. The same is true of your home."

Jack said nothing. What could he say? More to the point he was now certain he had heard this elf's voice before, but where?

"I'm sorry," Jack started, "but, I feel I know you somehow." The young elf smiled in response, a very disarming, warm smile, the like of which never crossed the face of Daniselle or any of the sombre mountain elves.

"That is because we have met before. I am Ellisenn."

"But, we can't have met before. I think I'd remember," Jack replied.

"You were asleep at the time," Ellisenn explained. "I carried you from the firewyrm field to Daniselle's home."

"You carried me?" Jack was mortified. Ellisenn was not much taller, though admittedly more muscled, nor seemingly older than him. The idea of being carried in the young elf's arms made Jack feel decidedly uneasy. He looked to Harriett for confirmation. She'd been awake for that part of the trip to Daniselle's home. Harriett smiled bashfully and shrugged her shoulders, as if to say 'I would've told you but I knew you'd be embarrassed'. The Druids all sat watching him, saying nothing. Jack's mortification deepened and he wondered what they were waiting for; were they expecting him to say something? Then Alva explained.

"We are awaiting Kashashem, the Head of the Order. She was detained by other business."

"Will she be very long?" Harriett asked, as if asking when dinner would be ready.

Before Alva could answer, the doors swung open and a tall, fierce-looking elvish woman with black skin and long, magenta dreadlocks entered the courtyard. Beneath her white hooded cloak she wore a long red coat-dress that fell to her feet. Jack started at the sight of her eyes, which were a bright yellow. Following Kashashem was Wadget and behind him, Aelf. Harriett jumped to her feet.

"Where have you guys been?" she demanded, tapping her feet on the flagstones, her hands on her hips. "I was so worried about you!"

"Forgive me, Harriett," Kashashem said in a deep, powerful voice. "I detained your friends so that they might relate all that occurred in the dells and at Oakholme these last nights."

"That's okay," Harriett said, going to Wadget and attempting to take his hand. He growled at her. She laughed and took Aelf's hand instead.

"You have a stout heart, youngling." Kashashem smiled. "It is a rare being who laughs off old Wadget's growl."

Harriett shrugged her shoulders as she sat down beside Aelf. "I just don't think he's that scary." At that the council members raised their eyebrows as one, many of them attempting to stifle smirks. Wadget's eyebrows shot up the furthest, either offended or just surprised by Harriett's boldness.

"I see now how it was that these children faced a dark sorcerer, the Oakling Mog and a goblin hunting party and survived," Kashashem said.

"Sheer dumb luck," Wadget growled.

"Perhaps the child sees instantly what many on the Council have taken decades to learn," Kashashem said, smirking, "that underneath it all Wadget has a heart as soft as butter."

"Butter me green butt," Wadget muttered.

Miss Butters flinched at the mention of Wadget's butt, yet Harriett merely chuckled and then whispered to Aelf, "How did you get here so fast?"

"We flew," Aelf answered.

"On a dragon?" she continued.

"Yes."

"What colour dragon?"

"A blue one."

"Oh, I love blue."

As Harriett and Aelf talked, Jack noticed that Wadget was the only druid in the room not wearing a white cloak. Instead he had what looked like a bunched up, old white rag tied around his waist. Apparently this was his nod to the formality of the Council meeting. While Jack was thinking this, Kashashem took her seat directly opposite him and looked straight into his eyes. It was as if she was looking right through him, seeing through body and flesh to his soul.

*It is as if she were Amallayne herself!* The voice at his ear said, making him flinch. He grabbed at his earlobe, hoping no-one noticed. Kashashem continued to look at him as before.

"You have the look of a Waycaller," she finally said.

"What do you mean?" Jack nervously covered his ear, fearful of being exposed as ear-whipped.

"The human Waycallers always carry the outer marks— hair as black as night, eyes the colour of sapphires, skin like cream—as well as the inner blessing of Amallayne."

"Blessing?"

"Yes, Amallayne has bequeathed your family line a part of herself. To those with the ability to see it, such as we elves, her light shines from within you like a sun shining from behind a veil of clouds."

"That'd be right," Harriett huffed loudly, "he's always thought the sun shines out of his—"

"Harriett!" Jack hissed, silencing her just in time.

"Be not envious," Kashashem said to Harriett, "for the light is within you also."

"What?" Jack gaped at his sister. "You mean she's a Waycaller too?"

"Not exactly. We do not know much of Faeden magic, they protect their secrets very well. We do know that there is only ever one otherworld Waycaller in each generation. However, if you were to die, the power to open the Way Between would arise in Harriett."

"Excellent!" Harriett looked very pleased with herself. "Not that I want you to kick the bucket, Jack."

"So, could any member of my family be a Waycaller?"

"No, the blessing falls to just a few," Kashashem explained. "In the generation before yours it was your mother who carried the blessing. It is exceedingly rare to have two in the one generation, but not unheard of. This is why we must protect you both, for Morrigan sees you both as keys to her prison. Now, we must appraise the whole situation we find ourselves in, for we have much to worry over. Jack, as Waycaller, you have the right to speak first."

Jack swallowed, terrified. What was he supposed to say? All the worries that had occupied his mind since they were first attacked by the skinwearer presented themselves in turn: Would he and Harriett ever be safe again? Would Morrigan ever stop trying to kill them when their deaths meant her freedom? Why was Serza hunting them? Could the dark prince be prevented from breaching the Veil again? Was he only so powerful because he had found Thullu's Gift, or was Thullu himself involved? Who or what was the creature with the red eyes that had followed them all the way from Bright, who seemed to be after Harriett? What was the voice in his ear? Was he really ear-whipped? Was he doomed to become a puppet to some evil sprite? Was that why he would one day be standing on a ruined battlefield with Harriett's body at his feet, her blood on a sword in his hand? Was there any way to avoid that coming true? It was all so overwhelming he hardly knew how he'd kept it all in his head. How could he possibly talk about any of it without jibbering like an idiot, like a lunatic? And then he thought of his mother. She was a Waycaller, but was she a murderess as well? Wadget had called her fierce and brave. If she had really killed their father, why had she done it?

"My, my mother ..." The words caught in his throat. He faked a cough and started again. "Our mother, why did she ... why did she kill our father?"

The druids' reaction to this question was not what Jack expected. Wadget jumped to his feet, growling. Aelf flinched and recoiled, his eyes wide with shock. Alva and a number of the others gasped. Ellisenn looked at Jack as though he had hit his head, hard, and was confused. Only Kashashem remained still, her yellow eyes boring into him.

"Is that why yeh never asked about yer mother?" Wadget's green lips were drawn tight. "Yeh think Eloise Gordon *murdered* Noble?"

"That's what we were told," Harriett said. "That she killed Dad and then drowned herself in the loch."

"What!" It was not just Wadget who shouted this, but Aelf and Alva and a number of the other councillors as well. Kashashem remained silent, her eyes digging deep into Jack so that it made him want to run out of the room and never come back. Anything but have to look into those yellow eyes any longer. She held up her hand and the room fell silent.

"Who told you this?" she asked quietly.

"The police. They found Dad's body in the circle, in the stone circle at Cairnbawn, his neck broken, and they found our mother's shoes and coat a few yards away on the shore of the loch."

"Eloise Gordon would *never* do such a thing," Wadget growled. "How could yeh believe it, boy, of yer own mother!"

"Please, Master Wadget," Kashashem said sternly. "Jack is not at fault here. If anyone is at fault, it is me. I should have crossed the Way and made contact with Jack soon after ... soon after it happened. I did not, knowing that Eloise had kept her children away from Anwynn for their own safety and had not told them yet that they carried the burden of Waycaller. I felt that, grieving as they surely were, adding a visit by one such as myself, a being from legend for all they knew, would have frightened them even more—"

"You should have come," Harriett blurted out. "We were all alone. We got put in a home. You should have come, you should have ..." Her voice trailed off. Jack put his arm around her but she shrugged him off, trying to be brave in front of the Council.

"Yes, it is clear now that I should have. I did not know that you believed that your mother had done such a thing."

"So, she didn't kill my dad?" Jack held his breath for the answer.

"I can assure you," Alva said, "that my cousin's wife did not kill him."

"Your, your cousin?"

"Yes, Jack. Your father was my cousin, well, the son of my mother's cousin. I grew up with Noble and was very fond of him. I knew your mother as well. There is no way Eloise would ever harm Noble."

"Well, what happened then?" Jack's heart thudded in his throat.

"I crossed the Veil soon after it happened." Kashashem began. "An ill feeling led me there. Noble's body was already being taken away when I arrived. It was raining heavily, as it often does in Cairnbawn. The rain had removed all trace of the struggle that occurred there. The otherworlders who found Noble's body must have assumed that Eloise killed him, as she was nowhere to be found herself. But elves and druids can see things that otherworlders cannot. I found amidst the standing stones the signs of a tremendous fight. I also found slight impressions, invisible to the ordinary eye, of three sets of footprints."

"Three?"

"Yes, Jack. I recognised Noble's and Eloise's prints easily. The other set I did not recognise, but it was clear that this third person had killed Noble and attempted to kill Eloise."

"Attempted?"

"Yes. Eloise survived. I know this because there was the trace of magic on the air, a trace only left when the Veil is parted. It seems that Eloise opened a Way after Noble was killed. She travelled here, to Anwynn."

"Mum's alive?" Harriett nearly shrieked the question. She was shaking, her eyes as wide as saucers. Jack's skin tingled all over. His heart pounded even more. His mother was alive! He and Harriett weren't alone after all.

"Yes, she is alive." Kashashem smiled at them both, her eyes showing them that she was not deceiving them.

"Where is she?" Jack looked over his shoulder, half hoping she was about to walk into the courtyard.

"Sadly, I do not know. I have not seen her, nor heard from her, since that awful day." For the first time, emotion played on Kashashem's face, a mixture of sadness and regret.

Jack's stomach sank. He'd gone from elation to disappointment in just a few seconds. His mother was alive, but missing. "So how do you know she's still alive?"

"We were very close, the link between us is strong. I feel her heart beating in the echo of my own. She is alive, of that I am certain."

"Why hasn't she come back then?" Harriett asked, her voice pained.

"That is a question I have long pondered. I have yet to find the answer. I feel that something deeply magical prevents her from returning. But believe me, Harriett, I have not stopped searching for her since the day she disappeared. Unfortunately I have found no trace of her nor discovered what happened in the circle of Cairnbawn that day. Until last night, I did not know who killed Noble. I believed it was a random act of violence, such acts being common in the otherworld."

"Until last night?" Jack asked.

"Yes. Ellisenn learned the truth of it only last night." Kashashem looked to the handsome young elf and nodded, giving him permission to tell them what he'd learned.

"A decade or so ago," Ellisenn began, "a sorceress devoted to Morrigan found Thullu's Gift and used it to send a Vellenor assassin across the Way to kill your mother, and also kill you, Jack, and your sister as well. The assassin failed, though your father lost his life in the attempt. Somehow Thullu's Gift then came to be in the Oakling Mog's possession. Serza learned of this and took it from her. Just days ago, the dark prince used the Gift to send a skinwearer across the Veil to kidnap Harriett, whom he believed to be the Waycaller. The prince intends to use the Waycaller to ensure Morrigan remains imprisoned, or to somehow destroy her, for he has turned against the Pale Mother and plans to subjugate all the Dark Ones, and all of Anwynn, under his own rule."

The room was silent. Jack's ears were ringing and he felt dizzy. So Serza didn't want him dead, but to use him against Morrigan. But, how could the dark prince possibly think Jack could help him to defeat Morrigan? She was a Faeden, a goddess to the goblins, and he was just a boy, Waycaller or not. Nothing he could do would have any impact on the Pale Mother. Serza must be mad, Jack decided, totally mad. He didn't have the chance to say anything or ask any questions. At that moment a horn sounded in the passageway leading to the courtyard. The druids all stood, looking towards the doors through which Jack and the others had just come. Anarra stood as well, quickly throwing back her hood and gesturing for Jack, Harriett and Miss Butters to stand as well.

"What's happening?" Jack asked. It was Anarra who answered.

"The Bright King, High Sovereign of all Elvinidd, approaches."

The horn blew again, closer now, and the doors opened. A dozen fearsome-looking elves strode out into the courtyard, all with black skin and brilliant yellow eyes. All but one was armed with spears and wore breastplates and helms of white metal over their long black dreadlocks, helms that took the shape of dragon-heads breathing flame. Jack recognised them at once from the vision of the Battle of Bright he'd witnessed with the aid of Aelf's memory stone. These were members of the Sovereign Guard. In the centre of them paced a seemingly young man, unarmed and unarmoured, his eyes more gold than yellow and his skin almost glowing, if the night sky could glow. Jack recognised him immediately. The ornate winged crown of Elvinidd kept his black dreadlocks in place, which otherwise hung well below his waist. The man's bearing declared him as the Elven Sovereign more than any crown or blaring horns.

Anarra and the elvish druids all dropped to their knees, the rest of the druids bowing their heads. Jack didn't know what to do. Harriett was staring open-mouthed, so he forced her head into a slightly respectful bow and then did the same. The king's guard positioned themselves at each entrance to the courtyard and the king strode over to Kashashem and laid his hand on her head.

"Stand, please, Kashashem, always you are so formal. Are we not friends?"

Kashashem stood and smiled at her king. There was more than affection in that smile, more even than love. It was complete devotion. When the king smiled back it was as if the air in the courtyard sparked with electricity. When Jack took his next breath he was sure the air in his lungs was warmer, more alive.

"Stand, please, all of you," the king said. "These old flagstones are not easy on knees." The elves stood but kept their heads bowed, only Kashashem was able to look the elvish king straight in the face. The other druids kept their heads bowed as well, except for Wadget, who for inexplicable reasons was vigorously scratching one of his feet. The noise drew the king's attention and, smiling, he walked over to Wadget and bent down on one knee so that they were eye to eye. "Oak Lord, long has it been since last we met. Are you well, apart from that itch?"

"Well enough." Wadget dropped his foot. "An' yeh, Dhudhannan, are yeh well?"

"I am well, but worried, as I am sure are you and all of the Council." The king stood and gestured for them all to take their seats. Then he noticed Jack, Harriett and Anarra and crossed the space between them.

"Anarra Settonett," he said. "Wadget sent me word of your coming. I dared not believe it nor rejoice until I saw you with my own eyes. Long has it been since my eyes have rested on one of your kin. So glad I am that your people are not lost to the night forever. I exult in the continuance of your line, Anarra Settonett, and in your own wellbeing."

"Thank you, my King." Anarra's voice was so quiet it could barely be heard around the courtyard. Her head bowed, her eyes full of tears, she looked overwhelmed. Jack wanted to reach out and comfort her, but he dared not in front of the king of Elvinidd.

"And you must be Jack and Harriett, Eloise's children. I am Dhudhannan. Pleased I am to meet you. I trust you are well?"

That King Dhudhannan knew their names surprised Jack, he would never have expected that. He certainly hadn't thought the king would speak directly to them. Too overcome with nerves to speak, he merely nodded that he was well. Harriett did the same.

"Glad I am." The king smiled at them, his black skin shining with an inner light. "That is one worry I can put to rest. I knew your mother only a little, but was fond of her. Your father I knew better. As a boy, Noble Senn spent time at Merielle. He was mischievous, but true of heart. You both resemble him greatly."

"Thanks," Harriett said, beaming. "But our dad's name was Noble Gordon, not Noble Senn."

The king looked to Kashashem, as if for explanation.

"Eloise and Noble took that name to protect the children's true identity," the druidess said, looking sadly at Jack and Harriett, aware that she was delivering another hard blow. Not even their name was real! Jack wasn't sure if he could take any more shocks.

"Ah, I see. Well, Jack, Harriett," the king began kindly, "I am sorry to strip you of that name, which I am sure is dear to you as it connects you to your parents, but it is my honour to grant you now your true name. You are the children of Noble Senn, sole heir of the House of Senn, an ancient family of the Kingdom of Pix."

Jack's mouth fell open. Harriett actually laughed, shocked and a little hysterical. Jack didn't care if it was rude, he had to sit down. He slipped onto a bench and stared around, his heart thumping in his dry throat. Alva was smiling at him kindly. He wished she wouldn't, he couldn't bring himself to smile back. The name 'Noble Senn' echoed in his mind. He had heard that surname before. Aelf had said it when reciting the prophecy about the rebuilding of Amaltor, and the final defeat of Morrigan. Was the prophecy about him? Wadget had said his mother had sacrificed much to see it made real. Was this why? Was Jack meant to face Morrigan and somehow defeat her? Was he the Druid King, the Oracle? But that was impossible! He looked over to Wadget, who was staring back at him, looking grumpy as usual but also thoughtful. It was clear now why Wadget and Aelf hadn't told him about this sooner. They'd been right to hold it back. This news was the last straw. Jack couldn't deal with it. His mind stuttered into horrified silence. His hands trembled and his chest ached.

King Dhudhannan, perhaps seeing the pain Jack was in, lay a warm but strong hand on his shoulder, filling Jack with a sudden and inexplicable calm. When the king lifted his hand, Jack felt a gentle tingling sensation where those ancient fingers had rested. The king then turned to Kashashem, saying, "You have done well, Kashashem. Your watch over Eloise and Noble's children has ensured that the House of Senn abides and will surely flourish." He smiled once more at Jack and Harriett, bowed to them and walked to an empty bench beside Wadget, where he sat down.

"You, you watched us?" Harriett whispered to Kashashem as they sat as well.

"Yes. Unseen, I spent much time in Cairnbawn. I watched you both grow up. Many times I wanted to introduce myself to you, but it was your mother's wish that you live the safe and ordinary life of otherworld children. I had planned to come to you on Jack's eighteenth birthday, which was when your mother had intended that you both learn of your destiny and your true name. The skinwearer ruined those plans, however."

The king cast his serene gaze around the group until they were all settled, then waited a moment before addressing them. "I apologise for intruding on this Council. Lady Kashashem has informed me of the Prince of Fellwood's ill deeds and intentions. My heart is still heavy with the news. As merely a king and no magic-wielder, I can do nothing about the Secret Gift, though wish dearly I could. I must leave that up to this Council. I come to you now to hear more of the Vellenor armies amassing in the south, for armies are something I can deal with."

"My King," Ellisenn said, "the Prince of Fellwood's armies are gathering on the far bank of the Great River, ready to move into the Empty Lands and then on to Pix, but it is the prince's desire to conquer all of Anwynn. From Pix he will surely move on Elvinidd."

"It is as it has always been," one of the elvish women said. She was clearly recognisable as an inhabitant of Songarielle, one of the mountain elves. "Every five hundred years or so they rise up against us. Every five hundred years we crush them and send them back to their vile nests in Fellwood and the Swampmere."

"If only it were as simple as that," Ellisenn said. "This time they have amassed a force the like of which we have never seen and the Secret Gift makes the Dark Prince of Fellwood most powerful in wicked sorcery."

The king thought for a moment. "If this Council concurs," he said, "I will send emissaries at once to King Mael, asking that the armies of Pix join the Sovereign Guard on the banks of the Great River to block Prince Serza's path north. If there is to be a war, I will have it at a place of our choosing."

Around the circle the druids all nodded in agreement. The king opened his mouth to speak again but fell silent. The light from above had dimmed and was growing darker. The king looked up. Following his lead, Jack and everyone else looked up at the same time, to see a vast black shape pouring over all four edges of the building into the courtyard. It was like a cloud of thickest ink pouring down on them, or a shadow made solid. Before Jack could comprehend what he was seeing, long tendrils of inky darkness, like phantom tentacles, shot out of the mass to strike toward King Dhudhannan.

Wadget, Kashashem and Aelf were at the king's side in seconds. Wadget slashed his wand through the air so fast it cracked like a whip, sending bursts of green energy at the shadow tentacles, making them recoil and preventing them from reaching the king. Kashashem and Aelf extended their arms, creating a sphere of light around themselves and the king, which the shadow tentacles coiled around but could not pass through. The king's guards formed a perimeter around this protective sphere, using their spears to jab at the shadow, but to no avail. The dark mass crept lower and lower into the courtyard, now blocking the sky completely. A tentacle shot out and stabbed one of the guards in the chest. He crumpled to the ground and did not move again.

Miss Butters grabbed Jack and Harriett by the collar and dragged them toward the nearest door out of the courtyard. Jack just managed to take hold of Anarra's hand and drag her along with them. A long tendril stretched out after them but stopped when it reached the doorway through which they'd just passed. Miss Butters pushed them all behind her and faced the open door, where the tentacles snaked and flailed like the arms of a mad octopus against an invisible barrier. She forced Harriett into a squat and pressed her between the wall and her own fleshy body, using her wide girth as a shield. She shielded Jack and Anarra with an outstretched arm. Three more tentacles attempted to stab at them but were stopped at the doorway, as if hitting a wall of glass.

"The hearth ward," Miss Butters said. "The hearth ward! Bless Eugene!"

Jack wasn't sure what she meant at first but then remembered that long ago the halfling god Eugene had placed a protective ward over all dwellings that had a cooking fire. Bless Eugene, Jack thought, and bless those druids making onion soup as well.

The shadow now completely filled the courtyard, covering it in pitch darkness, obscuring everything but the shining sphere of light surrounding King Dhudhannan, Aelf and Kashashem. Dozens of dark tentacles roiled over the surface of the sphere, seeking a way in. Wadget stood just outside the sphere, his wand whirring through the black air like a firebrand, fending off the shadow with a ferocity that took Jack's breath away. Another light sparked at the other end of the courtyard, revealing Ellisenn, arms outstretched, creating a dome of light to protect Alva, who sat slumped on the floor, and the other druids. A body lay just outside the edge of the light, that of the female mountain elf. As Jack watched a tentacle whipped out at Ellisenn's protective sphere, wielding a dead guard as a weapon. The guard hit the light and slid down it as if it were solid to join the other body on the floor. Harriett shrieked. Jack wanted to comfort her but she was completely covered by Miss Butters' body and he couldn't touch her. A loud bang drew all their attention.

Wadget had been knocked to the ground. His wand skittered across the flagstones into the darkness. The tentacles pressing down on the protective sphere over the king now numbered hundreds, perhaps thousands. The sphere actually bowed under the weight of them. Then, as if in slow motion, a single, needle-thin tentacle slithered its way through the dome of light. Once through, it shot forward so fast it was just a blur and struck King Dhudhannan directly in the heart. The king's golden eyes widened with surprise and then dimmed, as if drained of their light. He fell to the floor. The black mass immediately receded, drawing back up the courtyard walls and away, allowing the sun to shine in again. Aelf slumped to his knees, exhausted. Kashashem knelt beside the king, checking his pulse. Wadget staggered to his feet, shaking his head in a daze.

With the shadow lifted, Jack could see that all of the king's Sovereign Guards and one of the druids were dead. Only Ellisenn showed no signs of fatigue. The young elf dashed across the courtyard to where Dhudhannan lay, kneeling down beside Kashashem as she ministered to her fallen king. After a brief conversation with her, Ellisenn walked out into the passageway and up to Jack, his eyes wide with concern.

"Are you unharmed, Jack?" His hand involuntarily went to Jack's shoulder.

"I'm fine," Jack answered. "Is the king?"

"The king yet lives," Ellisenn said, "but is grievously injured."

Anarra stifled a small sob. Ellisenn looked into her face then down at her hand, still held in Jack's own. Something crossed the handsome elf's face that Jack didn't quite recognise. Was it disappointment? Or anger? Whatever it was made Jack uncomfortable.

"Miss Butters, get off me!" Harriett's voice was muffled by Dorothea's heavy flesh.

"Oh, so sorry dear." Miss Butters released Harriett but dragged her back in close when she attempted to move towards the courtyard.

"I want to see what's happening!"

"You can see well enough from here, young Harriett," Miss Butters hung on tight to Harriett's jacket sleeve.

"Let me go!"

"I will not. There's deaduns in there and anywhere there's deaduns is no kind of place for younglings."

"Your actions, Dorothea Butters of Bright, surely saved Jack and Harriett's lives," Ellisenn said. "For that, I am most, most thankful."

Jack wasn't sure why but the relief in Ellisenn's voice added to his discomfort.

"I'm not in the market for thanks from elves," Dorothea said. "Though a certain scrawny girl would do better to thank the fact that she's alive than fidget and pull and try to get away."

Harriett stopped trying to wriggle out of Miss Butters grasp and sighed, her shoulders slumping in defeat. "Thank you for saving my life," she mumbled, in what Jack thought was a very ungracious tone.

"Yeah, thanks Miss Butters," Jack added.

"We all owe you a great debt," Aelf said, walking out of the courtyard to join them. "That Sending had a power beyond any I have ever seen. We would have lost Jack and Harriett, and Anarra, if you hadn't thought to get them indoors."

Miss Butters flushed a little, apparently unused to receiving such heartfelt thanks. She went to say something but couldn't quite bring herself to do so.

"We must not linger here. Things are dire if a Sending can penetrate deep into Songarielle. I have conferred with Kashashem and Master Wadget. I am to take you, Jack and Harriett, straight to Amallayne's temple."

Jack felt his throat constrict, but was glad he was finally going to do what they had travelled all this way to do. He felt Anarra squeeze his hand and looked into her eyes. She smiled encouragingly.

"You will do well, Jack," she said. "Amallayne will hear you and come to our aid."

"I hope so." Jack thought a moment then asked Aelf: "Can Anarra come with us? If she wants to come, that is."

"Yes, I would like to come with you." Anarra smiled at Jack and then glanced at Ellisenn. Something passed between the two elves that made Jack's discomfort rise even more.

"I'm sorry, but no." Aelf said. "King Dhudhannan wants to see you, Anarra."

"The king wishes to see me? Now?"

"Yes. He is about to be moved to the royal apartments here in the senate. When that happens, you must go with him.

He is very weak, barely able to speak, so stay by his side."

Anarra nodded but did not let go of Jack's hand nor move. Now that they were holding hands she seemed unwilling to let go. Despite the recent terror Jack had just gone through, he couldn't help but feel uplifted by that.

"May I accompany you and Jack to the temple, Master Aelf?" Ellisenn asked. "I can offer protection if another Sending were to attack."

Jack was relieved when Aelf answered. "No, Ellisenn, Master Wadget needs you. The sorcerer responsible for that attack must be found and punished. Wadget wishes you to aid him in that task."

"Yes, Master Aelf, of course. I will do what I can." Ellisenn looked at Jack, nodded farewell and then went back into the courtyard to find Wadget.

"Now, Miss Butters, I know you will not like to hear this, but you are required to wait here. Kashashem will come to meet you soon. She has something she wishes to discuss with you."

"With me? What does she want to discuss with me?"

"I am not at liberty to say, but it is important, especially now."

Jack suspected that what Kashashem had to say to Miss Butters was what Aelf and Wadget had been keeping from the halfling all along, why they'd manipulated her into leaving her comfortable home in Bright.

"Well, this is all most irregular," Dorothea said, "but I didn't want to go to Amallayne's house anyway, so I suppose I'll wait here. Just make sure you take care of my younglings and bring them right back here when you're finished in that nasty temple."

Jack and Harriett glanced at each other. *My younglings?* Was Miss Butters taking ownership of them now? Jack wasn't sure how he felt about that, but, on balance, he thought he felt okay with it.

"You have my word, Dorothea," Aelf said.

As Aelf headed down the passageway, Anarra held Jack

back a moment.

"Jack," she whispered. "I must explain something to you, which as an otherworlder you might not understand."

"Okay, sure, go ahead."

"How much do you know about the way of elves?"

"Not much, why?"

"Elves are different to humans—"

"I've noticed; those cute ears for one thing."

She ignored that. "Unlike humans, elves couple for life and only once in a life."

Jack's mouth popped open. He closed it again as quickly as he could. Was she really talking to him about this now? They'd only held hands, and only then because their lives had been in danger. Surely it was way too soon for a conversation about lifelong commitment.

"Umm, okay," he said, not sure what else to say.

"Here in Anwynn, human children tell stories of love at first sight. Do the children in your world tell those stories?"

Jack swallowed, hard. This was getting a bit scary.

"Umm, yes, they do. Why?"

"Those stories are inspired by elves. For humans, love at first sight is just a fantasy, it is not real, but for elves, it is very real. Elves can fall in love at first sight and once in love, that is it: for the duration of their long lives they will love no other."

Jack felt his heart thumping like a bird desperate to escape a fleshy cage.

"Look, Anarra, I'm, I'm sorry, but, I mean, I like you, I like you a lot, a lot, but … Maybe it's because I'm human, I just don't believe in love at first sight. I didn't feel that, for you, not right away—"

Anarra frowned and dropped his hand. "I am not telling you this because *I* fell in love with you at first sight, Waycaller, but because someone else has—"

"Jack!" Aelf had stopped at the end of the passageway. "Jack, come at once!"

Jack motioned to Aelf that he was coming. When he

turned back to Anarra she had already gone through the door into the courtyard. Completely confused and still shaking his head, Jack caught up with Aelf.

"What's wrong, Jack?" Aelf asked.

"I will never understand women," Jack answered.

"That's not a surprise to anybody," Harriet said, smirking and taking his hand.

# FALLING LEAVES

As Aelf hurried Jack and Harriett across the square toward Amallayne's temple, Harriett took the opportunity to ask the druid more questions. It would take more than a horrific attack by a Sending with a thousand deadly tentacles to stop Harriett asking questions. Jack listened with only a part of his attention. His mind reeled with what had happened in the Druid Chambers, and with the fact that their mother was alive and hadn't killed their father. No matter what happened now, no matter what happened in Amallayne's temple, Jack would not rest until he found their mother.

"Will the king be alright?" Harriett asked.

"I hope so. Few elves have the same strength as Dhudhannan, which is the result of his vast age."

"How old is he?" she asked.

"Eight thousand years, give or take a few decades. He is the oldest of all the elves."

"What about Ellisenn?" Jack asked. "How old is he? Is he like a thousand years old or something, like Daniselle?" The thought that Ellisenn might be as old as a thousand years made Jack feel a little better about having been carried in his arms. It would make Ellisenn well and truly supernatural and not just a pretty boy.

"Goodness no," Aelf said, "Ellisenn is something of a prodigy. He is the youngest to qualify as a druid in the Order's long history and certainly the youngest druid ever to be invited to sit with the Council. He is really quite extraordinary."

"But how old is he?" Jack needed him to be at least a hundred years old. He wasn't sure why, he just did.

"I should think he's little more than a year or two older than you, about eighteen years old, which, for an elf, is practically an infant," Aelf answered.

This made Jack feel decidedly uncomfortable. He thought

he'd never be able to look Ellisenn in the face again, but if all went well in the temple he wouldn't have to. If Amallayne agreed to help, he would be leaving the druids to deal with Morrigan and Serza, he would be leaving Songarielle to find his mother and take her and Harriett home.

As they reached the steps leading up to the entrance of Amallayne's temple they joined small groups of other people heading in the same direction. Jack was surprised that they were calm and unhurried. They clearly did not know that a Sending had just attacked and seriously wounded King Dhudhannan, but none of these people were elves. They were the first humans, apart from Aelf and the druid councillors, who Jack and Harriett had been close to since they arrived in Anwynn. They were all dressed in what Jack would describe as medieval peasants' clothes – tunics and tights with long travelling cloaks. Many of them carried baskets brimming with flowers and food.

"Are they going on a picnic?" Harriett asked, staring at a small family mounting the steps ahead of them.

"These are pilgrims. The things in the baskets are offerings for Amallayne, who is their Goddess. Many believe that the Faeden appreciate the aroma of food and flowers and that by offering them their prayers will be heard. Most of these pilgrims are from Pix, but some are from as far away as Danussan, my original home." Aelf indicated a group of people whose features and hair were fair.

"Does everyone from Danussan worship Amallayne?" Jack asked, intrigued by the look of reverence and serenity on the faces of the pilgrims, even the children who carried their own little bunches of flowers as offerings.

"No. In the North Kingdom they officially worship only Danuss, but these days some among the poor have turned to Amallayne, even though it is prohibited. Some of these Northerners have come here in order to worship Amallayne without fear of persecution. My home country is very beautiful and rich, but the King of the North is narrow minded on questions of religion. I haven't been home for decades. Magic is not altogether popular in the North Kingdom, as druids do not bow down to Danuss. As a result, I am an exile, more or less homeless."

"I'm sorry," Harriett said, reaching out her free hand to take Aelf's. Jack smirked and shook his head. Having both hands held was Harriett's idea of perfection.

As they reached the top of the stairs and entered into the shade of the arched entrance, an aura of serene quiet overcame them. The pilgrims all bowed at the waist, then, with measured slowness, entered the temple through the large open doors. Aelf, Jack and Harriett entered also, behind a family of pilgrims whose daughter was about the same age as Harriett. The two girls looked at each other and smiled.

The circular interior of the temple was one huge, unfurnished space with light spilling in from high rectangular windows. On the other side of the space, directly opposite the entrance, was a dais. At the centre of this dais was another door, this one made out of beaten gold. The pilgrims all headed toward the dais and then, after placing their offerings to one side, bent at the waist to pray in silence. To all intents and purposes, it looked like the pilgrims were worshipping a golden door. Aelf whispered an explanation.

"The door leads to a smaller chamber where the effigy of Amallayne is housed. The effigy was given to the ancient kings of Pix by Amallayne herself. It was moved here at the time of the Doom War, to save it from the destruction that befell Amaltor, where it once stood. Most of the pilgrims are satisfied to make their prayers here, not wanting to disturb Amallayne by entering her private chamber. But, if one seeks permission from the temple caretakers, one can enter beyond this point through a side door."

Aelf led them quietly to the head of the great hall and over to a tall, austere looking Pixish man holding a long staff. Jack assumed he was one of the caretakers.

"Good tidings, friend," the man said to Aelf. "It is rare to find druids in this place."

"Indeed, but I am accompanying these human children

who have travelled from afar to see the effigy of Amallayne. May we enter?"

"Amallayne's house is open to all who wish to enter," the caretaker said, as if explaining the obvious to a child. "Follow me, friend." He led them to a corner at the side of the dais where, as they got nearer, another, smaller door became visible. The caretaker placed the end of his staff into a large round lock in the door and turned it. A clicking sound preceded the door slowly swinging open. The caretaker gestured for them to enter and said, in what Jack thought was a slightly condescending tone, "On behalf of those pilgrims who come to the house of Amallayne to make offerings but are too poor to do so, the temple caretakers have made available such provisions befitting an offering. You will find them within, to the left."

Jack attempted a thankful smile but thought he just looked intimidated. He waited for Aelf to lead them in. Instead, Aelf motioned that they come in close to him before entering.

"You should go in alone," he said.

"But, what am I supposed to do? How am I supposed to beseech Amallayne to help us?"

"You simply place yourself before the effigy and ask."

"Is that all?"

"That is all. You see, the power of the Faeden flows into the world through their effigies, which they gave to their disciples in the beginning of days. The effigies are likenesses of the Faeden themselves, in the form of statues. Amallayne's effigy contains great power. Through it Amallayne will be able to hear you."

"But, what if she doesn't answer?"

"Well, then we will have to face Serza and the threat from Morrigan on our own."

"But we'll lose." The volume of Harriett's voice made the caretaker frown.

"Perhaps," Aelf said, "but we will fight anyway. We have no choice and I, for one, would rather fight and lose than let the Dark Ones win without a struggle."

Jack thought the difference between being crushed by Morrigan or Serza was likely to feel much the same whether or not they put up a fight, but didn't say this to Aelf. He swallowed hard and, allowing Harriett to take his hand again, entered the private chamber of the Goddess Amallayne.

The chamber was not large and had the atmosphere of a small church. It was dimly lit, with no windows and just a few candles throwing meagre illumination. A life-sized statue of a young woman, carved out of a single ruby, was ensconced in an alcove in the wall opposite them. Before the statue was an altar of marble on which sat many offerings and, strangely, a small plant in a shallow pot. The plant looked to Jack like a perfectly formed tree in miniature. Its green leaves caught the candlelight and shimmered.

As Jack's eyes adapted he could discern the ruby effigy's features. The young woman's eyes were wide, her hair flowing upwards as if in a blast of wind, her arms outstretched, palms upraised. Jack recognised the image instantly as that of the Faeden who'd appeared at the Battle of Bright. The same young woman carved on the pillar at Amaltor: Amallayne the Conqueror. The sight of her sent chills down Jack's spine.

*Amallayne!* The voice in Jack's ear whispered.

"Quiet," Jack said out loud.

"I didn't say anything, Jack." Harriett frowned, confused.

"Sorry, Harrie," Jack apologised. "I'm just a bit on edge. I've never beseeched a goddess before."

"Oh, I beseech goddesses all the time," Harriett whispered.

"Very funny, Harrie, very funny. Not."

"Just get on with it, Jack, or are you chicken?"

"I'm not chicken. I just need to get myself sorted. Do you think we should make an offering, maybe it will help?"

"I don't know, maybe." She shrugged as she went to the table laden with offerings. There were flowers, fruit, jugs of steaming hot water and little bowls of tea leaves. "I suppose it can't hurt." She brought over some flowers and fruit. Jack took them and they both walked forward and placed them at Amallayne's feet.

*Do you dare call out?* the voice asked.

"Quiet!" Jack spat.

"Jack! I think you *are* ear-whipped! Are you ear-whipped, Jack? Tell me!"

"Not now, Harriett, I have more important things to do."

"Being ear-whipped is pretty important, Jack. Didn't you hear what Daniselle said? They kill people who are ear-whipped!"

"Shush! I have to call. If I call her, Amallayne will fix everything, even the earwisp."

At that Harriett gasped, realising that her brother was possessed by an earwisp.

"Oh, Jack, oh no!"

She was silenced as Jack whispered Amallayne's name. "Amallayne, are you there? Amallayne, I beseech you, please come ... Amallayne?" Jack wasn't sure if he was doing it right. He turned to Harriett for reassurance. She just shrugged. "Amallayne," Jack repeated, "please come."

The chamber remained silent, the effigy still and lifeless apart from the dance of candle flame reflected on its surface. He called out a few more times, but still nothing happened.

"Do you think she knows we're in Anwynn?" Harriett asked, fiddling with the sleeve of her jacket.

"Who? Amallayne?"

"No, Mum."

Jack looked into his sister's eyes. They were glassy, anxious.

"No, Harrie. If mum knew we were in Anwynn, she would have come to find us."

Harriett smiled at that. It was a small smile, soon overtaken by worry. "I hope she's okay," she said.

"Me too. Harrie, I'm going to find her. I don't care what the druids want from us. From now on, my first priority is to find Mum."

"I know you'll find her, Jack, but finding Mum won't

make Morrigan go away."

"I know that. I'm not saying I won't help the druids, but if helping the druids means we might not find Mum, then that's when I draw the line."

Harriett went back to fiddling with her coat sleeve, her eyes still worried. "Maybe you should go back to beseeching now."

Jack looked into the eyes of the ruby effigy again and summoned his will. "Amallayne," he repeated, "please come."

"I don't think you're doing a very good job of that," a female voice said from behind Jack and Harriett, making them both jump. They turned and saw a dark-skinned girl, maybe sixteen years old, leaning against the offerings table and eating an apple. "I think you're supposed to be all submissive and stuff."

"Thanks for the advice," Jack said, put off by a combination of the girl's off-hand demeanour and how pretty she was, "but I'm doing something important here."

"That's what they all say." The girl smirked. "They all think their prayers are *very* important. But I've heard it all and I can tell you they're all pretty much the same." She moved closer, pushing her long dark hair behind her ears, which were not long and pointy. Not an elf then, Jack thought. Her eyes, once illuminated by candlelight, were a glistening black.

"Excuse me, but who are you?" Jack asked, irritated that this girl wasn't taking his beseeching more seriously.

"My name's Laynie. I work here, collecting the offerings. Funny that nobody notices that Amallayne never eats any of this stuff."

"Maybe she's not hungry," Harriett said defensively.

"Or maybe she's not listening." The girl raised a punctuating eyebrow.

"Look, do you mind?" Jack asked. "I'm busy here and I can't concentrate with all this noise."

"Sorry," the girl said. "I didn't mean to disturb you. I just noticed you didn't look like your everyday Pixish pilgrim. You look *kind of* Pixish, but your clothes are all wrong. Where are you from?" She took another bite of the apple, waiting for Jack to answer.

"We're from the otherworld and this is my brother Jack and he's a Waycaller," Harriett said.

"Harrie!" Jack glared at his sister. "Quiet!"

"A Waycaller from the otherworld?" The girl looked mildly intrigued. "Well, that is interesting. I knew there was something strange about you. I thought you might be skinwearers. You aren't, are you?" Her voice had a mocking tone to it.

"Of course not," Jack said irritated. "Do we look like skinwearers to you?"

"Skinwearers can look like many things, even shabby otherworld children."

"Well, we're not," Harriett said. "We're Scots. Where are you from?"

"I am what you call a homeless waif. The elves have adopted me and given me a home. In return I have to clear up this lot." She indicated the offerings at the statue of Amallayne's feet. "Go on then," she said to Jack, "tell me what you're trying to do."

"It's kind of private," he answered.

"Okay, but I might be able to help," Laynie said. "I've seen a lot of this bowing and scraping stuff and I think I've got the hang of what works and what doesn't."

"Morrigan, and the Prince of Fellwood, are after us and we're trying to get Amallayne to help us," Harriett blurted out before Jack could stop her.

"Really?" The girl rolled her eyes, disbelieving. "Morrigan is entombed, everyone knows that."

"She's trying to escape, or at least her minions are trying to break her out," Jack explained, thinking the best way to deal with this situation was to give Laynie all the information so that she stopped asking questions. "A sorceress found this Thullu's Gift thing many years ago and now another sorcerer, Serza, has stolen it and sent a skinwearer into our world after us. It's all a real mess and we need Amallayne's help to fight

Serza and make sure Morrigan stays locked up."

"You've got a vivid imagination, I'll say that for you," the girl yawned. "Best you get on with it then."

"No more advice?" Jack asked.

"No, just try and sound a little more respectful. Amallayne's a sucker for that."

"Thanks a lot," Jack said sarcastically, wondering why all the gorgeous girls in Anwynn were either a million years old or totally nuts. Then he looked up at the statue of Amallayne and tried to centre himself again. Just before he called out to Amallayne once more, he heard Laynie whisper to Harriett,

"Is he always such a sour puss?"

"Pretty much," Harriett whispered back, "he's got hormones."

"Do you two mind?" Jack demanded. "I'm trying to commune with a goddess here!"

"Sorry," Laynie mouthed. "You go right ahead."

Jack spent the next half hour beseeching Amallayne. He hadn't realised what hard work beseeching a goddess would be, especially when she didn't answer. Laynie soon said she had work to do and wandered off, which was a relief to Jack. Her way of looking at him, as if assessing a mental defective, made him feel very inadequate. Harriett, tiring of the quiet and solemn atmosphere in Amallayne's chamber, went over to the offerings table and made herself a cup of tea.

"I don't think you should be doing that, Harrie," Jack said. "Those are offerings."

"Laynie helped herself," Harriett shrugged and took a sip of tea.

"I don't think you should be taking lessons from Laynie on how to behave, she's clearly nuts."

It was then that they heard a commotion outside. First the sound of swift moving feet, initially just a few, but soon dozens. This was followed by the sound of gasps and shouts of disbelief or fear. Clearest among the shouts was the voice of a woman repeating the same words over and over again, her voice trembling with terror: "They wither, they wither."

These words were taken up by others until finally an alarmed man's voice echoed these words in the temple itself: "They wither!"

Jack found himself feeling strange, the room spun around him and his vision blurred. Then it was as if he were looking out over Songarielle's central square from above. In the avenue leading through the city from Songarielle's main gate, small groups of elves and pilgrims gathered to watch in fear as the leaves on the sacred Alder trees yellowed, then turned brown and fell to the ground. At the same time, dark clouds gathered on the horizon and the sunlight inexplicably faded, as if the flames of the sun itself were being dimmed by some awful power. Jack's vision blurred and cleared again. He was back in Amallayne's chamber. He put out a hand and steadied himself on the offerings table.

"What's happening?" Harriett asked.

"I don't know, something bad." Jack turned to the statue of Amallayne and called again. "Amallayne, please, come to help us." Then he noticed that the leaves on the miniature tree on the altar had turned brown. As he watched, three of the leaves fell onto the altar and crumbled into dust. For some reason this frightened Jack nearly as much as the Sending that attacked them in the senate. His heart hammered in his chest. "Please Amallayne," he called out again, "something terrible is happening here!"

The door to the outer temple swung open and Aelf strode in. "We must go," he said, "the leaves of the sacred Alder are falling."

"What does that mean?" Jack asked, remembering that, according to Daniselle, the Alder trees were magically linked to the life-force of King Dhudhannan and part of the enchantments that protected Songarielle.

"It means that the Bright King, Lord Dhudhannan, is dead." Aelf's voice cracked with emotion. "The protections of Songarielle are broken." Jack had never heard fear in Aelf's voice before, but now the druid's voice positively trembled.

Before Jack and Harriett could do anything other than

look back at Aelf with apprehension, a series of loud sizzling thunder cracks echoed across the city. These were soon accompanied by screams and the sound of many running feet. Then there came the sound of explosions.

"Serza!" Aelf shouted just as a streak of blue lightning flashed through a window in the antechamber and struck the golden door with a deafening boom. "Take cover!" Aelf yelled, but too late. Another more powerful lightning bolt struck the door. The golden door exploded, sending debris flying through the air. Jack fell to the floor, his head throbbing with concussion and bloodied by the explosion, and slipped into black unconsciousness.

# TING

*Are you there?* A little female voice, somehow familiar, whispered, like the ringing of a miniscule bell. *Jack, are you there?*

Jack couldn't see anything or feel anything. Everything was black. He couldn't feel his hands or feet, nor his legs, nothing. It was as if he was just a mind, a mind without a body. Am I dead, he wondered, have I died?

*No, you are still alive,* the voice said. *But you are at the gateway of death, in-between life and what follows. Few return from here.*

"You're a liar," Jack said, recognising the voice in his mind, despite it no longer sounding like his own. "I don't believe anything you say."

*I know that you do not trust me, but trust me you must. The tide turns, Jack, the darkness grows. You cannot die. Without you we have no hope. Wake up, Jack, wake up and flee Songarielle. If not, Serza will surely destroy it and you with it.*

"You don't care about me!" Jack spat. "Or anyone else! You only want me to escape Serza so that Morrigan can kill me herself!"

*No! I do care! I have been in your mind, Jack! I have seen you like no-one else ever has. No-one knows you the way I do, Jack, no-one. Knowing you thus, how could I want any harm to befall you?*

"Lies," Jack said. "Just lies."

*I know that you do not believe me,* the tiny voice said, *because I have come into your mind uninvited. But I had to do it, Jack. There was no other way I could help you. Haven't I helped you, Jack? Didn't I help you escape the skinwearer? And Serza, and Mog? I have helped you, Jack. Over and over I have proven that I care about you.*

Jack silently laughed. The thought that the earwisp cared about him was ludicrous, but a part of him found the notion seductive. The idea of someone knowing his deepest, darkest thoughts, really understanding him, and caring about him nonetheless was compelling. Wasn't that what everybody

332

wanted underneath it all? But it was just lies, just lies to deceive him.

*No, Jack, not lies. It is the truth. I do understand you, and I do care about you. I will even tell you my name, Jack. We Tiqq never do that! We never tell anyone our name! My name is Ting, Ting the Earwisp.*

"I don't care who you are or what your name is. For all I know, I'm already dead and you're trying to turn me into a zombie," Jack accused, remembering what the scroll had said about earwisps; that they could speak to the dead and raise corpses to do their bidding.

*I'm not trying to raise the dead!* the voice shrieked. *I'm trying to prevent you from becoming one of them! I want you to live, you stubborn boy!*

"Don't call me a boy! I'm not a child."

*Then don't act like one. Don't give in, Jack. Fight, wake up!*

Jack felt the strong compulsion that normally accompanied the voice but resisted it. He pushed against it with all his might. He found that in this disembodied state, he had more ability to resist the voice than normal.

"No!" he shouted. "I won't do anything you ask!"

The little voice shrieked in frustration, *Jack! You will allow yourself to die rather than trust me! Don't you see how pointless that is?*

"I don't care! I won't wake up until you get out of my head! One way or another you're out of a host! If you care about me as much as you claim, then you'll get out and let me wake up on my own."

*I can't, Jack! If I leave your ear I will have to take my true form! The elves hate my kind! If they discover me they'll ... they'll hurt me.*

"Probably no more than you deserve," Jack said. "That's what you get for going around possessing people."

*I can't help it, Jack,* Ting cried. *That is how we live! We grow weak without a host and if we're without one long enough we fall into a terrible sleep.*

"You mean you die?" Jack felt a small pang of sympathy.

*Not die, worse, we go into an endless sleep of nightmares. All the worst thoughts of all our hosts haunt us and torment us.*

Jack couldn't quite believe he was thinking it, but he

wouldn't want that to happen to anyone, not even an earwisp. Ting the Earwisp must have detected his sympathy, for she seized on it. *You see, you see how kind you really are. This is why I could never harm you! Because I know you to be truly kind and good.*

"I, I don't know," Jack said. "Why should I live? It's all too hard, too painful."

*Why should you live?* Ting repeated in disbelief. *Can you value yourself so little?* The question hung in the air. Jack didn't know what to say. In the silence he sensed the darkness closing in on him and his mind grew tired. He had the sense of a creeping cold.

*Death comes,* Ting said. *You must wake soon! What if I show you? What if I show you why you mustn't die?*

"How? How can you do that?"

*I am an earwisp. I can show you things, using the magic of my kind.*

"Alright." Jack steeled himself. "Show me."

In the darkness a tiny, white speck appeared.

*Focus on the speck of white,* Ting said. Jack didn't find that difficult at all, as the speck drew Jack's attention rather naturally. It was the only thing that wasn't darkness. *Allow the vision to grow.* As he focused, the speck grew so that soon all his vision was transformed into a field of brilliant white. *Go into the vision,* Ting's little voice directed, and so Jack willed himself to move into the whiteness. As he did so, he felt as though he were coming up out of deep water until he suddenly emerged into a world of deafening sound and light.

He opened his eyes, or at least he thought he did, for now he appeared to have eyes again. Even though his eyes were open, his vision was still dominated by whiteness. As he stared at the whiteness, and became accustomed to seeing with eyes once more, he realised that he was looking at the white fur of some kind of animal. He lifted his head and saw with some surprise that what was now his face was resting on a big shaggy clawed hand. He looked down and saw not his own body but the body of a huge hairy beast covered in straggly white fur. He realised that he was lying on the ground and that his fur was covered in blood. He looked up and saw before him a sight that took his breath away.

Ahead of him was the walled citadel of Songarielle, much of it aflame. Pillars of black smoke billowed upwards to the sky from every quarter. Immediately in front of him was a mass of hundreds of other hairy white beasts that appeared part gorilla, part bear and part wolf. About eight feet tall, the creatures sported big, bear-like claws on their hands and feet, and long, needle-sharp teeth. They charged toward Songarielle howling like demons from hell.

*Trolls,* Ting said. *Under the command of Serza.*

"When is this," Jack asked, "is this now?"

*Yes, this is now. I am letting you see through the eyes of a dead troll.*

Something jumped over Jack's prostrate body, startling him. It was a heavily armed goblin wielding a stubby broadsword. Then another, and another, and another green-eyed goblin leapt over him, hurtling in the direction of Songarielle. Jack turned and saw rushing forward a vast company of goblins and behind them, moving toward him at a steady, military pace, a row dozens-deep of Dark Elves in full armour, their white hair, pale skin and pink eyes emanating menace. *Serza has used the power of Thullu's Gift to instantaneously transport these fiends here,* Ting hissed. *How can Songarielle stand against this?*

Jack's attention was drawn upwards as a blast of flame hit the ground near him, scorching half a dozen trolls, sending the acrid smell of burning flesh and fur through the air. In the sky above them were dozens of dragons, all mounted by a pair of Songarielle elves. One elf commanded the dragon and directed its flame as if it was a living flamethrower, while the other fired arrows, sending them hurtling down to kill and maim the advancing horde. The goblins drew bows and arrows and fired at the firewyrm riders but to no avail, they were far out of reach. The dragons blasted the ground with flame and more goblins and trolls were incinerated, but Serza's dark army just kept coming.

A powerful boom sounded in the distance. Jack looked toward Songarielle and saw on the walls of the city the distinctive robes of Kashashem, her yellow eyes ablaze. She clapped her hands and another sonic boom rolled forward as a visible haze. When it met the advancing army, hundreds of goblins and trolls were crushed where they stood and fell to the ground dead and bloodied. Jack realised that this had been the fate of the troll whose body he now occupied. He suddenly understood why Kashashem was so regarded. Her power was incredible. Then Jack spotted beside Kashashem the small figure of Wadget, standing on the parapet of the city wall. He had his wand drawn and with minute movements was sending thousands of tiny green sparks flying out amongst the advancing goblins. On contact with the goblins the little green sparks acted like acid and ate away at their flesh until only bones remained.

The sizzling sound of lightning caused Jack to duck his bulky head and cover it with his shaggy paws. A streak of blue lightning raced through the sky and connected with two firewyrms at once. The dragons imploded with a thunderous boom, leaving nothing but a cloud of ash-filled smoke that fell slowly to the ground as black snow. Jack turned his troll eyes in the direction from which the lightning came and saw Serza, the Dark Prince of Fellwood, hovering high in the sky, his arms outstretched, sending sheets of lightning in every direction to harry the firewyrm riders and bombard Songarielle. A deafening roar above caused Jack to look up again. Hurtling toward Serza was the silver firewyrm, Jossa, mounted by Daniselle and another of the elves. As they dashed overhead Jack recognised the other rider. It was Ellisenn.

Jack watched, amazed, as Ellisenn traced a sign in the air with his fingers. As his fingers drew the sign, a vivid pentagram of golden energy emerged. The pentagram hovered in the sky, emitting blinding rays of light. Ellisenn directed the pentagram to fly downwards into the onrushing mass of goblins, trolls and Dark Elves. At the mere sight of the golden pentagram the advancing beasts fled in terror. It was only seconds later that Jack saw why. When the pentagram's golden light made contact with the dark beings' skin they erupted into flames. Hundreds of them were burnt to cinders in this fashion. Clearly Jack was wrong about the pentagram, it *was* very powerful. But the pentagram soon faded and the dark army surged forward again.

As Jossa carried Daniselle and Ellisenn nearer to Serza, the dark prince cast a triple bolt of lightning directly toward the silver dragon and his mounts. At the last minute Jossa veered aside, just evading the lightning. Then, astoundingly, Ellisenn stood on Jossa's back and leapt into the air, nocking arrows as he spun and loosing them at Serza. Jack's stomach dropped, as if falling from a high space, his heart pounding. Surely Ellisenn would fall to his death? But then Ellisenn somersaulted in mid-air and landed deftly on another dragon's back, this one a huge, red-scaled beast. The red dragon streaked toward Serza at break-neck speed. Serza merely laughed and, pointing his long pale hand directly at Ellisenn, sent multiple bursts of lightning from his fingers that spiralled through the air like sizzling sea-snakes. The red dragon dodged sideways, but one of the snakes of lightning struck him on the wing and, screaming, he crumpled, falling in cartwheels toward the ground, carrying its rider and Ellisenn with it.

"No!" Jack yelled, though only an animalistic growl came out of his mouth.

Jack realised, as he shouted and squinted into the sun to see where Ellisenn had fallen, that something was terribly wrong. "How can this be? How can they be out in the daylight?" Jack demanded of Ting.

*Thullu's Gift*, Ting said. *Serza uses it as a ward against the sun and to break Songarielle's protective spells as well. The city is defenceless against it. If you remain, Serza will destroy it and all who dwell there.*

"No!" Jack growled. "No! We have to stop him!"

*There is but one way*, Ting said. *Wake up from your death-thrall and flee. Serza will not tarry here once you have gone.*

"But what about Harriett? I can't leave her alone."

*Harriett will be the Waycaller if you die. To protect her you must live and flee.*

Jack knew this was true. If he died Harriett would be the Waycaller and then she would face all these enemies alone. He couldn't let that happen. Normally he would never consider leaving his sister alone, but now he knew their mother was alive, alive and in Anwynn. Harriett would not be alone for long; Jack was sure their mother would find her. A loud explosion made him flinch. A massive plume of smoke billowed up into the sky from the centre of the citadel of Songarielle.

"Alright. I want to wake. I want to stop all this!"

Instantly, a warm sensation rose and spread through him, sending waves of heat throughout his body. His vision blurred and his hearing dimmed. His troll body slumped down on the ground, his troll head resting once more on his shaggy paws. Everything went dark. Jack's mind slowed to the point of no thought. Then there was nothing but blackness and silence.

❧ ❧

Jack's eyes shot open. The ground was still shaking from an explosion nearby. He scrambled out from under the offerings table, which had somehow fallen on top of him. Harriett lay nearby, face up, eyes rolled back into her head, her limbs askew, bleeding from the mouth and nose.

"Harrie!" He ran over to his sister and dropped to his knees, trembling. Please, he thought, please let her be alive. She was perfectly still and silent but breathing, though she seemed badly hurt. "Aelf, Aelf help!" Jack called, looking around the chamber for the druid. He spotted Aelf, pinned beneath a heavy section of the golden door, moaning, slipping in and out of consciousness. "No, Aelf, no!"

He cradled Harriett's head in his hands. "Harrie," he shouted into her ear, "Harrie, are you alright?" She didn't move and made no sound. He touched the skin of her forehead and was relieved to find that it was not cold, not yet.

"Harrie, Harrie wake up! Please, please don't be dead."

Another explosion struck the temple. Jack ducked and shielded his sister from falling debris. He looked out into the greater hall of the temple and out through the entrance doors into the square. There was a lot of smoke and fire. Every building in the square was burning. The trumpeting of dreadful horns and the horrid roars of a horde of monsters echoed throughout the city. In response, Songarielle's war drums boomed out. The sound of the drums was so life affirming that for a moment Jack had hope that the city would survive, but then he remembered the army of dark creatures assailing its walls, and the dark prince, hovering in the sky, seemingly as powerful as one of the Faeden.

He hugged his sister closer to him and caressed her face. She was going cold. Her breath now undetectable. His mind reeled. Harriett was dying, Aelf was trapped under the heavy golden doors that Jack hadn't the strength to lift. No-one else was there to help him, and probably wouldn't be as they would all be manning the walls. Then he thought of Laynie. If she were nearby, he could get her to cradle Harriett while he went to find someone to help him dig out Aelf.

"Laynie! Laynie, help! Help! Help!" But Laynie didn't come. The deafening sounds of battle were smothering his cries. He pounded the marble floor with his fists and in his despair started to thump at his own thighs. He felt so totally helpless. All hope had vanished and he dreaded that he would be completely alone in the world, without Harriett. Then a desperate thought came to him.

What use was it being a Waycaller if he couldn't save his own sister? Aelf had said there was vast power within him, more power than most druids could ever hope to attain. But was that power only to open the Way, to travel between stone circles and part the Veil between the realms? Could he use that power for other things, to save Harriett, to help Aelf?

He lay Harriett's head gently on the floor. Then, kneeling over her, held his hands over her chest. He summoned all his will, picturing Harriett healed, opening her eyes, smiling and talking. Then he tried to push his will and that image out through the palm of his hands. Nothing happened. He gathered his will again and pushed with all his might. A flash of silver light burst from his hands. The light surrounded Harriett, causing her whole body to glow. A few beads of perspiration formed on her brow. Jack watched, elated, as her skin blushed and paled and blushed again.

"Yes!" He punched his fist in the air. "Yes! Harrie, you're alive!"

Harriett moaned and moved her head to the side, her eyelids fluttering as if trying to open. She uttered the slightest of sounds.

"Jack …"

"Harrie! Harrie, I'm here, it's okay."

"Sorry … I left … you alone," she moaned.

"It's okay, Harrie. It's all going to be okay now." He looked to Aelf, deciding he would try to use magic to free him. He adjusted Harriett so that he could extend his hand towards the door crushing Aelf. He summoned his will, imagining the door lifting away. A hand came out of nowhere and slapped his hand down. Jack looked up and saw Laynie, her black eyes wild, her face transformed with rage.

"What are you doing?!" she demanded.

"Trying to save them!"

"Jack, you foolish *human*!" Laynie's face contorted with rage. "What you have done to bring back your sister is *forbidden*!"

"Why? Why is it forbidden? I had to save her!"

Laynie didn't answer. She grabbed Jack by the hair and bent down and took hold of Harriett with her other hand. Jack struggled to break free but Laynie's grip was incredibly strong. He looked into her face to demand that she release them. Her eyes had become swirling black whirlpools. Her black hair danced on-end in the air as if blown by an invisible wind. Her skin shimmered and sizzled, emitting dark electricity from every pore. Jack flinched and tried to scramble away as Laynie was consumed by flame, a bright ruby fire that then enfolded them all. The fire emitted a sound like a million voices, like a million mouths uttering a strange incantation. Jack's heart and mind filled with regret, as though they were one heartbroken organ. He had just discovered that his mother was alive and now he was going to die. The swirling flames quickened and closed in around him. Jack had just enough time to look over to Aelf, unconscious on the floor, before the chamber around them vanished and the battered druid was left alone in the devastated House of Amallayne.

# ABOUT THE AUTHOR

Family legends inspired D.J. McPhee to write *Waycaller*. The McPhee clan hail from the small island of Colonsay, off the west coast of Scotland. The name McPhee translates as 'children of faeries'. For centuries the McPhee clan has been associated with the legends of Celtic mythology and with magic. The clan symbol is an open hand – the sign of both peace and magic-making. In ancient times it was said that the eldest born of the clan were destined to be either warriors or wizards, shield-maidens or Celtic priestesses. Sometimes D.J. McPhee believes these family legends to be historical fact, which is why, perhaps, he is not altogether comfortable in the modern world. D.J. lives in a small town with two bossy cats and an amazingly supportive partner.

Note from the author: If you've enjoyed this novel, I'd greatly appreciate it if you could leave an honest review on Amazon, Goodreads or on my Facebook page. Reviews are very important to authors, and it only takes a few minutes to post one. Thank you in advance.

Join me on Facebook:
https://www.facebook.com/D.J.McPhee.Author

www.ingramcontent.com/pod-product-compliance
Lightning Source LLC
Chambersburg PA
CBHW010803250626
47156CB00010B/2989